PRAISE FOR MICHAEL MCBRIDE

"Thrilling entertainment."

— *PUBLISHERS WEEKLY* ON MUTATION

"McBride writes with the perfect mixture of suspense and horror that keeps the reader on edge."

— EXAMINER

"McBride's style brings to mind both James Rollins and Michael Crichton."

— SCI-FI & SCARY

"Highly recommended for fans of creature horror and the thrillers of Michael Crichton."

— *THE HORROR REVIEW*

"Michael McBride literally stunned me with his enigmatic talent and kept me hanging on right up until the end."

ALSO BY MICHAEL MCBRIDE

THE UNIT 51 TRILOGY

*Subhuman * Forsaken * Mutation*

THE VIRAL APOCALYPSE SERIES

*Contagion * Ruination * Extinction*

STANDALONE SCI-FI/HORROR

*Ancient Enemy * Burial Ground * Chimera * Extant ***
*Fearful Symmetry * Innocents Lost * Predatory Instinct * Remains*
*Subterrestrial * Sunblind * Unidentified * Vector Borne*

THE SNOWBLIND SERIES

*Snowblind * Snowblind: The Killing Grounds*

STANDALONE SUSPENSE THRILLERS

*Bloodletting * Condemned * Immun3 * The Coyote * The Event*

THE EXTINCTION AGENDA SERIES

(Written as Michael Laurence)

*The Extinction Agenda * The Annihilation Protocol*
The Elimination Threat

CHIMERA

MICHAEL MCBRIDE

PRETERNATURAL PRESS
DENVER, COLORADO

First paperback edition published by Preternatural Press

www.michaelmcbride.net

Cover Design by Deranged Doctor Design

ISBN 979-8-453-95496-4

First Edition: September 2021

10 9 8 7 6 5 4 3 2 1

For the Woonuses

.

1

Francis S. Gabreski Air National Guard Base
Westhampton Beach, NY
40.837880, -72.644385

Today

Senior Master Sergeant Dan Cameron strides down the corridor, his mind running through every possible scenario that would have warranted the abrupt termination of his confined space rescue training at the FDNY academy on Randall's Island and a police escort back to the base. His camouflage fatigues are covered with dirt, and his boots leave dusty prints on the otherwise pristine tile floor. A ring of soot encircles his face where the SCBA mask had been seated over his rugged features, and his chestnut hair is matted from the helmet he'd been wearing a mere twenty minutes ago. His hazel eyes focus upon the door at the end of the hallway, which opens at the sound of his approaching footsteps.

Lieutenant Colonel Richard Andrews emerges and ushers him into a conference room, where Colonel Jack Patrick is already seated at the head of a massive oak table. The commander of the Air National Guard's 106th Rescue Wing cuts an imposing figure in his dress blues, which he's donned for the man seated beside him, whose dark, hooded eyes latch onto Cameron as he enters and salutes his superior officer.

"Take a seat," Patrick says, inclining his chin toward the chair to his right. He swivels the laptop in front of him so that Cameron can see the screen. "We received this footage from the NSF just under an hour ago."

He taps a key, and the video recording plays. A woman appears, bathed in the red glow of emergency lights. Her ebon hair is wild and tangled. Wide blue eyes stare out from a face that fades in and out of the shadows. Twin lines of mucus glisten from her upper lip. Fractals of ice have formed on the inside of the slanted windows to either side of her, through the cracks in which a wicked wind howls.

A thudding sound erupts from behind her and the woman glances over her shoulder toward a barricaded door. The chairs piled on top of the table braced against it shiver with the impact from the other side.

"This is Dr. Mira Stone at Academy Station," she says. Clouds of breath plume from her lips and her voice trembles when she speaks. "We've lost primary power and the integrity of the complex has been compromised—"

Thud!

The door shudders, scooting the table inward. Its legs screech on the tile.

"Something is in here with us. Six of us are already dead. The rest—"

Crack!

The door bursts open. The woman looks back as the chairs topple to the floor amid splinters of wood from the broken trim. Sparks rain from an electrical conduit in the outer hallway, where the emergency lights stain the darkness.

There's no one there.

The woman turns to the camera, her eyes frantic.

"We're going to try to make it across the glacier to Station Nord. Academy Station is lost. Do not—I repeat—*do not* attempt to reclaim—"

Movement behind her. A wavering of the air, like heat rising from a desert highway.

The woman lunges toward the camera, causing the view to spin wildly and topple to the floor—

The image darkens and the communication ends. Cameron stares at the monitor in silence, trying to figure out precisely what he's just witnessed.

"Repeated efforts to hail Academy Station have gone unanswered," the man seated across from him says. He wears a suit that undoubtedly cost more than Cameron makes in a month and a visitor's badge that reads: Dr. Carter Young, NeXgen Biotechnology. "All systems are offline, so we can't access them remotely."

"You need a team to arrange for extraction from Nord?" Cameron says.

"We're talking about Peary Land in Greenland, the northernmost landmass on the planet," Patrick says. "The temperature's currently thirty below and Nord is reporting whiteout conditions. There's no way they're reaching it across a hundred miles of open arctic terrain."

"This will be a search and rescue mission," Andrews says. The medical group commander wears small round glasses that make his eyes appear too large for his face. "We've been in contact with a Canadian Coast Guard cutter on Baffin Bay and several commercial vessels in the Greenland and Norwegian Seas, but they lack your team's medical training and experience under these conditions."

The 103rd Rescue Squadron had performed extensive field exercises in the frozen wastes of Kangerlussuaq, Greenland with the 109th Airlift Wing, which operates the only ski-equipped LC-130 Hercules transport in the entire U.S. military, but they'd never attempted an actual retrieval operation.

"One of our subsidiaries operates a shipping fleet out of Norway," Dr. Young says. "We could dispatch a SAR team, but even if they set sail right now, you'd still beat them by a good eight hours."

"We can be airborne in thirty minutes," Cameron says.

"You'll be taking a scientific team from NeXgen, as well," Patrick says. "You're to locate Academy Station's personnel and secure the station, where Dr. Young's team will assume operational command."

Cameron furrows his brow.

"Are we not extracting the civilians, sir?"

"There are other objectives considered to be of critical importance to national security."

"At an outpost operated by the National Science Foundation, sir?"

"In conjunction with commercial interests aligned with the Department of Defense."

Cameron glances across the table at Young, whose expression remains unreadable.

"What were they doing at Academy Station?" he asks, his eyes never leaving those of the lone civilian. "I need to know what kind of situation we're walking into."

Young turns to Patrick, who nods and gestures for him to proceed.

"What I'm about to show you is classified top secret," Young says, swiveling his laptop just far enough that Cameron can see the monitor. "You are not to speak of it outside of this room, not even to your team."

Cameron didn't like withholding information from his men, especially concerning an operation where lives hung in the balance and so many variables were outside of their direct control. He's just about to voice his objections when Young opens a screengrab of Dr. Stone. The barricade has already fallen behind her and she's just warned them not to attempt to reclaim the station. The civilian contractor had enhanced the resolution, sharpened the detail, and zoomed in over her shoulder, where Cameron had initially detected the hint of movement. What had originally appeared to be a heat mirage was simply a distortion of the background, as though a localized section had been displaced by just a few pixels. If he leaned closer, he could almost imagine it looked like a figure running toward her from behind.

A figure with strikingly human proportions.

2

Three Months Ago

The red Airbus AS350 helicopter banked around Independence Fjord, offering its passengers a stunning view of the sheer granite escarpments and sparkling whitecaps, which stretched to the distant Arctic Ocean. Exposed rock gave way to hardpacked snow. Academy Glacier rose before them as a great wall of ice, its calving front in a perpetual state of decay. A great concrete dam had been constructed in the mouth of a side-channel, trapping a two-mile-long body of seawater known affectionately as Lake Tranquility. Ice floes drifted through the maze of jagged granite islands breaching its surface, which appeared as black as the sea on the moon after which it was named.

Dr. Mira Stone leaned against the window and looked straight down into it, hoping for a glimpse of the whales she'd heard so much about, but her breath fogged the glass at the least opportune moment. She wiped away the condensation with the sleeve of her parka as the lake once more vanished into the deep canyon, leaving her staring at her reflection, her amber eyes looking back at her from behind the strands of raven-black hair that had come untucked from her ski cap. In that moment, she was again the young girl who'd dared to dream of a better world, not the associate professor of climate science at Northern Arizona University's School of Earth and Sustainability who feared that even her best efforts to combat global warming would prove to be too little, too late.

The chopper passed over the glacier, its shadow streaking up the sheer face to greet them and chasing them across the seamless ice.

Everything was just as she'd imagined it would be, although never in a million years had she dreamed she'd actually be here. The other passengers appeared every bit as overwhelmed by the magnitude of their surroundings, although in different ways. Dr. Carrie Keyes pressed her freckled face against the opposite window, her auburn hair standing apart from the fur trim of her hood like little wisps of flame, her hands disappearing underneath it in an attempt to hold the cans over her ears. Dr. Rylan Moore sat between them, his face pale, his eyes fixed straight ahead, and his feet tapping a nervous rhythm on the floor. He hadn't spoken a word since they'd boarded the chopper at the airport in Qaanaaq, little more than a stretch of dirt on the shore of ice-choked Inglefield Fjord, although he'd frequently pressed the back of his gloved hand to his lips as though in an effort to keep something in.

"There it is," Carrie said through the microphone on her headset.

Mira leaned across Moore's lap and looked past Carrie as the helicopter circled back toward the fjord. Her heart raced when Academy Station came into view, the sun's golden rays glinting from its silver metallic surface. It looked like a hexagonal spaceship that had crashed onto the glacier, skidded across the ice, and come to rest hanging over the edge of the granite slope. The leading edge was perched precariously on a network of support posts, its tinted windows offering a view from which she could only imagine witnessing the aurora borealis. Photovoltaic solar arrays lined the slanted roof, from which multicolored prayer flags had been strung, the faded cloth flaring on the breeze. Wind turbines stood from the rugged ridgeline, their long blades turning, driving the power to augment the rows of thermal solar cells ascending the hillside. A radio antenna bristling with satellite dishes stood from the highest crest, quite possibly the tallest structure on the northern end of the continent.

The chopper descended onto the level ground behind the structure, its rotors whipping up a cloud of accumulated snowflakes, which momentarily swallowed it whole. Two silhouettes wearing parkas and balaclavas emerged from the station and tromped toward them, their arms raised to shield their eyes. The engine ramped down with a whine, and the snow settled once more.

Someone opened the door from the outside and cold air rushed into the cabin. Mira flinched as though she'd been struck. She thought she'd been prepared for the cold. The low-thirties hadn't sounded that bad at all, but when coupled with ninety-some percent humidity, it felt like the exposed skin on her hands and face had instantly turned to ice. She could only imagine how painful it would come winter, when the temperatures rarely rose above the negative double digits.

A heavyset woman with graying hair and a florid face leaned into the chopper, her breath billowing from her lips.

"Welcome to Academy Station," she said, her voice surprisingly deep and melodic. "I'm Amy and this here is Elroy, like from *The Jetsons*. I'd love to say we volunteered to be your welcoming committee, but—truth be told—we drew the short straws, so grab your bags and hurry the heck up. It's colder than a witch's tit out here."

Moore unbuckled, climbed over Carrie, and shoved past Amy and Elroy. He promptly doubled over and vomited onto the snow between his feet, spattering his boots.

"Now that's how you make a first impression," Elroy said, clapping him on the back. He had bright blue eyes and a bushy black beard flecked with red. Ice had already begun to form in his mustache and around his nostrils. "Kick some snow over that before we have every bear north of the Arctic Circle thinking it's dinner time."

"How can you even tell with this infernal sun in the sky all day and night?" Carrie asked.

"We maintain an artificial twenty-four-hour light cycle inside the station," Amy said. "The tinting of the windows varies by the time of day. Besides, we have our bellies to remind us when it's chow time. We might not have gourmet rations, but you'll be amazed what our cook can do with them."

The pilot unlatched the port-side compartment and handed out their bags, one at a time. The majority of their gear had been shipped ahead of them on the cargo transport out of Narsarsuaq, which serviced the station twice a year. With any luck, their equipment was already set up and waiting for them in their respective labs.

Mira slung her hiking pack over her shoulders and followed Amy and Elroy toward the entrance to the facility. She'd chatted with both of them in countless Zoom meetings leading up to their arrival, but this was the first time she'd seen either of them in anything larger than a tiny square on her laptop. Of course, she knew all about both of them. Dr. Amy Madigan was the chief scientific officer and ostensibly in charge of all of the various projects under her roof, which meant that she spent more time attending to administrative duties than her own research, which, fortunately, could be handled largely from her desk, where she tracked a native population of polar bears by satellite and surveilled their activities by drone.

Dr. Elroy Hudson was one of the world's foremost experts on renewable energy sources. He'd worked closely with the team of architects and engineers responsible for designing this station, which was the first of its kind not to utilize fossil fuels in any form or fashion. It was a marvel of industrial design, employing both thermal and photovoltaic solar panels to generate power during the endless days of summer and wind turbines to harness the energy of the tempestuous winter gales, the combination of which was so efficient that the system required an entire storage room filled with lead-acid batteries to capture the excess energy for later use.

Amy opened the station's front door, releasing a swell of heat that reminded Mira of entering a greenhouse. The warmth on her face felt positively divine. She passed through an anteroom adorned with framed blueprints of the facility and photographs taken during its construction and ascended a staircase to the residential level.

"Your suites are just around the corner to your right," Amy said. "I'll give you a few minutes to stow your gear before we embark upon the grand tour."

Mira followed Carrie and Moore down a narrow hallway. Someone had written her name on the whiteboard hanging beside the door to her room. Several of the other researchers had already scribbled notes of welcome and drawn little smiley faces. She paused to soak it all in, took a deep breath, and stepped into the eight-by-ten enclosure that would serve as her home away from home for at least the next year. There was barely enough room for a single bed and a closet, which wasn't much larger than the backpack she hung from the hook inside it. A wooden desk had been pushed up against the back wall, underneath the window, which afforded her a stunning view across the icecap, all the way to the jagged rim of Hagen Fjord on the far horizon, seemingly at the end of the world.

Few people in the history of humankind had ever laid eyes upon this magical landscape, let alone lived here for any length of time. It was heartbreaking to contemplate the ravages being wrought by climate change all around her at this very moment, melting sea ice and permafrost and driving already endangered species to the brink of extinction.

But that was all about to change.

3

"We have fifteen full-time residents," Amy said, guiding them through the residential wing, where the living quarters were crammed together on the opposite side of the hall from cramped communal restrooms. Heated air thumped through the exposed ductwork overhead, which ran perpendicular to the thick wooden support posts that formed the station's underlying framework. "The majority of them are researchers working on different climate-related projects under the auspices of the NSF. The remainder is composed of support staff hired on annual renewable contracts. We currently have a professional chef and two facilities engineers, one of whom also serves as our yoga instructor, should you be interested in joining our morning exercise group after breakfast."

Mira followed with her head on a swivel, silently taking in everything around her, the cylindrical silver cryogenic storage dewar she'd brought all this way cradled to her chest. The outer walls of the facility were slanted and arrayed with windows metered by angled wooden beams, while the inner walls were vertical and surrounded the two-story central core, which housed the climate control systems.

They passed from one room to the next as they traversed the circumference of the hexagon's upper level: a dedicated communications center that looked like the flying bridge of a ship, with racks of handheld transceivers on chargers, long-range video satellite systems, and monitors tracking everything from the weather to the winds and oceanic currents in real-time; a research library with sunlit tables on one side and bookcases on the other; a lounge with upholstered furniture, a television, and a shelf brimming with DVDs and video games for the dusty console perched on top of it; and a well-appointed kitchen with a serving bar, several small tables, and a narrow staircase leading down to a dry storage room filled with industrial-size containers of foodstuffs and supplies, including an entire wall of toilet paper.

"We keep the coffee pot percolating around the clock," Amy said. "You finish it; you start another. That's the most important rule here. Break it, and people will start going Jack Torrance in a hurry."

"Can we see our labs?" Carrie asked.

Amy turned and winked at the three of them.

"I was saving the best for last."

They funneled down the rear staircase, rounded a landing decorated with black-and-white photographs of ancient vessels locked in the broken ice, and descended into the lower level. Despite the recycled air blowing from the vents, it was markedly colder down here. Machinery hummed from behind a closed metal door, from which a distinct chill radiated. Amy opened it and led them into the climate control center. Inside, a man wearing navy blue cargo pants, a red parka, and noise-canceling headphones tended to monitors with flashing lights and equipment sprouting the pipes and aluminum ductwork that extended all the way up the hexagonal walls to the catwalk encircling the second story.

"This is Ed Dougherty, our chief engineer," Amy shouted over the mechanical ruckus. The heavyset man raised his goggles, tipped his hardhat, and offered a disarming smile that was barely visible through his thick beard. "He and Tom Nichols are the best friends you'll ever have, as they're the ones responsible for keeping you from freezing to death, which, I assure you, can happen a whole lot faster than you expect out here on this glacier, a world away from anything resembling civilization."

Amy guided them back to the main corridor, her footsteps echoing from the hollow space housing the ducts and conduits underneath the floor. The labs were all wedge-shaped—like slices of Bundt cake arranged around the engineering core—and two steps lower than the hallway. The first one they passed featured a counter with a clean hood, a PCR workstation, and a table upon which someone had anatomically arranged the skeleton of what appeared to be a whale.

"I was hoping to introduce you to Jen and Aaron, but they must have already gone down to the dam," Amy said. "You can find them out there pretty much every waking moment. I'm sure you'll run across them soon enough, though. They have to eat sometime."

Mira looked forward to meeting Drs. Jennifer Albert and Aaron Wallace, whose work with the whales she'd hoped to see from the chopper was truly fascinating, although the marine biologists sounded more than a little territorial about their precious lake, which they would soon be forced to share for the first time.

"The labs are smaller than I'd been led to believe," Moore said. He still looked a little green around the gills, but he'd regained at least a small measure of his dignity, which had probably come with his change of shoes. "I wish I'd been more suitably forewarned."

"I trust you'll find a way to make it work," Amy said, failing to hide the annoyance in her voice. She gestured to the next lab in the sequence. "Have a go for yourself."

Moore descended into a space that hardly seemed large enough to contain all of the equipment packed inside, and yet the volcanologist beamed as he explored workstations better appointed than any university lab, every surface shining with stainless steel and humming with electrical life. He waved them away without so much as a backward glance.

"I'll let the fact that he's sharing the lab with Anthony Martinez and Laurie Simmons, our resident geologist and oceanographer, be a fun little surprise," Amy said. She winked and led them out over the support posts. The wind howled from below them, producing a subtle, disconcerting vibration. She stopped in front of the next lab, which was stuffed with equipment, the majority of which Mira had never seen before, let alone worked with. Outside of the standard computer and microscope stations, she only recognized the mass and atomic spectrometers and the vacuum extraction lines used to prepare isotopic samples. "This is the climatology lab. Carrie, you'll be forced to work in such terribly cramped quarters with Dr. Leo Olafson. Brushing against you from behind, the warmth of his breath on your neck, his gentle touch causing the goosebumps to rise along your arms . . ." Her words trailed off and she appeared momentarily lost. "Where was I?"

"On the verge of needing a cold shower," Carrie said.

"You mock me now, but just you wait and see," Amy said, blushing. She turned and continued down the hallway, rounding the corner and stopping before the next open doorway, where a man in a white lab coat sat with his back to them. He swiveled around in his chair and offered a smile that didn't quite reach his eyes. His face was pale, his hair thinning, and his red eyes suggested that he didn't get nearly enough sleep. "This is the medical suite. Drs. Mira Stone and Carrie Keyes . . . meet Dr. Kyle Porter. Dr. Porter . . . Drs. Stone and Keyes."

"A pleasure," he said, returning to his work.

"While Dr. Porter is technically our staff physician, he sees patients by appointment only as they tend to distract from his research on how the human immune system copes with the bacterial load generated by living in such a confined space over an extended period of time." Amy lowered her voice to a whisper as she ushered them down the hallway. "I don't recommend asking him about it or you might never be able to eat again."

"I think it sounds quite interesting," Mira said.

"I'm glad you think so because he'll be taking weekly swabs and blood draws, whether that's what you signed on for or not." Amy stopped before the next lab, which was filled with computer equipment and offered a breathtaking view of the water and the distant mouth of Independence Fjord, framed by towering escarpments. "Elroy and I share this lab. We were here first, so we got to choose. Some days I think I spend more time staring out that window than actually working."

Mira's heart beat faster and faster as Amy continued down the hallway toward the lone remaining doorway before they again reached the stairs. She'd spent her entire life preparing for this moment. Time slowed around her. She turned and stood in the threshold, staring down upon the destiny she'd envisioned since she was a little girl on a ranch in the middle of nowhere, contemplating an apocalyptic future of rising temperatures, melting ice caps, and vanishing coastlines.

Her legs seemed to move of their own accord, carrying her down the stairs and past a giant aquarium situated below a blinding lighting array designed to mimic the sun's rays at this precise latitude. At twelve feet long, ten feet tall, and ten feet deep, it contained more than ten thousand gallons of water and had to be anchored directly to the underlying bedrock. Seaweed wavered on the artificial current beneath water hazy with tiny air bubbles and aquatic microorganisms. Rock formations stood from the pale gray sediment, all of which had been collected directly from Lake Tranquility. Enormous fans mounted to an elevated platform blew across the surface, simulating the prevailing arctic winds.

"Well, it's about time," someone called from behind racks of equipment piled so high they nearly blocked the windows. The voice was melodic and lightly accented. Finnish, Mira knew from their countless conversations over the phone and in online conference calls. "I was starting to think you weren't coming."

Dr. Sammie Rantanen stepped into view, her white-blond hair tied in a ponytail behind her head, her eyes like amethysts stomped into the snow. She bounded down the aisle, engulfed Mira in a hug, and twirled her loose.

"After all these months of working together online, it's nice to finally meet you in person," Mira said. "I see you've already set up everything and—"

"Do you have it with you?" Sammie asked, bouncing excitedly on her toes.

Mira smirked and held up the cylindrical container. She set it down on the nearest countertop, unlatched the lid, and raised it until it locked into place. A cloud of supercooled air dissipated, revealing the vials that hadn't left her sight on three airplanes and a helicopter, crossing two continents and nearly the entire northern hemisphere. She plucked one from the clip holding it in place and held it up to the light, which turned the water inside a rather vile shade of green.

"What is it?" Carrie asked, leaning over her shoulder to get a better look.

"The future," Mira said. "Or at least our best hope for it."

4

"You're certain all of the levels are within parameters?" Mira said. She crouched on the platform above the aquarium, near where the sealed vial floated. "Ammonia? Nitrates? Temperature? The slightest spike in any variable could kill the culture and contaminate the entire tank."

"Who do you think you're talking to here?" Sammie asked. "As you Americans say, this is not my first rodeo."

Mira glanced down and was surprised to see that only the slender Finn remained. How long had Amy and Carrie been gone? She hadn't even noticed them leave.

"I trust you, but we only have six—"

"Just do it already."

Mira took a deep breath and unsealed the container. An amorphous sludge slid out and floated several inches below the surface. It appeared almost fuzzy, like a gob of algae. Without the vial to contain it, it slowly expanded. For a moment, she feared that the organisms had died during transit, that months of intensive labor were now for naught, but as she watched, the filamentous appendages relaxed and spread out into the cold seawater, flattening to increase the surface area exposed to the artificial lighting. Its coloration subtly brightened before her eyes until it took on an iridescent purple cast, refracting the rays of light into a pale haze and casting a diffuse shadow into the water beneath it.

"We did it," Sammie said. "It's magnificent."

Mira couldn't find the words to respond. Magnificent was an understatement; what they'd done was magical. It was as though they'd reached through the veil and plucked their own chimera from mythology, only rather than a fire-breathing monster with a lion's head, a goat's body, and a serpent's tail, they'd created an aquatic biofilm using phytoplankton, purple bacteria, and spider DNA, a combination they hoped would prove to be the single most significant climate change combatant the world had ever known.

Whether one believed that climate change was anthropogenic or due to natural causes, there was no denying the empirical evidence: the oceans surrounding the polar ice caps were getting warmer and more acidic. Oceanic temperatures across the globe were maintained by the ceaseless movement of currents that transported warmer water to the poles and cooler water toward the equators. Any dramatic interruption of that cycle could cause the earth to abruptly freeze as it did during the Younger Dryas, 12,000 years ago, or heat up as it did during the mid-Holocene Warm Period, 6,000 years ago. Falling pH contributed to that feedback loop by diminishing the amount of carbon dioxide that could be absorbed by the ocean, in some cases even leading to its emission, releasing free hydrogen ions that caused the water to become increasingly acidic. Combined, the two formed the greatest variable for which climatologists couldn't account. Conservative estimates suggested that most climate predictions, which were notoriously unreliable to begin with, were inherently hampered by the unpredictable reactions of living microorganisms like phytoplankton to the changing environmental conditions around them.

While technically neither animals nor plants, phytoplankton were responsible for producing nearly half of the oxygen we breathed and consuming a full quarter of all CO_2 generated by the burning of fossil fuels. Given access to proper ratios of sunlight and nutrients, they bloomed in concentrations so dense they were visible from space, but as the oceans warmed, more distinct stratifications formed in the water column. One such layer, the nutricline, provided the nutrients that phytoplankton consumed as part of the process of photosynthesis, which dramatically increased the temperature of the water above it and contributed to the melting of sea ice, leading to deeper penetration of sunlight, further heating the water near the surface in a deadly positive feedback loop of increasing temperatures and rising acidity that was responsible for killing off more than forty percent of the global population of phytoplankton since 1950 and driving the remainder toward the cooler waters of the poles.

The key to halting the loss of sea ice, stabilizing the temperature, and returning the pH to normal levels lay in breaking that feedback loop, and the only viable way of doing so was through the phytoplankton themselves, specifically a type known as diatoms—disc-shaped algae with glasslike cell walls composed of silica—which trapped CO_2 and sank to the bottom of the ocean, where they decomposed into fossil fuel over the course of thousands of years, starting the cycle all over again.

One such species of diatom, *Chaetoceros gelidus*, utilized long spines called *setae* to attach to other individuals, forming colonies that functioned like microscopic carbon dioxide scrubbers and attracted mutualistic bacteria, which fed upon the waste byproducts of photosynthesis. These bacteria began the process of decomposition as the diatoms died and began sinking to the bottom, releasing an organic yield of phosphorus, nitrogen, and carbon—the very nutrients that phytoplankton needed to photosynthesize—that settled into the nutricline, where living specimens gathered to feed.

Mira's working theory was that by raising the level of the nutricline, they'd be able to reduce the amount of heat trapped above it, allowing the sea ice to refreeze and diminishing the penetration of solar radiation, thus decreasing the temperature, any slight change in which would effectively begin the process of not just stalling, but completely reversing climate change. The most critical factors were finding a way for the diatoms to photosynthesize at a shallower depth and slowing the rate at which the dead organisms sank, buying the bacteria more time to release the nutrients for the living organisms to feed upon, essentially creating a new, self-sustaining nutricline high above the existing one.

That was where Sammie had come in. She'd proposed the idea of creating a biofilm, which by definition was a community of microorganisms irreversibly attached to a surface and encased by extracellular polymeric substances that enhanced the community's ability to scavenge nutrients from the environment and promote metabolism under extreme conditions. The most significant limiting factor, of course, was what they could attach it to, as floating too near the surface would expose the diatoms to lethal levels of ultraviolet radiation and encouraging its growth upon any kind of object tethered at the proper depth wouldn't allow for the necessary lateral expansion of the biofilm. They'd needed to find a substate slightly denser than the surrounding water and yet light enough to float both within the photic—or sunlit—zone and below the shipping lanes, one with enough tactile strength to maintain its form in one of the harshest environments on the planet and porous enough to allow marine life to pass through it with minimal disruption, and one that would continuously expand to provide greater surface area for the microbes living upon it.

A semi-buoyant, self-contained food web.

Web being the operative word.

By inserting segments of DNA from an orb-weaver spider, *Nephila clavipes*, into the genome of a purple marine bacterium called *Rhodovulum sulfidophilum*, Sammie had been able to stimulate the latter species to express the major ampullate spiridion—MaSp—genes responsible for the production and secretion of microscopic strands of dragline silk, the structural component of spider webs and the lifeline by which they dangled, a high-molecular-density material stronger per unit weight than steel. Immersion in water caused the silk, which was naturally hydrophobic, to behave almost like rubber, helping it maintain its tensile strength down to -40 Celsius. And at one-sixth the density of steel, it was just buoyant enough to form a floating mat that adhered the diatoms and bacteria together at a depth roughly twenty percent higher than the existing nutricline. Throw in the refractive qualities of the iridescent purple bacteria, and they were looking at an immediate reduction of surface temperature and sea ice melting by a factor of two and cooling of the underlying water column by a magnitude of four, the combination of which, according to statistical models, would completely reverse the effects of climate change by the year 2053.

And now, here they were, on the cusp of seeing the dream they shared implemented on the grandest scale, but before they dared release it into the open ocean, they needed to make sure that it worked under controlled conditions, which was the whole reason they'd traveled halfway around the world to be here.

"What do you say we take this baby out on the road and see what she can do," Mira said.

"You mean release the organism into the biocube in the

lake?" Sammie said. "Don't you at least want to unpack first? Maybe, you know, take a shower?"

Mira blushed. She could only imagine how ripe she must have smelled, but at the moment, she simply didn't care.

"I don't know about you," she said, "but I didn't come all this way just to stare at a fish tank."

5

The staircase descended from the southwestern side of the station into a narrow crevice, which shielded them from the brunt of the wind. Their footsteps clanged from the metal steps, the grated surface preventing them from turning into miniature sheets of ice; however, the spikes of their crampons occasionally got stuck in the holes. At the bottom, the windswept snow gave way to bare granite and loose talus. A path traced the topography toward the sheer escarpment upon which the station sat, mercifully keeping them in its lee until they reached the rugged shoreline, from which they were finally able to see their destination.

"Watch your step through here!" Sammie shouted, a frigid gust ripping the words from her lips and carrying them over her shoulder on a cloud of breath. "These loose rocks slide across one another like ball bearings!"

Mira lowered her head against the wind and focused on her footing. She could already feel ice forming around her nostrils and see it riming the strands of hair that had worked their way loose from her stocking cap. What in the name of God had possessed her to leave Flagstaff to come to such a nightmarishly cold place? And this was the middle of summer!

The path terminated on a cliff overlooking the fjord, twenty-some feet down. A narrow walkway led out onto top of the dam, across the bowed surface of which the tempestuous gales screamed. Tattered flags snapped from poles mounted to either side of the boxlike research facility. It was positioned roughly a quarter of the way across the half-mile-long concrete structure, a convex barrier following the shoreline of the fjord and spanning the mouth of the outlet, trapping Lake Tranquility in a deep cul-de-sac of towering cliffs. The side opposite Academy Station was crowned with ice, like a frozen wave preparing to crash down on the human-made lake. Waves broke against the distant islands with a constant rumbling sound.

Mira watched for the humped backs of the whales or spurts of air from their blowholes as she crossed the icy concrete, clinging to the railing. A cloud of steam billowed from the roof of the research center, its windows lighted and fogged over from the inside. Sammie had to chip a layer of ice from the frame to open the door. A glorious aura of heat enveloped them as they crossed the threshold.

The building was roughly the size of a mobile home. It contained furniture strewn with pillows and blankets, a table piled with notebooks, and a dedicated computer system that monitored the dam's structural integrity. A television mounted above the picture windows, which offered an unobstructed panoramic view of lake, rolled through screens displaying the current weather, an hourly forecast, and a doppler image of a storm front advancing across the glacier from the southwest. At the far end were two closed doors, one of which presumably led to the restroom, the other onto the continuation of the dam.

Mira and Sammie hung their parkas on hooks beside two others, beneath which rested matching pairs of boots: one large, the other small. There was no sign of whoever might have worn them.

"They must be down on the observation deck," Sammie said, leading Mira around consoles with inset monitors, dials and gauges, and banks of switches and flashing lights to a staircase framed by an iron railing that had been invisible from her previous vantage point. "The system is fully automated; however, our engineers service it twice a day and carry remote monitors with them at all times. A failure wouldn't be catastrophic, by any means, but good luck getting someone out here to repair it."

The stairs were steep and doubled back upon themselves several times, like those of a skyscraper. Mira and Sammie were well below the waterline when a faint bluish light spread across the landing below them. Their footsteps echoed from a space far larger than Mira had expected.

"Anybody down here?" Sammie called, ducking underneath the low concrete ceiling and stepping out into a narrow room built directly into the dam.

"Over here," a deep voice responded. It sounded like it originated from somewhere on the other side of a maze of pipes and conduits.

Thick Plexiglas viewports were set into the walls on both sides, revealing the turbulent black water of the fjord on one side and the greenish brown salt lake on the other. Air bubbles and bits of organic material tumbled past the figure seated at the small desk in front of the central window, silhouetted by the glow from the screen of his laptop. He removed a pair of headphones and tapped several keys before turning to face them. His skin was dark, his head freshly shaved, and his eyes red from staring at the screen in the pale light passing through the murky water. He wore a flannel jacket over bib snow pants and tennis shoes he must have had waiting for him when he kicked off his boots.

"Where's your partner?" Sammie asked.

As if to answer her question, a woman wearing a drysuit and scuba gear drifted past the window. She held a diving camera, from which a blinding light diffused into the water.

"Jen's documenting the introduction of Teng, a rehabilitated male we acquired from a zoo in Shanghai, to the rest of the pod —which is technically called a blessing—while I record their vocalizations and map their movements." He glanced up at them as though seeing them for the first time. "Dr. Stone? I'm glad you were finally able to join us."

"It's great to finally meet you in person, Dr. Wallace."

"Call me Aaron. Formalities quickly disappear when you have to share a communal bathroom." He offered a playful wink. "Sammie here's told me all about your work. Crazy sci-fi stuff."

"And I'm excited to learn about yours," Mira said. "I find whales fascinating. Especially the way they communicate."

Aaron beamed like a child and unplugged his headphones. A barrage of rapid clicking sounds, metered by eerie, haunting noises, erupted from the speakers of his laptop and reverberated from the concrete walls.

"I thought whales sang," Mira said.

"Blue whales sing," Aaron said. "Narwhal vocalizations range from low-pitched sounds reminiscent of the buzz of a playing card in the spokes of a bike's tire to high-pitched whistles that sound like someone blowing on the reed of a woodwind instrument. They use that clicking you hear as a form of echolocation, but we're only now beginning to investigate their social interactions and how they play a role in migratory behavior. With the addition of Teng, we now have six narwhals and eight beluga whales. A few have already established breeding pairs and we're expecting our first calves in the spring."

A shadow passed across the viewports. Mira turned in time to see an eight-foot-long creature swim past. Its smooth skin was mottled in shades of gray. A giant horn easily long and sharp enough to spear a man protruded from its face. She gasped as it veered toward Jen, who easily moved out of its way and ran her palm along its length as it passed.

"Narwhals are gentle creatures," Aaron said. "That horn is really just a big old tooth that grows right through its upper lip. While they've been known to stun fish by clubbing them with it, they don't use it for hunting. It's actually a sensory organ with millions of nerve endings so sensitive that they can detect subtle changes in the water, like salinity, pressure, and especially temperature, which alert them to the possibility of the ice beginning to freeze above their heads. While they can hold their breath for nearly half an hour, they still have to breach the surface for air at some point or they'll drown. In a pinch, they can use their tusks to punch through a thin layer of ice, but breaking it would be extraordinarily painful. And likely fatal."

Jen tapped the window, waved to them, and gestured for Aaron to put on his earphones. She spoke through the headset she wore underneath her diving helmet for several seconds. He nodded and turned to face Mira and Sammie.

"She says she'd be happy to release your biofilm into the cube, if you brought it with you."

Mira smiled, whipped the container from the pocket of her parka, and held it up to the glass. She glanced at Sammie, who deferred with a smirk and a sweep of her arm.

"The honor is yours, Dr. Stone."

"There's a pass-through box over there," Aaron said, inclining his chin toward a stainless-steel hatch set into the concrete between two of the windows.

Mira opened the door, set the vacuum-sealed container on the grated drain inside, closed the door, and engaged the air seal. Jen opened the hatch on the other side, flooding the interior with water, and removed the container. She held it up for all of them to see and closed the hatch again.

The wall vibrated and produced a whirring sound as the water trapped inside the pass-through box was flushed back into the sea.

Jen swam away from them, toward the farthest window on the left, against which a Plexiglas cube had been mounted. It utilized dozens of tiny, semi-permeable forward osmosis membranes on each of its exposed surfaces to selectively filter out organic material, allow water to circulate unimpeded, and prevent the larger organisms contained inside from escaping. She screwed the cap of the container onto an external nozzle, which broke the vacuum seal and released the biofilm into the cube.

Mira shone a flashlight through the viewport and watched the sludge float into the murky water, tumbling on the current. The biofilm unfurled and spread out until it was so thin that she couldn't see it at all. Her stomach fluttered. She glanced at Sammie, whose expression mirrored her own. She obviously felt it, too. The significance of their accomplishment. The magnitude of the moment.

They were going to change the world.

6

20,000 Feet Above Lake Melville
Labrador, Canada
53.692908, -59.437899

Now

Cameron leans back in his seat and rubs his eyes. His head aches from the roar of the turboprops, the pressure from the headset over his ears, and the strain of concentrating on the countless files open on the screen of his tactical tablet. He needs to learn everything he can about the scientists and the station itself, including the technical schematics and layout, in case his team's mission suddenly changes from a routine rescue operation to the engagement of an unknown enemy.

And that was the problem; they simply didn't know what awaited them at Academy Station.

Information was the key to any successful operation. Going in unprepared increased the chances of leaving someone behind. Or worse, risking the lives of everyone involved. Any variable for which they didn't account could ultimately prove catastrophic. An ice shelf could calve beneath their feet, dragging them down into the frigid sea. An unstable structure could collapse, pinning them beneath the rubble while they slowly froze to death. A power source could explode. And in an environment like the one they were rapidly approaching, there were far worse things that could happen to them and there was no one left to come to their aid.

"You okay, Sergeant?" a voice asks through his headset.

Cameron glances up at the man strapped into the side-facing dropdown seat across the aisle from him, so close their knees nearly touch. Staff Sergeant Steve Ryder has the long, lithe body of a swimmer, a shock of dark hair, and the sun-leathered skin of a man who's spent years on the open sea. The rescue combat officer wears MultiCam fatigues and an expression of concern.

"Everything's copacetic," Cameron says. He can't afford to let the others sense his unease. "Just wishing I'd had the chance to shower after training at the FDNY academy this morning."

"That's what we're all wishing right about now," Senior Airman Todd MacDonald says, laughing hysterically. His thick red hair and pale skin have cursed him to a lifetime of being called Ronald, a constant frustration he channels into inappropriate humor and weightlifting. Now, the only people who called him by that name did so at their own risk, which the men harnessed in the seats around him took great pleasure in doing, knowing they were the only people in the world he allowed to get away with it. "I was starting to think something had died and started to rot in here."

Major Aadan Bashir, slouching in the seat beside him, tips up the brim of his cap and opens one eye.

"You're smelling yourself, Ronny," the paratrooper says. A heavily muscled man whose parents immigrated from Somalia, he's completed more than a thousand jumps, including one where he landed on a burning Chechen tanker, his flaming chute in tatters, and rescued the crew trapped belowdecks. The hair had never grown back on the left side of his head, so he'd started shaving and polishing that mahogany dome of his until it shined. "You'd need a chisel to scrape that funk off your tiny sack."

"Leave the poor guy alone," Major Joe Gonzales says, stowing his tool kit and strapping himself in next to Cameron.

"Thank you," Ronny says. "At least one of you doesn't always have to be a total douchebag."

"I mean, can't you see Little Mac's already got Whopper envy."

The vehicle operations specialist leads a chorus of laughter. He's considerably shorter and thinner than the rest of them, wears his omnipresent camo cap so far back on his head that the brim stands nearly straight up, and has the wispy mustache of a thirteen-year-old boy. He couldn't have looked more like "The fastest mouse in all Mexico" if he tried, hence the reason everyone called him Speedy. That, of course, and the fact that he was the most skilled driver any of them had ever worked with, especially when it came to the SUSV—small unit support vehicle—parked behind them in the cargo hold.

The Bandvagn 206 armored all-terrain vehicle might have looked like two miniature snow-camouflaged boxcars linked together by a single coupling, but with its tank-like tracks and six-cylinder Mercedes diesel engine, it could go positively anywhere, which they just might have to do if they're going to find and retrieve Dr. Stone and the other scientists. Fortunately, before he'd transferred across the country to be closer to his elderly mother, Speedy had spent countless hours operating this very model in the Colorado Rockies, rescuing hikers and skiers lost in the backcountry from certain death. Of course, as remote as those locations might have been, they weren't thousands of miles from the nearest trauma center.

The four men from NeXgen Biotech sit inside the lead car, the doors closed and the microphones on their headsets disengaged so that no one can hear what they're discussing. They wear matching black thermal undergarments beneath white-and-gray drysuits, the upper halves of which hang open at the waist. Cameron had barely gotten a look at them when they boarded and certainly hadn't received an introduction. Judging by their stature and bearing, they were obviously former military—maybe even private contractors—which begged the question, what in the name of God had those scientists been working on in that station?

The entire plane lurches, as though struck by a giant fist of air. Cameron glances over his shoulder through the porthole window but can barely see the ocean below through the dense cloud cover.

"Might want to strap in, boys," the pilot says through the comm. "Looks like things are going to get kind of dicey for a while."

Major Tim Dancer and his co-pilot, Captain Paul Brooking, are around the corner and up the ladder on the flight deck, seemingly isolated from the rest of the plane. As are the flight engineer and navigator, Senior Airmen Phil Thomassi and Omar Kattan, respectively, who were responsible for keeping this massive bird airborne and on course.

Tech Sergeant Bryan Rush emerges from the curtain surrounding the toilet, carrying his laptop open in front of him. He braces himself against the SUSV and staggers toward them, the floor rising and falling underneath him. While he looks like any anonymous grad student you'd find at a hipster coffee-house, he was a Tri-State Golden Gloves champion as a teenager and a defenseman on the Air Force hockey team. Needless to say, his smile is startlingly white, thanks to all of the dental implants.

"We finally have imagery," he says, harnessing himself into

the seat beside Cameron's. "It's snowing pretty hard up there, but the satellite managed to capture a few good shots with thirty-centimeter resolution. The pictures should be arriving on your tablets right about . . . now."

Cameron opens the incoming file and studies the aerial shots, one by one. Most of the images are marred by the storm, although several decent pictures had been captured through gaps in the clouds. Each individual pixel covers an area of roughly one square foot, phenomenal resolution for a camera thousands of miles above the surface of the Earth, but not quite sharp enough to distinguish fine details. He zooms in on the station, searching for any sign of what had happened or where the staff might have gone. The building itself appears largely intact; however, several windows on the front are a different color, presumably broken or missing entirely. No plumes of exhaust seep from the vents on the roof and whatever tracks might once have crossed the snowpack have been scoured away by the wind. He doesn't have decent imagery of the stairs descending through the narrow crevice or the path leading down to the lake, although he has a good shot of the rim of the dam.

"Does the satellite have thermal capabilities?" he asks.

"No, sir," Rush says.

Cameron brings the tablet closer to his face. It does kind of look like there's exhaust funneling from the roof of the small building, but with as hard as the wind's blowing—

Something catches his eye. On the ground. Just outside the entrance.

A human shape barely stands apart from the snow, its contours defined by shadows. There's no doubt in Cameron's mind that he's looking at a dead body, slowly vanishing beneath the accumulation, although the limited resolution prevents him from seeing any recognizable details.

Speedy glances down at the image and grunts. He sees it,

too. There's no point in dwelling on it now, though. They've all been on search-and-rescue missions that ultimately boiled down to the retrieval of remains, but they can't let it get in their heads, not while there are potentially living people in dire need of their help.

Ryder unfastens his harness, stumbles across the aisle, and grabs a conduit for balance. He notes which image the others are looking at and brings it up on his tablet.

Cameron scours the picture for any indication as to what might have happened. Without being able to visualize the vertical surfaces of the dam and the building on top of it, all he can see is a rooftop set against a stripe of snow-covered concrete.

"There's another body," Ryder says. "In the water."

Cameron adjusts his centering to better see the vague shape floating on the surface of the black water. A ring of ice has formed around it, partially obscuring its appendages. Another body floats maybe twenty feet away. It's twice the size of the first and, based on its immensity, undoubtedly one of the whales mentioned in his briefing.

"What the hell happened up there?" Rush asks.

"Get ahold of Colonel Patrick," Cameron says. "Let him know we're looking at two confirmed casualties. And tell him I want remote access to communications and data logs from that station. We need to figure out what we're dealing with before blindly walking into a situation we can't control."

"Yes, sir."

Rush heads toward the flight deck and Ryder eases into his vacated seat. He swivels the microphone away from his lips and leans closer to Cameron.

"Something doesn't feel right," he says.

Cameron nods. He can barely see the NeXgen contingent through the reflection on the window of the SUSV. There's obviously critical information they aren't sharing with him, and he'll be damned if he's risking the lives of his men until he knows exactly what they're up against.

He recalls the reaction of the woman in the video to the shimmering air behind her.

And shivers.

7

Academy Station
Greenland
81.906296, -29.744960

One Month Ago

Mira glanced up at the downward-facing, wide-angle digital camera, mounted in the middle of the array of LED lights above the aquarium, and then back at the monitor beside the tank. It was impossible to believe that she couldn't see the biofilm right in front of her face from any conceivable angle, and yet the proof of its efficacy was staring her right in the face.

More than one hundred color-coded temperature probes—one for each vertical inch of water above the substrate—had been affixed in a diagonal line to the back wall of the tank, from behind the wavering kelp to the turbulent surface, where the corresponding readouts were mounted to the outer lip. The bottom was a full four degrees cooler than the top, which was truly astounding considering that the water was only ten feet deep. The most exciting development was the formation of an artificial thermocline—a thin but distinct layer of fluid beneath which the temperature changed more drastically with depth than it did in the water immediately above and below it—at a point precisely 22.6 inches beneath the surface.

In a nutshell, their experiment had worked perfectly. At least under controlled conditions.

Mira hit the switch to kill the overhead lights, paused the program on the LED array, and turned on the nitride-based green diodes, which produced light at a wavelength of 540 nanometers—the same shade utilized by night-vision technology—and caused the web-producing purple bacteria to iridesce. A nearly indetectable green line, no wider than a single stroke from a pencil, formed right in front of her. She snapped a quick picture and entered its exact depth in her notebook, which she'd input into her computer later that evening when she recorded her video log. The overhead camera, however, captured a much more exciting image, one she memorialized with a wide-angle screenshot.

From above, the biofilm looked like a metallic green oil spill, which shimmered with shades of yellow and orange around the edges. It already spanned the width of the enclosure and was now within inches of reaching the ends, a surface area of just under 120 square feet. She wondered what would happen when it ran out of space to expand, a problem it wouldn't face in the ocean.

"Still growing?" Sammie asked.

Mira had been so wrapped up in what she was doing that she hadn't thought to check with her colleague before darkening the lab. She hit the overhead lights, resumed the day cycle on the LED canopy, and offered an apologetic smile to Sammie, who sat at her workstation on the far side of the room, preparing slides for her array of microscopes, as always.

"Visibly," Mira said. She didn't need to upload the screenshot into her program to know that the biofilm had grown since the previous day.

"And the sea ice?"

"Still there."

"Which, after two months of dropping it in and watching it melt, is a victory in itself," Sammie said. "How about the kelp?"

"Proliferating out of control," Mira said. "We're going to have to look long and hard at thinning it out, regardless of its impact on the biome."

They'd been hesitant to mess with anything at the bottom of the aquarium and not just because of the damage they would inflict upon the biofilm while attempting to do so. The water and soil samples they'd been able to collect around it revealed the presence of microbes they hadn't even known were in the sediment when they first set up the tank. Several species of formerly dormant coralline algae had begun colonizing the rock formations, from the crevices of which tiny tubes containing annelid worms poked at odd angles. All thanks to the rising pH and diminishing acidity, which broadened the spectrum of marine life the tank was able to sustain.

If only they could replicate the results at the dam.

It wasn't that the biofilm in the cube was failing, per se; it simply wasn't thriving. Its overall biomass had increased a hundredfold, but it had yet to truly establish itself in the turbulent water.

"Maybe the membranes in the Plexiglas aren't conducive to proper circulation," Sammie said, seemingly reading her mind. The longer they worked together, the more they started to think and talk alike. When they weren't getting on each other's nerves, anyway. One could only spend every waking second with the same person for so long before the urge to scream became overwhelming. "I'll bet if we released it—"

"We'd be compromising the experiment," Mira said, interrupting. "We've been over this a thousand times and I just can't see any way around it."

"Maybe a bigger cube?"

"That wouldn't change the dynamics of the internal circulation."

"We could use a system of buoys to float a giant net made from the same forward osmosis membrane as the vents in the cube—"

"We'd be taking a huge risk. If the organisms were somehow able to get out—"

"Isn't that our ultimate goal anyway?" Sammie asked. She loaded a prepared sample into the scanning electron microscope, clicked her mouse, and initiated the scan. "It would still be contained behind the dam."

Mira sighed. She was tired of having this same conversation. They went round and round and never found any common ground. The problem was they were coming at the issue from opposite angles. Sammie was a genetic engineer. She could insert, delete, modify, and replace entire genes without dwelling on the consequences of playing God. In her mind, she genuinely believed that she knew best, that every organism whose genome she'd altered was better for it, while Mira understood that any ecosystem was inherently fragile, that the slightest change in the behavior or physical appearance of a single, seemingly inconsequential microbe at the very bottom of the food chain could cause the whole thing to collapse.

That was the reason the world was in this mess in the first place. She and Sammie needed to take baby steps—even if they knew in their hearts that they were right and could prove it in the lab—or else they risked destroying everything they hoped to save.

"I guess we both know what they say about good intentions," Sammie said, perusing the black-and-white image generated by the SEM. "Maybe we just need to take a different approach. We're dealing with an environmental system in a constant state of flux; there are any number of variables that change on a daily basis and . . . "

Her voice trailed off.

"And what?" Mira asked, glancing back at her partner.

When Sammie didn't reply, Mira set down her laptop and crossed the lab to see what had derailed her train of thought.

Sammie furrowed her brow and bit her lip as she stared at the monitor of the SEM, the rectangular light reflecting from her eyes. The magnified organism on the screen was one Mira had seen countless times before. *Chaetoceros gelidus*, their photosynthetic diatom, was unmistakable with its circular body and whiplike appendages, which protruded from both poles like the antennae of an old TV and gripped another specimen, forming the foundation of a chain. Oval-shaped *Rhodovulum sulfidophilus* surrounded them, their outer surfaces frayed as though they were made from old rope stretched to the point of breaking. The fibrous strands extended from the bacteria, fanning out and adhering to the diatoms and other bits of organic debris, forming an irregular mesh that more closely resembled woven fabric than a web.

"I've never seen anything like it," Sammie whispered.

She looked over her shoulder at Mira, an expression of confusion on her face. When she recognized that Mira hadn't noticed what she obviously had, she tapped the screen beside the body of one of the bacteria.

Mira leaned closer and squinted to better see an amorphous organism that looked like a crumpled wad of cellophane, only with nearly imperceptible fingerlike protrusions, several of which appeared to be reaching for the neighboring diatoms.

"What is it?" she asked.

Sammie could only shake her head.

"I don't know."

8

M ira slapped a pile of oatmeal on her plate, decorated it with dried cranberries and raisins, and offered the man standing over the chafing dish, arms crossed over his chest, a polite smile of thanks. Calling Terry Swearengin a professional chef was perhaps a tad generous. While the diminutive man with the stringy beard and long hair technically qualified, since he did make his living cooking for other people, he often acted as though it were a distraction from his true purpose in life, which appeared to be huddling in a natural rock formation underneath the station and filling their labs with the scent of whatever he rolled and smoked, be it tobacco or plant material of a more exotic variety.

She felt his eyes on her rear end as she carried her plate toward the tables.

"Over here," Carrie said.

Mira veered toward the open seat between Carrie and Dr. Leo Olafson. It was understandable how Amy had practically melted just talking about him. He had shaggy blond hair, fathomless blue eyes, and the kind of dimples that positively cried out to be touched. Not to mention the fact that he was also a perfect gentleman. He stood when he saw Mira coming and pulled out the chair for her.

"Thank you, kind sir," she said.

"The pleasure is mine, m'lady."

Carrie's eyes narrowed with a momentary flash of jealousy. She looked toward the kitchen, then at the door.

"Where's Sammie?" she asked.

"Back in the lab," Mira said. "She found a microbe she couldn't immediately identify on the SEM, so she's running its DNA through the sequencer to see if she can figure out what we're dealing with."

"How exciting," Leo said. "Do you think you've discovered a novel species?"

"I hope so. We're grasping at straws trying to figure out why our biofilm is thriving in the lab but barely surviving outside."

"Don't let it get you down. The interaction between oceans and glaciers is notoriously unpredictable, especially in fjords like this one."

"How so?" Mira asked.

"Take that manmade lake of yours," Carrie said, gesturing with her spoon as she spoke. "You have the dam on one side and the glacier on the other. That ice is constantly melting and feeding freshwater into a closed system. Ordinarily, that cold freshwater would ride across the heavier layer of saltwater moving toward the shore, slowly mixing in as it's being carried out to sea, but that dam stops it."

"As a result," Leo said around a mouthful of oatmeal, "that freshwater continually circulates, decreasing the salinity ever so slightly with each passing day."

Mira blanched. She knew all about thermohaline circulation, the process by which water flowed through the world's oceans. As a rule, cold water was denser than warm water and saltwater was denser than freshwater, forming natural stratifications whenever they came into contact with one another.

With the dam containing that circulation, the currents now flowed in a circular pattern. The colder glacial runoff would be carried near the surface toward the fjord, where it would meet with the dam. Unable to go any farther, it would be sucked under, mixed with the heavier saltwater, and ushered back toward the shore, lowering the temperature and diminishing the salinity as it went.

Suddenly, everything made sense.

"We put the cube right in the densest concentration of cold freshwater." She shoved back from the table, nearly knocking over her chair in the process. "How could I not have seen it?"

Mira kissed both of them on the tops of their heads and hurried back to her lab.

"Glad to have been of help," Leo called after her.

She hit the hallway at a sprint, skipped down the stairs two at a time, and burst into the lab. Sammie gasped in surprise.

"There you are," she said. "I—"

"I figured it out," Mira blurted.

"So did I."

Mira wanted to tell her to go first, but she couldn't contain her excitement.

"We took the readings more than a year ago," she said, blowing past the aquarium and sidling up to Sammie, who swiveled around in the chair to face her.

"What are you talking about?"

"The temperature and salinity. All of the chemistry. We took the readings at the point in the lake where we decided to set up the cube more than a year ago. And since then—"

"Glacial runoff," Sammie said, slapping her forehead. "Nearly two full summers of melting and the chemistry in that spot is off by just enough to stunt the biofilm's growth."

"Exactly."

Mira beamed and held up her palm. Sammie slapped it and spun a circle in her chair.

"So what do you propose?"

"We take the cube out closer to the center of the lake."

"It won't float," Sammie said.

"We'll use buoys and tether it to the sea floor."

"I'm sure one of the facilities engineers could easily make the necessary modifications to the cube."

"And he could probably rig a five-hundred-and-forty nanometer light source and digital camera to the top so we can monitor the growth rate remotely," Mira said, clapping her hands. This was it. She'd cracked the code. It was all smooth sailing from here. "I'll bet if we asked nicely enough, we could have the whole setup in place by this time tomorrow."

"You're a bad girl," Sammie said, smirking.

Mira wiggled her hips, struck a pose, and giggled at the silliness of it.

"So what did you figure out?" she asked.

Sammie gestured to the monitor. She'd broadened the view to reveal several other specimens of the unknown organism and sharpened the resolution just enough to reveal faint linear depressions on their surfaces. They appeared to have become trapped in the webbing.

"I was able to sequence its genome without much difficulty." She swiveled her laptop so that Mira could see the screen, which displayed a circular design with three concentric rings composed of what looked like colorized barcodes. "This specific species isn't in any of our databases, but I have no doubt it's a type of archaea."

Mira nodded. A part of her had suspected as much. Along with bacteria and eukaryotes, archaea were one of the three basic domains of life on the planet, incorporating the more advantageous elements of the other two. They looked like bacteria and were similarly prokaryotic—lacking a cellular nucleus—and yet they had genes that coded for the enzymes responsible for the transcription and translation of DNA like eukaryotic cells, which formed the basis of all higher orders of life, from the tiniest diatom to the largest whale, and everything in between. Unlike either, though, archaea didn't need oxygen to survive. Every species had adapted to a specific role within its established ecological niche, exhibiting complex functions and fascinating mutualistic behaviors with other microbes that researchers were only now beginning to investigate.

Various species had learned how to metabolize complex organic compounds like ammonia, metal ions, and even hydrogen gas, allowing them to survive in environments where no other organisms could, from the heart of the coldest glacier to the caldera of the hottest volcano, where they played an integral role in carbon fixation, nitrogen cycling, and the reclamation of organic material. Strains known as methanogens even lived inside the intestines of human beings and ruminant animals like cattle, where they aided in the process of digestion and essentially produced their own toxic atmosphere of methane gas, which was responsible for the rotten-egg smell of flatulence and the rising concentrations of CH_4 in the atmosphere.

Of course, it was also the presence of methane gas on other planets that led scientists to speculate that colonies of archaea-like organisms already flourished in the soil and that they were the key to unlocking the mystery of extraterrestrial life.

"What are you saying?" Mira asked. "That we've discovered a new species in our aquarium?"

"One that we either transferred into the tank with the substrate or the water, technically," Sammie said. "But, yeah, that's exactly what I'm saying. The problem is that I don't have the slightest idea what it does."

9

Mira watched the dam draw closer over the bow of the inflatable Zodiac, which rose and fell on the whitecaps. The spray bursting from the chop patterned the visor of her diving helmet. She scraped away the residual salt and burgeoning ice and focused on the two figures standing on top of the dam near the observation center, silhouetted against the mist rolling into the fjord from the distant sea.

Jen sat in the stern, controlling the outboard motor and steering them around jagged crests of sea ice and exposed granite. Her tinny respirations hissed from the speaker mounted beside Mira's ear, which kept them in constant contact with each other and the team on dry land, just in case anything went wrong. Most of the precautions seemed like overkill to Mira, although with the way the frigid wind cut through her drysuit, she could only imagine how cold she'd be once she was actually in the water.

"It's about time you guys got here," Aaron said through the speaker. "If I'd known it was going to take you so long, I'd have waited to inflate the buoys so I wouldn't be standing out here freezing my nuts off."

"Oh, quit your bitching," Jen said. "At least you get to go back inside once they're in the water."

"My nuts?"

"The buoys, dummy."

Jen laughed. It was the first time Mira had heard her do so. The marine biologist was always so serious and dour that it undoubtedly caught everyone by surprise.

"Have I mentioned how much I appreciate your help?" Mira asked.

"I'm sure we could both stand to hear it again," Aaron said.

"On behalf of Sammie and myself: thank you both, from the very bottoms of our hearts."

"Where is that blond goddess anyway?"

"She's obsessed with that new microorganism of hers," Mira said. "I don't think she's left the lab since she found it."

"She just wants to make sure no one found it before her so she can name it after herself."

"Can we focus on the task at hand?" a gruff voice said. "Some of us have actual work to do."

"We all have actual work to do," Jen said.

"But everyone won't freeze to death if you don't do yours."

"I hope you know how much—" Mira started to say, but the man cut her off.

"Stow it, kiddo," Dougherty said. The massive facilities engineer looked like a modern-day Viking with his narrow eyes, thick gray hair, and bushy beard, but get him talking about his grandkids and he glowed like he must have when he played Santa Claus for them on Christmas. "That chocolate bar you brought with you is all the thanks I need."

Mira smirked. When she'd packed a small box filled with candy to savor, one bite at a time, over the next six months, she'd never anticipated having to use its contents as currency, like cigarettes in prison.

The dam rose above the raft until all she could see were

two faces peering down at her over the railing, twenty feet up. The side of the Zodiac scraped against the icy concrete, the clapping of water against it echoing all around them. Another eighteen feet down was the cube, mounted over the viewport by a series of latches that secured it to the support platform and the dam itself. Dougherty had used an acrylic adhesive to seal a waterproof, remote-controlled, battery-powered lighting hood, like the one suspended over the aquarium in her lab, onto the top of the cube. He'd also affixed eight eye rings to the sides so it could be attached to both the buoys that would keep it suspended eighteen feet below the surface and the anchor that would prevent it from drifting.

Mira leaned back and looked straight up.

"Ready when you are," she said.

One by one, four inflatable buoys—each easily four feet in diameter—rolled over the railing, trailing eighteen-foot lengths of steel cable. They plummeted to the water and bobbed on the surface.

"I'm just the chauffeur," Jen said. "It's all you from here. Just remember everything I told you and you'll be fine."

"All you said was 'Don't drown.'"

"I stand by that advice."

Mira rolled her eyes and swung her legs over the side. This wasn't her first time diving. In fact, she'd participated in several winter dives off the coast of Nova Scotia, where the water was so cold that even the lobsters turned blue, but this was a different animal entirely.

"Focus on your breathing and keep your fingers moving so they don't lock up," Aaron said. "And try not to panic."

"Easier said than done," Mira said.

She took a deep breath, counted to three, and rolled backward into the frigid water. The cold struck her like a blow to the chest, knocking the wind out of her. She concentrated on the air flowing through the regulator in her helmet to ensure she didn't pass out.

"How're you doing down there?" Aaron asked.

Mira's teeth were chattering so badly that she couldn't respond, so she released one of her hands from the pontoon and gave him a thumbs up. The bulk of the thermal underlayer and the drysuit restricted her movements to such an extent that she hardly would have been able to swim, even if she'd been able to make her shivering appendages do her bidding. Were it not for the buoyancy compensator—a vest lined with inflatable air bladders—she would have sunk straight to the bottom.

"The sooner you get those buoys hooked up, the sooner you can warm up," Jen said.

Her words rang in Mira's head as she let go of the Zodiac, released some air from the compensator, and slowly descended into the dark water. She barely had enough dexterity in her frozen fingers to switch on the light mounted to her helmet, which cast a diffuse glow into the water. The cords attached to the buoys dangled beside her, shimmering strands of silver wavering in the water. She grabbed one loosely in each hand and slid down to the bottom, where the carabiners affixed to the ends swung back and forth. A flick of the wrist and they easily snapped onto the eye rings. She similarly fastened the other two and hurried to unlatch the cube from its moorings before she lost the use of her fingers altogether.

The cube swung away from the dam, like a wrecking ball in slow motion. It clipped her heels as she swam out of the way.

"Are you okay out there?" Aaron asked. He'd gone down the stairs to the observation deck and stood on the other side of the viewport, silhouetted against the interior lights, his breath fogging the glass.

Mira again gave him a thumbs-up, inflated the bladders on her vest, and floated back up to the surface.

"Grab onto one of those buoys and hold on," Jen said. "I'll try to go slow."

Mira did as she'd been instructed. Her fingers were so cold that she had to wedge them into one of the small handholds on the pontoon and wrap the cable around her arm, but she managed to hang on as the Zodiac puttered away from the dam, lurching on waves that threatened to drag her back down. The rocky islands seemed so small in the distance. She closed her eyes and tried to think about anything other than her rapidly falling core temperature or the cable that felt like it was cutting through her arm, the weight of the filled cube like towing a boulder. The buoy tapped a drumbeat against the back of her helmet, a counterpoint to the water slapping her face shield. The rhythm made her drowsy, forcing her to open her eyes before she fell asleep.

Giant crests of granite towered over her, jagged pillars carved by the same ancient flow of water that had cut the sheer cliffs cradling the lake. She glanced back and saw the dam, little more than a gray line in the distance.

"S-s-stop h-h-here," she sputtered.

Jen killed the engine and the raft drifted toward the formation. They were roughly two hundred feet away, at a point where the bathymetric map showed a flat, solid seafloor.

Mira released the cable. The buoy floated away from her, the settling wake slapping against it with a chuckling sound. From where they were, Academy Station was little more than a silver glint on the horizon. The towering stone walls surrounding her gave way to the glacier in the opposite direction. A frigid gust moaned through the canyon, bringing with it the first snowflakes of the impending storm.

"Better hurry up," Jen said, lowering a bundle of cable over the side of the boat.

Mira nodded, cast one last look at the dark clouds creeping across the gray sky, and sank into the depths, unspooling the cable until she found the carabiners clipped to the end. Latching them onto the underside of the cube was considerably more challenging, but she figured out a system quickly enough. She'd just secured the final clasp when she felt movement against her legs, a distinct change in the water currents that caused her to twist sideways. She glanced down in time to see a dark shape vanish into the darkness beyond the reach of her light.

"All f-f-four latches s-s-secure," she said. "G-g-go ahead and d-d-drop the anchor."

"Copy. Stay clear."

Mira pulled herself around the far side of the cube and looked up at the boat. The anchor broke the surface and appeared to hover for several seconds before streaking toward the bottom, trailing a slipstream of bubbles and swirling debris. The loops in the cable slowly tightened as the anchor plummeted, drawing the cube away from her in the process.

She willed herself to memorize every minute detail: every sight, every sound, every sensation. This was the defining episode of her life, the singular moment when she changed the—

A shadowed form streaked past her, the turbulence in the water buffeting her to the side. She caught the swoosh of a flipper, and then it was gone.

"Wh-wh-what was th-th-that?" she gasped.

"Beluga whales are naturally curious," Jen said. "They're just trying to figure out what you're doing."

Mira smiled at the thought of the whales swimming through the water around her. She would have loved to stick around and observe them in their element, but freezing to death wasn't on today's agenda. Dialing up the air in her vest, she caught a cable attached to one of the buoys and used it to guide her to the surface, all the while watching the dark depths, which seemed to writhe with life.

10

Mira had milked every last drop of hot water from the shower, and yet she still couldn't seem to get warm. It felt like the cold had just burrowed deeper into her body, tunneling into her bones. She wished she'd thought to bring an electric heating pad or blanket, but it wouldn't have mattered if she had. Right now, the only thing she cared about was getting to her lab and checking on the video footage from inside the cube.

Sammie was right where Mira had left her, staring at the screen of the scanning electron microscope with a mug of coffee growing cold at her elbow. She didn't even look up as Mira crossed the room and took a seat at her desk. Mira wanted to tell Sammie all about setting up the cube in the open water, but she didn't want to break her partner's concentration. There was nothing more annoying than being interrupted while on the brink of a revelation, which she really hoped Sammie was about to make. An unclassified organism that had inadvertently found itself trapped in their aquatic web was a curious anomaly, but one that interacted directly with their biofilm created a variable for which they couldn't account, one that threatened to derail their entire experiment.

Mira opened her laptop and logged into the live feed being broadcast from the lake. Aaron had checked it while she was huddled in the Zodiac, shivering against the bitter wind and snow, and had confirmed that everything appeared to be in working order. Now that she'd seen it with her own eyes, she allowed herself to breathe a sigh of relief. The image was dark and grainy and offered little in the way of resolution until she turned on the white light, which defined the contours of the cube and cast a murky pall over the water inside. A beluga whale emerged from the darkness and nudged the bottom with its bulbous snout before quickly swimming away.

She couldn't help but smile.

With the tap of a key, she turned on the 540-nanometer green light and watched the organism iridesce. It appeared to have stabilized roughly a third of the way from the top and close to the level of the small holes housing the forward osmosis membranes, through which water circulated between the cube and the lake. It had spread out, forming a shimmering green mat that wavered like a six-inch-long flying carpet. A quick screengrab and she loaded the image into the program that would measure its growth rate. She had no doubt that it would fill the entire width of the cube within a matter of—

"We need to get it out of there," Sammie said.

She abruptly stood, knocking her mug from the desk. It broke on impact and sent ceramic shards skittering across the floor.

"Get what out of where?" Mira asked.

"The cube. We need to get it out of the lake."

"What are you talking about? We finally have it in a location where the biofilm will actually grow—"

"It doesn't matter," Sammie said. She looked around the lab with a confused expression on her face, as though she'd just awakened from a deep sleep. "We can't risk environmental exposure until we know exactly what we're dealing with."

"If we pull that cube out of the lake, the biofilm will die."

"We have more in the dewar. And those samples haven't been tainted."

"That's not the point," Mira said. "We'll have to start all over."

"We need more time to observe the interactions between the biofilm and the archaea."

Mira was about to argue that they'd already spent months observing the biofilm in the lab and that while they messed around the environment was actively dying, when she recognized the terror in her friend's eyes.

"What did you find?" she whispered.

Sammie collapsed into her chair and scooted back under her desk.

"Let me show you something."

Mira glanced at the shimmering film one last time and switched off the green light. She needed to separate her emotions from the situation. A delay wouldn't be the end of the world. She had to take a step back, hear out her partner, and make an informed decision based on whatever new information she'd discovered. Chances were Sammie just needed a good night's sleep to clear her head. It wasn't like Mira hadn't been in the same position countless times before.

She rolled her chair across the room and sat next to Sammie, who tilted the monitor so they could both see it. The screen displayed what appeared to be the same unclassified microbe, only it had taken on a rodlike shape. The parallel striations she'd noticed earlier had elongated.

"What does that look like to you?" Sammie asked.

"The same organism with different physical morphology."

"Look harder."

Mira leaned closer to the screen, squinting her eyes to better see—

She jerked her head back and looked at Sammie, who swiveled around in her chair to face the workstation behind her. The magnification of the digital microscope wasn't nearly as impressive as that of the SEM, but it allowed them to view the organisms while they were still alive. The tiny 4K viewscreen mounted on top of it showed strange microscopic creatures wriggling against a gray aqueous background. The strands of webbing looked like cracks in a shattered windshield. She immediately recognized the diatoms, as they resembled semi-transparent sand dollars, and the bacteria, which reminded her of clear grains of rice. As she watched, a crinkled archaeon shivered right up to a bacterium, slowly expanded, and engulfed it whole.

"It's an Asgard archaeon," Sammie said.

"Like from Norse mythology?"

"The first specimen was discovered not far from here, near a hydrothermal vent known as Loki's Castle. It was named Lokiarchaeota. Several other species were subsequently identified—Thor-, Odin-, and Heimdallarchaeota—and filed under the superphylum Asgardarchaeota. We still know very little about them, outside of the fact that they possess genes we once believed were unique to higher orders of life."

"Like what?"

"Genes that code for the proteins responsible for forming internal cell membranes, constructing skeleton-like fibers, and repairing damaged DNA. They can swallow bacteria and utilize them for energy production, like mitochondria inside a human cell, a trait that many researchers speculate might be responsible for the genesis of the first eukaryotic cells, the origin of higher life itself."

Mira cocked her head and contemplated the implications. The theory that an entire order of life had evolved from the mutualistic relationship between two single-celled organisms —that somehow aggregates of these primitive eukaryotes had arisen from the primordial stew and developed over countless generations into specialized cells capable of thought, motility, and breathing the atmosphere their ancestors had created through their own metabolic processes—was fascinating. Of course, that was all it was. A theory. And one that didn't seem entirely relevant to their current situation.

"Be that as it may, I don't understand why the interaction between these archaea and our bacteria necessitates the removal of the biofilm from the lake. I mean, once we release it from the cube, it's bound to interact with all kinds of organisms to which we couldn't expose it under controlled conditions in the lab."

"Did you look at the aquarium on your way in?"

Mira shook her head.

"I was in a hurry to check out the imagery from the camera in the cube."

Sammie rose from her seat, offered Mira her hand, and guided her across the lab. From the side, the aquarium looked precisely as it had when she'd last seen it. The kelp still wavered, the tiny worms still thrust their feathery mouths from their tubes, and tiny aquatic organisms still crawled across the substrate. The temperature readings didn't appear to have fluctuated in the slightest.

"Go ahead," Sammie said, inclining her chin toward the ladder.

Mira climbed to the top, ducked her head under the lighting array, and stared down into the water. The biofilm, as always, was so thin that it was invisible to the naked eye.

Sammie killed the overhead lights and darkened the tinting on the windows.

"I don't know what I'm supposed to—" Sammie hit the green light, and Mira's words died on her lips. "Oh my God."

11

20,000 *Feet Above the Labrador Sea*
60.284768, -56.219521

Now

"We've been granted access to the station's video archives," Rush says through the headset.

Cameron nods to himself. He stands apart from the others, watching the NeXgen contingent from a distance. The four men appear oblivious to everything transpiring outside of the SUSV, where they lean closer together and speak in conspiratorial tones, covering their mouths to prevent anyone from reading their lips. Only once had one of them emerged from the front car of the vehicle, and then just long enough to use the facilities and cast an imperious eye upon the Air National Guardsmen.

Rush hadn't been sitting on his thumbs while he waited for Colonel Patrick to railroad the NSF into approving his request for access to the station's communications and data logs, though. He'd attempted to penetrate Academy Station's mainframe, but he hadn't even been able to locate it. Either it had been deliberately isolated from the network or there was simply no power to it, an explanation that made them all more than a little nervous, although not nearly to the extent of the civilian contractors who'd been foisted upon them. Their dossiers would have been impossible to access for someone lacking Rush's skills, and even he had barely been able to gather more than superficial information about each of them.

The tall man with the white hair, aquiline nose, and tinted glasses was Dr. Trey Waller. A former program manager in the Biological Technologies Office of the Defense Advanced Research Projects Agency, he held postgraduate degrees in chemistry and microbiology and had been lured to the greener pastures of the private sector more than a decade ago. He'd accrued a small fortune during that time, the majority of it held in various offshore accounts.

Seated next to him, with the buzzed hair and caterpillar eyebrows, was Dr. Hinote Kato, who'd also worked for DARPA, specifically in the Tactical Technology Office, where he'd over-seen the Mobile Force Protection Program. With advanced degrees earned on three different continents and the ability to speak as many languages, the former Japanese national appeared to be a classic overachiever who belonged in an office, not in the field, and yet he seemed wholly in his element.

The two men sitting across from them, with their backs to Cameron, both hailed from the research and development department at NeXgen. The man wearing the fleece trapper hat and constantly looking back over his shoulder, revealing his hawklike profile, was Dr. Harrison Grant, chief research officer for the entire company and the direct supervisor of the man with the round head and large ears to his right. Dr. Rendon Silver, who resembled a dark-haired Alfred E. Neuman, had been snatched from the clutches of the U.S.

government's Advanced Undersea Technology Department and brought into the fold as the director of its Biomanufacturing Division.

Together, they painted a picture not of a bureaucratic envoy tagging along to minimize the corporation's liability but of a highly trained team of scientists dispatched to handle something that only they would recognize, something that NeXgen was desperate to recover and terrified of allowing anyone else to discover.

Suddenly, Cameron understands exactly what Colonel Patrick had meant when he said that these men would assume operational command once the station had been secured. NeXgen hadn't called in favors to ensure the presence of its team on this transport; it was in league with the Department of Defense. Whatever awaits them in Greenland has national security ramifications.

Cameron turns away from the SUSV. He needs to view those video logs.

"Start with the scientist in charge of the station," he says into his microphone.

"Dr. Amy Madigan," Rush says. "Arctic ecologist and chief scientific officer."

"What does her communications log look like?"

Cameron assumes the seat next to Rush and tilts the tech specialist's laptop so he can see the screen. Rush hands him an earbud, which he plugs into his right ear, underneath his headphones.

"No direct contact with anyone outside of the station in the past seventy-two hours," Rush says. "Her most recent video log is from thirty-six hours ago. The night before last."

"Let me see it."

Rush breezes through several different screens, and a video player appears. An older woman with a full red face and frizzy gray hair appears. The wall behind her desk is adorned with watercolor paintings, at the heart of which is a Garfield calendar.

"November twenty-first," she says, theatrically crossing out the date with a red marker and spinning around in her chair to face the camera again. "As anyone with even a rudimentary understanding of polar bear behavior knows, they're solitary creatures that spend the majority of their lives alone on the ice. That's why a gathering of any number is called a 'celebration,' and the reason why I'm considering breaking out the party decorations—"

"Fast forward to the end," Cameron says.

Rush does as he's asked.

"—telemetry demonstrates the erratic inland migration of our tagged polar bears, suggesting the storm we're following on doppler has the potential to be considerably worse than antici-pated," Dr. Madigan says. She hits a key and a map with zigzag-ging lines appears. "And while that might justify their staggering pace, it doesn't explain why their paths have started to overlap. As you can see, Nanook and Nukka are within a quarter of a mile of one another. Miska and her cubs, Shila and Suka, are hot on their heels. Try as I might, I can find no plau-sible explanation for their continued proximity to both the station and one another. And without his tracking collar, Chinook continues to evade our best efforts to locate him by satellite—"

The woman's interrupted by a muffled voice from some-where barely within the microphone's range. She glances up and frustration registers on her face. She reaches toward the camera and stops the recording.

"What about the woman who sent the SOS?" Cameron asks.

"The final entry in her video log is from, again, roughly thirty-six hours ago," Rush says. His fingers buzz across the keys and another video starts to play.

Dr. Mira Stone sits at a desk in a poorly lit room, her face a study in shadows. She draws a breath and lowers her brow, as though contemplating how to begin. It's hard to believe that this is the same woman he'd seen earlier. She looks so calm and composed, her hair drawn back in a ponytail, her slender neck sloping gracefully into the furry collar of a parka.

"This is all my fault," she finally says. "Believe me when I say that I only ever had the best of intentions. I never meant for any of this to happen. Everything just spiraled out of control, and now I don't know how to fix it. Or even if I can."

She leans back in her seat and closes her eyes. Several seconds pass in silence before she continues.

"I'm worried about Dr. Rantanen," she finally says. Her tone is one of genuine concern, and perhaps a touch of guilt over what she believes to be the betrayal of a colleague's trust. "Sammie doesn't look well. Dr. Porter, our staff physician, isn't overly concerned, but I'd be lying if I said that I wasn't. You don't work in such close proximity to someone for so long without being able to recognize when something's seriously wrong with her, especially after everything I've seen. And definitely not after what happened to—" Her eyes snap open and she glances up. Cameron hears another voice, but it's not loud enough to make out the speaker's words. "Are you certain? You find Porter and I'll—"

Dr. Stone reaches toward the camera and the recording abruptly ends.

"There's nothing after that?" Cameron says.

"No, sir," Rush says.

"Show me Dr. Rantanen's most recent video log."

Rush again works his magic and Cameron finds himself looking at a woman with white-blond hair and a face so pale that the rings around her eyes look like bruises. Her lips are bluish-purple, her shoulders sloped with fatigue.

"This is from sixty hours ago," Rush says. "Three nights ago."

Cameron nods and the footage rolls.

"I think I'm finally starting to understand how the novel species of archaea we discovered works." She speaks slowly, sluggishly, as though utterly exhausted, but her blue eyes are sharp and seem to bore through the screen. "I believe the silica-based striations produced by the surface proteins of the S-layer are responsible for the lenticular properties of its cell walls—"

"Lenticular?" Cameron asks.

"Something having to do with a lens," Rush says. "I don't understand the implications, though."

"—although that doesn't entirely explain the visual phenomena or the excessive production of major ampullate spiridions," Dr. Rantanen continues. She switches on a hand-held green light, momentarily blinding the camera on her laptop, which she carries across the room to an aquarium that takes up half of the lab. Inside is one of the ugliest fish that Cameron has ever seen, a species that looks like a horned toad with sharp, fanlike fins projecting from seemingly everywhere at once. It appears to have become ensnared in a massive aquatic spider web. "As you can see, our project has exceeded our wildest expectations, but I fear it's only a matter of time before we lose containment. And when that happens . . . "

Her words trail off. She records the tank for several more seconds before heading across the room, the camera capturing a bouncing view of the shoulder of her lab coat, her untamed hair, and the equipment behind her. She sets down her laptop and turns it so that the camera faces a dissection tray, where a fish with a trio of dorsal fins, whiskers protruding from its lower lip, and a yellow stripe down its side is pinned to the wax. At first, it looks like someone or something has taken bites out of its flank, but the edges of the wounds lack the distinct ridges of teeth. They look more like deep lesions, or perhaps full-thickness burns. The flesh inside appears almost melted.

"There's been another development," she says. Her voice sounds distant, as though she's speaking from another time and place entirely. "One I can't quite qualify. All I can say is that the tissue samples collected from the wounds reveal the presence of a number of hydrolytic enzymes, among them proteases primarily associated with digestive fluids, although it's worth noting that in the case of predacious arthropods, there's considerable overlap with those found in venom." She zooms in on the wounds to better display their eroded edges. "I await advisement."

The recording ends. Cameron stares at the black screen, replaying Dr. Rantanen's words in his mind. Dr. Stone had been so worried about her that she'd convinced her to see the staff physician, who'd claimed that nothing was physically wrong with her, and yet here they were, mere days later, streaking toward the north pole with a team of corporate scientists who'd cut their teeth at the Department of Defense.

Cameron casts a glance through the windshield of the SUSV. Waller stares back at him from behind his tinted lenses, their eyes meeting across the distance, taking each other's measure.

"I want to know what they were working on at Academy Station," Cameron says. Waller smiles, offers a mock salute, and returns his attention to his colleagues. "I mean, what they were *really* working on."

12

Academy Station
Greenland
81.906296, -29.744960

One Month Ago

Mira could hardly believe her eyes. Never in a million years would she have imagined that the biofilm was capable of proliferating to this extent in such a short period of time. It had to have grown several inches in the last few hours alone. Strands of webbing clung to the glass, forming a filamentous mesh that had begun creeping slowly toward the surface, the structural strands like so many gossamer vines.

"That's a full week's growth since this morning," she whispered.

"More than that," Sammie said. "Computer measurements indicate a ten percent increase in total biomass."

"Ten percent? That has to be a mistake."

"I ran the digital image through the program three times,"

Sammie said. She switched off the green light and the biofilm became translucent once more. "We need to remove the cube from the lake. At least until we have a better understanding of what's going on in there."

"You think this Asgard archaeon is responsible for the dramatic increase in growth rate?"

Sammie sighed and leaned against the front of her workstation. She stared at Mira through eyes that appeared to fix on some unknown point in the distance.

"The bacteria weren't designed to produce silk in the same way that a spider does," she said. "They don't have conscious control over their actions and have no way of determining how much silk they make. They constantly express the MaSp gene, excreting a small amount of webbing all the time, almost like a snail leaving a trail of slime everywhere it goes. We designed them that way in an effort to produce biopolymers with advanced mechanical properties from renewable resources like sunlight and seawater. The fact that they metabolized nitrogen and carbon dioxide was simply a beneficial side effect."

"I didn't realize that you'd engineered it with a specific commercial purpose in mind."

"We created it as part of a project we'd hoped would lead to the production of a flexible polymer with the tensile strength of steel."

"But it didn't work?"

"Of course it did. The problem was that for all its vaunted strength, it was still a spider web. You can tear through it with your bare hands. Transforming it into a functional material is a different story, one that belongs to the research and development department."

"Whose R and D department?"

"NeXgen Biotech. I might have helped engineer the bacterium, but it's their trademark stamped on it."

Mira had always known who Sammie worked for—after all,

her university had technically negotiated the partnership with Sammie's employer—and yet somehow she'd failed to consider the corporation's motivations in entering into the agreement, nor had she so much as speculated that her partner's participation might be for reasons other than altruism. Not that it mattered in the grand scheme of things. As long as Mira achieved her goal of reversing climate change, did it matter how she did so? Now that she actually thought about it, though, she had to wonder if she'd ever really had any control over the project at all.

"What does NeXgen have to gain from our experiment?"

"Combating climate change is a multi-trillion-dollar industry," Sammie said. "That's more than healthcare and manufacturing combined. And roughly comparable to oil and gas. We're talking research into alternative power sources. Solar and wind energy. Mitigation, remediation, and education. And it's not the public that cuts the checks to pay for that research; it's the governments of the world, shoveling inexhaustible piles of cash at every company invested in the research and development of any kind of technology that promises to decrease the production of greenhouse gases and combat the global consequences of their accumulation."

"That's an incredibly cynical way of looking at it."

"It's a simple statement of fact. Corporations are in the business of making money. That's the bottom line. Last year, NeXgen received more than fifty billion dollars in investment capital from the U.S. government alone. Add in another fifty from Europe and Canada, and you're looking at a total investment of one hundred billion dollars in a single company. That's the equivalent of the GDP of a small country. Now, that's not to suggest we're taking that money and offering nothing in return. There are countless projects like ours that offer genuine hope for future generations, but to justify its funding, NeXgen needs to be able to provide a return on that investment."

"And just what kind of financial return can our biofilm possibly offer?" Mira asked. "Once we release it out there, it'll belong to the world. It will spread throughout the Arctic Ocean at no cost to anyone."

"Of course it will," Sammie said, taking Mira by the hands and looking her directly in the eyes. "And this miracle we've worked so hard to create will change the world. We're the beneficiaries of billions of dollars of research invested elsewhere. Our biofilm is the end-product of an experimental program with limited applications that could be re-capitalized by expanding its potential into a new market. This project doesn't need to make money because it already has and will continue to do so, in a roundabout manner."

"I don't follow."

"Consider the millions invested into engineering a marine bacterium that's capable of producing spider silk. On one side of the balance sheet is an asset with limitless profit potential in the production of biopolymers; on the other side, we have an organism that won't earn a dime as a biofilm. We essentially take that initial government funding, invest it into research with dual applications, and produce two separate products, one for the corporation and one for the government. The former generates income for the company, while the latter serves as the return on investment: the delivery of a product, as promised. And once we demonstrate the efficacy of our biofilm, every government will want to invest in NeXgen's other projects, securing the corporation's future and funding for even more experiments like ours, experiments that will change the world for the better."

"So it's all a big game."

"With impossibly high stakes. It might look like governments throw around money like they don't have a care in the world, but, I assure you, that's not the case. We need to produce something amazing in return or our funding dries up."

"If we pull the biofilm out of the lake, we're setting ourselves back at least six months and jeopardizing our own funding from the NSF." Mira searched Sammie's eyes for the truth, which she sensed her partner was carefully skirting. By putting their project on hold, they risked costing NeXgen billions of dollars in future government investments. Not to mention the profit that came with it. Sammie had to have a really good reason for potentially endangering their entire experiment. "What aren't you telling me?"

Sammie released Mira's hands and turned away. She walked across the room and stared at the newfound organism on the screen of the scanning electron microscope.

"I've spent years developing this bacterium, tinkering with variables and fine-tuning genes until it was able to do exactly what I wanted it to do. Until I felt as though it had reached its full potential. And then this random microorganism comes along and makes it do things I couldn't. This archaeon is one of the most simplistic organisms on the planet, and yet it's also one of the most adaptable. It can breathe without oxygen, generate its own atmosphere, metabolize heavy metals, and live inside ice."

Mira studied the image of the archaeon engulfing the bacterium in a new light. Her partner was right: this was no simplistic relationship that could be written off without further investigation. It was an interaction wholly unseen in the history of humankind.

"What exactly are you trying to say?" she asked.

"This archaeon is like any other organism," Sammie said. "Its sole biological imperative is to perpetuate its species. To survive and replicate. We're talking about one of the three primary domains of life, one we didn't even know existed until fifty years ago. And even after all that time, we're only now beginning to understand how it works. But if the theory that archaea are responsible for the genesis of all higher orders of life on the planet is correct, then what are the implications of an unclassified species engulfing our bacterium within seconds of introduction? What are the consequences of it being able to trigger uncontrolled proliferation and silk production?"

Mira furrowed her brow. She finally understood why Sammie seemed so scared and why she was so desperate to remove the biofilm from the environment.

She feared the organism was evolving.

13

Mira tossed and turned for hours before finally giving up on the idea of sleeping. She opened her laptop and watched the live feed from inside the cube, the submerged lighting fixture casting a green glow over the entire room, limning the bare walls and the empty closet. She spent so little time in here that she hadn't even bothered to unpack. No one cared that she recycled the same few outfits over and over, mainly because they did the same thing, not that any number of them were in the same room longer than it took to stuff their faces before hurrying off to their labs. There were people she saw maybe once or twice a week, and still others she never saw at all.

She'd expected Academy Station to be something like campus faculty housing, where she'd meet new people who shared her interests, fellow scientists with whom she'd grow close over the course of her tenure, remember fondly during the intervening years, and look forward to catching up with at sporadic reunions down the road. Instead, she'd found a collection of individuals so focused on their work that they hardly stepped out of their own heads long enough to engage in conversation, let alone connect on anything resembling a meaningful level. Sure, they were all friendly enough, and she got along with every one of them, but she was beginning to feel isolated and lonely, even in their company.

Although she wasn't a social butterfly by anyone's definition of the word, she had a core group of friends back home in Arizona. Coworkers, mainly. A neighbor and an old roommate from grad school. She missed them all terribly, even if they hardly seemed to notice her absence. It was the daily interactions that staved off the feeling of desolation, which had become a crushing weight that grew heavier with each passing day, one that they all bore within the confines of the station, trapped by falling temperatures and storms that increased in both frequency and ferocity.

"It'll all be worth it in the end," she whispered, knowing full well that she wouldn't be going home anytime soon.

Sammie was right: it would be impossible to plow ahead with their project while that unclassified organism was out there. They'd worked too hard and come too far not to take a step back and carefully study the interaction between two species that never would have come into contact in the natural world. It wasn't as though they hadn't anticipated such events, though. Statistical models had predicted a high degree of interaction with other species of phytoplankton and bacteria, especially as the existing nutricline slowly rose to merge with the artificial one created by the biofilm. They'd only been able to account for existing species, however, and none of them posed the kind of existential threat that the archaeon did, assuming that the conjoining wasn't entirely benign. For all they knew, they'd found a biocatalyst that merely accelerated the production of dragline silk, which would be a freakishly positive development they could never have predicted. And that was probably precisely what it was, but what if it wasn't?

They'd know for sure soon enough, although with as

rapidly as the length of the day shortened, it was only a matter of time before the sun set for the final time. The phytoplankton needed the sun to proliferate and they were already down to two hours of daylight. By the end of the coming week, they'd be stranded in a state of perpetual twilight for an entire month, until darkness fell in earnest. If they pulled the biofilm now, they wouldn't have any hope of establishing it outside again until the sun rose in March.

She watched the biofilm waver on the gentle current passing through the tiny membranes in the walls of the cube and felt a tug of sadness.

There were no other options. Tomorrow, Mira would don her diving gear once more, take the Zodiac out onto the lake, and retrieve the cube. She'd bring another buoy to attach to the anchor, marking the spot for next spring. They'd transfer the biofilm to another aquarium and grow it just like the one in the main tank. Surely there'd be enough subtle differences between the two to drown them in data for the foreseeable future. Maybe they could even—

The camera shook, causing the entire image to tilt sideways. The biofilm folded in on itself. It slowly expanded as the camera once more leveled off.

Something must have struck one of the buoys. Probably an ice floe, or maybe one of the whales. The cube was designed to withstand direct impact from objects weighing thousands of pounds; knocking around the cables wouldn't cause the slightest—

Again, the camera shook. The view canted forward and the cables went momentarily slack. The biofilm crumpled against the Plexiglas.

Mira turned on the white light and flooded the water with a pale glow, illuminating tiny bubbles and floating sediment. A shadow drifted through the darkness far below.

The cube slowly swung back into place, tightening the cables trailing it into the depths.

Several minutes passed without any sign of whatever had caused the disturbance.

She switched back to the green diodes, and the emerald illumination retreated to the confines of the cube. The biofilm bobbed on the current, crumpled like an iridescent ball of foil.

A dark silhouette shot upward from the depths, rising straight toward the cube, spiraling around the cables until it came fully into view. The beluga whale slowed before impact and nudged the transparent bottom, its bulbous forehead flattened, its mouth pursed as though it were blowing her a kiss.

It quickly swam off again, leaving the entire cube rocking in its wake.

Mira realized with a start that the creature was playing with her. Such amazing animals. She couldn't help but smile.

She triggered the white light again and left it on for thirty seconds before switching back to the green light.

The whale appeared as if from nowhere, its white form streaking across the screen. It nudged the cube and the camera swung sideways.

Again, Mira hit the white light, which illuminated a cloud of silt rising from the seafloor, where the anchor had shifted in the sediment.

That was probably enough fun for tonight; she didn't want to encourage the whales to play with her setup any more than they already did. At least she knew she had friends out there, friends who'd be available anytime she needed them.

It might not have been much, but it made her feel better.

Maybe even well enough to fall asleep.

14

Mira awakened to a clattering sound. She sat up and looked around the small room, searching for the source of the sound. Her laptop lay on the floor beside her bed. She grabbed it and checked to make sure she hadn't cracked the screen. She must have fallen asleep with it on her lap, sitting up, as her aching neck would attest.

Relieved not to have damaged something so valuable and impossible to replace in her current situation, she set it aside and changed her clothes. The lights were already on in the outer corridor, the timer set to replicate the daytime hours on the eastern coast of the U.S. The window afforded a view of snow rising in swirling clouds from the accumulation at the behest of the howling wind, marring the darkness like television static. It wasn't arctic night, at least not technically, but rather one of the various states of twilight, as defined by the degrees of the sun's position below the horizon, although she had yet to learn how to distinguish one from another. Soon enough, it wouldn't matter anyway.

There were only a couple of other people in the cafeteria when she arrived. She must have slept through what passed for the morning rush. Swearengin was nowhere in sight, although he'd left a chafing dish filled with scrambled eggs and sausage links on the serving bar. He was likely underneath their feet at that very moment, huddled against the bitter chill, a cigarette clutched in his shivering hand.

She scooped a pile of eggs onto her plate and headed for the tables. Tom Nichols, the nightshift engineer, had slumped over onto one of them beside his empty plate, his head resting on his folded arms, snoring softly, as he tended to do after finishing his job and leading his daily yoga devotional. Elroy and Moore sat at the other table, talking in hushed voices so as not to wake the man who kept them from freezing to death in their sleep.

The affable bearded man kicked out the chair beside him and gestured with a flourish for Mira to take a seat.

"Top of the morning to you, Dr. Stone," he said. "No offense intended, but you look like you just crawled out of your own grave. Having trouble sleeping?"

"You could say that."

"I just did."

He boomed a laugh and glanced guiltily over his shoulder at Nichols. The night engineer shifted in his seat and leaned to the side, drool dribbling from the corner of his mouth.

"It's colloquially termed 'polar insomnia,'" Moore said. "And you're not the only one it currently afflicts."

"I think there's more to it than that," Mira said. "Sammie and I have hit a snag in our research. We're going to have to take a step back and reevaluate."

"You have my sympathies," Elroy said. "I was in your shoes not so long ago with this very station. We'd originally thought the combination of the wind turbines and the photovoltaic solar panels would be enough to power the station year-round, but we—I should say I, if I'm being completely honest— underestimated the amount of heat required to melt snow in large enough quantities to maintain the volume of water necessary to keep the showers running and the toilets flushing through the dark winter. We only narrowly survived what most of us old-timers affectionately call 'The Brown Death.' Between our respective funks and the delightful aroma emanating from the bathroom, many of us risked life and limb out in the elements, if only to escape for a few precious moments." Another hearty laugh thundered from his massive chest. "Needless to say, we installed the thermal solar panels to provide a continuous supply of water just as soon as we were able."

"That's terrible," Mira said. She tried to contain her laughter but failed miserably. Elroy was just one of those people who had the natural ability to bring it out of those around him. "I can only imagine how awful that must have been."

"You have no idea," Nichols said, rising from his table. He stretched out a yawn, scratched his stubbled face, and headed for the residential wing without another word.

"While I shoulder my share of the blame, I wasn't the one who served chili seemingly every other day," Elroy said. He returned his attention to Mira. "The point of my tragic tale is that you're not the first to face adversity within these hallowed aluminum-paneled halls."

Mira smiled and, before she even knew what she was going to do, started talking at a million miles an hour. She explained how the Asgard archaeon had potentially compromised their control sample, how they would have to remove the cube from the lake, and why they couldn't move forward until they'd thoroughly qualified the relationship between the microorganisms. By the time she'd regurgitated the entire mess, her eggs had grown cold on her plate and she felt awkward for having unloaded on these poor men, whose only crime had been choosing to have a late breakfast.

Neither spoke for several moments, compounding her embarrassment.

"As a volcanologist, I find archaea fascinating," Moore finally said. "Believe it or not, there are no volcanos on Greenland, and yet the evidence of prehistoric volcanic activity is all around us, from the sediment carried by the glaciers to the exposed rock of the coastlines, which we've dated to more than two billion years old. We theorize it's the result of eons of accumulated magma welling from the unstable divergent boundary to the east of here, where the North American and Eurasian tectonic plates are slowly pulling apart. The whole undersea ridge is rife with volcanic activity in the form of hydrothermal vents, the sulfurous discharge from which can reach temperatures as high as seven-hundred-and-fifty degrees Fahrenheit, and yet numerous species of archaea thrive within its toxic black smoke. Chemolithotrophs that metabolize sulfur and iron. Diazotrophs responsible for nitrogen fixation. Methanotrophs that consume methane before it can be released into the atmosphere."

"Is that what your team is studying?" Mira asked.

Moore offered a charming smile, his customary abrasiveness momentarily vanished. He was so much different in his element.

"In a roundabout way," he said. "As you obviously know, I'm working with Anthony and Laurie, our resident geologist and oceanographer, on a study correlating undersea volcanic activity and climate change. In fact, our project dovetails quite nicely with yours. You see, those hydrothermal vents flood the ocean with toxic gasses and minerals, which are then consumed by unique species of archaea and bacteria, and strange creatures like tube worms, giant crabs, and colonies of mussels and barnacles. Together, they're responsible for eliminating ninety percent of the methane—a greenhouse gas twenty-five times more potent than carbon dioxide—released from the Earth's core. Were these ecosystems to fail, we would literally be looking at a doomsday climatic event. That's not hyperbole. We would no longer be able to breathe our atmosphere and would die choking on our own vomit."

"And on that cheery note . . . " Elroy said, standing. "Someone needs to go outside and spray deicer on the turbines. Any volunteers?" He looked from Moore to Mira and gave a playful wink. "Everyone's all about renewable energy until it comes time to brave a blizzard."

His laughter trailed him down the hallway.

"I should very much like to see this biofilm of yours," Moore said.

Mira beamed and opened her laptop. She was still logged in to the live feed from the cube. The water was dark and clear, the Plexiglas subtly defined by the sparse ambient light that penetrated the lake to its eighteen-foot depth.

"There's not really a whole lot to see," she said. She switched on the green light, and the contrast grew sharper. "It's maybe four inches in diameter and invisible to the naked eye, at least until you cause it to iridesce."

"I don't see it," Moore said.

Mira swiveled the laptop so she could better see. There was no sign of the biofilm. Her first thought was that it must have died, but even the deceased bacteria would retain some small measure of iridescence.

The truth struck her like a blow to the gut. She jumped to her feet, forgetting all about her laptop as she ran down to the lab and burst in to find Sammie shining a handheld green light across the surface of the aquarium, revealing the tiny filamentous appendages that had grown up the glass walls and over the rim of the tank.

"It's gone," Mira gasped, doubling over to catch her breath.

"What's gone?" Sammie asked.

"The biofilm. It's no longer in the cube."

15

The Zodiac skipped across the waves, throwing frigid water into the air as it sped toward the cluster of buoys, little more than red dots bobbing against the backdrop of the island, its spires rimed with ice, like the towers of some mythical castle. Mira ducked her head against the spray and struggled to seat her diving helmet. She was already drenched underneath her drysuit, although she appeared to be in better shape than Sammie, who positively shook from the cold. Her lips were purple, her philtrum glistening with frozen mucus. She clung to the opposite pontoon with one trembling hand and attempted to buckle her compensator vest with the other.

Aaron manned the helm, while Jen stood beside him, leaning over the short windshield in her drysuit, her jaw muscles bulging in frustration. They'd rushed to meet Mira and Sammie at the boathouse the moment Mira had hailed them on the remote transceiver at the observation center. Neither of them had been thrilled that the microorganisms had somehow escaped into the open water with their whales, but that was the least of their worries. The odds of the biofilm harming such enormous creatures were infinitely smaller than the chances of it finding its way to the other side of the dam.

And once it was in the fjord, there would be no stopping it from reaching the Arctic Ocean, from which the unpredictable currents would spread it far and wide.

"We're just being overly cautious," Mira said, although she wasn't sure whom she was trying to convince. "We probably could have released it into the lake on our own without any adverse effects."

"Assuming it's truly no longer in the cube," Sammie responded through the speaker in Mira's helmet. "That containment unit was designed to withstand a lot more than a whale can dish out."

Mira bit her tongue. The enclosure itself might have been, but the membranes hadn't.

The thumping of waves against the hull grew louder. Curtains of water splashed down on them. Mira clung to the rope strung down the length of the pontoon, her knees leaving the bottom every time the boat lurched from one swell to the next, rapidly closing the distance to the island, its towering formations stabbing into the belly of the advancing storm.

Aaron ramped down the motor and they floated toward the buoys. The wind screamed through the canyon, the bitter cold passing straight through their suits, the outer layers of which were already crisp with ice.

Mira leaned over the side. She could barely see the cube down there, its faint green outline at the farthest extent of her vision, at the point where the steel cables tethering it to the buoys converged. She'd left the light on and replaced the white LEDs in their diving flashlights with green diodes. If the biofilm were outside of the cube, its iridescence would be their only means of finding it, assuming it hadn't been ripped apart by the current and scattered throughout the lake, seeding it with specimens too small to be detected by the human eye.

At least until they started proliferating out of control.

"These collection devices are airtight and more than large enough to accommodate the specimen," Sammie said, removing four containers reminiscent of enormous canning jars from her drenched backpack, one at a time. "If you find it, be careful to capture it in its entirety. The webbing is more than strong enough to hold its biological components together, but it will tear upon contact if you so much as brush against it."

Mira felt the press of time. With each passing second, the current carried the biofilm farther and farther from the cube. She hooked one of the containers to her diving belt, grabbed a flashlight, and, without a word, rolled back into the water. This time she was prepared for the cold shock, although it didn't make the slightest bit of difference. Her entire body clenched, her muscles locking up and her teeth beginning to chatter. The water trapped underneath her drysuit immediately started to freeze. Not that it mattered; she wouldn't be down here for very long. If they didn't find the biofilm right away, they'd never find it at all.

She released air from the compensator and turned on the green light as she sank, shining it toward the cube below her. By the time she reached it, it was readily apparent that the biofilm was no longer contained. Between the overhead light and the four handheld beams shining into it from as many different angles, it would have lit up like an emerald if it were still inside.

Mira pulled herself right up against the Plexiglas and inspected the dozen pencil-sized holes in each of the sides. The circular membranes looked almost like bubbles trapped in the tiny orifices.

"They all appear intact," Sammie said through the speaker, unable to hide the surprise in her voice.

Mira nodded, but she couldn't seem to bring herself to speak the words they were both thinking. The biofilm had crossed one of the barriers on its own, which shouldn't have been physically possible.

"Fan out," Jen said. "Just don't stray too far. Without someone on the surface to coordinate our movements, we could easily become separated."

"This water is so cold that your body will start to shut down very quickly," Aaron said. "And it won't give you very much warning when it does."

Mira watched the specks of microorganisms drifting on the current. It flowed slower than she'd expected, which was just about the only thing working in their favor. She drifted away from the others, using the cables to propel herself toward the distant island. She'd heard the waves breaking against it and knew that if the biofilm had floated that far, their hunt was already over.

She deflated the air bladders, just a touch, and sank into a haze of nutrients. The microscopic organisms sparkled in her light, like tiny bits of glitter in the pale green miasma, distant stars in a nebula millions of miles away, universes unto themselves.

The current abruptly shifted and the cloud dissipated.

"Not now," she whispered.

"What is it?" Sammie asked, her voice tinny inside Mira's helmet.

"The green lights attract the whales."

As if to prove her point, a beluga whale fluttered past her, the light reflecting from its smooth white flank. A slow-motion wave of its tail fin and it was gone, leaving the water swirling in its wake.

"Whales are colorblind," Aaron said. "They see in gradations of gray."

"I wonder if this particular frequency of light appeals to them more than others," Jen said. "Like how cats are drawn to red laser dots."

"Or perhaps they're responding to the temperature of the light, with green being a far warmer color than white, like diffuse rays of sunlight suddenly penetrating to their depth."

Mira tuned them out and focused on the water around her. She was already so far away that she couldn't see the others' lights behind her. Her fingers and toes were growing colder by the second. She wouldn't be able to stay down here much longer. With miles of open water surrounding them, finding a single gob of sludge was like trying to find a needle in a—

A flicker of green light caught her eye.

There it was. Maybe six feet away. Fluttering like a leaf of kelp as it rode the current.

Mira couldn't take her eyes off of it for even a moment, nor could she risk calling the others, whose exertions would alter the already fluctuating hydrodynamics. She unhooked the container and fumbled with the lid until she was sure it was open. The mouth was maybe six inches wide, leaving her little room for error, especially with as badly as her hands were shaking.

The current carried her closer, until the biofilm was just barely out of her reach. She would need to use both hands, but she wouldn't be able to see it without the green beam, so she wedged the flashlight underneath her arm and pinned it to her side. Her eyes burned from her refusal to blink as she drifted closer . . . and closer . . .

Voices crackled in her ears, stuttering from the cold. She couldn't allow them to distract her.

The biofilm rippled. A shifting current struck her a split-second later.

She knew what had caused it.

A dark shape swooped through her peripheral vision to her right, passed behind her, and then appeared to her left. The beluga whale flashed past, the disturbance in the water buffeting the biofilm toward her like a plastic bag on the wind.

It was too close now. She couldn't allow it to hit her or it would break apart on impact.

The whale circled again, tightening its spiral around her back and appearing once more in front of her. It hovered in place, the green light reflecting from the tiny eyes on the sides of its head, its mouth curled into an almost comical smile. Without warning, it propelled itself straight toward her.

It was going to hit her, and it was going to tear right through the iridescent webbing first.

Mira lunged toward the biofilm, dragging the open container through the water as though in slow motion. The whale's face grew larger behind it, bearing down on her.

She focused on the faint green glow and released the flashlight, the iridescence fading as the lens tipped down toward the ocean floor. The biofilm passed through the orifice as she closed the lid, sealing it a split-second before the whale dove after the falling light, its tailfin slapping her legs and flipping her head over heels in the water.

"I th-th-think I g-g-got it," she said, righting herself and turning in what she hoped was the right direction.

She raised the container, but she saw only clear water inside. Her heart sank. Had she gotten it? If she'd somehow missed . . .

A greenish glow materialized ahead of her. She swam toward it as best she could in the restrictive suit. The silhouette of a diver appeared behind it, face shield reflecting the hand-held light, which shone into the container, illuminating the iridescent green mass trapped inside.

16

Now

C ameron paces the frozen tarmac, his boots crunching on the ice. The wind chases his breath over his shoulder and cuts straight through his parka. He finds that the cold helps him think, sharpens him mentally, although he fails to reach the epiphany he seeks. There's something he's missing, something of critical importance that he needs to figure out before they arrive at Academy Station, where he can only imagine how bad the weather must be. Even down here, at the southwestern end of the country, it feels like the bare skin of his face might freeze, and his team is still nearly three thousand miles from its destination, way up above the Arctic Circle.

The engine of the fuel truck grumbles behind him. He hadn't noticed that the refueler had finished his job. A fresh application of deicing and anti-icing agents once they were ready to taxi and the plane would be good to go.

He glances up at the terminal, a three-story gray building set into the naked hillside, where his men have been stretching their legs and loading up on coffee. They must have been watching from behind the tinted windows. As if on cue, they emerge from the bottom of the ramp and strike off across the apron toward him, bracing themselves against the tempestuous gales blowing across the frozen fjord, glazing the ice with a fresh application of sleet.

Ryder offers Cameron a steaming paper cup, ducks his head, and guides the others toward the crew steps leading into the belly of the Hercules. Cameron savors the warmth in his bare hands and nods to each of the men as they pass, his eyes never leaving the NeXgen contingent as they pick their way across the concrete apron. He takes a drink of the brew, which, given the situation, is far better than he'd expected, and precedes the four men into the plane, waiting for them to pass before closing the door behind them. The propellers roar to life as soon as he throws the latch.

"You guys are welcome to join us in the forward cargo compartment," Cameron says, following the civilian contractors down the central aisle. "I promise we won't bite."

"Speak for yourself," Ronny says.

Waller turns around and smiles at Cameron, his expression that of a parent with only so much patience left to give.

"We appreciate your offer, but we must return to our work," he says. "There is much we still need to do before we arrive."

The other three have already assumed the same seats inside the lead car of the SUSV. Cameron catches a glimpse of Dr. Stone on Kato's tablet. The man across from him, Grant, has his laptop open on his thighs and an image on his screen that doesn't look like any of the video logs Cameron has seen so far.

It shows a hallway bathed in the red glare of emergency lights from an overhead vantage point, a blur of motion frozen in the middle.

Waller catches him looking, steps in front of him, and offers that same cloying smile.

"Well," Cameron says. "The offer stands if you change your mind. Might be nice to all be on the same page when we land on a glacier in the middle of nowhere."

"You just focus on doing your job, Sergeant. We'll take care of the rest."

Cameron nods in parting and heads toward the front of the plane, which slowly begins to taxi. He grabs the netting on the wall for balance and raises his cup to keep it from spilling as he navigates the narrow aisle, shouldering back and forth between the SUSV and the fuselage.

Rush glances up from his seat. Cameron raises the question with his eyebrows. His tech sergeant grins and moves his laptop so that Cameron can sit beside him. While everyone else was in the terminal, Rush had patched into the video camera inside the SUSV. It lacked sound and broadcast in black and white, but it was the next best thing to having someone physically inside the vehicle with the NeXgen crew.

"Those guys wouldn't even hit the head at the same time as the rest of us," Speedy says. "Like their shit doesn't stink."

"They're just not the kind to slum around with the help," Bashir says.

"There's more to it than that," Ryder says, his brow furrowing. "They know something—"

Cameron presses his index finger to his lips to prevent his rescue combat officer from saying anything more. While the men from NeXgen might have turned off their microphones, that didn't mean they couldn't still hear every word that passed through their headsets. For whatever reason, Cameron isn't inclined to share his suspicions about the nature of the civilians' involvement. At least not yet.

"I don't care what those ass-hats hear," Ronny says. "They can think whatever the hell they want about me. I won't lose any sleep over it."

Silver looks back over his shoulder, his eyes locking onto those of the senior airman. Ears aside, the two of them could have been brothers.

"What are you looking at, you ugly mother—?"

Cameron silences Ronny with a glare, slips off his headset, and speaks to Rush so that no one else can hear.

"I need you to find a specific video log entry for Dr. Stone. I don't have the date, but I can tell you that she's wearing . . . " He closes his eyes and concentrates on remembering the freeze-frame he saw on Kato's tablet. " . . . a gray hooded sweatshirt. Her cheeks are red and her hair is damp."

"I'm on it," Rush says. His fingers buzz across the keyboard. Images of Dr. Stone seated at her desk blur past, her outfits changing with blinding speed, until she appears in a gray sweatshirt. "This one?"

"No. That's the right outfit, but we're looking for a recording where she appears flushed, like she just got out of the shower." Rush flips past several more images. "That's it. Right there."

"October twenty-second," the tech sergeant says. "You can access it easily enough from your tablet."

Cameron nods his thanks and leans closer, his words barely audible over the thunder of the high-pressure spout hosing down the plane with an anti-icing agent.

"Also, I want you to see if you can find something for me. Discreetly. I think there are security cameras inside the installation. See if you can access them."

"The mainframe's offline and convincing the NSF to let us view the video logs was like pulling teeth," Rush says. "There's no way they're granting us access to surveillance footage, not without someone even higher up the chain of command than Patrick exerting some pressure."

"If I'm right," Cameron says, studying the men in the SUSV from the corner of his eye, "there are other ways to get into those archives."

A smile slowly spreads across Rush's face.

"That will take time," he says, "but it can definitely be done. I've been itching for an opportunity to flex my cyber muscles. Hacking into NeXgen ought to do the trick."

"Just don't get caught."

"Who do you think you're talking to here?" Rush winks and closes his laptop. "I'm going to need a little more space and a whole lot less supervision to work my magic, though."

He tucks his computer under his arm and heads for the flight deck, where he'll be able to patch into the communications network, leaving Cameron to watch Dr. Stone's video log on his own. The senior master sergeant plugs in his earbuds, seats the cans over his ears, and presses play.

"At approximately ten this morning, we discovered that the biofilm was no longer in the cube," Dr. Stone says in a tone of resignation. Her eyes are red as though she's been crying. "We were able to recover it shortly afterward, although I'm afraid the damage has already been done."

She hits a key on her laptop and a gray-scale image resembling a textured concrete wall appears on the screen beside her.

"This is the top layer of a forward osmosis membrane as viewed under a scanning electron microscope," she says. "As you can see, there are no apparent disruptions to allow anything larger than a water molecule to pass through." She taps her keyboard and the image is replaced by another. It looks almost like the surface of the moon, with subtle ridges, craters, and dark holes. "This is one of the membranes we excised from the cube. Its integrity has been compromised to such an extent that it's little more than a biological sieve. The majority of these holes are easily large enough to facilitate the movement of microorganisms as large as diatoms from one side to the other."

Dr. Stone rubs her temples and stares blankly into the camera for several seconds before continuing.

"Our working theory is that the damage was inflicted by a recently discovered species of archaea. We believe that organism to be methanogenic, meaning that it produces methane gas as a byproduct of carbon metabolization. This process also produces a small amount of formate, a simple carboxylate anion that hydrolyzes with water to produce formic acid, the substance responsible for the burning sensation of an ant bite or a bee sting. While considered a relatively weak acid, its corrosive properties are more than strong enough to damage such a delicate membrane."

She lifts her laptop from her desk and carries it across the lab, the view jostling chaotically.

"While such a development is troubling on its face," she says from offscreen, "more concerning is the fact that the individual components of the biofilm would have had to dissociate —presumably as a result of the acid dissolving some unknown amount of the spider silk holding it together—in order to cross the membrane. This implies that the microorganisms were able to reintegrate on the other side to form the intact specimen I collected in the lake."

She sets down the computer so that its camera faces an enormous aquarium and kills the overhead lights. Kelp wavers in silhouette near the bottom. There doesn't appear to be anything in the water above it.

"I fear that any amount of material I failed to collect, no matter how small, will thrive in the environmental conditions for which it was specifically designed and within a matter of weeks will look like this . . . " A green glow blossoms above the tank, revealing a glimmering film floating where there had been only water before. It looks like thousands of spiders had spun a mat of emerald webbing, tendrils of which creep up the glass like ivy. "And once it does, there will be no way of stopping it from reaching the open ocean."

17

Academy Station
Greenland
81.906296, -29.744960

Three Weeks Ago

Mira piloted the Zodiac away from the rugged shoreline, rising and falling violently on the rough chop. Thanks to Aaron's tutelage, she'd gotten considerably better with the controls during the past week. He'd been kind enough to free up a little time every afternoon to take her out on the lake, while Jen remained at the observation center and in constant contact via a remote transceiver, just in case they needed assistance in a pinch. The precaution hardly seemed necessary since they weren't actually getting in the water. Not that they stayed any warmer or dryer in the boat with the way the spray burst from the bow and crashed down upon them.

"Adjust your angle so you're not hitting the waves head-on," Aaron shouted from the seat beside her. Mira turned the wheel ever so slightly and the boat fell into a rhythm with the waves. She beamed at the marine biologist. "There you go. You're getting the hang of it."

She'd also gotten better at physically preparing herself for her daily sojourns, wearing multiple layers of undergarments and microwaving homemade pouches filled with dry rice to stuff into her gloves and boots, but no matter how hard she tried, she couldn't get used to so few hours of sunlight. She'd thought herself better prepared—after all, she'd read countless studies and transitioned her sleeping cycles weeks in advance —and yet no amount of research or foresight could have prepared her for the reality of the situation.

The depression and anxiety triggered by the shortening days were instinctive reactions, honed to a razor's edge by innumerable generations of evolution. Primitive cultures had feared the darkness and enacted rituals designed to reverse the lengthening of the night, offering sacrifices to appease the gods. It wasn't until now, however, that she truly understood why they'd done so. It wasn't the fear of the unknown or the things that went bump in the night that caused such unease; it was the hindbrain's response to the diminishing light cycle, the body's reaction to the lack of vitamin D, and the psychological impact of the falling temperatures and increasing isolation that set the entire nervous system on edge.

There were nights when she fell asleep praying to awaken in her bed back home and mornings when she woke up feeling so depressed that she wasn't sure she'd survive the coming day, let alone three months of complete and utter darkness. Somehow, however, she forced herself to crawl from beneath the covers and soldier on. She had a job to do, and she wasn't about to walk away from it, although the excitement she'd felt about the prospect of her project changing the world had been replaced by the fear that it would do just that, and with potentially unpredictable and detrimental consequences.

Mira cut the engine and the Zodiac drifted into the eddying waters in the lee of a small island. There were nineteen of them in all, ranging in size from maybe fifty to several hundred feet in diameter. She'd named them after the castles they most closely resembled from the animated Disney movies she'd loved so much growing up. She was able to recognize the shape of each by sight, even after the sun had set and she could see only its silhouette against the canyon wall. Every pinnacle and outcropping was rimed with a layer of ice that would just keep getting thicker and thicker through the long winter.

Arendelle Island spared them from the brunt of the wind's assault, if only momentarily. Mira leaned over the pontoon and shone her green light down into the water, while Aaron did the same thing on the other side. The facilities engineers had taken her request to build more powerful flashlights as a challenge. Dougherty and Nichols had jointly presented her with two that could penetrate the water to a depth of roughly twenty-five feet. While that wasn't quite as deep as she'd initially hoped, it was theoretically deep enough to identify any burgeoning colonies of biofilm, although they had yet to see a single glimmer of iridescence, a fact that encouraged them to move faster and clear larger sections of the lake with every passing day.

"Still nothing," Aaron said. "Do you really think we'd be able to see small bits of biofilm so far down there anyway?"

Mira pretended not to hear him. It was the same question he'd asked several times already, and one for which she didn't have a good answer. They likely wouldn't be able to see a small colony, but what was the alternative? The fact that the biofilm had essentially disassembled itself to pass through the membrane and reassembled itself on the other side didn't sit well with her, although not nearly to the extent that it troubled Sammie, who hadn't left the lab for any length of time in a week.

There were only three variables that could be responsible

for the bizarre behavior. Diatoms were essentially single-celled plants that drifted aimlessly on the currents and photosynthesized when environmental conditions were right. Bacteria, on the other hand, were motile creatures known to exhibit sophisticated communal actions, like aggregating to form biofilms, but they lacked what one might even loosely consider consciousness. Under normal conditions, anyway. The presence of the spider's DNA dramatically altered the paradigm. This bacterium was no longer a naturally occurring species. It was a genetically engineered organism that could never have evolved on its own, one capable of producing webbing like the golden orb weaver spider from which its genes had been harvested, but its apparent sentience wasn't the most frightening part of the biofilm potentially taking root in the wild. Of greater concern was its ability to create environmental conditions conducive to the proliferation of the mysterious archaea, which Sammie had officially named Ymirachaeota, after the ice giants of Norse mythology from whom Loki descended.

Sammie theorized that the microorganisms had been preserved in a state of cryptobiosis—a condition of metabolic inactivity just this side of death—brought on by either rising global temperatures or carbon dioxide levels. Their genetically engineered biofilm had reversed these conditions in the aquarium, essentially triggering their spontaneous revival. The same thing could happen out here in the lake, which was why it was critical to make sure that the archaea didn't interact with the biofilm in a setting outside of their control. At least not until she and Sammie had a better understanding of what they were dealing with.

They just needed a little more time to study the bacterium's nascent abilities and its interactions with the newly discovered archaeon. That was all. Then they could get back to focusing all of their energies on saving the world.

The Zodiac drifted out from behind the island, where the

current caught hold of it and carried it onto the harsher waves. Sleet clamored from Mira's drysuit. Her light shook in her hands. Neither she nor Aaron would be able to last very much longer out here. They needed to complete their circuit of the islands before the elements drove them back inside, where she had more than her share of work waiting for her. Despite the one glaring setback, the biofilm was performing better than she and Sammie ever could have imagined, and they were collecting data faster than either of them could process it. Someone was going to have to correlate it and write it up, and it was starting to look like it was only a matter of time before Sammie's eye merged with the lens of her microscope, so that responsibility would likely fall squarely on Mira's shoulders.

"Moving on," she said, setting down her light and taking the wheel. She glanced at Aaron as he crawled into the set beside her. "Have I mentioned how grateful I am for all of your help?"

"Only every day."

She studied his face, searching for the answer to a question she wasn't sure how to ask. After several awkward moments of silence, she just spit it out.

"Why are you doing this? You should be back on the observation deck with Jen, not freezing out here in the snow with me."

"I like to think of Academy Station as our fortress of solitude," he said, smiling wistfully. "And we're all superheroes trying to save the world in our own unique ways. More than that, though, we're a family. Or at least I like to think of us as one. And families help each other, regardless of how close they come to freezing to death in the process. There will always be more work waiting in the lab, but there are only so many opportunities to make a difference in the lives of the people who matter to us."

Mira felt herself tearing up and had to look away. She cranked up the outboard motor and sped toward Corona

Island. It was impossible for any number of people to scrutinize a lake this large, so she'd developed a pattern of searching in the lees of the islands, where the currents were the weakest. The water flowed so fast out in the open that any collection of microorganisms would race past before she caught a hint of their iridescence anyway.

She once more killed the engine and drifted behind a formation reminiscent of a giant sandcastle, its towers white with seabird droppings, its parapets prickling with desiccated reeds from last spring's abandoned fulmar nests.

"Back to it," Aaron said, climbing over the seat and grabbing his light.

Mira leaned over the opposite side and aimed her beam into the depths. A school of fish streaked past, the reflective scales on their flanks flashing green. A narwhal cruised lazily behind them, rising toward her like a knight preparing to lance the tiny green bulb with its pointed tusk. She turned off the light, but not before catching an emerald glimmer from the corner of her eye.

"Hold up," she said.

"Did you see something?" Aaron asked.

Mira switched on her beam and shone it toward the point where she was certain she'd seen a flash of iridescence.

There was nothing there.

It must have been just another fish startled by the boat.

"Never mind."

The narwhal crested the waves and then dove into the darkness beyond her light's reach. She was just about to crank up the engine again when she heard a buzzing sound, distant at first, but growing closer by the second.

A black shape knifed through the clouds overhead.

Mira caught a glimpse of eight slender appendages, the ends of which were blurred by the motion of small rotors. A camera protruded from its belly, framed by twin landing skids.

She smiled and watched the drone disappear over the horizon.

"Well, what do you know?" she said.

"What is it?" Aaron asked.

"We're heading back. I think we're done out here."

Mira brought the engine to life and accelerated toward the shore. Behind them, the sun slunk beneath the horizon, abandoning them to another increasingly long night.

18

W hile Mira wanted nothing more than to climb in the shower and absorb every last drop of hot water, she was too excited to wait for a single second longer. She changed out of her drysuit and thermal underlayers, put on sweats and a pair of fuzzy slippers, and rushed down to the lower level, only this time with a different destination in mind.

"I need to borrow your drone," she blurted out as she entered Amy's lab.

The chief scientific officer gasped in surprise and spun around in her chair, clutching her chest.

"Christ almighty, Mira. You just about gave me a heart attack."

Mira bounded down the steps, grabbed the chair from Elroy's workstation on her way past, and rolled it right up to Amy's. There were three computer monitors on the desk: the screen in the center displayed some sort of video manipulation software, while the outer two showed the same live aerial footage, only one was in digital HD, and the other was in the strange colored hues of the thermal register. On the left screen, an enormous polar bear trundled across the glacier with two cubs in tow, nearly invisible through the blowing snow. The sow abruptly stopped, rose to her full height, and stared up into the sky toward the camera. On the right screen, she looked positively demonic, her body standing apart from the black ice and snow in shades of purple and pink. Her facial features glowed orange, and her eyes and mouth burned bright white as though about to shoot fire.

"Your drone," Mira said. "Tell me you'll let me borrow it."

Amy looked at her as though she'd asked for her firstborn.

"Do you have any idea how long and hard I had to fight to acquire that Matrice Six Hundred Pro unmanned aerial vehicle? This isn't some toy you might buy your nephew for his birthday. This is a fully customized octocopter with a top-of-the-line battery management system capable of extended flight times and a range of more than three miles. Its camera exceeds all professional broadcasting requirements, including four-K resolution at one hundred and twenty frames per second, while simultaneously capturing imagery in the infrared range. To be blunt, it cost more than my car, and it's likely more valuable to the NSF than both you and I combined. I had to take virtual classes with the manufacturer, log five hundred hours of flight time, and earn a commercial license from the Federal Aviation Administration before they'd even submit the requisition."

Mira sighed and tugged her fingers through her damp hair.

"What could you possibly need it for anyway?" Amy asked.

"I was hoping I could attach a green lighting fixture to the bottom and use it to surveil the lake for the presence of our biofilm remotely."

Amy looked sideways at her.

"I thought you retrieved your sample."

"I did. Or at least I think I did. The drone would just help confirm as much and allow us to more carefully monitor its growth when we do formally release it."

Amy nodded and spun a circle in her chair.

"While that's a clever idea, I'm afraid I simply can't risk flying the drone that low over the water, especially with the winds in that canyon. If it were to crash or become immersed, there would be no hope of repairing, let alone replacing it." Amy must have seen the disappointment on Mira's face. She rested her hand on Mira's shoulder and directed her attention toward the computer setup. "Let me show you why this is so important to me."

She brought up a map centered over Baffin Bay, the body of water separating northeastern Canada and Greenland. Clusters of jagged colored lines marred the coastal regions, occasionally stretching inland and out across the ice masses.

"Each of these lines represents an individual polar bear that researchers like me have been tracking via satellite," Amy said. "There are fewer than twenty-five thousand left in the world, divided into nineteen distinct subpopulations, the majority of which reside in northern Canada. Their numbers continue to decline at the lower latitudes as rising temperatures force a continuous northward migration." She turned around and looked Mira directly in the eyes. "You have to remember that polar bears are the largest terrestrial marine carnivores in the world. The primary component of their diet is seals, which don't just swim to shore and serve themselves on platters. Polar bears have developed a system by which they use the sea ice to hunt their prey on the open ocean, but with the decline in sea ice and the resulting shift from multi-year to annual ice packs, many have been forced to seek alternative forms of sustenance."

"By heading inland," Mira said, recognizing where Amy was leading her.

"And up the coastlines, where they increasingly come into contact with human settlements." Amy sighed and returned her attention to the screen. "These aren't semi-domesticated animals content to rummage in garbage bins; they're apex predators conditioned to hunt any available species in a harsh and unforgiving environment where weeks at a time might pass between meals. More than thirty have been killed in quote, unquote 'self-defense' by villagers along the eastern coast of Greenland over the past five years—a statistically significant number from a subpopulation that numbers fewer than two hundred—including the mother of the very individual you're looking at now."

The expression on Amy's face was one of a proud parent showing off pictures of her child.

"Meet Miska," she said. "I rescued her as a cub from a village called Ittoqqortoormiit—try saying that five times fast—where six adults were killed when they strayed too close to habitation. She alone survived the massacre, and only because she fetched a price I was able to pay from my personal bank account. I've watched her grow from an orphan who could barely feed herself to a ferocious mother who always ensures that her cubs eat first. I witnessed her birthing and weaning them on a remote camera installed inside her den. The first footage I recorded on this drone was of them emerging from the darkness and tentatively crawling away from their home, growing increasingly comfortable until they were playing in the snow without a care in the world."

She smiled and traced her fingertip across the monitor, where the mother bear nudged her wrestling cubs to separate them.

"They're adorable," Mira said.

"We all make tremendous personal sacrifices in the name of science. Some of us more than others. This is not an easy life up here. It's important to savor the simple joys whenever and wherever you can. As corny as it sounds, I think of these amazing animals as the children I'll never have. My big white furbabies."

"What a beautiful sentiment."

"That drone's my only real connection to them," Amy said. She wiped a tear from her eye and laughed at herself. "Someone has to look after them and make sure they're all taken care of."

"And no one could ever do it better than you do, mama bear," Elroy said from the entryway. He walked up behind her, squeezed her shoulders, and winked at Mira. "As you can probably tell, we old-timers won't ever be accused of being the sanest people in any room and likely wouldn't be welcomed back into civilized society with open arms—"

"Speak for yourself, you old goat."

"—but we do have a pretty good thing going, don't we?"

Amy placed her hand on top of his, and Mira suddenly realized that she'd overstayed her welcome. She excused herself and was nearly to the door when something Amy had said hit her.

"You said you had to log five hundred flight hours before the NSF would approve your requisition for a new drone," she said. "Did you do that up here?"

"Of course," Amy said. "It's not like they could make me return to the States to do it."

"Do you still have your old drone?"

"I think so, but it's crashed so many times that I'd be surprised if it flies anymore."

Mira smirked.

"Maybe it doesn't have to."

19

"I'd forgotten this thing was even back here," Dougherty said. The massive facilities engineer lifted a dusty crate from the top shelf, set it on his workbench, and carefully extricated the old drone from the polyethylene foam insert. "Ah, yes. The Phantom Two Vision-plus. While this model was the top of the line in its day, it simply wasn't designed with arctic conditions in mind. I can't tell you how many times Amy brought it down here—rotors busted and guts hanging out—begging me to put it back together again. It's almost a shame we had to put it out to pasture."

"Does it still work?" Mira asked.

Dougherty removed the quadcopter's casing and set it aside, exposing the inner workings. He seated a pair of magnifying lenses on the tip of his nose, leaned his head back, and studied the components.

"If I remember correctly, the power distribution board is fried, which means there's no way of sending equal amounts of juice to each of the rotors. The infernal thing just spins like a top."

"Can you fix it?"

"Well, sure . . . but without a new board, I'd have to rewire the whole thing so that the battery distributes power to each rotor individually, which would increase its weight and decrease its responsiveness to such an extent that it wouldn't stay aloft for more than a few minutes in this wind, let alone with the precision you'd require for it to hover just a few feet above the water."

"What if it didn't have to fly at all?" Mira asked, offering a crooked half-smile.

Dougherty stared at her for several seconds, his bushy brows furrowed, until he finally realized what she was suggesting. He beamed and looked at the Phantom in a new light.

"Why didn't you say so in the first place? That changes everything."

"Can you do it?"

"Is it safe to assume there will be more chocolate in my immediate future?"

"I have a hunch that can be arranged."

"Then I relish the challenge."

"I that a 'yes'?"

"Has anyone ever been able to tell you 'no'?"

Mira hopped up on her toes, wrapped her arms around his neck, and gave him a flurry of pecks on the fuzzy cheek, each punctuated with a "Thank you."

"Go on now," he said. "You're making me blush."

Mira exited the workroom in the rear of the climate control center and headed for her lab. She could hardly contain her excitement and couldn't wait to tell Sammie about her idea for the drone. If Dougherty could really retrofit the old drone for their purposes, then they would have a way of confirming that the biofilm wasn't colonizing the lake and a means by which they could monitor its growth once they did officially release it.

She skipped down the stairs toward the giant aquarium and was just about to share the good news when Sammie looked up from her microscope, stopping Mira dead in her tracks. Sammie looked like she hadn't eaten or slept in days. Her face was ashen and the rings around her bloodshot eyes were as dark as a raccoon's.

"It's about time you got here," she said, rising from her desk. "There's something I need to show you."

She grabbed a box from the counter behind her and carried it over to the aquarium in hands that positively shook from caffeine overload.

"Are you okay?" Mira asked.

"Kill the lights, would you?" Sammie said, dodging the question.

Mira hit the switch just as Sammie reached the top of the ladder and turned on the green lighting array. The biofilm materialized from the open water, clinging to the glass walls above the wavering kelp, beneath which crabs scuttled across the sandy substrate and tube worms tentatively extended their feathery appendages from the rocks.

"It's grown even since this morning," Mira said.

"That's not all, though. What else do you notice about it?"

Mira leaned right up against the tank. It was readily apparent that the bacteria were producing dragline silk at an unprecedented rate. Countless individual strands connected the biofilm to the glass and formed overlapping layers reminiscent of pictures she'd seen of spider webs that carpeted entire meadows or filled the rafters of abandoned barns. She was just about to ask Sammie what she'd noticed when she made the connection for herself.

"It has to be nearly a quarter of an inch thick," she whispered, looking up and finding Sammie staring back down at her with an unreadable expression on her face. "It should be visible to the naked eye."

"Exactly. The microorganisms themselves would only be identifiable by their communal iridescence, but the sheer amount of webbing binding them together should be impossible to miss."

"So why can't we see it?"

"I have a theory," Sammie said, glancing over her shoulder at the box she'd brought with her. "Mind handing me the flashlights labeled 'green' and 'white'?"

Mira passed them up to Sammie, who switched off the lighting fixture, darkening the room. A green glow blossomed from the first flashlight as she shone it down into the water. The beam created a circle of emerald iridescence that diffused outward through the biofilm, fading near the periphery. She moved it back and forth, illuminating different sections.

"Look at it from underneath," Sammie said.

Mira crouched and peered upward, but the light on the biofilm looked just as it had from above.

"It's the same," she said.

"But it shouldn't be. Sure, some amount of light should pass through the webbing and refract from the organisms at tangential angles, but the superficial bacteria should act like mirrors and reflect the light. They shouldn't be transmitting that iridescence to the inferior surface. Now, watch what happens when I turn on the ordinary flashlight with its full-color spectrum of white light . . . "

Sammie shone the second beam onto the exact same spot as the first. The white light seemed to erase the green, turning the biofilm invisible once more. She drew the two flashlights apart and the organisms underneath the green light appeared on one side of the tank again.

"Now, hand me the blacklight."

Mira retrieved a third flashlight, labeled 'Black UV,' from the box and exchanged it for the other two. The blacklight blossomed a heartbeat later, casting a purplish-blue glare over the lab. The biofilm appeared once more, only it looked like a particulate mist trapped in a chaos of translucent spiderwebs.

"That's the Ymirarchaea," Sammie said. "It's resistant to light in the ultraviolet range, which causes damage to the DNA of most microorganisms, hence the reason that marine bacteria iridesce and diatoms die when they're too near the surface." She climbed down the ladder, picked up her box, and returned to her microscope. A quick glance through the eyepiece confirmed that she could still see what she expected, even under only the blacklight bulb. "Now, look at the slide and watch how it reacts."

Mira looked through the lens and saw an archaeon that had engulfed both a bacterium and a diatom, forming a single pentagonal organism reminiscent of a human cell. Fibrous strands of webbing surrounded it, adhering it to the slide. The linear grooves on the surface of the archaeon glowed faintly blue in the ultraviolet wavelengths. Sammie moved the flashlight to the other side of the lens, and the lines appeared to shift.

"It's like the light reflected from one set of lines when you were on my right," Mira said, "and then from the lines in between them when you stepped to my left."

"Keep your eye on that archaeon."

Sammie turned off the blacklight, momentarily allowing the lab to fall into complete darkness. She switched on the green flashlight and the archaeon vanished as though it had never been there at all, leaving behind a single iridescing bacterium within its body mass.

"And now the white," Sammie said.

Something in her voice made the hairs rise on the backs of Mira's arms.

The ordinary white light filled the view through the microscope. Sammie pressed the flashlight against the side of the aperture and shone it directly onto the slide, producing a reflection from the thin glass. When it resolved, only a vague shape of roughly the same dimensions remained, as though the communal organism—archaeon, bacterium, and diatom—had been replaced by a fluid of slightly different density than the fixation solution.

"It disappeared," Mira whispered.

Sammie moved the light and the organism reappeared.

"What in God's name have we done?"

20

Dougherty eased out onto the floating dock, the resin-coated aluminum slick underfoot. Waves thumped against the underside and vanished beneath the ice rimming the shallows. The wind blew straight into the open boathouse from across the lake, the far side of which was invisible through the sheeting sleet. Arendelle Island materialized from the storm, marking their initial target.

"How's the video?" he called back over his shoulder.

"Perfect," Mira said. She stood at the foot of the dock, her back to the lake to shield her laptop from the elements. Her screen displayed the live feed from the drone's camera, which jostled wildly in Dougherty's grip. The clear plastic housing caused a fisheye distortion and there were numerous dead pixels, but she couldn't have been more pleased. "I can't believe you were able to modify the drone so quickly."

Dougherty knelt at the end of the dock and glanced back at her. His cheeks were red and chafed, his beard frosted with ice, and yet the expression of pride on his face was unmistakable.

"Oh, how I relish a challenge," he said. "Not that I don't

enjoy my role at the station. It's just that I'm rarely afforded the opportunity to dig into my bag of tricks."

He'd looked like a little kid with a new toy when he tracked her down on her way to the lab this morning, holding his monstrous contraption in his arms. Mira hadn't even recognized the drone at first, as it had almost looked like a gyroscope mounted inside a motorcycle tire, at least until she'd seen the tiny propellers protruding from the top. He'd rewired the current from the batteries directly to each of the rotors, encased the wiring in spare PVC pipes, and built a clear waterproof housing that he'd fitted into a ring of the same closed-cell poly-ethylene foam insulation that lined the inside of the station's walls. He'd even upgraded the drone's antenna array and the remote control so that it would be able to cover the entirety of the lake from the comfort of her lab, even the far southwestern shore, where the runoff from the melting glacier eroded the granite hillside.

A crackling sound burst from the transceiver in the pocket of Mira's parka.

"How's it going down there?" Sammie asked.

Mira set down her laptop on a nearby crate and brought the two-way to her lips.

"We're just about to find out," she said through a cloud of breath.

Dougherty took that as his cue and set the drone in the water. The image on the screen blurred before, then resolved into crystal-clear footage of smooth gray sediment spotted with the occasional rock or seashell from which brown macroalgae grew in hair-like clumps, shifting gently on the current.

"So far, so good," Mira said. "What about the green light?"

Dougherty scuttled back down the icy dock and retrieved the remote control from where he'd left it on top of the crate. A flick of a switch and the color darkened to a deep green. The domed casing produced refractions of light that wavered near the edges of the screen.

"Now, let's take her out and see what she can do," he said, toggling the twin sticks with his gloved thumbs. The rotors buzzed and the drone streaked away from them, riding the waves. On the monitor, the seafloor passed in a blur until it dropped out of sight. "The controls will take some getting used to, but once you've got it down, it's a piece of cake. Just be careful not to push too hard or"—the drone screamed and rose several feet from the water in the distance—"it will actually take flight."

Mira caught a glimpse of open air and plastic spotted with water on the monitor. And then she saw only green-tinted darkness once more.

"Amazing," she whispered.

Dougherty blushed and offered her the controls.

"It's all yours," he said.

"You built it," Mira said. "Play with it for as long as you like."

Dougherty didn't need to be told twice. He stepped right up beside her and piloted the drone straight toward the island, which appeared in outline on a satellite map in the lower right corner of the screen.

"Listen," Sammie said from the transceiver. "I didn't call just to check up on you. I think I figured out how the archaeon creates the illusion of invisibility."

"Do tell," Mira said, her eyes never leaving her laptop, where green water roiling with disturbed silt and microbes streaked past beneath the camera's lens.

"You remember how when the archaeon ingested the diatom, a chemical interaction occurred between the two species that created what looked like parallel striations on the diatom's cell wall? That outer layer is called a frustule. It's made of silica, which is a type of quartz with both reflective and refractive properties. I believe those striations are actually raised ribs that serve as microscopic magnifying lenses, which, based on their columnar shape, change what you can see through them when viewed from different angles, just like those optical illusions that transform from one picture to another as you walk past them. Or remember those little cards that used to come in Cracker Jack or cereal boxes? Tilt them from side to side to make a butterfly's wings move or a cartoon character dance?"

"I'm familiar with the concept," Mira said, watching the red dot marking the drone on the map as it neared the island. "They used to put them on the covers of horror novels when I was a kid. Faces turning into skulls and that kind of thing. I had to close my eyes when I walked past them in a bookstore."

"Exactly, and in the process of researching my theory, I came across a magician on YouTube who used a sheet of lenticular plastic to build an invisibility shield. By bending the sheet at just the right angle, he utilized Snell's law of refraction to make anything directly behind it disappear. What you see is the white light striking the bowed surface of the shield being redirected toward the center of it by all of those thin, corduroy-like lenses, effectively hiding the magician crouching behind it by refracting the light around him, creating an artificial blind spot."

"And you think this chimeric organism—or, more specifically, the sum of its parts—causes the biofilm to function the same way?"

"That would explain why the white light essentially makes it invisible, while the green and black lights reveal its individual components."

On the monitor, the passage of water slowed, and the organic matter suspended in it coalesced into the familiar nebulous cloud in the lee of the island.

"So what are the implications?" Mira asked.

"At this point, I don't have the slightest clue," Sammie said.

"It could be merely an intriguing coincidence in need of further exploration or . . . "

Her voice trailed off. Mira was about to ask her what she was going to say when something caught her eye. A glimmer in the water, at the farthest reaches of the camera's range, where the green light dissolved into the darkness.

" . . . or maybe we're witnessing the evolution of an entirely new species," Sammie said, finishing her thought.

Mira's pulse rushed in her ears. The entire world seemed to slow around her.

"We'd better figure it out," she heard herself say, her voice distant, as though originating from the bottom of a well.

"Why?" Sammie asked. "What's wrong?"

"It's in the lake."

21

20,000 Feet Above the Southwest Greenland Ice Sheet
70.399835, -47.735173

Now

"We've been poring over the satellite imagery, but we can't find any indication as to where the scientists might have gone," Ryder says. "Assuming they left at all. Of course, with as hard as it's snowing, their tracks would already have been erased and they'd have been forced to seek shelter."

"It's also possible that they've returned to the station and they'll be waiting when we arrive," Bashir says. "If not, our only choice will be to track them blindly across the glacier by Susvee."

Cameron nods and glances at the NeXgen contingent through the window of the all-terrain SUSV. He feared that whatever their priorities upon landing might be, tracking and rescuing the scientists wasn't near the top of the list. He needed to figure out what kind of mess they were walking into, and he was running out of time to do so.

"Keep looking," he says. "We're searching for highly educated individuals—"

"Which means somewhere between jack and shit in weather like this," Ronny says.

"His point is that they have a better than average chance of survival," Speedy says. "If they're still out there, they'll find a way to signal us."

"If they were as smart as everyone seems to think, they wouldn't have left the infernal station in the first place."

"Just keep looking," Cameron says. "There has to be some sign of them."

"You mean other than the bodies on the satellite images?" Ronny says.

Cameron glares at the senior airman, who holds up his hands in surrender and resumes his perusal of the satellite photographs on his tablet. As their commanding officer, he feels a pang of guilt for not sharing his suspicions with the men he's asking to risk their lives for him, but at the same time, he has no idea what they're up against. While he'd initially believed that the threat to the scientists was human in nature and that someone had digitally altered the footage he'd seen in Colonel Patrick's office to conceal the identity of the person attacking Dr. Stone, he's beginning to think they're dealing with something else entirely, something beyond his limited ability to comprehend. And the more video logs he watches, the more convinced he becomes.

He resumes playback as soon as his men have returned to their assigned tasks.

"This is Dr. Mira Stone." She wears a hooded sweatshirt she's already worn in several other entries and an expression of utter exhaustion. "The date is October twenty-seventh. It's now been three days since we confirmed the presence of the biofilm in the lake, and its growth rate has already surpassed our most ambitious projections. While accurate measurement is impossible under field conditions, we've detected a total of eight amorphous biomasses between twelve and sixteen feet in diameter. Each of them is larger than the specimen in the aquarium, confirming Dr. Rantanen's theory that, like many other species, the biofilm's ultimate size is dictated by the available space it has to grow."

She hits a key and the screen splits in half. A video recorded by some sort of submersible vessel plays beside her, demonstrating a wavering emerald carpet of slime. It's patchy and misshapen, but, after everything he's learned from the previous entries, truly magnificent in every other way.

A narwhal passes through it as though it isn't even there, strands of webbing floating outward in its wake as it races toward the camera. The green light shuts off, and Dr. Stone stops the footage.

"Thus far, samples collected from each of the individual biomasses—identified by Greek letter, from alpha through theta—have failed to demonstrate the presence of any species of archaea." She breathes a long sigh and allows her shoulders to slump. When she again speaks, it's in a tone that mirrors the expression of discomfort on her face. "I suppose that should be good news, but I can't imagine the presence of the Ymirarchaea in the aquarium is an anomaly since it originated in the substrate collected from the seafloor of the lake. Maybe I'm wrong—scratch that; I *hope* I'm wrong—but I believe that once the biofilm is established, it's only a matter of time before conditions favor its awakening, if you will, from its state of cryptobiosis. And once that happens, I'm afraid it will be impossible to predict how it will respond in the open water."

She nods to herself and terminates the recording.

Cameron opens the index for Dr. Rantanen's logs. He's begun alternating from one scientist to the next as it seems like each of the women is privy to a subset of the information he needs and approach their work from different perspectives. He's also beginning to think that their motivations don't entirely align, which is somewhat alarming considering Dr. Rantanen's prior relationship with NeXgen, and presumably the four men quietly plotting inside the SUSV.

The blond microbiologist appears on the screen. With her green T-shirt and her hair piled on her head, she looks remarkably like an overworked Tinkerbell. She speaks more formally than in previous entries, as though communicating directly with a specific audience, rather than merely recording her day's work for posterity.

"This is Dr. Sammie Rantanen. Date: October twenty-seventh. Subsequent experimentation on the three mutualistic organisms—which I shall collectively refer to as 'the chimera' from this point on—has demonstrated the very results we had originally hoped to achieve with Project Araneidae. The Ymirarchaeon appears to have independently conquered some of the limitations of our bacterium. The dragline silk generated by the chimera is five times as thick and ten times as strong as that of the purple marine bacterium alone. Given more time to work with it, I believe we can achieve the goal we envisioned when we originally devised our project. Throw in its lenticular properties, and suddenly we're looking at success beyond our wildest imaginations. Not only will we be able to secure inexhaustible government funding for its use as a climate change mitigant, but we'll also be able to harvest unlimited quantities from the open ocean. The potential profits for a polymer with such staggering physical properties are incalculable."

Dr. Rantanen smiles, dons a pair of rubber gloves, and produces a bowl from somewhere off-camera. She holds up a small canister with color-coded values on the side, removes a slender length of studded paper, and turns it over and over, presumably to demonstrate that it's an ordinary chemical test strip. With a theatrical flourish, she dunks it into the bowl, which appears to have been filled with some sort of acid, because when she removes it, only half of the test strip remains. She grabs a tissue, wipes down the test strip, and the missing half once more appears, only now it features a range of colors aligning with those on the label of the container.

"What the hell . . . ?" Cameron whispers.

"I'm in," Rush says through the headset. "You need to see this."

Cameron casually checks to make sure the men in the SUSV aren't watching and makes his way to the ladder leading up to the communications center situated behind the flight deck. His tech specialist sits before a bank of satellite and radio equipment, his networked laptop propped on the table in front of him and an indecipherable expression on his face.

"I was able to hack into NeXgen and access the surveillance footage from inside the station without much difficulty," Rush says. "I figured I'd start at the point where they lost power and watch it in reverse until I found something useful. I notified you the moment I saw it."

He unpauses the recording on his computer and the video begins to play. The perspective switches from one camera to the next every few seconds. There's a staircase, at the bottom of which is an open door, through which the blowing snow has drifted; a hallway, the floor smeared with dark fluid and littered with plastic shards from the broken lenses of the overhead light fixtures; and a cafeteria, the tables upended below shattered windows that admit the gusting wind.

Rush pauses the playback and points at the top left corner of the screen, where a man lies on the ground behind the serving bar. His face is blistered, his teeth bared, his skin seemingly melted to the consistency of candle wax. Ice clings to the sparse clumps of hair sprouting from his scalp and chin. A tatter of flesh curls away from the exposed tendons and muscles in his neck.

"Jesus," Cameron whispers. He looks up at the monitor displaying the Hercules' cargo hold, past his team and to the SUSV, inside of which the four men from NeXgen are little more than dark silhouettes. "What in God's name were they doing up there?"

22

Greenland
81.906296, -29.744960

Two Weeks Ago

M ira watched the fluttering green mat pass beneath the camera, glimmering at the very edge of sight. Yesterday, there had been several disruptions in the biofilm known as Beta, but the webbing appeared to have knitted itself closed overnight. There was only a single new hole inflicted by one of the whales, which she'd become quite skilled at distinguishing from the different shapes of ripped biofilm caused by schooling fish, swirling currents, and diving seabirds, which she feared would be the source of the chimera's initial spread beyond the dam. They had yet to find any trace of it in the fjord on the other side of the dam, although the current could have easily carried it several miles farther inland and swept it under the glacier.

Despite the laser tape measure Dougherty had installed on

the drone, it was becoming harder to accurately gauge the dimensions of the biomasses with every passing day. The growth rate wasn't quite exponential, but the individual colonies had nearly filled the lees of their respective islands and had begun testing the more tumultuous waters. She'd witnessed the currents tear sections from the edges of the film and usher them toward the shoreline, where the shallows, including those surrounding the dock, were already carpeted beneath the ice. It was only a matter of time before the biofilm either adapted to the currents or reached the limits of its proliferation.

Either way, they'd passed the point of no return long ago.

At least it was doing everything they'd hoped it would. There was already a demonstrable difference in temperature between the water immediately above and below the biofilm, and the laser thermometer registered a three-degree decrease at the bottom of the lake in the last three days alone. The water chemistry had also changed dramatically. The pH had risen by a measurable amount, and the concentration of diatom frustules collected from the silt had increased by five percent, both of which were proof that the biofilm's efficacy was well on its way to surpassing even their most ambitious projections.

The problem was that if they were right about the origin of the archaeon, it was only a matter of time before it awakened from its eons-long metabolic stasis and began absorbing the individual components of the biofilm. If that happened, their only option to ensure the extermination of the resulting chimeras would be to turn the lake into an uninhabitable toxic stew and hope to God they didn't contaminate the fjord and the Arctic Ocean in the process. But before they could even consider taking such drastic measures, they'd have to arrange for the relocation of the whales, which would be too expensive for the NSF to shoulder alone, and based upon the current perception of keeping such noble creatures in captivity, it would prove a public relations nightmare that would drag on indefinitely. So all they could do was hold their breath and pray—

A tendril of silt passed through a hole in the biofilm and dissipated into the water. One of the whales must have disturbed the sediment on the bottom.

Mira carefully toggled the miniature joysticks on the remote and guided the quadcopter out from behind the island. Water rushed past on one monitor while the red dot of the drone's GPS beacon crossed the satellite image on the other. She'd already spent too much time surveying the previous biofilms and she'd nearly burned through what little daylight she had left.

Documenting the chimera's growth patterns grew more monotonous by the day. It would have been nice if Sammie had been willing to spell her from time to time, but, like Dougherty had said, the controls took some serious getting used to and she wanted her partner focused on the bizarre mutualistic relation-ship between the bacterium, the diatom, and the archaeon. They needed to understand everything about the chimeric organism and Sammie was the only one with the skill to ascer-tain the truth, not that she was very good at sharing what she'd learned. In fact, she almost seemed secretive about her research.

Mira glanced at her partner's unattended station. Where was she anyway?

The drone rose and fell on the waves before swirling dizzily into the lee of Arendelle Island, where they'd first discovered the biofilm known as Alpha. It had grown so large that it had folded back upon itself in several areas. Ridges and valleys had formed, creating river-like seams through which the current passed unimpeded, carrying larger nutri-ents that would have otherwise become trapped in the webbing.

Again, a cloud of silt billowed through the gaps and drifted away.

Mira heard footsteps on the stairs behind her and whirled around in surprise, knocking a pencil and notebook from her desk in the process.

"Sorry," Carrie said, holding up her hands in mock surrender as she crossed the lab. "I didn't mean to startle you."

"I guess I just got a little too wrapped up in what I was doing." Mira smiled and gestured for the paleoclimatologist to pull up a chair. "I'm sure you know how that goes."

"And then some." Carrie inclined her chin toward the monitor. "Not that I work with anything as cool as that biofilm of yours. It looks like something from a different planet."

"It's sure growing like it is."

"And it's working?"

"Better than we ever could have hoped."

"Then why don't you look like this is cause for celebration? It's not every girl who gets to say she's saving the world."

Mira offered a halfhearted smile. She wasn't entirely sure how to answer without dumping all of her problems on Carrie, who'd already been on the receiving end once, so she changed the subject.

"How's your research going?" she asked.

Carrie's face lit up.

"That's why I came down here," she said, jumping from her seat and staring out across the lake toward the opposite ridge-line. "Moore and his team found a void anomaly during their magnetometric survey of the glacier. They think it's probably a cave, so they called Leo, who's already getting everything ready to head out at first light tomorrow. I figured you needed a break and might want to come with us to do a little exploring."

"I don't know," Mira said. "I have a lot of work to do."

"It'll still be here when you get back. You've been given a once-in-a-lifetime opportunity. What's the point of traveling all

the way to the top of the world if you're not going to go out
there and set foot where no other human being has ever tread
before?"

Mira's heart raced at the prospect. How many men had
given their lives to chart a course through this cold and unforgiving part of the world, searching for a northwestern passage
that might not even have existed? And here she was just sitting
in her lab, staring at a computer screen. She could probably
spare a few hours to explore a cave that no other human being
on the planet—living or dead—had ever seen before. Besides,
there was nothing she could do but watch helplessly as her
creation overtook the lake.

"I guess it doesn't technically need to be light outside for me
to observe the biofilm."

"That's the spirit," Carrie said. "The theoretical cave's only
twelve miles away. We can take the snowmobiles and be back
before dinner."

The silt billowing from underneath the biofilm grew so
thick that Mira could barely see the emerald iridescence
through it. She switched off the green light. The biomass
vanished and the cloud took on a pinkish hue.

It wasn't sediment.

"Oh, no," she whispered.

Mira rose from her chair and stumbled toward the window
on numb legs. She stood beside Carrie and stared down at the
lake. The water surrounding the islands and rimming the
shoreline turned red, as though the earth itself were bleeding,
its lifeblood burbling up from the depths and diffusing into the
lake.

"Red tide," she whispered.

"What's that?" Carrie asked.

"Red tides are harmful algal blooms caused by upwellings
of nutrients from the seafloor following major storms. They
release enough toxins to decimate entire marine ecosystems."

Mira's heart sank as the reality of the situation came crashing down on her.

There hadn't been a major storm.

And those organisms weren't algae.

They were archaea. She'd seen similar blooms in the hot springs of Yellowstone and the salt ponds of San Francisco Bay.

The biofilm had awakened the Ymirarchaea from their cryptobiotic slumber.

Whatever was going to happen, there was no way of stopping it now.

23

Mira pounded on Sammie's door. When no one immediately answered, she called out to her partner.

"Sammie!"

The door swung inward just as Mira was preparing to hammer it with her fist again.

"Jesus, Mira," Sammie said. Her eyes were bloodshot, her hair matted on one side. "What are you—?"

"There's an archaeal bloom in the lake."

Sammie blinked several times as though questioning if she were truly awake.

"You're sure?" she finally said.

Mira hit the switch to lighten the tinting on the window and dragged Sammie across the bedroom. They had to lean against the glass and crane their necks to see a mere sliver of the lake over the rim of the canyon, but that was more than enough.

Sammie's face blanched.

"There's a black hardshell case in the closet behind my desk in the lab," she said. "Grab it and meet me in the dry room."

Mira turned without a word and ran back down the hallway

toward the stairs. She nearly bowled over Amy and Elroy on their way to the cafeteria and had to sidestep Dr. Porter, a breadstick hanging from his mouth and a fistful protruding from the pocket of his lab coat, on her way through. She descended the staircase and hit the corridor at a sprint. The windows lining the back walls of the labs blew past in her peripheral vision, revealing a sky that had already started to darken. They'd be lucky to have half an hour of useful light by the time they got down to the lake.

She shouldered past the aquarium and rounded the desk. The case was right where Sammie had said it would be, only far heavier than she'd expected. She grabbed a transceiver from the charger and ran back upstairs, her legs burning from the exertion.

Sammie was already in the dry room—a narrow heated chamber off the main entrance where they hung their wet clothing and diving gear to dry over a series of floor drains—when Mira arrived with the case containing the portable micro-scope. Five minutes later, they were both wearing their drysuits and staggering away from the station across the icepack. They braced themselves against the wind and descended into the narrow crevice housing the steep metal staircase. In her hurry, Mira had forgotten her crampons and slipped on practically every other step, but she clung to the railing and somehow managed to keep herself upright.

The stairs deposited them on the windswept dirt, only rather than following the path along the ridge to the dam, they doubled back and took the winding route down to the boathouse.

Mira stopped in her tracks when she caught her first unob-structed view of the blood-red lake. The color had darkened even in the few minutes since she'd seen it last, with little more than stripes of clear water flowing between the islands on the fastest currents.

A crackle of static erupted from the two-way.

"What the hell is wrong with the lake?" Jen shouted.

"We're working on it," Mira replied. "We're nearly to the boathouse now. I'm going to take out the Zodiac, and I'll need you to spot me."

"What's this going to do to my whales?"

Mira didn't answer. She burst through the door and headed straight for the inflatable boat, which hung from the rafters by a series of pulleys. She lowered it to the ice and dragged it down the length of the slick dock to the open water.

"Here," Sammie said, handing Mira one of the green flashlights and a collection container with a vacuum seal. "You're going to need these."

Mira loaded them into the Zodiac, climbed behind the wheel, and roared across the choppy waves toward the nearest island, leaving Sammie stomping through the frozen shallows to collect a sample of the discolored water. The archaeal bloom looked more pink than red from down here, but it darkened to a rich rust color in the deeper water. She knew precisely where she was going and how far down she needed to dive. A sinking sensation in her stomach confirmed that she also knew exactly what she'd find.

This was like a nightmare from which she couldn't awaken, one in which everything she did, despite the noblest of intentions, invariably turned into a disaster of unmitigated proportions. She heard a voice inside her helmet and realized that she was talking to herself.

"It's all right. Everything's going to be fine."

Mira slowed as she neared her target, killed the motor, and drifted into the lee of Arendelle Island. She rolled backward over the pontoon before the boat had even stopped, bleeding air from her compensation vest as she sank straight toward the bottom. The cold squeezed the breath from her lungs and prickled her flesh with goosebumps. A flick of a switch and the green beam turned the red cloud black. She caught the faintest hint of the biofilm below her and watched it rise toward her feet, parting as though it weren't even there as she passed through it. The moment she had a sample sealed within the collection device, she inflated the vest and swam toward the wavering sky.

Sammie's voice burst from the speaker inside her helmet as she breached the surface.

"It's definitely the Ymirarchaea."

"You're sure?"

"Without a doubt."

"What does that mean?" Jen asked.

"Quite probably nothing," Sammie said. "These organisms aren't foreign to these waters. They've undoubtedly been down there in the sediment since long before our first ancestors descended from the trees. Try not to worry—"

"Try not to worry? These whales are like my children, and you expect me not to be alarmed by the fact that the entire lake looks like it's turned to blood?"

"We'll figure this out," Mira said, splashing toward the boat. "Everything's under control."

"Somehow, I'm not overwhelmed with confidence."

Mira tossed the canister into the Zodiac and hauled herself over the pontoon. She cranked the motor and sped back toward the boathouse, bouncing from the waves and careening toward the dock, which she narrowly averted as she crashed through the layer of ice that had already reformed in the shallows.

"Did you get a sample of the biofilm?" Sammie asked.

Mira tossed her the canister and wrenched off her helmet to make sure that no one could overhear their conversation.

"What are we going to do?" she asked.

"Keep a level head, for starters," Sammie said. "You and I both know that while we're dealing with a novel microorganism, the chances of it being detrimental to an environment in which it's existed for eons are beyond slim."

"That doesn't change the fact that we're dealing with an unpredictable relationship between three distinct species that have never come into contact before, one of which was engineered in a lab using spider DNA."

"We're still talking about a biofilm, Mira. Living slime. These things occur naturally in the wild. You wouldn't think twice about wading through one in a swamp or wiping it from the bottoms of your shoes on the floor mats of your car."

"Be that as it may."

Sammie sighed and visibly collected herself.

"Let's just take this one step at a time," she said. "There's no point in panicking unless we find something that's genuinely cause for concern."

Mira met her partner's stare and slowly nodded her agreement. Sammie was right. In fact, it almost looked like the archaeal bloom was fading with the setting of the sun. The water was already a lighter shade of red than it had been when they'd first arrived.

"Good," Sammie said. "Now let's find out what we're dealing with."

Mira paced the dock while her partner prepared a slide to view under the microscope. By the time she'd finished, the sun had slunk beneath the horizon. It would set for the final time in less than two weeks, abandoning the sky to the stars that would shine around the clock for three long months.

Sammie looked through the lens for several seconds before stepping aside and gesturing for Mira to take a peek. She leaned right against the eyepiece and adjusted the focus the tiniest bit until the various microscopic creatures on the slide came into view. The archaea had already begun consuming the bacteria and diatoms, producing the same multicellular chimeras they'd discovered in their lab.

For better or worse, this singular new species had broken containment.

Whatever happened from here was their responsibility.

And they didn't have the slightest idea what it did.

Let alone how to stop it.

24

Mira smelled Swearengin coming before he even entered the room, carrying a five-gallon bucket by the handle.

"Where do you guys want this?" he asked.

"Anywhere is fine," Sammie said, rising from her station. Her eyes were so red that it looked like she was the one who'd been down at the fjord smoking hand-rolled cigarettes. "What did you catch for us?"

The skinny man beamed and gestured to the bucket with a flourish. Mira rolled her chair closer, peeked into the murky water, and recoiled. When the chef had volunteered to catch some fish for their tank so they could study how another species interacted with the biofilm, she'd assumed he'd return with some cod or char, some normal edible fish, not whatever these . . . *things* . . . were.

"What in the world are those?" Sammie asked. "They look like a horned toad mated with a frog and grew fins for legs."

"What did you expect?" Swearengin said. "It's not like I was going to sit down there on the dam with a fishing pole in this bloody weather. I grabbed a pair of hip boots and a net, waded out into the shallows, and caught whatever I could find."

"What are those things anyway?" Mira asked.

"Arctic staghorn sculpins. They live on the bottom and use those pectoral fins like little feet to hop around on the sand."

Now that she really looked at the strange creatures, they more closely resembled the lionfish her dentist kept in his office aquarium, with its orange stripes, spiked fin rays, and mohawk of dorsal spines, only these were squat and bony, with a reddish coloration to their horned faces. There appeared to be five or six of them in the bottom of the bucket, the largest of which was barely longer than her hand.

"We need fish that will interact directly with the biofilm," Sammie said. "You know, the kinds that actually swim?"

"The chimeras are more concentrated in the shallows," Mira said. "A benthic species like this one should provide a solid foundation we can expand upon when we get a chance to add more pelagic species."

"Better in our tank than in our bellies, I guess," Sammie said.

"Don't think I haven't got a stack of recipes for critters like these in case we burn through our rations," Swearengin said. He winked, but he didn't appear to be kidding. "Just be careful of those spines along its back. They have a tiny bit of poison—"

"Venom," Sammie said, interrupting. "Poison is ingested; venom is injected by a bite or a sting."

"Whatever." The chef rolled his eyes. "Anyway . . . it'll hurt like a mother if you get stung, but it won't do any real harm. Beyond the pain, of course. If you prick your hand, just soak it in some hot water to neutralize the toxins. Anywhere else on your body, and I'd be happy to pour you a bath—"

"We've got this from here," Sammie said, turning Swearengin back toward the door and ushering him to the stairs.

"The offer stands," he called over his shoulder as he rounded the corner.

Mira waited until he was gone to get up from her desk.

"So would you like to do the honors or should I?" she asked.

"You're better with the camera," Sammie said. "Why don't I release them while you try to record them passing through the biofilm?"

"You just want to handle those little cuties, don't you?"

"That's what these are for," she said, grabbing a pair of elbow-length rubber gloves from the corner of her desk. "Shall we?"

Mira retrieved the case containing the digital video camera from the cabinet. The NSF had equipped each of the labs with a state-of-the-art recording device so the scientists could film their daily logs in crystal-clear 4K resolution. However, after poring over research and staring at computer screens and microscope slides all day, most of them lacked the energy to set up the tripod and the lighting array, so they just recorded directly onto their laptops and called it good enough. Documenting the introduction of two species that had never met in the wild was a much better use of its technical capabilities, anyway.

She killed the overhead lights and waited for Sammie to switch the lighting array on the aquarium's hood from white to green before setting up the tripod so that the camera looked straight across the biofilm. Her goal was to capture roughly eight inches of water above and sixteen inches below the iridescent mat, allowing plenty of room for it to stretch and recoil when the fish passed through it. Sammie grabbed one of the fish in her gloved hands and climbed the ladder, using her elbows for balance. She reached the top, leaned over the edge, and held the fish right above the surface, its spiny fins poking through the gaps between her fingers and its tail slapping her wrists.

"Ready?" she asked.

"Whenever you are," Mira said, pressing the button to start the recording.

Sammie lowered the sculpin into the water, squeezing it as it thrashed to free itself from her grasp. She reached as far as she could into the tank, until she held the fish mere inches above the glimmering green layer. With a glance through the water at Mira to confirm her readiness, she released the sculpin. It streaked straight toward the bottom, passing through the biofilm as though it weren't even there and vanishing into the kelp. Green tatters swirled in the fish's wake, marking its passage into the depths like a slipstream of glitter.

"One down," Sammie said. "Did you get it?"

"Oh, yes," Mira said. "I was looking right into its beady little eyes as it tore through the biofilm."

"Why don't you try to capture some more footage of it while I grab the next one?"

Mira removed the camera from the tripod and circled the aquarium until she caught a glimpse of the sculpin, resting on the bottom among the rocks, nearly concealed by kelp, its mouth opening and closing. A patchy iridescent skein clung to its scales, confirming that some residual amount of the biofilm had transferred to the fish. While they'd expected that to be the case, they'd hoped it wouldn't be. The last thing they wanted was for the chimeras to interact directly with Aaron's and Jen's whales, but now that there was no way of preventing it, they needed to study how the organisms interacted with higher orders of life if they wanted to avert a potential disaster.

As soon as she heard Sammie's foot hit the bottom rung of the ladder, she reseated the camera on the tripod and prepared to record the introduction of the second individual, which was a whole lot feistier than the first. It squirmed and flopped in a desperate attempt to wriggle out of Sammie's hands.

"Damn it," she snapped, wincing and nearly dropping the fish. "It got me with one of those stupid spines."

"You need to soak your hand before the toxins kick in."

"Too late for that. It's already starting to burn. Just keep that camera rolling so the pain won't have been for nothing."

Sammie struggled to maintain her grip on the frantic sculpin as she leaned all the way over the edge. She nearly fell in while trying to keep from prematurely releasing it, inadvertently thrusting both her hands and the fish through the biofilm before regaining her balance.

"That was close," she said, the wet end of her ponytail clinging to her shoulder. "Are you ready?"

"You should move one way or the other," Mira said. "The biofilm looks pretty torn up through there."

Sammie nodded, scooted to her left, and released the fish, which raced straight to the bottom to join its kin. She leaned back and started to raise her hands from the water—

"Wait!" Mira called. "Don't move. Let me get a shot of those gloves."

Sammie's hands iridesced under the green light. She turned them over and over, examining the slimy surfaces. Once Mira had recorded several seconds of good footage, Sammie pulled them out of the water and held them in front of her face.

"Hit the overhead lights, would you?" she said, nudging the switch on the aquarium's lighting fixture with her elbow, turning off the green light.

Mira flipped the switch and looked up at Sammie, whose hands appeared to have been raggedly cut off at the wrists.

"Oh, my God," Mira whispered. "Are you all right?"

"What a strange sensation," Sammie said, tilting her head from side to side. "I can't see them, but I can still feel them."

Mira stepped closer and saw that her partner's hands hadn't vanished entirely; there were slight disturbances in the air where they'd been, almost like heat mirages rising from the desert highways back home.

"Get a good shot of this," Sammie said.

Mira recovered from her initial surprise and ascended the ladder to get a better shot of Sammie's hands. The microbiologist slowly raised them in front of her face. Her features remained visible, only subtly distorted, as though viewed through water. A crimson rivulet trickled down her forearm and dripped from her elbow.

"You're bleeding," Mira said.

"Stupid fish," Sammie said, peeling off her gloves and rushing to the sink. "Why don't you document the behavior of the ones in the tank while I rinse out this infernal puncture wound."

Mira nodded and turned the camera on the aquarium once more. She zoomed in and visually scoured the kelp and rocks for any sign of where the sculpins had gone, but either she couldn't find them . . .

Or she couldn't see them.

25

M ira seated her diving helmet and stared down into the aquarium. The biofilm iridesced below her, obscuring her view of the bottom. They'd released a total of five sculpins, all of which had promptly disappeared. It had taken seemingly forever to find them, but before calling it a night, she and Sammie had discovered them hiding among the tangles of vegetation and in the crevices between rocks, shimmering ever so softly under the green light. Of course, by the time they'd returned to the lab this morning, the blasted fish had been nowhere to be found. Not just invisible beneath the white light, as they'd been the night before, but impossible to detect across the entire color spectrum.

There hadn't been bodies floating on the surface or rotting into the substrate, no bits of flesh in the pincers of the crabs or trapped in the filtration units, no spikes in the levels of ammonia or nitrates. It was as though the sculpins had somehow managed to escape the tank. A quick search of the lab had confirmed that wasn't the case, which meant they had to be hiding, and there was only one place they could be.

"Try to balance on the rocks," Sammie said. She wore a

headset and spoke into the microphone so they could stay in contact while Mira was in the water. "If you step into the sediment, you're going to find yourself enveloped in a cloud of silt."

"I'm going to create one when I start digging through the sand anyway," Mira said. She lowered herself over the edge and gasped when the cold hit her through her suit. "Let's just hope the lights are strong enough to pass through it and make the bacteria iridesce."

She let go and sank straight down into the biofilm. It clung to her boots like cellophane, pulling the entire sheet inward and dragging it down with her until she finally punched through. Tatters clung to her suit and hung in the water around her. She shone her handheld green light past her feet and aligned herself with one of the rock formations peeking through the kelp. Her heels struck the slick surface and nearly slid right off before she managed to brace herself against the glass wall.

Carefully, she crouched and sifted through the vegetation, looking for a flash of emerald among the deep shadows. She turned in a circle, moving slowly so as not to disturb—

A shimmer of iridescence caught her eye.

Mira leaned closer and aimed her beam directly at a tiny protrusion that almost looked like the quill of a feather. She gently brushed away the surrounding silt, which billowed up into her face like smoke.

Long spines stood from the back of the ugly fish, which had extended all of its fins to lodge itself in the sand, but that was all she could clearly discern through the tangle of silk woven around it, like the carcass of an insect in a spider's web. Filamentous strands fanned outward through the silt like roots, mooring it to the surrounding rocks and the bottom of the tank. Its tiny eyes stared up at her from between the narrow gaps in the webbing.

"Can you see this?" she asked.

"It appears as though the biofilm has become attached to the sculpin's scales and begun proliferating," Sammie said.

Mira nodded to herself. A more concise explanation was that the chimeras appeared to be weaving a cocoon around the fish, but she couldn't bring herself to speak the words out loud.

"Can you tell if it's alive?" Sammie asked.

"I think so," Mira said. "It's hard to tell in this dim green glow, though. Try turning on the white lights."

"Give me a second."

Sammie's distorted silhouette passed on the opposite side of the glass. She appeared again near the stairs when the overhead lights snapped on. Mira switched off her green light and watched the bizarre fish practically disappear. It was weird knowing that it was still there but that she was able to see little more than its dark little eyes and slivers of its flank and fins. Its body appeared almost aqueous, as though the rest of it were made of an oily substance with a slightly heavier density. The settling sediment gave form to the strands of silk tethering it in place.

"We need to get a closer look at it," Sammie said, her voice strangely flat.

"Do you need me to move so you can get a better camera angle?"

"No. I need you to extricate it from the sediment."

"You want me to tear it out so you can see it better?"

"I want you to detach it, with as much webbing as possible still attached, and remove it from the tank so that I can study it."

"But that will kill it," Mira said. It took her several seconds to realize what her partner intended to do with it. "You're going to dissect it."

"I'm going to figure out exactly what's happening to it."

"By killing it."

"That's obviously not my primary objective," Sammie said.

"I need to examine how the chimeras interact with living tissue. There's an entire lake filled with marine life forms out there, any number of which could already be experiencing the same reaction. What if the condition turns out to be fatal? What if it infects the whales?"

Sammie was right. They needed a better understanding of what was happening, and there was only one way to do so.

"Grab the bucket," Mira said.

She delicately removed the cocoon from the silt and floated to the surface, where Sammie knelt, tipping the five-gallon container out over the water. Mira handed off the sticky fish and pulled herself up onto the platform. By the time she climbed down, removed her drysuit, and swaddled herself in the blanket she'd brought down from her room, Sammie had already excised a section of the sculpin's dorsal fin and commenced examining it under the microscope. The fish itself lay motionless at the bottom of the bucket, iridescing faintly beneath the glow of the green light Sammie shone onto the slide under the lens.

"The individual chimeras appear to have bonded directly to the scales, kind of like a microscopic exoskeleton," Sammie said. She leaned away from the eyepiece so that Mira could take a peek. "See how coarse it looks, almost like the keeled scales of a venomous snake?"

"Which is physically dissimilar to its normal presentation as a biofilm."

"Exactly."

Mira stepped back from the microscope.

"So what would cause something like that?" she asked.

"I don't know," Sammie said. "An interaction with the epidermal layer of the sculpin's scales? A reaction to the mucus secreted by the goblet cells?"

"Have you examined the scales from elsewhere on the fish's body?"

Sammie finished preparing a second slide and held it up for Mira to see.

"I collected this sample from its flank, just behind its gill." She placed it under the lens and looked through the eyepiece. "The level of colonization is roughly the same, only it almost looks like . . . "

Her words trailed off.

"Almost looks like what?" Mira asked.

"Take a peek and tell me what you see."

Mira glanced curiously at Sammie before taking her place at the microscope. The sample collected from the fish's body was markedly different than that of its fin. It looked like a flattened pinecone, only the individual scales resembled the feet of so many geese. The chimeras stood apart from them, distinct overlapping shield shapes with linear striations, which formed a sludge-like film. A thin layer of webbing anchored it to the scales, raising the edges ever so slightly.

"I'd swear it appears as though . . . " Mira said, struggling to find the right words.

"The biofilm's attempting to peel up the fish's scales so it can get underneath them?"

"Yeah," Mira said. "But that can't be right, can it? It ascribes a measure of sentience we don't traditionally associate with microbial life forms."

"And the archaeon absorbing the bacterium and the diatom to form a single self-sustaining organism capable of producing its own food and energy doesn't?" Sammie reclaimed her seat at the microscope and nibbled on her lower lip while she composed her thoughts. "This arrangement benefits all three species by allowing them to survive under conditions ordinarily fatal to each of them separately. The diatom converts light energy to chemical energy, producing organic carbon as a byproduct. The bacterium consumes that carbon and releases a small amount of carbon dioxide, which the archaeon then reduces to formate and methane, creating the microclimate it needs to thrive, even as the diatom is continually converting that methane back into the oxygen that would otherwise cause it to revert to a state of cryptobiosis. Is it so hard to believe that the sculpin could be incorporated into that mutualistic environment?"

"As a symbiont or a host? The former implies that the fish maintains some measure of autonomy, which hardly appears to be the case"—Mira gestured toward the cocooned sculpin in the bucket—"while the latter suggests a parasitic relationship, and the only constituent of the chimera with even a tangential relationship to a higher order of life capable of parasitism is a bacterium with the DNA of an orb weaver—"

"Hold up," Sammie said, interrupting. She grabbed a pair of forceps and prodded the exposed flesh behind the fish's gills, where she'd excised the scales. She tweezed the tissue away from the underlying swelling until she exposed an engorged vesicle encased within a veiny silver sheath. A gentle tug and a wormlike tube bulged out behind it, bringing with it a fresh dribble of blood. "The ultimobranchial gland is distinctly swollen and it appears to have formed a fistula with the esophagus, connecting the two structures."

"What does that mean?" Mira asked.

"The ultimobranchial gland is a small endocrine body in the pharynx," Sammie said, turning the tray so that she was looking at the sculpin head-on. She parted its lips and thrust the tips of the forceps between them. "It's largely been incorporated into the thyroid gland in mammals, but in fish it remains separate and produces the hormone calcitonin, which reduces the amount of calcium in its blood. In this sculpin, however . . . " With a twist of her wrist, she withdrew the forceps, pulling a mass of sludge with it. She grabbed the goo between her fingers and fanned it out until there was no mistaking what it was. "It produces dragline silk that can be expelled from its mouth via the esophagus."

Mira's jaw fell slack. She could only stare in shock.

A crackle of static from the transceiver tuned to their lab's channel cut her off.

"Mira? Are you there? It's Carrie. Pick up if you're there."

"Carrie?" Mira said, grabbing the two-way from the charger. "Where are you?"

"At the cave, remember?"

Between the archaeal bloom in the lake and the introduction of the fish, Mira had completely forgotten about Carrie's invitation to join her and Leo on their adventure across the ice cap.

"I'm so sorry," she said. "I totally spaced—"

"No worries, Mira. There's just something you need to see."

"What is it?"

"I'm streaming on channel four. You should be able to see it on the internal network."

Mira grabbed her laptop and opened the feed. The image was dark and grainy, the footage repeatedly freezing due to the poor signal quality across the glacier.

"I'm watching it now," she said. The image resolved into a flashlight shining onto a thick layer of ice, casting the faint shadow of something frozen within it onto the underlying stone wall. "What am I looking at?"

And then it clicked.

"Oh, my God," Mira gasped.

26

20,000 Feet Above the Central Greenland Ice Sheet
73.652043, -45.429926

Now

"Tell me you were able to isolate the feed from the security camera in the kitchen," Cameron says, ducking underneath the ladder leading up to the flight deck.

Rush and Ryder wait for him in what the maintenance crew affectionately call the "hell hole," a cramped space filled with avionics equipment that makes such a racket that it sounds like he's crawled into a wind tunnel. Like the others, he's switched off the microphone on his headset to prevent anyone, specifically the NeXgen contingent, from overhearing their conversation.

"Yes, sir," Ryder says, his voice barely audible over the background noise, "but the footage isn't especially helpful."

"Why not?"

Ryder nods to Rush, who hands Cameron his tablet. He'd

dispatched his two top men to find out how the dead man on the floor in the video had come to be in such a state, sending them one at a time so as not to arouse suspicion from anyone covertly surveilling them. In the meantime, he'd discreetly apprised Speedy, Bashir, and Ronny of the situation, or at least as much of it as he could.

"Because there's nothing to see," Rush says, starting the playback.

Several seconds pass, during which the kitchen stands empty. There's shattered glass on the floor and overturned chafing dishes on the serving bar. The red glare of the emergency lighting casts shadows so deep they're impregnable to the camera. A dark form streaks down from the top of the image and lands behind the eating bar. The dead man's eyes stare blankly at the camera from a face glistening with blood. He makes no effort to rise.

"Where the hell did he come from?" Cameron asks.

Rush opens his mouth to speak but instead closes it without a word and retrieves bookmarked footage. A tap of the screen and it starts to play. The timestamp in the bottom corner marks the video as three and a half hours earlier. There's still glass on the floor, but the chafing dishes sit upright on the island. Sheets of snow gust in front of the camera and faint shadows move in the red light, although their source isn't readily identifiable.

A door in the back right corner opens inward and a man stumbles out. Cameron catches a glimpse of long hair and a stringy beard as the man trips and goes down hard. He lunges to his feet and abruptly jerks upright. Grabs his throat and opens his mouth to scream as he rises into the air, kicking and flailing, toppling the serving dishes and scattering their contents onto the countertop. He reaches for anything to slow his ascent as he disappears from the top of the screen, beyond the camera's range.

Cameron stares at the tablet, struggling to formulate his thoughts.

"Now show him what you showed me," Ryder says, his expression uninterpretable.

Rush rewinds the footage to the point where the man has just pushed himself up from the floor and zooms in on the air above him. There's a strange distortion, a ghostly displacement of pixels, as though some sort of vapor flows over the top of the doorway and billows upward toward the ceiling.

"Look at the cupboards above the counter behind him," Rush says.

A faint shadow, barely discernible in the wan light, passes straight down the cabinet behind the blurring. It bleeds into the man's shadow as he's ripped from his feet and lifted into the air.

"What in God's name was that?" Cameron whispers.

"We were hoping you'd be able to tell us," Ryder says.

Cameron recalls the video that Colonel Patrick had shown him, but he's unable to give voice to his suspicions, or perhaps he fears what will come out if he tries.

"We went back through the footage until we found this," Rush says, opening a new bookmark.

Everything in the kitchen appears to have reverted to normal. The overhead lights die, and the screen goes momentarily dark. The red emergency lights bloom and a figure streaks past the camera, passing from one side of the image to the other. Shattered glass cascades over the tabletops and washes across the floor. The tables topple and the chairs tumble away from them. A distortion appears at the bottom of the screen and one of the tables breaks in half. A blur and it's gone.

Rush pauses the recording and turns on Cameron.

"What aren't you telling us, sergeant?"

Cameron shakes his head. He's just about to order his men

to continue evaluating the archived security footage from NeXgen's database when a new video box opens on the tablet. A man with white hair and an aquiline nose stares back at them through tinted glasses, a self-impressed smirk on his face. Dr. Trey Waller. The former DARPA scientist cocks his head and speaks in a voice even sharper than his features.

"Senior Staff Sergeant Cameron," he says. "Perhaps the two of us should have a little chat."

"Agreed," Cameron says. "It's about time my team and I got some answers."

Waller vanishes with a nod.

Cameron passes the tablet back to Rush.

"They terminated my connection to the NeXgen mainframe," the tech sergeant says. "I've only managed to download maybe three hours of footage."

"Do you think you can clean up that imagery so we can get a better look at what we're dealing with?"

"Yes, sir."

"Then get on it," Cameron says, turning to Ryder. "Keep going through those security recordings and find me something we can use. Do you get my meaning?"

Ryder nods his understanding. Waller had just defined the terms of their relationship. He'd staked his claim to the high ground, which meant that Cameron and his men needed to find leverage they could use to level the playing field. They weren't about to walk into a potentially hostile situation without getting the answers they needed first.

Cameron ducks out of the hell hole, rises to his full height, and cracks his neck, first one way and then the other. Speedy and Bashir glance up at him as he strides past their seats. Ronny lounges with his feet up and his eyes closed, but his posture suggests that the three civilians emerging from the SUSV haven't escaped his attention. They clear a path for Cameron to climb into the vehicle with Waller and close the door behind him. He takes a seat across from the man who believes himself to be in charge and looks him squarely in the eyes.

"I have to admit I'm impressed that your man was able to hack into our system," Waller says, "but our cybersecurity team is the best that money can buy."

"As I'm sure are you, judging by the fortune you've squirreled away in offshore accounts," Cameron says.

Waller smiles in amusement.

"Despite what you think, we're all on the same side here."

"And which side is that?"

"The side that wants to see the staff of Academy Station returned safely to their families."

"Those who are still alive anyway," Cameron says. He's dealt with men like Waller before, men with all sorts of fancy degrees who think they're so much cleverer than everyone around them. Their vanity always proves to be their Achilles' heel. "I know I'm not nearly as smart or as well educated as you are, but—"

"Let's not waste what little time remains playing games," Waller says. "I know which daily logs you've viewed, and I've seen the security footage your tech sergeant downloaded. I think you have a pretty good idea what our scientists discovered at that station."

"A biofilm that appears to produce a cloaking effect."

"Excellent," Waller says, stroking his chin. Cameron wishes he could see the man's eyes so he could better read his intentions. "I had requested that your colonel dispatch his top men; I'm pleased he didn't disappoint."

"Appealing to my ego will get you nowhere."

"Nor will playing upon my vanity."

"Then what do you say we cut to the chase," Cameron says. "Tell me what the hell my men and I are walking into, or you'll be going in there alone."

Waller smiles and opens the laptop resting on the seat beside him. He turns the screen so that Cameron can see the video log. Dr. Rantanen wears a pair of rubber gloves and holds a scalpel in one hand and a pair of forceps in the other. A green lighting fixture illuminates the cocoon-like mass of biological matter on the dissecting tray in front of her. It takes several seconds for Cameron to realize that it's a fish, which, judging by the T-shaped pins affixing its fins to the tray, is no longer among the living.

"We're now at approximately thirty hours post-introduction of the sculpin," she says. "As you can clearly see, the production of dragline silk has run rampant, encasing the entire fish within an asymmetrical, chrysalis-like construct."

Dr. Rantanen cuts a straight line with the scalpel down the fish's head, from the base of its dorsal spines to its bulbous lips. She pinches a gob of webbing with the forceps and peels the layer of scales covering half of its face outward, past its cloudy eye. A skein of blood rises from the pinkish tissue. She sets down the scalpel and uses an eyedropper to irrigate the wound. The blood clears and reveals tiny hairlike filaments connecting the scales to the flesh. She pulls on the scales and the filaments stretch until they snap.

Cameron glances at Waller from the corner of his eye and finds the other man watching him, gauging his reaction. He concentrates on maintaining a neutral expression so as not to betray the fact that he recognizes that the spider silk has worked its way through the scales and knitted itself into the underlying tissue.

"While I have yet to establish whether this physical intrusion is structural or functional," Dr. Rantanen continues, "I have no doubt that the relationship between the chimeras and the sculpin is not mutualistic as we'd hoped, but rather parasitic in nature, although I have yet to establish what the chimera gains from this interaction as it's already self-sustaining. Perhaps it merely adheres to the fish and uses it as a means of locomotion, much like an anemone that grows on a snail's shell or a barnacle that clings to a whale, or maybe . . . "

Her words trail off and she leans back in her seat, her brows lowered in concentration. She grabs her parka from where it hangs on the back of her chair, bunches it in her lap, and looks around her desk until her eyes settle on something off-screen. With a faint smile, she grabs a thin Plexiglas stirring rod and stares down at it for several seconds, momentarily lost in thought.

"Surely you've seen how a spider web billows toward you when you get too close," she says, looking up into the camera once more. "That's because the glue-like substance coating the silk has electrostatic properties that cause it to reach out and grab charged particles or objects, like pollen and flying insects. It also functions like a water magnet, sucking in humidity and converting it into tiny droplets that increase the electrical conductivity of the silk."

Dr. Rantanen bunches up the hood of her parka and rubs the stirring rod back and forth through the fur lining, building up a static charge. She aligns it with the filaments passing through the intact scales on the opposite side of the fish's skull and carefully touches them—

The fish flops on the tray, tearing its fins free from the pins holding them in place.

Cameron looks at Waller and then back at the monitor, his mind reeling with the implications.

27

One Week Ago

Mira stood as close to the edge of the glacier as she dared. From this vantage point, she looked directly down upon a sloping boulder field that vanished into the shallows of the artificial lake. Runoff flowed between the massive stones, eroding the earth and causing the water level to continuously rise and creep up the face of the dam, little more than a gray crescent against the black ribbon of the distant fjord. The sun barely breached the horizon, its diminishing rays reflecting from the silver saucer of Academy Station and glimmering from the choppy waves. The bloodred stain of the archaeal bloom had nearly dissipated, leaving faint pink shapes in the lees of the islands, where the biofilm was undergoing its chimeric transformation before her very eyes.

Her hands trembled as she turned away from the lake and headed back toward the snowmobiles.

"We need to get moving," Leo said. The exposed skin around his goggles was already windburned. Ice clung to his balaclava where his breath passed through the neoprene. "The sun might have just risen, but we only have an hour and a half before it sets again. And, believe me, once it does, the temperature will start falling in a hurry."

Mira nodded her understanding. She probably shouldn't have asked to stop, but she'd needed to see the lake from this perspective to truly understand the consequences her actions had wrought. No seabirds swooped low across the ice or bedded down on the shore. Not a single fish rippled the surface. Only the tracks of a lone polar bear wended downhill into the water, the massive pawprints preserved in the frozen mud. It was almost as though the animals could all sense what had happened and wanted nothing to do with whatever biological processes were transpiring in the depths.

She climbed onto the slick black Arctic Cat Bearcat and started the engine. While she'd never actually driven one before, the controls weren't all that much different than the dirt bikes she'd ridden as a teenager, and she picked them up quickly. Carrie and Leo often pulled away from her, trailing rooster tails that merged with the blowing snow. She kept their bright orange parkas in sight, or at least as well as she could. The occasional gale kicked up with such ferocity that they disappeared when they were barely ten feet away, forcing her to throttle down so she wouldn't slam into them from behind while going twenty miles an hour across a sheet of glazed ice.

It would have been exceedingly easy to lose her bearings out here. There were no mountains or trees or landmarks of any kind, only snow as far as the eye could see. She tried not to imagine the horror of being lost out here a week from now, when the sun no longer rose and temperatures rarely climbed out of the negatives. If she somehow managed to get turned around, she could very well freeze to death before she found her way back to the station, mere miles away.

Instead, she focused on the memory of the live feed that Carrie had broadcast from inside the cave. Mira had so many questions for which there were simply no answers, chief among them what in the name of God was frozen in the ice and why had she only been able to see its shadow? She had a pretty good idea what caused the latter, but the answer to the former terrified her. A part of her wished Sammie could have torn herself away from her microscope, if only long enough to come with them. At the same time, however, she knew that her partner's time was better spent in the pursuit of answers, especially if this little expedition revealed what she expected.

The intonation of Leo's snowmobile changed as he slowed, materializing from his own wake and driving into the shadow of a rocky crest, on top of which a tattered red flag snapped on the wind. Attached to its base was the geolocation beacon that Moore and his team had used to mark the spot where they'd remotely sensed the subterranean void.

Carrie pulled into the windbreak, turned off her Arctic Cat, and removed her helmet.

"We have to go on foot from here," she shouted.

Mira silenced her engine. The wind screamed in its stead, blowing a fin of snow into the air from the edge of a cliff maybe fifty feet ahead of them.

"We cut a path down through the ravine," Leo said. "It's steep and slick in places. Just take it slow and you'll be fine."

"You make it sound so easy," Mira said, following him toward what looked like the edge of the world, beyond which she could see only storm clouds, darkening as the premature dusk crept inland from the east.

The path zig-zagged between ice formations that Mira didn't realize were actually made of stone until she descended from the wind and snow onto the bare granite and hardpacked dirt. Loose talus, slicker even than the ice, slid out from beneath her with every step, clattering down the steep hillside and plummeting to the bottom of the ravine. The stream at the bottom flowed beneath the ice, its crystalline waters appearing every so often as they wended across nearly a hundred miles of rugged terrain toward Danmark Fjord, on the far side of which stood Station Nord, a Danish defense command post staffed by a handful of non-commissioned officers and a few seasonal researchers.

Mira followed Carrie and Leo from the makeshift trail onto a narrow ledge, where they were forced to scoot sideways. The mouth of the cave yawned before them, maybe five feet wide and two feet tall, like a crooked smile slashing the face of a frozen waterfall. Leo lowered himself to his chest and slithered into the darkness. His flashlight blossomed a heartbeat later, limning the interior with an ethereal blue glow.

Mira waited for Carrie to squirm through the orifice before squeezing in behind her. The pressure on her back and chest made her feel like she was suffocating. On the verge of panic, she dragged herself through to the other side and stood up the moment she was finally able to do so. She removed the trio of mini LED flashlights she'd brought with her from her parka, read the labels, and stuffed the green and black lights back into the inner pocket. A flick of a switch and she shone the white light upon walls made entirely of ice, which had grown so thick that it looked like blue glass with wavy striations corresponding to the different eons that had come and gone since the Earth was new.

"Back here," Leo said. His voice sounded like it simultaneously originated from far away and all around her at once. "You should really check it out before I start drilling."

Mira followed the sound of his voice deeper into the cave, alternately shining her light onto the rocky ground to keep from rolling an ankle and exploring the amazing world around her. The differences in the thickness and appearance of the ice as she advanced into the darkness were staggering. At first, the walls and the ceiling looked like they were made of chipped glass, and then waves somehow suspended all around her. Finally, they took on a warped texture as soft and smooth as limestone. She ran her palms along the ice as she walked, the cold passing straight through her gloves as though she weren't wearing them at all. The rock underneath was still visible, like the bed of a clear creek, only distorted to such an extent that it was impossible to tell how many feet of ice had frozen over it.

She found Leo around a blind corner that reminded her of a turn in a funhouse maze. His light and the orange of his coat reflected from seemingly everywhere around her at once as he knelt over his handheld drill. The coring auger was only three inches wide and three feet long, but it was portable and would serve his purposes until he determined if it was worth the effort to haul the larger electromechanical drill from the station.

"Where is . . . ?" Mira started to ask, but the moment her light struck the wall to her right, the answer became clear.

The beam illuminated a hazy shape that looked almost like a collection of fluid trapped within the ice, which cast a curiously deep shadow onto the bedrock behind it. This was what she'd seen on the video. This inexplicable shadow was the reason she'd braved the storm and the falling temperatures and traveled all the way across the glacier with little more than a trio of flashlights stuffed into the inner pockets of her parka.

"Would you guys mind shutting off your lights for a second?" she asked, exchanging her ordinary flashlight for the green one.

Mira hit the switch and pressed the lens right up against the ice. She couldn't even tell if the 540-nanometer wavelength was strong enough to penetrate more than a few inches until the others turned off their white lights. The shape took form, seemingly out of nowhere, along with a dozen others she hadn't seen until that very moment, scattered throughout the ice all around her, glimmering iridescent creatures unlike any she'd ever seen before. They resembled trilobites. Only rather than ridged carapaces reminiscent of horseshoe crabs, they had eleven broad, leglike protrusions extending from either side of their slender bodies and long stingers jutting from their rear ends.

"What in the world are those things?" Carrie asked.

"I have no idea," Mira said. "Can one of you take some pictures for me?"

Mira waited until she no longer heard the clicking of Leo's camera before trading her green light for the black, which caused all of the tiny bacteria covering the creatures to glow faintly purple, like magic dust coalescing into vague constellations.

She could only stare at these prehistoric creatures, which must have been hundreds of millions—if not billions—of years old to have existed at the same time as the Ymirarchaea. It felt as though a weight had been lifted from her shoulders. Granted, nothing remotely resembling this species currently existed, but the mere fact that it had interacted with the naturally occurring form of the chimera without utterly derailing the course of global events meant that the accidental release of their own genetically engineered version might not destroy the local environment after all.

Of course, she couldn't account for the spiridion genes that had been inserted into the bacterium's genome, but how much harm could the addition of spider DNA to a microscopic communal organism really do?

28

Mira had been so excited to share the news of her discovery that she'd tried hailing Sammie on the transceiver at least ten times, but her partner hadn't answered. She'd assumed that Sammie's exhaustion had finally caught up with her and the microbiologist had passed out in her bed. Instead, she found Sammie sitting on the floor of the lab, staring into the aquarium, looking significantly more worn down than she had mere hours ago. Her eyes were dark and recessed, her face a pasty shade of white. She appeared haunted, as though something was consuming her from the inside out.

"Let's get you up," Mira said, taking Sammie by the hands and pulling her to her feet.

Sammie blinked several times, as though seeing her for the first time. The microbiologist's eyes were so bloodshot that her irises looked like sapphires sinking into pools of lava and her lips had taken on a bluish cast. She was in desperate need of a shower, but at least she was still eating, if the small of hard-boiled eggs on her breath were any indication.

"There's something I need to show you," Sammie said.

"I have something to show you too, but it can wait until you're able to catch up on a little sleep," Mira said. "Why don't I help you to your room—"

"They eclosed."

"What are you talking about?"

"The sculpins," Sammie said. "They emerged from their chrysalises while you were gone."

Mira glanced at the aquarium. The white lights were on, rendering the biofilm invisible. There was no movement inside the tank, save for the wavering of the kelp on the artificial current, the crabs scuttling across the sediment, and the tube-worms opening their feathery mouths—

Her breath caught in her chest when she saw a pair of tiny black eyes staring back at her from an ugly little face resembling that of a horned frog. She'd seen eyes just like them looking up at her from between the gaps in the webbing cocooning the specimen she'd exhumed from the substrate.

"Don't make any sudden moves," Sammie said.

Mira leaned closer to get a better look. The fish vanished into a cloud of disturbed sediment. She crouched and peered through the vegetation, searching for where it had gone. It wasn't until the silt settled upon its nearly invisible form that she realized it hadn't moved more than a few inches. It had simply vanished in plain sight. Its spiny dorsal fins formed a mohawk down its back, its pectoral fins expanding to frame its face like the frill of a *dilophosaurus*, its mouth gulping dramatically.

"It can control the cloaking effect," Mira whispered.

"Which implies a relationship between the chimeras and the sculpin beyond simple parasitism," Sammie said. At the sound of her voice, the fish hopped behind a rock. "Remember what happened when I applied static electricity to the dragline silk that had passed through the fish's scales and perforated its flesh? It's as though those filaments have tapped into the fish's central nervous system and the chimeras have become an extension of it, a living skin connected to the neural network by strands of silk capable of transmitting faint electrical currents."

"You think the chimeras used their webbing to hijack the fish's brain?"

"Like a hacker into a mainframe." Sammie sat on the edge of her desk and finished off the last of the coffee from her thermos. "On its most basic level, thought is nothing more than a series of electrochemical impulses passed along chains of sensory and motor neurons that cause the body to detect sensations, interpret their meaning, and act upon them. Surely a similarly conductive material could substitute for those neural pathways if it could transmit the same impulses. The animal kingdom is full of examples. There's a species of fungus—*Ophiocordyceps unilateralis*—that infects ants and uses chemical signals to control their brains, forcing them to climb to a suitable height from which to disperse its spores. Another kind of fungus—*Massospora cicadina*—infects cicadas and produces a psychoactive compound that triggers their mating instincts, causing them to spread the spores throughout the swarm. A species of parasitic wasp known as *Hymenoepimecis argyraphaga* stings other insects, lays its eggs inside them, and then stabs their brains with its stinger, using it as a joystick to control their movements."

"This isn't necessarily a catastrophic development," Mira said. "A primitive version of our chimera existed millions of years ago. I've seen proof with my own eyes."

"But the bacterium we incorporated into ours contains the genes of an arachnid, a class of life that has never existed in a marine environment."

Mira fell silent. She'd so desperately wanted to believe that the frozen creatures she'd found in the cave proved that they had no reason to worry.

"On the positive side," Sammie said, "the engineered

bacterium allows the chimeras to do things we would never have dreamed possible."

"Like what?" Mira asked.

"Think about it. That sculpin is essentially covered with biofilm and yet we can still see it, which implies that not only can the cloaking effect be turned on . . . it can be turned off."

Mira looked into the tank, searching for the fish she knew had to be in there somewhere, while she struggled to wrap her mind around the implications.

"Mind turning on the green lights?" Sammie said.

She waited until Mira had done as she'd asked before killing the overhead lights.

The biofilm appeared inside the aquarium, now nearly three inches thick and surrounded by webbing that ascended the glass like vines. Ghostly strands connected it to the surface of the water, where they adhered to the aquarium's rim. Impossibly thin filaments also traveled in the opposite direction, clinging to the rocks and the tips of the kelp. Broken lengths of dragline silk and tattered clumps of shredded cocoon floated on the current. One of the sculpins appeared as if from nowhere, its spiked form shimmering with iridescence as it clung, upside down, to the biofilm. It scrabbled across it, using its fins like hands and the spines jutting from them like fingers.

"Now watch this," Sammie said. She climbed the ladder to the top of the tank and crouched on the platform beside a five-gallon bucket. "In the wild, a sculpin's diet consists primarily of crabs, mollusks, and the occasional minnow. Basically, anything small enough to fit in its mouth."

She thrust a net into the bucket, swished it around, and held up what appeared to be a juvenile cod, larger than any of the individual sculpins. Its tail slapped at the mesh as it tried to escape.

"Where'd you get those?" Mira asked.

"Swearengin managed to catch a few for us, although I'm not sure what it'll end up costing us yet."

"Perfect."

Sammie smirked and, for the briefest of moments, looked like her old self. She leaned over the tank and inverted the net. As soon as the cod hit the water, it streaked straight down, passing through the biofilm—

The sculpin struck at it the moment it was within range, impaling it with its spines and driving it toward the bottom, where the other sculpins appeared as if from nowhere. The cod struggled valiantly, but it was no match for the ferocity of the benthic fish and the toxins they pumped into its body, its movements growing increasingly sluggish until its tail merely flicked at the kelp tangled around it. The sculpins attacked it with open mouths, latching down upon it and jerking at its flesh, like so many hyenas with the remains of a gazelle. When they were done, the desiccated carcass floated away, mealy white flesh disgorging from the ragged wounds.

The entire process had taken less than thirty seconds.

Mira couldn't seem to form a single coherent thought as she watched the dead cod drift on the current, which carried it upward toward the biofilm. It finally came to rest near a bulge in the webbing, which contained the body of another cod, presumably the specimen Sammie had used as her first test subject.

Sammie again turned on the light, and the entire scene vanished, transforming into an amorphous liquid mirage that blended into the surrounding seawater.

Mira thought about the extinct creatures she'd seen in the ice cave, their bodies concealed by the chimeric organisms. Either every single one of them had frozen while the chimeras were demonstrating their ability to refract light, or the ancient microorganisms hadn't been able to control the expression of their lenticular properties. If that were the case, then the life forms she and Sammie had inadvertently created were nothing like their extinct ancestors.

Their chimeras had subsumed the bodies of the sculpins and established a relationship that went beyond mere parasitism.

They were using the cloaking effect as a defensive mechanism.

The implications struck Mira all at once.

"The chimeras have evolved sentience."

29

"They're called *Kerygmachela kierkegaardi*," Amy said. Mira had forwarded the photos she'd taken inside the cave to the chief scientific officer in hopes that she'd be able to help identify the creatures.

"So you've seen them before?" Mira said.

"Of course." Amy swiveled around in her chair and gestured to her computer monitor with a flourish. On the screen was a detailed image of a stone slab, at the center of which were the petrified remains of a creature resembling those they'd discovered frozen in the ice. "One of our former researchers chiseled this fossil from the talus downhill from where the boathouse now stands, back before we erected the dam. It might look like a trilobite crossed with a scorpion, but it turns out that it's actually an ancestor of modern arthropods like lobsters, butterflies, and spiders, if you can believe that. Carbon dating revealed this one to be somewhere in the neighborhood of five hundred and fifty million years old, more than three hundred million years older than the dinosaurs."

"And around the same time that levels of atmospheric

oxygen rose high enough to sustain cellular respiration, leading to the Cambrian explosion and—"

"All forms of terrestrial life," Amy finished for her. "Without the photosynthetic powers of the phytoplankton in the very waters below us, life as we know it wouldn't exist today, but I don't suppose I need to tell you that. It's the whole reason you're here, isn't it? To essentially trigger the same reaction that caused nightmarish creepy-crawlies like these to evolve in the first place?"

Amy rocked back and laughed. Her humor died when she realized that Mira wasn't laughing along with her.

"Why the Gloomy Gus routine?" she asked.

"I'm worried about Sammie," Mira said. She wasn't sure how much she should share with the woman who wielded the power to cancel their grants and send them home, but the bottom line was that her partner was burning the candle at both ends, and it was only a matter of time before she flamed out.

"Anxiety, irritability, depression, difficulty sleeping, changes in grooming habits?" Amy asked.

"Yes." Mira pulled up a chair and took a seat beside the chief scientific officer at her computer. "All of the above."

Amy smiled patiently and took Mira's hands in her own.

"We see that a lot here, especially during a new resident's first few months. They're all classic symptoms of cabin fever, which isn't technically a formal psychological diagnosis, but it's real enough up here. People don't realize how reliant they've become on their daily routines until they're taken away. We're social animals. We thrive on sunlight and human interaction, on being able to do whatever we want, whenever we want to do it. With the UV-B bulbs, timed lighting, and automatically tinted windows, we've done our very best to replicate the circadian rhythms of life back in the States, but it's simply not the same thing."

"So what am I supposed to do to help her?"

"Just keep an eye on her. If her condition worsens and you start to genuinely fear for her health or—God forbid—her life, then you need to drag Dr. Porter away from his work to examine her. Otherwise, it's only a matter of time before her body succumbs to exhaustion and she crashes hard for a few days. I can't count how many researchers have practically gone into hibernation on my watch. Once she stops fighting it and allows herself to rest, she'll be up and about and as good as new."

Mira nodded and offered the best smile she could muster. She'd never been a big fan of letting events run their course. Still, it was comforting to know that Amy had encountered this kind of apparent physical deterioration plenty of times before and didn't seem at all worried.

"You're a good friend for looking out for Sammie," Amy said. "She's lucky to have you. Just be careful not to internalize her problems, or you'll find yourself suffering right along with her. It wouldn't be the first time I've seen that, either. The most important thing to do here—especially right now, as the days are getting shorter and shorter and you're staring down the barrel of three months of night—is to take care of yourself. Make sure you're eating well and taking your vitamins. Do your best to exercise every day, even if it's just climbing those infernal stairs. And—for the love of God, child—stop trading away all of that chocolate you brought with you and indulge yourself a little bit every now and then."

She winked at Mira, who had to admit that she did feel better. As usual, she was probably just overreacting.

Amy sat up straight and clapped, startling Mira.

"You know what always brightens my day?" she asked. "A couple of roly-poly polar bear cubs. What do you say we take a peek at the satellite and see what kind of trouble Shila and Suka are getting themselves into this morning?"

"I'd love to," Mira said. "I could use a little cuteness in my life right about now."

Amy swiveled back to her computer and awakened the sleeping monitor on the right. A few clicks of the mouse and she brought up an image of the northeastern coastline, from Academy Glacier through the finger-like fjords projecting into the Arctic Ocean. Dozens of colored dots stood out from the seamless white expanse. Each represented an individual polar bear from the population roaming this region. They spread farther apart as Amy zoomed in until there were only six of them within the frame, which covered an area encompassing the station, the lake, and several miles of inland terrain.

It struck Mira that she'd likely driven right past these polar bears on her snowmobile without having the slightest idea that they were lurking in the storm. For as cute as the cubs were, the adults were undoubtedly equally ferocious, especially when startled.

Amy adjusted the view until it was centered over three tracking beacons in various shades of red, with a fourth blue dot in the upper left corner. She clicked the mouse several times and the glacier came into sharp focus. The mother polar bear, Miska, stood apart from the blowing snow thanks to a yellowish streak along her back. It took several seconds for Mira to find the cubs. Shila and Suka wrestled downhill, nearly indistinguishable from the accumulation, especially in the civil twilight before dawn.

"They're just too adorable," Mira said.

"Enjoy it while it lasts," Amy said, although Mira suspected the older woman was talking to herself. "It's only a matter of time before they strike off on their own. Maybe I'll be fortunate enough to still be here when they have cubs of their own."

One of the balls of fluff clobbered the other, burying it under the snow, and then ran to her mother's side before her sibling could retaliate. It was a universal behavior that Mira

had experienced with her own brother, seemingly a lifetime
ago.

"I don't see anything where the blue dot was," she said.

"That's Chinook," Amy said. She adjusted the centering and
leaned closer to get a better look. Sheets of snow gusted across
the ice, alternatingly concealing and revealing broad swaths of
the underlying hillside, which ascended to a glacial steppe
hidden beneath the storm. "Miska's den is somewhere through
there. I wonder if he crawled inside, although none of the other
adults has ever done that before . . . "

She bit her lip as she backed out of the satellite feed and
scrolled through the list of available live cameras until she
found the one she wanted. Mira recognized the interior view of
the den as soon as it opened.

"There you are, you sneaky bugger," Amy said. She turned
the camera ever so slightly until the massive ursine mound was
right in the middle. Chinook's fur had a subtle golden
coloration and appeared clumped, as though he'd recently
emerged from the water. He'd buried his muzzle under his
enormous, upturned paw, which was easily the size of a dinner
plate. A crust had formed in the lashes of his closed eyes.
Brown fluid leaked from the corners. His nose ran and his
mouth frothed.

"He doesn't look so good," Mira said.

Amy looked blankly at the screen, her face etched with fear.

"No, he doesn't, does he?"

She abruptly stood, grabbed a medical kit from the cabinet,
and headed for the door.

"Where are you going?" Mira asked.

"Where do you think?"

And without another word, Amy was gone, her footsteps
trailing her down the corridor toward the staircase.

Mira stared at the giant paw of the polar bear on the monitor. It was just about the same size as the tracks she'd seen heading down to the lake.

30

The cafeteria was busier than usual when Mira arrived. Swearengin was conspicuously absent; however, he'd left several sleeves of crackers alongside heated drums of chili and containers of shredded cheddar cheese that hadn't quite thawed. She filled bowls for Sammie and herself and was just about to head down to her lab when she saw an empty chair between Carrie and Leo at one of the tables, where they huddled around a laptop with Moore. They were so wrapped up in whatever they were doing that they didn't even notice when she joined them.

"It's impossible to tell," Leo said. "Based on the relatively shallow depth of the ice, I'm confident that the cavern was filled with water for the majority of its existence, which makes accurately dating any core sample a whole lot trickier than one taken from, say . . . the top of the glacier, where ice accumulates at a fairly steady, if not entirely predictable, rate."

"That layer right there," Moore said, tapping the screen. "That's tephra. No doubt about it."

"What's tephra?" Mira asked.

"Tiny shards of a glass-like material that accumulate in the wake of volcanic activity. Finding tephra inside of our cave means that at some point, it was open to the air during an eruption. I'm just trying to figure out when that was, and I can't just assume that it was at the same time that those . . . whatever the hell they are—"

"*Kerygmachela kierkegaardi*."

"They named an extinct sea creature after the Father of Existentialism?" Leo said.

"What they're called isn't important," Moore said. The volcanologist slapped his palm on the table for emphasis. "What matters is that we can't simply assume that the foundation ice corresponds to the same timeframe that the bloody monsters were frozen."

"We ran a sample of the tephra through the GC-mass spec," Carrie said. "It showed elevated levels of sulfates—"

"Which could have been caused by any volcanic eruption throughout the planet's history."

"But it also revealed extraordinarily high concentrations of methane."

"Now we're getting somewhere."

"The last time atmospheric concentrations were that high was roughly five hundred and fifty million years ago," Carrie said.

"Amy told me that the researcher who first discovered the *kierkegaardi* fossils dated them to that same time period," Mira said.

"And voilà," Leo said, leaning back in his chair and lacing his fingers behind his head. "There you have it . . . confirmation of our dating of the ice core."

"But there's a flaw in that logic," Moore said. "You're still working under the assumption that there couldn't have been more than one atmospheric shift—"

"And you keep insisting that everything we say is wrong."

A hand settled on Mira's shoulder. She felt the warmth of breath on her ear.

"We need to talk," a woman's voice whispered.

Mira glanced back and found herself staring into Jen's eyes. Aaron hovered over her shoulder, an indecipherable expression on his face.

"Sure," Mira said. She excused herself and rose from the table. "Is everything all right?"

"Can we go someplace more private?" Aaron asked.

"I need to run this food down to Sammie. Will our lab work okay?"

Aaron glanced at Jen, who nodded her consent. Neither spoke as they followed Mira down the stairs, around the arched corridor, and into her lab. Sammie sat at her desk in the purple glow of a single black light bulb, her teeth and lab coat glowing bright white.

"This'll just take a minute," Aaron said. "And then we'll be on our way."

Sammie looked up at him and repeatedly blinked, as though awakening from a deep sleep.

"Sorry," she said. "I didn't hear you come in. What's going on?"

Mira hit the overhead lights and set the bowl of chili in front of her partner, who eyed it for several seconds before trying a tiny spoonful.

"Here's the deal," Jen said, pacing back and forth in front of the aquarium. "That biofilm of yours has to go."

"What do you mean?" Mira asked.

"What my less-than-tactful associate means to say is that none of our whales will go anywhere near it," Aaron said. "You have to remember that they're mammals and need to breathe air to survive, but they're only breaching the surface in specific areas where the currents are the strongest. And, even then, only when absolutely necessary."

"They don't want anything to do with that slime of yours," Jen said.

"It's not like they can see it," Sammie said.

"We're still trying to figure out how they even know it's there," Jen said. "I'd love to be able to study the interaction up close, but they haven't let me within fifty feet of them in days. So, I repeat, you need to get your film out of our lake."

"And how do you propose we do that?"

"I don't give a rat's ass how you do it, as long as it gets done."

Aaron took Jen by the hand and communicated something to her with his eyes. She sighed in frustration, but she ultimately assented with a nod and handed him her cell phone.

"Let me show you something," he said, opening the video player on Jen's phone and setting it on the table. The paused image was dark and grainy. He pressed play, and Mira recognized the dam below the waterline. Aaron stood silhouetted in the viewport. He waved as the camera sunk past him and toward the bottom of the lake, following the concrete barrier. "Jen recorded this maybe an hour ago."

"I don't understand what we're supposed to be looking at," Mira said.

"You will," Jen said.

On the small screen, Jen turned away from the dam and her diving light diffused into the depths. Dark shapes moved in the distance, whales passing through clouds of silt mere feet above the ground. The view tipped straight down and filmed the seafloor rising to meet Jen's boots. Clumps of brown macroalgae grew from the exposed surfaces of buried rocks. A field of kelp lay wilted and flattened at the side of the screen. Jen headed toward it, puffs of silt billowing every time she stepped on the soft earth, which transitioned to a gravel of seashells, dead starfish, and broken bits of coral. She crouched and exhumed a handful in her open palm.

"They're all dead," Jen said. "Every mollusk and echino-
derm. The lakebed is littered with their remains."

"And you think our biofilm's to blame?" Sammie said.

"We tested the water quality," Aaron said. "We're talking
about levels of nitrates and dissolved methane more than ten
times their baseline levels. Something in that lake is killing
them, and the more that die, the worse those levels get."

Mira was afraid to ask the obvious question, but it burst
from her lips before she could stop it.

"What about the whales?"

"Keep watching," Jen said.

On the cell phone, the marine biologist strode away from
the dam and toward the massive shapes moving through the
silt, which grew thicker by the second. A narwhal appeared
from nowhere, swimming straight at Jen. She sidestepped it,
but not quickly enough. It slammed into her shoulder and
spun her sideways. She stumbled and went down, the seafloor
rising as though in slow motion and exploding into a brown
cloud when she hit. The narwhal materialized from the haze,
its tusk aimed right at the camera. Jen ducked at the last
possible second, stirring up the sediment even more.

Visibility constricted to mere feet as the cloud closed
around Jen, sealing her in near darkness. She crawled forward,
the camera affixed to her helmet sweeping from side to side.
There was no sign of the narwhal that had nearly impaled her,
no indication as to where—

Movement. Ahead and to her right. Low to the ground.

The narwhal lay in a depression of its own making,
thrashing as though in an attempt to free itself from an invisible fishing net. She cautiously reached for it, but it panicked,
slapping its tailfin and further clouding the water.

Mira caught a glimpse of the whale's milky eye and the gray
tatters of skin that had once been its eyelids, the weeping
lesions on its flank and the blood diffusing from its injured fins,

and then it was gone. There was nothing she could say, no words to express how sorry she was, but could her biofilm really have been responsible for that kind of physical deterioration?

"We came to you first as a professional courtesy," Aaron said. "We need you to come up with a plan for how to remove the biofilm, or we'll be forced to talk to Amy."

"And if any of my whales die, there'll be hell to pay," Jen said.

She grabbed her phone and stormed out of the room.

"We both know this isn't your fault," Aaron said. "But we need you to fix it."

He nodded in parting and followed his partner into the corridor, their footsteps fading into the distance.

"What are we supposed to do?" Mira asked. She dragged her chair over beside Sammie's and slumped into it. "We're dealing with microscopic organisms that can pass through a selectively permeable forward osmosis membrane. There's no way we can collect more than the tiniest fraction of them."

"Then I guess we'll just have to kill them," Sammie said. The way she said it made the hairs stand on the back of Mira's neck.

"And just how do you propose we do that without killing everything else in the lake?"

"Hit the overhead lights, would you?"

Mira was beginning to feel as though she spent the majority of her waking hours flipping switches, but she did as her partner asked and returned to find Sammie aligning a petri dish filled with a thin layer of fluid under her microscope. She shone a handheld green light onto it.

"Look through there and tell me what you see," Sammie said.

Mira peered through the eyepiece and saw a sight she would have recognized anywhere.

"Our biofilm," she said.

"Correct. Now . . . watch."

Sammie turned off the green light and aimed a blinding blue light onto the petri dish. It reminded Mira of an ordinary black light bulb, only considerably more powerful. At first, the chimeras appeared unaffected, and then they started dissolving. Slowly at first. Little gobs of fluid leaking through ruptured membranes. And then faster and faster as the cell walls ruptured and the contents spilled out, the bacteria shriveling and the frustules of the diatoms hardening.

"Ultraviolet light with a wavelength of two hundred and eighty nanometers will kill nearly all microorganisms," Sammie said. "This is the same UV-B and UV-C radiation that the sun naturally produces, which causes everything from sunburns to skin cancer, only concentrated into a single bulb."

"That's great and all, but we're down to barely an hour of sun a day, and its rays can't penetrate the surface to the depth of the biofilm at the height of summer."

"Then I guess we have a real problem," Sammie said. She brought a spoonful of chili to her lips, made a face, and then dumped the meal—bowl and all—into the trash can. "The only other option I can think of is to chemically sterilize the whole lake."

"Which would wipe out all animal life and contaminate the entire ecosystem."

Sammie stood and walked away without another word, leaving Mira staring after her, unable to fathom how her dream of saving the environment had gone so terribly, terribly wrong.

31

20,000 Feet Above the Northeast Greenland Ice Sheet
77.823372, -40.064935

Now

"We'll land on the glacier right here," Waller says. The head of the NeXgen contingent points at the screen of his laptop, which displays satellite imagery demonstrating a faint linear demarcation vaguely resembling a runway on the ice sheet southwest of Academy Station. He switches to a detailed floorplan of the interior. "Your job will be to secure the station. There are two levels, each of which is ring-shaped, with rooms on both sides of a central hallway. The innermost rooms surround the engineering core, while the outer rooms have exterior access via a wall of windows, several of which appear to have been broken. Once we control the station, and assuming the scientists are no longer inside, you are free to take this vehicle and search for them."

"What about the four of you?" Cameron asks, glancing

through the window of the SUSV at Kato, Grant, and Silver, who stand outside the door, talking quietly among themselves.

"We will no longer be your concern."

"So make sure there's nothing inside that building that can hurt you and then get the hell out of your way so you can do . . . whatever it is you intend to do . . . without any witnesses."

"Something to that effect."

Waller offers a smarmy smile that Cameron barely resists knocking off his face.

"I've seen Dr. Stone's emergency broadcast and the security footage from inside the cafeteria," Cameron says. "Now, I might not be the smartest person in any room, but when I think about the video logs of Dr. Rantanen making a test strip disappear and using a static charge to reanimate a dead fish, those strange distortions of pixels start to make me nervous. We haven't been able to qualify their source, let alone identify the figure they conceal, nor have we detected any forces, hostile or otherwise, within a hundred miles of the station. And we're sure as hell not equipped to handle an unknown biological agent we haven't the slightest idea how to contain. I need to know that I'm not leading my men into a situation we have no hope of controlling."

Waller offers a subtle nod to Kato, who climbs into the vehicle and once more takes the seat beside his superior.

"Perhaps it's time we briefed the senior master sergeant on our little project," Waller says.

Kato takes his cue, opens his laptop, and turns the screen so that Cameron can see it.

"Project Araneidae is a joint venture between NeXgen Biotechnology and the Department of Defense," he says, flipping through photographs taken in a massive warehouse resembling a fish hatchery. There are rows upon rows of rectangular pools filled with water in shades ranging from green to reddish-purple. Equipment of all shapes and sizes surrounds them. Dr. Rantanen is in several of the pictures, although hers is the only familiar face among the dozens of men and women in lab coats. She appears deferential in most of them, as though she's merely a bit player. "As I'm sure you already know, we spliced the spiridion genes responsible for the production of dragline silk from a golden orb weaver spider into the genome of a purple marine bacterium with the intention of producing an inexhaustible supply of webbing with extraordinary tensile properties, which could be used in the manufacture of a lightweight, flexible polymer."

"That you could make into a breathable exoskeleton for our troops," Cameron says.

"As one of those troops, I'm confident you can see the value of a protective layer of clothing with the defensive capabilities of Kevlar at a fraction of the weight," Waller says.

"So what went wrong?"

"Nothing," Kato says. "The experiment is still up and running, albeit more slowly than any of us had hoped. While we've been able to produce even more silk than we'd initially expected, weaving the strands into a functional material has proved somewhat more challenging, as you can imagine."

"Then how in God's name did the product of your research end up in Greenland?" Cameron asks.

"After reading an article published by one of our chief geneticists, detailing her early successes in using the bacterium to produce spider silk, Dr. Stone reached out and proposed utilizing it to help create a mitigant for climate change. We recognized our opportunity to experiment with its growth in the wild, not to mention the potential for entire oceans filled with silk we could harvest for our polymer."

"While convincing the government to pick up the tab for the development of the raw material, which you would then refine and sell right back to it. At an insane profit."

"It's a shrewd business model," Waller says. "But don't think for a second that taking the lead in the war on climate change wasn't our primary motivation for contributing Dr. Rantanen's experience and our patented organism—free of charge, I might add—to Dr. Stone's experiment."

"Don't try to sell me that altruistic garbage. Combating climate change is a multi-trillion-dollar business paid for by governments and financed by a never-ending string of new taxes." Cameron looks from Kato to Waller, who shrugs as if the truth is of no consequence. "I don't care about any of that. The only thing that matters to me is the safety of my men and the missing researchers, so I ask you again, one final time, what the hell is waiting for us in that station?"

Kato glances from the corner of his eye at Waller, who nods for him to proceed.

"The truth of the matter is that we simply don't know. At least not conclusively. I'm afraid the discovery of the unclassified Asgard archaeon and its interaction with the biofilm caught us all by surprise."

"Especially its apparent cloaking abilities," Cameron says.

"Lenticular properties, technically. But yes, I'm sure you can imagine the value of a polymer that refracts light in such a way as to render its wearer invisible."

Cameron recalls the spectral figure behind Dr. Stone on her emergency broadcast and the strange distortion of pixels that lifted the man in the kitchen from his feet.

"It appears you were able to create a fabric after all."

"No," Kato says. "We haven't even begun experimenting with the biofilm's material applications. However, we believe it's safe to assume that physically coating oneself in it produces the desired effect, as evidenced by both our biofilm and the ancestral form of the microorganism discovered in the ice cave near the station. At this juncture, though, we have no idea why anyone would deliberately do so, let alone why they would destroy the station and attempt to kill everyone inside."

"You think that one of the scientists is using this . . . biotechnology," Cameron says.

"Someone definitely is," Waller says.

Kato opens a new file and scrolls through screengrabs from security footage that Cameron hasn't seen before. There's a blurry image of a hallway, sparks raining from a shattered light fixture and limning the ghostly apparition underneath it. Snow gusting through a broken window, a human-shaped void at the heart of the billowing flakes. A haze of smoke, the figure moving through it defined in silhouette.

"There are others that are considerably more troubling," he says, scrolling through even more images, although of an entirely different nature. An overhead shot of a man lying on the floor, the exposed vertebrae of his neck standing apart from flesh that appears melted. Spatters on an interior wall, through which someone has smeared a palm, drawing a long arc toward a doorway, where the hand has gripped the frame. A body sprawled, facedown, in the snow, the parka shredded from its back, its extended arms resting in a frozen pool of blood. A dead woman slumped against a wall and a man hanged in a stairwell, his back to the camera, his skeletal face in profile.

"You should have warned us," Cameron says through bared teeth. "My men should have been given the opportunity—"

"To do what?" Waller asks. "Decline their assigned mission? Last I knew, you were the Air National Guard and you followed orders—"

"Given by our commanding officer, not some corporate lackey." Cameron stands and reaches for the door. "I'm turning this plane around."

"That's entirely your prerogative, sergeant, but if you do, everyone in that station will die."

Cameron stares down at his fist, with which he squeezes the handle so hard that his knuckles grow white. Waller's right and he knows it. He and his team have been outmaneu-

vered by these civilians from the start. Worse, they've been
manipulated by their own government, which would sacrifice
his entire team for a chance to recover this biotechnology.
And for what? More war? The ability to kill even more of its
enemies?

"I've dedicated my life to saving people with little or no
hope for survival," he says. "I won't leave those scientists to die,
but I'll be damned if I'm going to send my men into an environment outside of our control without allowing them to choose to
do so of their own free will. Should they decide to stay on this
plane, you won't share that information with Colonel Patrick or
any other senior officer. That's the cost of your deception. And I
swear to you—right here and now—that if you've withheld any
information or lied to me about anything, I'll leave you in that
station until you can find another group of suckers to fly
halfway around the world to extract you. So this is your last
chance to tell me what kind of nightmare we're walking into, or
you're going in there alone."

He turns and spears Waller with a glare that could have
could have stopped a charging bull. The older man's face
betrays no emotion whatsoever, let alone a hint of the thoughts
passing behind his tinted lenses.

"You can expect to encounter an unknown number of
hostile actors you'll be unable to see," Waller says. "We don't
know if we're dealing with members of the station's staff or if
the facility has been compromised by agents of governments at
odds with our own. The rules of engagement are clearly
defined: secure the station at all costs."

"How are we supposed to shoot someone we can't see?"

Kato retrieves a case from underneath his seat and opens
the hinged lid. Inside are a dozen helmet-mounted optical
apparatuses resembling goggles.

"These lenses have both thermal and night-vision imaging
capabilities," Waller says. "The biofilm might be able to conceal

a man from visual detection, but it can't mask his heat signature."

"Assuming it's a man."

"What else could it possibly be?" Kato asks. "You saw those pictures. None of the women in that station could have inflicted that kind of visceral physical damage on her own."

"In my experience, no one man could have either," Cameron says. "From the moment this plane touches down until the station is secure, you will do exactly what I say, when I tell you to do it. No questions asked. And if I catch so much as a whiff of you trying to hide anything from me or plotting to undermine my authority, the consequences will be severe. Is that in any way unclear?"

Cameron looks from Waller to Kato and back again, making sure they understand that his threat is not an idle one. He exits the SUSV, slams the door behind him, and shoulders past Grant and Silver without a backward glance. His men see him coming and stand at attention when they recognize the expression on his face. He turns on his microphone and speaks in a tone of command.

"In just over an hour, this plane will land on the northernmost landmass in the world, thousands of miles from the nearest emergency medical center. The surviving men and women of Academy Station are in desperate need of our assistance, but there's more you need to understand—"

"We know everything we need to know," Speedy says. "This is what we've been trained to do."

"Where you go, we go," Bashir says.

Rush and Ryder nod their agreement.

Cameron looks at each of them in turn and sees the firm resolution of men willing to do whatever it takes to save lives, even if it means laying down their own.

He couldn't be prouder.

"Then I need to bring you up to speed in a hurry," he says,

unlatching the straps securing the tactical cases to the fuselage. "And you're not going to like what I have to say."

Ronny steps forward, opens the lid of the nearest case, and removes an M4 carbine from its slot beside the others. He grabs a magazine from the adjacent case and slaps it into the base of the rifle. His eyes sparkle and a smile spreads across his freckled face.

"Lock and load, motherfuckers."

Cameron smiles, but the expression doesn't reach his eyes. Deep down, he knows there's something Waller isn't telling him.

And he fears it will cost all of them their lives.

32

72 Hours Ago

M ira sealed her helmet, dialed up the flow of oxygen, and lowered herself into the tank. Her thoughts were racing so fast that she could hardly keep up with them, and even then, nothing seemed to make the slightest bit of sense. All five of the sculpins had been in the aquarium when she'd gone to bed last night, and yet she hadn't been able to find any of them this morning. Not one. She'd tried every possible combination of lights, and when that hadn't revealed them, she'd resorted to looking outside of the tank, but she hadn't found so much as a drop of water on the floor. She'd even tried to get Sammie to help her search, but her partner hadn't answered her door, no matter how hard she'd knocked.

She passed through the suspended layer of biofilm, which

clung to her drysuit in iridescent tatters as she sank toward the bottom, her teeth chattering from the sudden immersion in the cold water. The walls of the tank were nearly covered with webbing in fractal-like designs resembling frost. Strands criss-crossed the interior like laser beams in a booby-trapped corri-dor, but she tore right through them, leaving the untethered remains drifting in her wake.

The sudden surge in the biofilm's growth rate was more than a little alarming, especially considering all that had been left of the dead cod she'd cut from it were scales clinging to the underlying bones. It had somehow incorpo-rated the fish's mass, feeding on it by means she had yet to identify. She was beginning to fear that the biofilm had done the same thing to the sculpins, in which case there could be no more stalling; they'd be forced to take permanent measures to make sure that the chimeras never left the lake. Considering the sun was preparing to set for the next three months and there weren't enough UV lights in the entire country to cover an area that large, any permanent solution likely meant killing every living organism in the lake and making it uninhabitable for years to come, potentially upset-ting the entire local ecosystem and risking the contamination of the fjord—and quite possibly the Arctic Ocean beyond it—in the process.

Mira fell to her hands and knees and combed through the kelp, brushing aside the leaves and pressing on the substrate around their roots, hoping that the sculpins had once more buried themselves in the dirt. She dug up every suspicious lump and searched under every stone. Just as she was about to give up, she scooped away the silt from the base of the largest rock formation and found a small cave. A faint emerald irides-cence emanated from within. She put her shoulder into the rugged stone and tipped it back just far enough that she could see into the shadowed warren. A tracery of webbing lined the narrow walls, between which, if she shone her light at just the right angle, she was able to see—

A sculpin streaked out of the hole and struck her facemask. The claw-like tips of its ventral fins latched onto the Plexiglas with such force that they scratched the surface. Its mouth snapped mere inches from her eyes and disgorged a viscous fluid—

Mira instinctively swatted it aside, but it vanished before she could see where it had gone. She directed her flashlight into the hole, which was positively riddled with webbing, so much in fact that there was barely enough room for the bodies of the other four sculpins crammed inside. Their ugly little faces peered from the funnels woven around them, what little she could see of their bodies so desiccated that they looked like they'd been baked in the sun. One of them suddenly wriggled and gasped. Startled, she recoiled and let the rock fall back to the sediment, producing a billowing cloud of silt.

A dark shape appeared in her peripheral vision, slicing through the haze. The sculpin that had attacked her earlier struck at the side of her face. She knocked it away and swam toward the surface, grabbing the platform the moment it was within range and hauling herself out of the water.

Mira felt a sharp pinching sensation on her back, near her shoulder blade. Just beyond her reach.

She threw off her helmet and shed the top half of her drysuit. The fish hung from the neoprene, the sharp tips of bone protruding from its fins embedded in the rubberized fabric.

It twisted and flopped until it freed itself and plummeted down to the floor, where it flipped from one side to the other. Finally, it stilled and lay there helplessly, gulping for air.

Mira scrambled down the ladder, grabbed the empty five-gallon bucket, and scooped up the fish, which beat against the sides with its tailfin as she climbed back up to the platform. She upended the bucket and watched the sculpin vanish into the settling silt.

Heart hammering in her chest, she plopped down on her rear end and ran her trembling fingers through her hair. What in the name of God had just happened? What had the sculpin done to the others of its species, and why had it attacked her? She knew precious little about fish behavior beyond the fact that she'd never seen one act like that before.

Mira climbed down the ladder and finished changing out of her drysuit. The face shield was scratched to hell. Worse, there were amoeboid shapes on the outer surface where the Plexiglas almost looked melted. She made a mental note to examine it more closely when she returned and rushed up the stairs to the residential wing. If Sammie was finally catching up on some sleep, the last thing Mira wanted to do was wake her, but she needed to understand what had just happened. The sculpin's sudden surge in aggression was hugely unnerving, especially if the chimeras were in any way responsible.

She hesitated outside Sammie's room before talking herself into knocking. She waited several seconds, and when she didn't hear anything from the other side, knocked again.

"Sammie?" she called.

There was no answer.

She knocked harder, waited for a reply that never came, and then knocked harder still. Nothing. She checked the knob, which turned easily in her hand. Slowly, she opened the door upon the dark bedroom.

"Sammie?" she said. "Are you all right?"

The overhead fixtures in the hallway cast a pale glow upon the small room, which was considerably colder than the outer hallway. There were books open on the desk and a mess of clothes at the foot of the bed, on top of which Sammie appeared to have cocooned herself within the blankets, drawing them all the way up over her head. Her pale face peeked out from a small gap in the covers, her breath whispering past her parted lips in faint clouds. She furrowed her brow, tugged up the blankets, and, with a soft moan, rolled away from the light.

Mira debated dragging her out of bed. She'd become increasingly frustrated with her working relationship with Sammie, who never seemed to be available when Mira needed her the most. Either she couldn't be torn away from her microscope, or she was simply too exhausted to be of very much help. The two of them needed to have a serious conversation, but right now, Mira required answers, and it was apparent that Sammie wouldn't be able to provide any. It wasn't like she was an expert on marine animal behavior, anyway. Fortunately, Mira knew two people who were, although neither would be excited to see her, especially when they heard what she had to say.

She found Sammie's thermostat, dialed up the temperature, and struck off toward the dry room once more, willing herself to absorb every last ounce of heated air for the trek ahead. She changed into her parka, snow pants, and boots and struck off across the glacier toward the staircase leading down to the lake. Time passed in a blur as she descended, her mind a chaos of warring thoughts. The wind shifted when she reached the bottom, and she noticed how quickly the sea ice on the lake had expanded, forming rings around the islands and thickening in areas where the sluggish current permitted. It was immensely gratifying to see the proof of the biofilm's efficacy, but she couldn't seem to bring herself to enjoy the success while she trudged down the snow-dusted path for an entirely different reason, one that sat like a rock in her gut.

The observation center faded in and out of the blowing snow as she set out across the dam, the exhaust seeping from the vents on its roof swirling on the tempestuous gales. When she finally arrived, her hands were so cold she could barely turn the doorknob. The warmth inside made her face hurt, but she wouldn't have traded the sensation for anything in the world. She hung her parka beside the other two on the rack, kicked off her boots, and headed across the room in her thermal socks. Voices rose from the stairwell at the back. She followed them all the way down to the observation deck, where two figures sat silhouetted against the viewports, the faint light from their laptops the only illumination in the otherwise dark room.

Jen turned at the sound of her approach.

"Oh," she said. "It's you."

Mira approached and stood at the window between the two marine biologists.

"You mind?" she asked. Aaron gestured for her to take a seat, but he said nothing. The tension radiating from them was palpable. "I need your help."

Jen scoffed.

"Let me show you something," she said, storming past Mira and grabbing a flashlight from the sill in front of Aaron. She switched it on and shone the green light through the window. A capillary-like network of iridescent webbing had grown over the glass. "Did you know there's a whale out there that we haven't been able to locate in nearly twenty-four hours?" Her voice rose with every word until she was shouting. "Do you even care that it could be sick or dying because of the infernal microbes *you* released into our lake?"

Mira recalled the narwhal she'd seen lying on the seafloor in the video.

"I'm sorry," she said.

"You're sorry," Jen snapped, slamming the flashlight down on the sill. "You hear that, Aaron? She's sorry."

"Let her speak," Aaron said.

"Fine. Here's your chance, Mira. Never mind the fact that

we came to you, asking for *your* help—which you didn't give, I might add—but please, tell us, what can *we* do for *you*?"

"It's about one of the sculpins in our tank," Mira said. "I'm not even sure how to say this." She paused to formulate her thoughts. "It appears to have killed three of the other four sculpins. I found it inside a hollow in the rock formation with their bodies. When I tried to get a closer look, it attacked me."

"What do you mean, 'it attacked you'?" Aaron said.

"Just what I said. I leaned closer, and it struck at my face. It even latched onto my drysuit and wouldn't let go until I was out of the water."

Aaron shared a glance with Jen. Something unspoken passed between them.

"We've noticed certain . . . anomalous . . . behaviors as well," Jen said.

"Like what?" Mira asked, looking between the two of them.

Jen sat down and swiveled her computer so that Mira could see the screen.

"Like this," she said, hitting the play button on a paused video.

It took several moments for Mira to understand that she was viewing footage from the vantage of the underwater camera affixed to Jen's diving helmet. With as dark as the water was, it was impossible to tell if it was day or night, not that there would be any difference in a few days anyway. Through the churning silt, she saw a shadow, which slowly took form as a deep pit at the base of the dam. A beluga whale knifed into view and hurled itself into the hole, thrashing as though in an attempt to burrow underneath the concrete barrier. The camera approached it slowly, its white flank flashing from the heart of the cloud of disturbed sediment. The whale must have sensed it was being filmed. It whirled toward the lens, blood diffusing into the water from the ruin of its bulbous forehead, and sped away from the camera, along the bowed surface of the dam toward where three other beluga whales lay, half-buried underneath the dirt. The moment the camera moved toward them, they scattered into a cloud of silt.

"I recorded this yesterday," Jen said.

"What am I looking at?" Mira asked.

"Keep watching."

The camera turned away from the dam and faced the vast expanse of open water leading deeper into the canyon. Jen swam low to the ground, staying below the invisible layer of the biofilm, glancing occasionally upward in its direction as though to make sure she didn't stray too close to the surface. Curtains of tiny bubbles rose from the seafloor, where jagged rock formations spiked with brittle corals stood sentry over seamless fields of brown kelp.

A dark shape moved in the distance. It was significantly smaller than a whale, maybe the size of a full-grown cod. A fish with a streak of gold on its flank materialized from the shadows. It abruptly changed direction and raced beyond the range of Jen's light. She swam after it and suddenly stopped. The cod floated at a strange angle, its mouth opening and closing even as its guts spilled out of the gaping wound in its abdomen.

The camera panned away and another carcass drifted into view, bits of flesh diffusing into the water around it. Jen turned and swam in the opposite direction, her arms flailing in front of the camera. A school of tiny silver fish raced past her. The view suddenly tumbled, revealing a jumble of bubbles and alternating glimpses of the seabed and open water.

"Something hit my legs," Jen said. "It felt like I got punched in the thighs. Even tore my drysuit. But I never saw—"

Thunk.

A heavy object struck the opposite side of the viewport, mere feet away, but by the time they looked, nothing was there.

"We theorize that she was hit by a chunk of sea ice that had been swept under by the current—" Aaron started to say.

"But that's not the point," Jen said, interrupting. "Did you see how those belugas were behaving? Or what about the cod? What the hell could take a bite from its belly in the three seconds it was out of my sight? It almost looks like a shark somehow got into the lake."

"And before you ask . . . no," Aaron said. "We would have known long before now if there were a shark trapped on this side of the dam."

Mira furrowed her brow and looked at the screen again.

"Then what could have—?"

Thunk.

Mira glanced at the viewport. There was a divot in the center, around which several tiny cracks had formed. Either she hadn't noticed it, or it hadn't been there a few seconds prior.

She picked up the flashlight, flicked the switch, and the green light bloomed from the lens. It barely illuminated the water directly on the other side. Nutrients swirled on the current, which swept them downward and churned them back across the bottom of the lake, unable to escape into the fjord. The darkness beyond the light's range shifted and—

A massive shape streaked toward the viewport.

Mira threw herself backward just as it struck, chipping the glass with a loud *thunk*. She caught a flash of black eyes staring at her down the broken length of a gnarled tusk.

With a swish of its tailfin, the narwhal was gone.

33

Mira ascended the stairs from the observation deck on numb legs, her mind a blur of images as she tried to make sense of everything. The sculpin streaking from the small cave where it had concealed the bodies of the other fish and latching onto her facemask. The punctures in her drysuit and the amoeboid patterns of melting on her visor. The beluga whales attempting to burrow underneath the dam and the mauled carcasses of the cods floating in the dark water. The narwhal rocketing straight at her and hammering the viewport with its already broken tusk.

Something was seriously wrong. Mira could feel it, deep down, a sensation like the entire world was falling apart around her. Her heart rate accelerated, and each breath came faster than the last. Numbness spread through her body as she stumbled onto the landing and staggered toward the wall of frosted windows overlooking Lake Tranquility. The sky rippled with ribbons of emerald and violet, the northern lights stretching from one end of the horizon to the other. She could have lost herself in its almost magical movements . . . had she not been distracted by its reflection, not from the ice or the surface of the water, but rather from beneath them.

The biofilm iridesced faintly from the depths. While the green light of the aurora borealis was perhaps of a slightly lower frequency than the 540-nanometer diode they used in the lab, it was strong enough to demonstrate that the chimeras had spread throughout the entire lake.

Mira felt sick to her stomach.

She averted her eyes and stared at the monitor mounted overhead, which showed a storm front creeping inland across the Arctic Ocean, one so immense that it eclipsed the entire right side of the screen. By this time tomorrow, it would be upon them, and judging by the fact that the temperature readout dropped before her very eyes, it was going to be worse than any she'd experienced so far.

Static crackled from the transceivers charging on the rack. Amy's voice erupted from all three of them at once, echoing throughout the room.

"Jen? Aaron?" A long pause. "I think I figured out what happened to your missing whale."

Mira's heart sank in her chest. The way Amy had said it . . . the tone of her voice . . .

Footsteps thundered from the stairwell, coming up fast.

Without thinking, Mira grabbed one of the transceivers and sprinted for the door, pausing only long enough to don her boots and parka. Jen and Aaron were right behind her by the time she charged across the slick dam, the rising wind buffeting her with sleet and forcing her to grab the railing for balance.

She was only peripherally aware of the whine of the drone streaking through the blowing snow overhead and the sound of Amy's voice through the speaker, cutting in and out from the gusts of wind screaming across the bluffs and threatening to send her tumbling down the loose talus and into the icy shallows. She ascended the switchbacking metal stairs in a blur, her chest heaving and her thighs burning as her clanging footsteps reverberated from the canyon.

The engine of a snowmobile roared overhead.

"Wait," Mira gasped into the transceiver. "We're almost there."

She rounded the final landing and crossed the windswept accumulation. Amy sat, hunched down, behind the windshield of an Arctic Cat, its headlights diffusing into the falling snow. Gasping for air, Mira climbed on behind her and wrapped her arms around the chief scientific officer's midsection. Without so much as a backward glance, Amy opened the throttle and sped away from the station. Mira caught a glimpse of Jen and Aaron —squeezing onto the seat of the second snowmobile behind Elroy—before they faded into the blowing snow.

The rugged edge of the canyon blew past beside her, offering sporadic views of the ice-rimed islands. As they rounded the southern rim of the canyon, the lake came into full view. Ice floes clogged what little flowing water remained open, their surfaces sparkling in the wavering light like the facets of gemstones. A pattern of broken ice extended from the deeper water into the shallows. The muddy shore cradled frozen pink puddles that could be only one thing.

Blood.

Amy braked hard and the Arctic Cat skidded sideways. She grabbed a heavy-duty Maglite from underneath her seat, switched it on, and shone it downhill. Mira joined her at the edge of the glacier and studied the trail of blood. It led up the slope from the shoreline, through the field of boulders, and vanished a dozen feet to their right, where the wind had already buried it beneath the accumulation.

"Jesus," Amy whispered, a cloud of breath filtering through the ice that had formed on her balaclava.

Mira read the truth in the older woman's eyes, even before she saw the pink pawprints in the snow, spared from the constant gales in the lee of a rock formation, mere feet from where they stood.

"Chinook couldn't have done this," Amy said, her voice barely audible over the roar of the incoming snowmobile. She removed a portable GPS tracker from the pocket of her parka and brought the screen to life. A blue beacon appeared in the bottom right corner, miles to the southeast across the glacier, well outside of the concentric circles radiating from their current position. She toggled the time-lapse function, and a blue line connected the two locations. "There are more than enough seals in the bay to support the entire polar bear population. Plus, they only hunt whales out of desperation, and never this close to habitation. Man is much easier prey."

Elroy pulled up behind them. Jen jumped off before the Arctic Cat even came to a halt. She stepped up to the ledge and stared down upon the scene of the attack, memorialized in ice. Tears froze in her lashes. She clenched her fists and rounded on Amy.

"You promised me those damn bears of yours wouldn't hurt my whales!" Her eyes were wild beneath the fur trim of her hood, her cheeks red and raw. "You were supposed to be tracking them at all times!"

"I was!" Amy shouted, but Mira knew that wasn't the complete truth. The chief scientific officer hadn't been able to physically locate Chinook since they'd seen him on the camera inside Miska's den. She'd driven straight out there, but he'd been gone by the time she arrived, his pawprints already wiped away by the wind. And while his GPS beacon had been easy enough to track via satellite, she hadn't been able to capture any useful imagery of him, even with the drone. "I . . . I'm so very, very sorry."

Mira recalled how sickly Chinook had looked on the remote camera, and how the sculpin she'd exhumed from beneath the sediment had appeared on the verge of death. She couldn't help but think of Sammie—lying in bed, wrapped in blankets—and felt a sinking sensation in the pit of her stomach.

"I should really back to the station," she said.

"Not unless you're walking," Amy said, climbing back onto the snowmobile.

"Where are you going?" Elroy asked.

"To find Chinook."

Amy hopped onto the snowmobile, mounted the tracking device below the windshield, and brought the engine to life.

Mira made an instinctive decision. Her butt had barely hit the seat when the snowmobile rocketed away from the lake. She grabbed Amy around the gut and hung on for dear life as the skids launched from every icy ripple in the snow. The wind chafed her face and the snowflakes stabbed her eyes like tiny needles. She ducked her head and, for the first time, noticed the tranquilizer rifle strapped to the side of the seat.

Amy slowed as they passed a faint swatch of pink ice, spared from the elements by a jagged crest of granite. Strips of gray flesh were frozen in it, their edges serrated by claws. She accelerated again and zeroed in on Chinook's beacon, the pulsating blue dot growing closer and closer to the center of the monitor.

A tattered flag materialized from Mira's peripheral vision. She knew exactly where they were going.

They stopped abruptly and skidded right to the edge of the canyon. Amy grabbed the remote tracker and the rifle, hit the switch on her flashlight, and headed straight for the path leading down into the valley, following a trail of pink droplets and pawprints the size of frisbees.

"You can't go down there!" Mira shouted.

Amy didn't even slow down, forcing Mira to slip and slide on the ice in her hurry to catch up. She grabbed Amy by the shoulder and spun her around.

"There's not much room to move in that cave," she said. "If Chinook's inside—"

"Then I have to tranquilize and relocate him," Amy said. "Don't you get it? If he didn't hesitate to hunt so close to the station, then it's only a matter of time before ... "

Her words trailed off. She obviously couldn't bring herself to finish a sentence that ultimately ended with her having to euthanize an animal she thought of as one of her children.

Amy shrugged out of Mira's grasp and continued down the path, clinging to every available surface to keep from falling. The distant hum of the second snowmobile reached them as they stepped out onto the narrow ledge leading to the cave. The icy granite was smeared with blood and scored with claw marks.

Mira prayed the polar bear wasn't still inside.

Amy shone her beam into the mouth of the cave and, without hesitation, crawled through the slender opening in the frozen waterfall. Mira fished her own flashlight from the inner pocket of her parka and followed.

The smell hit her first: a coppery, biological scent that hadn't been here before. She knew exactly what it was.

Her hands trembled at her sides. What in God's name were they doing? Amy had a tranquilizer rifle and knew how to use it, but how long would it take for the sedative to work? Could they possibly evade a full-grown polar bear in such close confines?

Mira chased away the thought and focused on regulating her breathing, listening for any sound to betray Chinook's presence. The snuffling of his enormous snout. The clatter of claws on stone. She watched for any indication that the polar bear was lying in wait as she followed the rust-colored bloodstains on the earthen floor. They led deeper into the cave, where Amy stood silhouetted in the glow of her flashlight, her beam directed onto the remains of a beluga whale.

Its skin was desiccated, its flanks riddled with claw marks and lesions that resembled acid burns. The wounds were so deep that the crescents of the ribs and the bulges of the vertebrae were visible. It had been gutted from vent to snout and absolved of its viscera, which appeared to have liquefied into a frozen puddle.

The blue beacon on Amy's handheld device flashed right at the center of the crosshairs. She stared at it for several seconds, and then looked down at her feet.

A tracking collar rested on the bare granite.

She turned around and, without a word, shoved past Mira, who watched the older woman's light fade into the darkness.

Mira waited until she was sure she was alone before exchanging her ordinary flashlight for the green one she'd left in her parka. She switched it on and aimed it at the dead whale, revealing the intricate network of webbing connecting it to the ground and the icy surfaces surrounding it.

34

Mira blew through the front door and headed straight for the dry room. She shed her parka, kicked off her boots, and grabbed the helmet from her drysuit on her way to the sublevel. Surely Sammie was up by now. She needed to hear about the sudden changes in the animals' behavior, although if Mira's suspicions were correct, the news wouldn't come as a shock to Sammie, whom she was suddenly certain knew a whole lot more than she let on. She'd spent every waking moment over the past few days in the lab, studying the interactions between the chimeras and the nervous systems of the sculpins. And while Mira had been content to let her share whatever she'd learned when she was ready, the time had come to demand answers, assuming it wasn't already too late.

She descended the stairs two at a time, ran down the arched corridor, and burst into her lab.

"Sammie!"

There was no reply from the dark lab, only the thrum of water circulating through the giant aquarium's filters.

It had been nearly eight hours since Mira had found her

partner swaddled in blankets in her cold room and a full day since she'd seen her outside of the residential wing. Sammie had looked like she hadn't slept in days, but she couldn't possibly still be asleep . . . could she?

A faint glow emanated from Sammie's laptop.

Mira crossed the room and stared at the screensaver on the monitor, watching one photograph fade and another appear. Sammie with a woman who could have been her sister, a rough sea breaking against a rocky shoreline at their backs; dressed in hiking gear and holding hands with a dark-haired man, the forest behind them swirling with mist; wearing a tiny black dress that complemented those of the other women crammed into the selfie, preparing to embark upon a night on the town. And in that moment, Mira realized that she knew next to nothing about the woman with whom she shared a lab, and even less about her role in the project that had produced the genetically engineered marine bacterium. And if Sammie didn't trust her enough to share the most basic details of her life, what else wasn't she telling her?

There was only one way to find out.

Mira glanced at the open doorway and listened for foot-steps in the hallway. Her heart beat faster and faster, until all she could hear was the rushing of blood in her ears. She took a steadying breath, tapped the spacebar, and woke the computer. All of the files Sammie routinely worked with were still open, although she hadn't updated any of them since yesterday evening. Mira aligned the arrow with the video log icon and rested her fingertip on the mousepad.

Viewing any of the recordings would be an invasion of privacy and a breach of trust. Besides, what did she expect to find anyway? Evidence that Sammie knew something was wrong with their project? Proof that she was covering up the cause of the behavioral anomalies? It seemed so absurd, and yet since breakfast, Mira had been attacked by a sculpin, nearly skewered through a solid foot of Plexiglas by a narwhal, and discovered the remains of a whale that had been dragged across the glacier and slaughtered by a polar bear in a manner unlike any she'd ever seen before. Something was seriously wrong with the animals that had been exposed to the chimeras, and she needed to figure out why.

Damn the consequences.

Mira opened the most recent video log and Sammie appeared on the screen.

"I think I'm finally starting to understand how the novel species of archaea we discovered works," she said, her voice little more than a whisper. Mira stared helplessly at the woman with whom she'd lived for all of these months, her physical appearance such a shock that Mira couldn't focus on her words. Her eye sockets were dark and recessed, her skin a pasty shade of white that made her lips appear blue. This was more than mere exhaustion; this was genuine cause for concern. " . . . only a matter of time before we lose containment. And when that happens . . . "

The camera blurred across the lab, from the green-lighted tank with the sculpin scuttling across the underside of the biofilm to Sammie's workstation, where a cod exhibiting extensive dermal lesions was pinned to the wax on a dissection tray.

"There's been another development," Sammie said, her disembodied voice echoing from the empty room. "One I can't quite qualify. All I can say is that the tissue samples collected from the wounds reveal the presence of a number of hydrolytic enzymes, among them proteases primarily associated with digestive fluids, although it's worth noting that in the case of predacious arthropods, there's considerable overlap with those found in venom." The camera zoomed in on the cod's wounds. "I await advisement."

The recording ended, and the screen went black. Mira

stared blankly at it for several seconds, allowing the implications to sink in.

Sammie had known and hadn't said a word. At least not to Mira. And whose advisement did she await? Certainly not the National Science Foundation's. But if not theirs, then whose? Who else held a stake in the success of their project?

Mira opened the file containing Sammie's notes and attacked the entries, her partner's words practically jumping from the screen.

. . . initially believed the acid the chimera used to erode the membrane of the cube was a simple chemical reaction, but formic acid can't burn through a fish's scales on contact . . .

Mira glanced at the erosions on the facemask of her diving helmet. She opened the photo gallery on her cell phone, studied the pictures she'd taken of the lesions on the dead whale's flank, and recalled the cod's wounds from the video log.

Digestive enzymes, on the other hand, are designed to do just that.

She looked at the whale's liquefied viscera, frozen to the bare earth around it. The chimeras couldn't have been responsible. They utilized photo- and chemosynthesis to generate energy and, thus, had no need for a stomach, let alone digestive enzymes, so where had they . . . ?

"Their host," she whispered. "The chimeras cause their host to excrete stomach acid."

. . . suspect the sculpin regurgitated its stomach acids onto the cod as either a defense mechanism or a form of aggression, one designed to expedite the process of consumption or, more specifically, to initiate the process of extra-oral digestion . . .

That wasn't possible, though. Fish processed their food in the same way as nearly every other animal on the planet. In fact, Mira could think of only one order of life that used its stomach acid to begin the process of digestion outside of its body . . .

"*Araneae,*" she whispered.

Spiders trapped insects in their webs, vomited stomach acid onto their exoskeletons, and then sucked out their liquefied insides. But if the chimeras were responsible for stimulating that behavior in their hosts, then that implied their infestation went beyond integration with the host's nervous system; they'd incorporated their DNA into the host's very genetic code.

. . . thought we'd spliced only the genes responsible for the production of dragline silk into the marine bacterium's genome, but we failed to take into account that those same sequences include the proteins that code for the digestive acids required to consume that very same webbing as part of the recycling process, among them hydrochloric acid, high concentrations of which will eat through metal.

That explained why the dead sculpins inside the rock had looked desiccated. Their insides had been removed and their carcasses left behind, like the whale in the ice cave, which meant—

"Oh, my God," Mira said. If the chimeras had infested the polar bear to the same degree as the sculpin, then there could very well be a staggeringly aggressive, thousand-pound killing machine out there right now, one that was capable of spewing hydrochloric acid and utilizing the lenticular properties of the chimeras to make itself invisible to the naked eye. "That's why Amy hasn't been able to find Chinook with the drone."

Mira jumped up from the stool and ran for the door. She veered left, rebounded from the corridor wall, and pulled up short when she heard Amy's voice from inside her office.

" . . . I can find no plausible explanation for their continued proximity to both the station and one another. And without his tracking collar, Chinook continues to evade our best efforts to locate him by satellite—"

"Try the drone again," Mira said, barging into the room.

Amy glared at her for several seconds before tapping the key to stop the recording.

"I wouldn't be able to see Chinook in this storm if I were staring right at him," she said.

"Even with thermal imaging?"

"With as fast as the snow is undoubtedly accumulating on their fur, I'd be lucky to capture more than vague, distorted heat signatures from any . . . of . . . them . . . ."

Amy's words trailed off, understanding dawning in her eyes as she mentally fitted the pieces together. Chinook's aberrant behavior . . . her inability to find him by either satellite or drone . . . the abnormal movements of the other polar bears. Her jaw muscles clenched and unclenched.

"You'd better hope he's all right," she said.

Without another word, Amy opened the drone archives and started with the most recent recording, captured right before they set off across the glacier. She brought up the aerial imagery, switched to the infrared camera, and fast-forwarded through the footage. The black glacier raced past, the rugged crests rolling like dark purple waves, until a violet blur materialized on the screen. Amy slowed the playback and revealed a massive polar bear, loping across the open glacier, a pink plume of breath trailing from its orange snout. Two smaller violet shapes followed, struggling to keep up with their mother, who abruptly stopped, rose to her full height, and surveyed the ice cap. She dropped to the ground, lowered her head, and appeared to issue a roar. As soon as her cubs were past her, she turned and urged them to run faster with the crown of her head.

"Miska and her cubs," Amy said. "I remember watching them in real-time and wondering where they were going in such a hurry."

The drone continued its southwestward course over the icecap until Amy suddenly paused the footage and started rewinding, one frame at a time. A rock formation appeared in the corner. The ice projecting from the pinnacle was a deep shade of purple and partially concealed the subtly lighter shape underneath it. Amy zoomed in on it until it became pixilated, then applied one filter after another until the detail came into sharp focus. A caribou's head projected from underneath the ice formation at an odd angle, as though suspended upside down. Its furry antlers would have been indistinguishable from the snow were it not for the amoeboid violet shape below it.

Blood.

The caribou had been strung up by its heels and slaughtered.

It didn't take long for Amy to locate the animal responsible. Chinook was maybe a quarter of a mile to the south, standing on his hind legs and staring up at the drone through the blowing snow. His muzzle was orange, his eyes like golden suns. The remainder of his face, a swatch on his chest, and his raised paws were the same shade of violet as the fluid beneath the caribou.

Amy tapped a few keys and the image reverted to the normal video.

Chinook vanished before their eyes.

She switched back to the infrared image and he appeared once more, those horrible eyes boring through the screen.

"Get out," she said, her voice thick with emotion. A single tear streaked down her cheek.

"I'm sorry," Mira said. "I—"

"You need to leave. Right now. Before I do something we'll both regret."

Mira stood and headed for the door. She turned around and started to say something reassuring, but she was suddenly assaulted by memories.

The sculpins . . . cocooned beneath the sediment . . . emerging invisibly from their weblike chrysalises . . . dead carcasses packed inside the hole in the rock. Chinook . . . his pawprints leading uphill from the lake . . . his sickly form on the live cam from inside Miska's den . . . the way he'd killed the whale. And Sammie . . . cocooned in blankets . . . her health visibly deteriorating . . . breath pluming from her blue lips . . .

"Grab Dr. Porter and meet me in Sammie's room!" she shouted, bolting for the hallway.

The walls blurred past in Mira's peripheral vision as she sprinted up the stairs and into the residential wing. She shouldered through Sammie's door and rushed to her bedside, only peripherally aware of the frost that had formed on the inside of the window and the droplets of condensation frozen to the ductwork. Sammie had once more dialed the thermostat all the way down and pulled the covers up over her head, leaving a gap just large enough for her mouth and nose. Wisps of steam seeped from her nostrils. Her skin was so pale that the underlying veins were visible.

Porter shoved Mira aside and opened his emergency medical kit on the edge of the bed.

"How long's she been like this?" he asked.

"I'm not sure," Mira whispered. "Since sometime last night, maybe? She's been working non-stop. I thought she'd finally succumbed to exhaustion, so I figured I'd just let her sleep."

The doctor donned a pair of examination gloves, grabbed an infrared thermometer, and pointed it at Sammie's forehead. The readout flashed 104.2.

"Did she complain about any specific symptoms?" he asked. "Lethargy? Headache? Sensitivity to light?"

"Headache for sure. And she did appear lethargic, although I chalked it up to—"

"Nausea and vomiting?" he asked, interrupting.

"I don't know. She hasn't really been eating."

Porter leaned across the bed, palpated the lymph nodes below Sammie's jawline, and nodded to himself. He plugged the ends of his stethoscope into his ears, tossed aside the blanket, slid the chestpiece under Sammie's shirt, and listened to her breathe.

"She's tachycardic," he said, an expression of concern forming on his face. "Rapid heart rate. Swollen glands. Loss of appetite. Fever. Headache. All symptoms common to a broad range of infections. Everything from a mild case of gastroenteritis to any number of serious, life-threatening conditions. I'll need to run some tests to determine which bacterium's our culprit, but considering an aggressive pathogen could spread through this entire facility in a matter of hours, I need to figure it out in a hurry, so if you can think of anything she's been exposed to . . . "

Mira remembered Sammie holding up her transparent hands. The blood dripping down her forearm. The hole in her rubber glove. The puncture wound from the infected sculpin's spine.

"Our chimera," she whispered.

35

"How's she doing?" Dr. Porter asked.

Mira turned at the sound of his voice. She hadn't heard him enter the dark room, where she sat at Sammie's bedside, holding her friend's hand, shivering against the cold as the room slowly warmed up.

"Her temperature's hovering right around a hundred and two," Mira said, "but she seems to be resting peacefully."

"Then you should probably think about doing the same."

"It doesn't feel right, you know? Leaving her alone when we still don't know what's going on inside of her."

"I'll sit with her for a while," Carrie said from the doorway behind her.

Mira glanced back and nodded her thanks.

"I've given her tetracycline," Porter said. "It's a broad-spectrum antibiotic that not only acts against both gram-positive and gram-negative bacteria but also effectively kills mycoplasmas and protozoan parasites, like that eukaryotic organism of yours."

"Are you sure it will work?" Mira asked.

"Time will tell," Perter said, resting his hand on her shoulder. "In the meantime, I'm going to need to get a sample of your blood. If you've been similarly infected, I want to get you started on a regimen, too. And I suggest you limit direct physical contact and try to get some rest yourself. I'd be happy to prescribe a sedative—"

"I'll be fine," Mira said, never looking away from Sammie's face. It was hard to tell in the dim light from the open doorway, but Sammie did appear to have gained a little color in her face. Or maybe that was just wishful thinking. She looked so small and helpless, buried under the blankets, her exposed skin glistening with sweat. "Just give me another minute, okay? I'll be right behind you."

Porter took a breath, as though he were about to say something else, but instead took his leave, his footsteps trailing him down the hallway.

"Feel better, okay?" Mira whispered. She rose from the chair and carefully extricated her hand from Sammie's. It came away sticky and left Mira's palm feeling as though it had fallen asleep, the skin under the assault of pins and needles. "I'll be back soon."

Mira tucked Sammie's hand under the blankets, mopped the sweat from her brow one last time, and stared down at her friend, her mind a jumbled mess of conflicting emotions. She was still furious with Sammie for not sharing her findings, but never in a million years would she have wished her ill. If the antibiotics didn't work their magic, she'd raise hell at the NSF until they sent a plane to airlift her to the nearest hospital.

"She's going to be all right," Carrie said, giving Mira's shoulder a reassuring squeeze. "You'll be the first to know when she wakes up."

Mira nodded, but she couldn't bring herself to meet the paleoclimatologist's gaze. With a glance out the window, which was still frosted around the edges and under siege from the other side by snowflakes the size of moths, she headed back down to the sublevel, stopping in the dry room only long enough to grab her parka. The outer shell was still damp, although after sitting in Sammie's freezing room for so long, the inside felt miraculously dry and warm. She found Porter waiting outside the medical suite. He guided her inside and gestured for her to take a seat in the chair beside the examination table, where his blood draw kit was already set up and ready to go. While she loathed the idea of slipping her arm out of the warm jacket, she'd done this enough times by now to know just how quickly the doctor worked.

Porter settled into the chair opposite her, tied a tourniquet around her upper arm, and swabbed the skin. Mira averted her eyes when he removed the cap from the needle.

"It really is an amazing organism," he said, inclining his head toward the computer monitor on his desk, which displayed a live image of the chimera squirming through a maze of human blood cells. As she watched, it engulfed a leukocyte, rupturing its membrane and squeezing out gooey strands that resembled strings of pearls. "That cellular fluid serves as a signal to the other white blood cells that there's a pathogen in their midst. You can see the other leukocytes already beginning to respond."

Mira felt a sharp pinch and watched her blood flood into the vacutainer from the catheter in her arm. By the time she returned her attention to the screen, the chimera had been overwhelmed by white blood cells.

"As you can see," Porter said, "the immune system is capable of fighting off the microbe on its own, but only in elevated numbers. Sammie's WBC count is less than three thousand per microliter, or roughly half the number from her last blood draw, while her platelet count is through the roof."

"What would cause a reaction like that?"

"The organism resembles a virus in its action, attacking at the cellular level where the immune system can't detect it, while simultaneously activating the extracellular autoimmune response, like a bacterial infection. And the whole point of distracting the immune system while it invades the host's cells is to—"

"Insert its DNA into the host's genome," Mira said, the room spinning around her with the implications.

"Fortunately, an antibiotic like tetracycline binds to the bacterial ribosomes and prevents the organism's RNA from interacting with the host's. Neutralizing it, for lack of a better term, until the immune system can purge the infection."

"You sound so confident," Mira said, accepting a cotton ball and pressing it against the tiny puncture wound in her arm. "What if the damage was already done before the antibiotic could do its job?"

"You're worried that the organism might have already infected Sammie's DNA with its genetic code?" Porter said. "The worst thing a bacterium can do is manipulate the immune response into creating conditions favorable to its survival. If that's already happened, then we should easily be able to counteract it with a round of more aggressive antibiotics."

Mira nodded. She drew a small measure of comfort from the doctor's words, although she couldn't help thinking of the sculpins and how quickly their physiology and behavior had changed in response to the chimeras. Of course, they were fish with bodies the size of a softball and Sammie was a full-grown woman, but she'd seen what they'd done to Chinook. And what he, in turn, had done to the whale and the caribou.

She recalled watching Sammie use the UV light to kill the chimeras on the microscope slide. Would the same thing work on those that had infected the polar bear? More importantly, if she gathered enough of the lights and exposed Sammie to them directly, would they augment the action of the antibiotics and help her immune system fight off the chimeras?

It was worth a try.

Porter returned to his workstation and didn't even look up when Mira left. She peeked into the adjacent lab as she passed. Amy was still seated at her desk, staring blankly at the footage from the drone. Elroy stood behind her, rubbing her shoulders. He glanced back at the sound of footsteps in the hallway, but he averted his eyes when he saw her. And in that moment, she realized that there was no salvaging the situation. Amy was going to have to hunt Chinook, a polar bear she thought of as one of her children, and hope to God they could treat him. Or else she was going to have to put him down.

But how could any number of people track and tranquilize the largest terrestrial predator on the planet if they couldn't even see it?

Mira paused in the next entryway and stared into her lab. The green glow from the aquarium lights limned the workstations and surrounding machinery. She remembered the first time she'd entered this room, how fast her heart had been beating, how her hands had trembled at her sides, how Sammie had rushed to greet her, and how she'd triumphantly held up the cryogenic storage dewar containing the bacterium she'd brought all the way from America.

They'd set out to save the world. How had everything gone so wrong?

She switched on the overhead lights and descended into the lab, passing the tank without a sideways glance. The last thing in the world she wanted to see was the biofilm or that horrible sculpin, which served as reminders of the magnitude of her failure and the consequences of trying to outsmart Mother Nature. She found the UV light on Sammie's desk and stuffed it inside her jacket with the other flashlights. Maybe one of the facilities engineers would be able to round up a few more for her. She was just about to head down the hall to find out when she saw her laptop sitting on her desk.

Before she realized what she intended to do, she'd taken a

seat and opened the computer. She stared at the screen for nearly a full minute before starting the recording. It seemed somehow important to document her thoughts for posterity, or perhaps to lighten her burden by taking responsibility for her role in everything that had gone wrong.

Her own face looked back at her from the screen, but she hardly recognized the person she saw there. Gone was the fierce woman hellbent on changing the world, leaving in her stead a frightened girl who couldn't even begin to express how sorry she was.

"This is all my fault," she finally said. "Believe me when I say that I only ever had the best of intentions. I never meant for any of this to happen. Everything just spiraled out of control, and now I don't know how to fix it. Or even if I can."

She leaned back in the chair and closed her eyes while she struggled to find the words to explain that her partner had been infected by the organism they'd created and that it was quite possibly killing her.

Or worse.

"I'm worried about Dr. Rantanen," she said, her voice echoing from the empty lab. "Sammie doesn't look well. Dr. Porter, our staff physician, isn't overly concerned, but I'd be lying if I said that I wasn't. You don't work in such close prox-imity to someone for so long without being able to recognize when something's seriously wrong with her, especially after everything I've seen. And definitely not after what happened to—"

Footsteps thundered down the hallway. Startled, Mira opened her eyes just in time to see Carrie lean through the doorway, breathing hard from running down to the lab, her eyes wide with panic.

"Sammie's gone," she said. "I looked everywhere, but I couldn't find—"

"Are you certain?" Mira asked. She jumped up from her seat

and hit the button to stop the recording. "You find Porter and I'll meet you upstairs!"

She ran across the lab and brushed past Carrie, who caught her by the arm.

"I just stepped out of the room for a few seconds," she said. "I swear to you."

Mira jerked her arm free and raced up the stairs toward her partner's bedroom, nearly barreling through Moore and Anthony.

"Sammie!" she shouted down the corridor.

Laurie poked her head out of her room, and Leo leaned back in his chair so that he could see into the hallway from the cafeteria.

Mira threw Sammie's door all the way open. Light spilled across the unmade bed, the covers bunched up just as they had been earlier. She cast them aside and stared down at the empty bed.

"Sammie?"

She turned in a circle, but there was nowhere to hide in such a small room. The closet door stood open, revealing nothing more than clothes and a small stack of books. She dropped to her hands and knees. Looked under the desk. Nothing. Under the bed. Again, nothing. She stood and glanced out the door. Surely if Sammie had left the room, someone would have . . . seen . . . her . . .

Mira froze and stared at the bed. At the dimple in the pillow and the impression on the sheet.

Blood rushed in her ears—*thoosh-thoosh-thoosh*—and her mouth suddenly went dry. Her hand shook when she reached into her jacket, removed the green flashlight, and pointed it at the mess of covers.

She swallowed hard.

And hit the switch.

Sammie materialized before her very eyes, her lower half

still concealed beneath the covers, her upper half drenched with sweat, her damp hair splayed across the pillow. Tatters of emerald webbing clung to both her torso and the blankets. Lengths of silk radiated from her body, connecting her to the bed and ascending the wall behind her. A patina of webbing resembling a fine layer of down covered her skin. Her face looked gaunt, her cheeks hollow.

Porter barreled into the room and fell to his knees beside Sammie's bed. He turned and shouted something at Mira, but she couldn't focus on his words. She watched Sammie's chest for any sign that she was still breathing, at her neck for the beating of her pulse, at her face—

Sammie's eyes snapped open.

Porter leaned over her, eclipsing the green light and causing her torso to disappear, revealing the sweat-soaked sheet.

Sammie arched her back and bared her teeth.

Porter threw open his emergency medical kit, reached for a needle and an ampoule of diazepam.

Sammie's chest lurched and her throat bulged. She made a retching sound, as though she were about to throw up. Her head snapped forward and she vomited onto Porter's face.

The doctor bellowed in agony and turned away, fluid dripping from his chin, flesh melting from the underlying bone.

Mira screamed and ran for the door.

36

20,000 Feet Above the Northeast Greenland Ice Sheet
77.823372, -40.064935

Now

"We're starting our descent now," Dancer says.

Cameron braces himself on the headrests of the pilot's and copilot's seats. The floor bounces underneath him as the Hercules battles the storm. The windshield wipers beat back and forth, clearing streaks through the ice. All he can see between them are the dense clouds and snowflakes that appear and disappear so quickly it's as though they never existed at all. Despite all of his training and the countless hours spent mastering his fear, he can't imagine having the nerves to fly a juggernaut like this, especially under these conditions.

"How long until we're on the ground?" he asks.

"Twenty minutes," Thomassi says from behind him.

"Assuming the weather doesn't force us to land before then," Kattan says.

"Your orders are to stay on the plane until I radio that we've secured the station," Cameron shouts so that everyone in the cockpit can hear him without their headsets. He glances back at the navigator and the flight engineer to make sure they understand the gravity of the situation before returning his attention to the pilot. "The moment I give the word, I need you boys to get thus plane refueled and ready to take off again. With or without us. Am I clear?"

Brooking peers back over his shoulder. An unvoiced question dies on the copilot's lips when he sees Cameron's face. He nods his understanding and reaches for the console. The ski-equipped landing gear deploys with a hydraulic whine.

"You kids are going to want to strap in tight back there," Dancer says. The nose of the Hercules suddenly dips. He pulls back on the yoke and the plane stabilizes with a scream of wind shear. "Things are going to get a little rocky from here."

Cameron claps him on the shoulder, nods to the other three men, and makes his way out of the cockpit. The ladder seems to jump in his grasp as the plane hits a wall of turbulence. The second his feet hit the ground, Ryder grabs him and pulls him into the hell hole, where Rush kneels, his laptop open on his thigh. Cameron crouches beside his tech sergeant and looks expectantly at the monitor.

"I went through the three hours of footage I was able to download before NeXgen booted me from its system," he says, his voice barely loud enough to be heard over the racket of avionics equipment. "And I found this . . . "

He hits play on the paused screen, and an image of a hallway from the vantage of a ceiling-mounted camera appears. Cameron recognizes the main corridor in the residential wing. There are open doors on both sides, but he can't see far enough into any of them to determine where they lead.

"Watch the bottom of the screen," Ryder says.

A woman with long black hair bursts from one of the outer

doorways, slams into the opposite wall, and uses it to propel herself down the hallway, where a woman with red hair is already descending the distant staircase. Cameron recognizes Drs. Mira Stone and Carrie Keyes a heartbeat before a man stumbles from the room behind them, his face buried in his hands, blood sluicing between his fingers. Dr. Stone rushes back to him, grabs him by the arm, and pulls him toward the stairs. He stumbles and falls. Dr. Stone glances behind her, tears streaming down her panicked face, and hurriedly drags the man to his feet. An indistinct haze passes through the doorway behind her and her mouth frames a silent scream.

Rush pauses the footage and zooms in on the blur, the pixels distorted in a vaguely human shape, as though someone had attempted to erase the figure from the recording. Blood gives form to an invisible hand. Spatters lend substance to a cheek here and a shoulder there. A thigh and a foot. A snarled tangle of hair.

"That's Dr. Rantanen's room," Rush says. He allows the recording to play again. The cloaked figure slaps its bloody hand against the wall, drags it along the surface to the next doorway, and grips the frame. "Now watch this."

A blur of movement, like steam rising up the wall, and the pixelated figure clings to the ceiling, shattering the lighting fixtures in sequence as it scurries toward the stairs, where Dr. Stone helps the injured man down the first flight. Sparks and shattered glass rain from the broken bulbs, obscuring the image.

Rush cuts to another camera, which displays the main corridor of the sublevel, looking back toward the bottom of the staircase. Dr. Keyes streaks straight toward the camera, glancing over her shoulder between unheard shouts. A middle-aged woman with graying hair—Dr. Amy Madigan— leans into the hallway from one of the doors on the bottom of the screen, just as Dr. Stone descends into view, the injured man's arm draped over her shoulders. Exposed bone is visible between his splayed fingers, his molars showing where his cheeks should have been. He abruptly stops and clutches his throat. Dr. Stone tumbles down the steps as he's lifted from his feet and rises, kicking and screaming, out of the camera's range.

The video abruptly ends, leaving Cameron staring at the blank monitor, recalling the screengrab of the hanged man with the skeletal face that Kato had shown him inside the SUSV. He shakes his head to dispel the image and finds himself overwhelmed by others that he can't seem to wrap his head around. The bloody, discorporate hand. The blur racing across the ceiling, shattering bulbs as it went. The man being lifted into the air. He feels a fresh swell of rage at the men from NeXgen, who've once more withheld critical information from him, doling out just enough to pacify him until it was too late to do anything about it.

"Sack up, boys," Dancer says through their headsets. "Commencing final approach."

"I'm done playing games," Cameron says. "Coordinate with the others. I want a set of eyes on those corporate pricks at all times. If any of them so much as think about stepping out of line, they're to be escorted back to the plane. By force, if necessary. Finding and rescuing the civilians is our sole priority."

Ryder nods and ducks out of the hell hole. Rush starts to follow, but Cameron grabs him by the shoulder.

"Kato mentioned something about an ice cave," he says. "If the scientists managed to escape the station, they might try to reach it. See if you can find its location."

"Yes, sir," Rush says. He pauses as though debating whether to say something weighing heavily on his mind. When he speaks, it's in little more than a whisper.

"What's inside that station?"

"I don't know," Cameron says, "but we're about to find out."

The plane bucks and the floor drops out from under their feet.

Cameron ducks back into the main aisle and shoulders his way toward the cargo hold, where the rest of his team is strapped into their harnesses, looking over their shoulders through the ice-rimed porthole windows. The men from NeXgen have donned parkas and boots over their drysuits and wear their thermal goggles perched high on their foreheads. They sit in the jump seats closest to the SUSV, as far away from the national guardsmen as they can get. Waller smiles and slides a serrated blade into the sheath underneath his left arm as Cameron assumes his seat and buckles himself in.

The plane lurches and the wings dip. A gust of wind tosses it like a child's toy.

Cameron glances through his window in time to see the glacier emerge from the clouds, far closer than he would have expected. He looks at each of his men in turn. Ryder speaks directly into Ronny's ear. The redhead's freckled face is uncharacteristically serious. He readjusts his grip on his M4, offers a nod, and turns to Speedy, who clenches his harness so tightly that his fists turn white, his lips curling back from his bared teeth with every sudden change in altitude. Only Bashir appears unfazed, although the paratrooper would undoubtedly rather take his chances with a parachute on his back than harnessed to seventy-five thousand pounds of frozen steel plummeting toward the icecap at hundreds of miles an hour.

The ragged edges of the canyon yawn below them, affording Cameron his first glimpse of the artificial lake, although it's now frozen solid. Snow has drifted up the faces of the rocky islands, which disappear as the ground races to greet the plane. The skis touch down and the props roar. The Hercules bounces and is momentarily airborne before slamming down once more.

Wind turbines race past the windows, their stilled vanes

heavy with ice. Rows of solar panels, nearly buried beneath the snow, quickly follow.

The men strain against their harnesses as the Hercules skids to a halt.

Cameron grabs his rifle from underneath his seat and looks at his men. Their eyes have turned inward, readying themselves to move on his orders, to act without hesitation, to do whatever it takes the save the lives of those depending upon them. He casts aside his harness, jumps to his feet, and starts barking orders.

"Bashir, lower the ramp. Ronny, you're on point. Rush and Ryder, you're with me. Speedy, that Susvee better be ready to roll out the moment we've retrieved anyone still in that station. If there are any survivors out there in this weather, they aren't going to last long."

He and his men all move as one, shouldering their gear and fitting the thermal night-vision goggles to their helmets. Cameron strides straight toward Waller and gets in his face. The older man removes his tinted lenses and reveals his gray eyes for the first time. Cameron doesn't like what he sees there.

"This is your final reminder as to who's in charge once we step off this plane," he says.

"Oh, I know exactly who's in charge," Waller says, the corners of his mouth curling into the faintest hint of a smile.

Bashir brushes past them and approaches the ramp station. He disengages the locks and begins to lower the ramp. The hiss of hydraulics gives way to the howling of the wind. Snow blows through the opening on gusts so cold that they pass right through Cameron, whose stare never leaves Waller's.

"Rescuing those scientists is all that matters right now," he says. "And I'm counting Dr. Rantanen among them. If she's still alive—"

Cameron detects movement in his peripheral vision and looks over Waller's shoulder. The shifting winds hurl sheets of snow in every direction, but there's something else . . . a void at the heart of the swirling flakes, like the eye of a tornado . . . only growing larger by the second. Its outline takes form, rimed with ice, its haunches bunching, its massive girth shuddering as its claws strike the ramp with a clattering sound that causes all eyes to turn in its direction.

"Magnificent," Waller whispers under his breath.

Bashir screams and flips into the air, his head rebounding from the fuselage and his spine folding backward over the roof of the SUSV with a resounding crack.

"Seal the cockpit!" Cameron shouts.

Silver turns to run and cries out as he's lifted from his feet. He slams into first the ceiling and then the floor, before tumbling down the ramp.

"Everyone down!" Ronny shouts.

Cameron and Waller dive out of the way as the senior airman bellows and fires. A crimson starburst appears as if from nowhere, the spattered blood outlining the broad chest of a great beast.

Waller jumps out of its path, throwing open the door of the rear car of the SUSV and lunging inside. Kato sprints after him, but Grant's too slow. He's slammed to the ground, as though run over from behind by an invisible truck. Claws tear through his clothing and shred his flesh, his blood giving form to giant paws and a belly covered with fur that hangs nearly to the ground. Kato clambers into the vehicle a split second before the door folds outward and snaps from its hinges.

Cameron propels himself to his feet and races in the opposite direction. His men are already scrambling into the lead car.

"Go!" Ronny shouts. He fires again and strikes the charging beast, but doesn't even slow it down. "I'll cover—!"

It charges straight through him, folding him in half and hammering him to the ground, his rifle skittering past

Cameron, who turns to rush to his subordinate's aid. Ryder tackles him into the SUSV and slams the door behind them.

"Get us out of here!" he shouts.

Ronny's cries abruptly cease. Jump seats snap from their moorings and cargo nets tear from the walls as the nearly invisible beast skids across the floor, its nails screaming for traction.

Speedy guns the engine, hits the gas, and the SUSV rockets backward down the ramp, bounding over Silver's body and sliding across the ice.

The polar bear rounds on the rapidly receding vehicle, lowers its chest, and opens its bloody jaws to issue a ferocious roar. It vanishes into the blowing snow behind them, the storm swallowing the plane whole.

37

Academy Station
Greenland
81.906296, -29.744960

36 Hours Ago

"You're going to be all right," Mira said. Porter's blood flowed unimpeded from his face, staining her parka black. She felt its warmth on the arm she used to support his weight as they hurried down to the sublevel. "Just a little bit—"

A sudden tug, and he was wrenched from her grasp, throwing off her balance. She caught a fleeting glimpse of Porter's feet rising out of sight as she fell down the stairs and slammed to the ground on her shoulder. Blood rained from the top of the stairwell, pattering the landing and spilling over the top step.

Carrie's scream echoed from deeper in the corridor. Shouts erupted from seemingly everywhere at once.

The reality of the situation came crashing down on Mira.

Porter was dead and Sammie had killed him. The chimeras had spread beyond her immune system's ability to combat them, and she'd killed the only one among them who possessed enough medical knowledge to treat her.

"Get up!" Amy yelled, grabbing her by the hand and dragging her to her feet.

Elroy appeared from the lab behind her, his bearded face crinkled in confusion. He turned toward the blood-spattered stairs as something struck the landing with a solid *thump*.

"What in God's name is happening here?" he yelled.

Mira shoved Amy and Elroy ahead of her, down the hallway toward Carrie. She risked a glance over her shoulder and saw an ill-defined figure on the landing, partially silhouetted in shimmering crimson, rise from a crouch. Her heart skipped a beat. She felt the weight of its stare upon her, the fire of its hunger, even from a distance.

Her friend was gone, leaving in her stead something else entirely, something . . . predatory.

The bloody form lunged for the wall, scurried up to the ceiling, and raced toward them on all fours.

Mira screamed and sprinted after the others. Bulbs popped and glass tinkled to the floor behind her. Amy looked back and her eyes grew wide. Carrie caught her by the sleeve and pulled her through the closest door, with Elroy hot on her heels. Mira ducked in right behind him. Slammed the door. Threw her shoulder into it. Reached for the lock—

Thud!

Impact from the other side, knocking her backward. She regained her balance and drove with her legs, holding the door closed while she locked it.

Thud! Thud! Thud!

Sammie hurled herself against the other side, over and over, as Mira stumbled down the stairs into her lab, unable to take her eyes off the slab of wood shivering in its frame.

A jumble of voices crackled from the transceivers charging on the rack. Amy rushed over and grabbed one. She hit the button and spoke in a tone of command.

"This is Dr. Amy Madigan. I'm declaring a state of emergency inside the station. You are to move quickly and orderly to the nearest room and lock yourselves inside. Those of you in the cafeteria and day room should head straight for the engineering core. Shelter in place and await further instructions."

"If you're coming to engineering, you'd better hurry," Dougherty said through the handset. "We've already sealed the entrance to the lower level and started barricading—"

Thud! Thud! Thud!

The trim beside the lock cracked. It wouldn't last much longer.

Mira detected movement from the corner of her eye as she backed away and turned toward the source. The sculpin repeatedly hurled itself against the wall of the aquarium, its ugly face smashing against the glass until—

The banging stopped. As did the fish's futile attack. It floated motionless in the water, its blood diffusing into a cloud around it.

Footsteps rumbled overhead as the other scientists followed Amy's orders.

Mira heard a *thud* against the outer wall, followed by the sounds of shattering lightbulbs, receding into the distance.

"I need your computer," Amy said.

Mira gestured vaguely toward her desk, unable to look away from the sculpin, which grew increasingly agitated. It swam violently back and forth until it suddenly stopped and fixed its beady little eyes on her. There was a sentience behind them, an intelligence that she hadn't seen there before. It streaked diagonally toward the surface, burst from the water, and—

Disappeared.

Water splashed the ground at her feet. Mira retreated

several steps and watched in horror as the puddle inched toward her, making clicking sounds she recognized right away. The sculpin was using the bony protrusions from its extended fins like feet, just like it had on the sandy substrate.

It was nearly upon her, S-shaped patterns of water trailing its swishing tail, when Elroy upended a wastebasket and slammed it down over the fish. He slid a file folder underneath it, scooped it up, and stared down at the invisible creature, which furiously beat against the rubber siding. His face remained expressionless, as though there were nothing unusual about what had happened.

"Do you want me to . . . you know?" he asked, gesturing toward the tank.

Mira remembered how Sammie had shone the ultraviolet light onto the microscope slide and suddenly had an idea. She rushed to the cupboard and grabbed the flashlight.

"Not yet," she said. "Just set it down for now."

Elroy carefully placed the trash can on the floor and backed away from it, while Mira rummaged through the mess on Sammie's desk until she found a test tube holder. She clamped the UV light between the metal pincers, fed the metal dowel from a support stand through the other end, and suspended it over the fish, which appeared once more in faint iridescent color. It fell still, opening and closing its broad mouth, and then resumed thrashing against the container.

"I found Sammie," Amy said, the glow from the laptop flickering on her face. "North stairwell. Going up fast."

Mira leaned over the older woman's shoulder and found herself staring at security footage from a camera she hadn't even known existed. Porter's body hung in midair above the landing, connected to the ceiling by filamentous strands glistening with blood. A blurry form passed beneath him and continued up the stairs.

"Dragline silk," Mira whispered. "She can produce it at will."

"How the hell could she possibly . . . ?" Amy started to say, but her words trailed off when the camera switched to the hallway outside the day room, where Leo and Moore funneled through the doorway onto the upper catwalk surrounding the engineering core. Anthony was just about to follow them when a shadow passed across the wall behind him. He went down hard, his forehead hammering the floor. The shirt tore from his back. A splash of fluid and his bare skin started to blister and melt. "Jesus."

The view changed again. Laurie stood in the day room with her back to the camera. Frozen in place. A dark pool slowly spread across the mouth of the open doorway in front of her. She turned and ran toward the camera, her face contorted by a scream. Bloody footprints appeared on the floor behind her, trailing a slender shadow—

Another switch and the kitchen appeared. Laurie emerged from one side of the screen and sprinted toward the other. Her head snapped backward, her long dark hair pulling taut. Fluid spattered against the side of her neck. She clasped her hands over the wound, blood gushing out from underneath them, and staggered past the tables, toward—

The residential wing appeared. Laurie collapsed to the floor outside of Nichols's room. The night engineer stepped out into the hallway, rubbed his eyes, and looked down at Laurie, who slid backward across the floor, trailing a broad smear of blood. He whirled and bolted in the opposite direction.

Once more, the camera angle changed, revealing the main entrance. Nichols entered at the top of the screen, looking back over his shoulder. He missed the top stair, stumbled halfway down, and jumped to the bottom. Two long strides and he was at the front door, fumbling with the latch. Bloody palmprints appeared on the wall, heading straight toward him. He threw open the door. A white drift toppled inward, burying his feet. Shielding his face with his arm, he charged out into the blowing snow—

The image switched again, starting the rotation from the beginning. Mira watched helplessly as the carnage scrolled past—Porter hanging in the stairwell, Anthony bleeding the floor red in the day room, Laurie crumpled against the base of the wall in the hallway—until she finally saw the main entrance, where a dark puddle had formed in the open doorway, melting through the snow and expanding toward the stairs. Spatters drained down the outer surface of the front door.

"What the hell is going on out there?" Dougherty asked, his voice bursting from the receiver.

"Lock the doors," Amy said, her voice strangely flat.

"There are only four of us—"

"Lock the goddamn doors!" Amy took a deep breath to compose herself and switched to the direct channel for the observation center down at the dam. "Aaron? Jen? Is anybody down there?"

"Amy?" Aaron asked. "What in the world is going on up—?"

"You and Jen are to stay right where you are, lock the doors, and—"

A thumping sound from behind her. She turned and looked at the window, beyond which there was only darkness. Snowflakes assaulted the tinted glass.

"Talk to me, Amy. What's happen—?"

"Just do as I tell you," she snapped. "I'll check in again as soon as—"

Tha-thump.

"Something's out there," Elroy said.

Mira walked slowly toward the window, watching the gusting wind alternately drive the snow toward her and rip it away again. She detected movement within it, something she couldn't quite define. A negative space. An absence where there should have been substance. She thought of all of the blood in the main entryway . . . and the complete lack of footprints tracking it back into the building. Slowly, she reached into her coat, removed the green flashlight, and shone it at the window.

Sammie appeared on the other side, her palms and toes pressed against the glass, her long hair and tendrils of webbing whipping on the violent gales. She rocked back and spewed digestive fluids onto the window.

Nothing happened.

Sammie paused only long enough to raise her fist and hammer the glass. A starburst of blood marked the point of impact.

"Out of the way!" Elroy shouted. He pushed past Mira, dragged Amy away from the desk, and flipped it onto its back. "Help me lift this!"

He grabbed one side of the desk, while Mira and Amy took the other. The three of them raised it high enough to shove it onto the narrow ledge and lean it against the window.

Sammie continued beating her fists against the glass.

Elroy dragged Sammie's desk across the room, stood it on end, and braced it against the other desk, bolstering the barricade.

"Get to engineering with the others!" he shouted. Sammie struck the other side of the window with a resounding crack that sent fissures racing through the glass. "Go!"

Mira turned to run and tripped over the wastebasket, sending the flashlight and the sculpin skittering up against the base of the aquarium. The outer coating of webbing and the tough layer of scales had turned to a substance resembling ash, which flaked away and revealed the exposed tissue underneath it. Blood welled to the surface and dripped to the floor. The fish attempted to crawl across the tile, its motions jerky and uncoordinated. Its tail slapped against the floor once . . . twice . . . and then stilled.

Amy ran past her, threw open the door upon the empty corridor, and veered toward the engineering core, shouting into her transceiver for someone to hurry and open the door for them. Elroy shoved off from the barricade, which shivered behind him with every subsequent blow.

Sammie put her fist through the window, admitting the screaming wind, but the desks miraculously withstood the assault.

Mira caught a fleeting glimpse of her partner's spectral green form crawling straight up the outside of the station. A window shattered on the upper level and something heavy thudded to the floor overhead. Mira turned and sprinted after the others, conscious of the drumroll of footsteps keeping pace in the hallway above her. She ducked into the engineering core right as Dougherty started to close the door.

He slammed it shut with a metallic clang that reverberated throughout the two-story chamber.

Mira leaned against the wall, slid down to the ground, and started to cry.

38

Mira couldn't hear anything outside of the engineering core over the racket of the machinery forcing heated air and water through the networks of ducts and pipes running up the walls and across the ceiling, but at least she and the others could surveil the station beyond the barricaded doors, not that it did them much good. Amy had opened the video surveillance system on the desktop computer and turned the monitor so that the rest of them could see from where they sat on the floor, leaned against the walls, or nervously paced the room.

They'd grown numb to the sight of their colleagues' bodies and watched helplessly as snow accumulated on the broken tables and toppled chairs in the kitchen and in the main entry-way, where Nichols's blood had vanished beneath a drift so deep it had begun to ascend the stairs. Dougherty had the equipment working overtime in an attempt to combat the influx of freezing air, even a small portion of which would have been a blessing in this suffocating chamber. At least they could be confident that if the cold couldn't find its way in, then neither could Sammie.

They spotted her on the security cameras every so often, although with nowhere near the kind of precision they'd need to pin down her location or anticipate her movements. The occasional watery distortion or vague shadow appeared on one camera, only to disappear before it reached the next one. A fresh trail of footprints materialized from the shattered glass on the floor, only to fade to nothingness as the blood transferred from her invisible feet. Something would fall from a countertop or already be on the ground when the footage cycled back to that vantage point. No one dared vocalize what they were all thinking . . .

Sammie was searching for a way to get in there with them.

Amy remained in constant contact with Aaron and Jen down at the observation center, but there was no way of reaching Swearengin. Every so often they caught a glimpse of him on the security camera, peeking out of the door leading down to dry storage—the only room in the facility without a full complement of transceivers on a charging station—and then quickly closing it again. Undoubtedly, he'd sneaked downstairs to grab a smoke. None of them envied him being trapped by himself, especially not without the slightest idea of what was going on beyond the screams he'd surely heard and the blood he saw every time he peeked out into the cafeteria. At least he had food, though. The rest of them didn't have so much as a stick of gum between them. And while water still flowed from the faucets on the industrial sink, Dougherty continually reminded them that it was only a matter of time before the pipes in the cafeteria froze and burst. Once that happened, the station was designed to recognize the danger and switch from primary power to the emergency generators, in hopes of preventing inadvertent electrocution or starting a fire they couldn't put out while the pipe was being repaired. What he was really trying to say is that they'd be left with basic life-support functions, and even those would last for only so long before leaving them at the mercy of the elements.

"She's just a person, like any other," Leo said. He sat on the floor beside Carrie, who leaned her head against his shoulder, her mascara staining her cheeks. "If we worked together, we could—"

"Do what?" Moore said, interrupting. He stormed back and forth between the monitor and the barricade. He constantly readjusted the wooden cases and shelving units they'd stacked against the door to ensure maximum structural integrity. "We can't even see her."

"You saw what she did to Porter," Carrie said. "She's nothing like the rest of us."

"What if we all took off in different directions?" Elroy said. He stood behind Amy, rubbing her shoulders as she stared at the security footage, the weight of her responsibility adding a decade to her face. "She can't possibly follow all of us at once."

"You'd be passing a death sentence on one of us," Moore said.

"We just have to wait her out," Amy said.

"Once the power fails and we're running on the emergency generators, this is one of the few rooms that will retain heat for any length of time," Dougherty said. "If I manually take the battery cells offline now, we can easily outlast her. She won't survive for very long in that cold."

"We're talking about killing one of our own," Mira said. They were the first words she'd spoken since taking a seat in the corner, from which she could still see the chief engineer's monitor without having to suffer the others' accusing stares. She'd seen what Sammie had done to their friends, but killing her for actions outside of her control had to be their final recourse. "There has to be another way. And besides, the organisms inside her thrive under freezing conditions."

"But she doesn't," Leo said. "The fact remains that she's a human being and possesses the same frailties as the rest of us."

"Does she, though?" Moore said.

All eyes fixed upon Mira, who could only shake her head. The truth of the matter was that she simply didn't know. Both the polar bear and the sculpin had become increasingly aggressive and attempted to kill everything in their paths, including members of their own species, and the only thing that had inflicted any kind of damage was the ultraviolet light. She couldn't imagine Sammie holding still long enough for them to use it on her, and the thought of burning off the top layers of her skin with the chimeras made her physically ill.

"I'm with Dougherty," Carrie said. "We have a better chance of making it through this if we act now. And really, we only have to wait another what, ten hours before the satellite's in range? Once the NSF tries to download our daily logs and sees that none have been recorded, they'll realize something's wrong and send help."

"They'll assume that the data failed to upload because of the storm," Amy said. "It wouldn't be the first time it's happened. And even then they probably won't call for emergency evacuation for another twenty-four hours." She paused and furrowed her brow. "If we can get to the communications center, however, we can record a message that will transmit the moment the satellite's in range. The problem is we'd have to take down the barricade and someone would have to go out there."

"Once we kill the main power, the temperature will fall so quickly that every pipe in this station is going to burst," Dougherty said, his voice distant, his eyes focused on something only he could see. "With the power limited to emergency functions, I can probably make the generators last for thirty-six hours, but if they don't dispatch someone to evacuate us right away, none of us will be alive when they arrive."

The room fell silent, save for the thumping of heated air through the ductwork overhead.

"We'll set a deadline," Amy said. "And if no one's arrived by then, we take the snowmobiles across the glacier to Nord."

"That's more than a hundred miles away," Moore said. "Assuming we can even find it in this weather. Plus, we'd be exposed to the elements the whole time. And that's assuming we can all get out of here and make it to the garage."

"The communication center's barely fifteen feet from that door," Leo said, inclining his chin toward the door at the top of the spiral staircase. "If we created a distraction, surely one of us could make it."

"But who's going to do it?" Carrie asked. "What if she sees through our ruse? What if she gets in here?"

All eyes turned toward the monitor. One feed after another passed without giving so much as a hint as to where Sammie was.

Mira realized that contacting the outside world and hunkering down inside the station provided the best chance not only for their survival, but Sammie's as well. Surely if the chimeras failed to keep her alive, she'd at least find a way to keep from freezing to death. After all, there were blankets on the beds in every one of the bedrooms. And only one of them needed to take the risk, one of them who was already wearing her parka and desperately wanted to make up for everything that had gone wrong.

She was just about to volunteer when she saw movement on the screen. Swearengin, slowly opening the door from the dry storage room and peeking out into the kitchen. He leaned out far enough for them to clearly see his face—

The camera switched to the residential hallway.

"Go back," Elroy said. "Isolate that feed."

Amy clicked through a series of prompts and the kitchen appeared once more. Swearengin ducked out of the stairwell.

Tripped and went down. Lurched back to his feet. Suddenly stiffened, grabbed his throat, and rose straight up toward the ceiling. His flailing legs kicked the serving trays from the countertop. And then he was gone.

"Jesus," Carrie gasped.

They were all going to die in here.

Minutes passed in shocked silence. The thumping from the ductwork grew louder, as though the furnace had suddenly ramped up. Or perhaps the temperature was dropping faster than they'd anticipated, causing the aluminum panels to contract and produce popping sounds as they cooled. Whatever they decided to do, they needed to do it soon.

Mira's hands shook at she pushed herself to her feet.

"I'll go," she said. The thunder of her heartbeat in her ears was so loud she could barely hear the words coming out of her mouth. "How do I use the communications equipment?"

"Look for the computer connected to the battery pack in the yellow case," Amy said. She glanced up at the sound of more thumping from the ductwork. Louder this time. Closer. "There's an emergency contact icon on the main screen. Click it and you'll bypass the security protocols and immediately start transmitting."

"You'll be killed if you go out there," Carrie said.

"Not if you guys create a big enough distraction."

"What if you can't get back?" Leo whispered.

A thunderous cracking sound echoed from the first floor, followed by the rushing noise of liquid flooding across the floor overhead. One of the pipes in the kitchen had burst. Water poured down the walls into the utility and storage rooms. Droplets formed on the undersides of the pipes and conduits traversing the ceiling. The lights flickered and, with a thud from the generator, died. The darkness was sudden and complete, although it didn't last long. The emergency lights and backup power kicked on mere seconds later, stranding them in a crimson glow.

"Whatever we're going to do, we'd better do it now," Dougherty said. "This room isn't airtight. We'll stay warmer than anywhere else in the station, but we'll be hemorrhaging heated air as fast as the furnace—"

A popping noise. From directly overhead, inside the room. The sound of aluminum buckling and snapping back into place. Everyone looked up at the heating duct. There was a bulge in the metal, near the wall. It flattened before their eyes and the adjacent panel bowed downward.

Mira glanced at the screen and once more saw the empty kitchen, where Swearengin had just risen straight up to the ceiling and out of sight.

"Oh, God," she whispered. "She's in the ductwork."

The next panel in the sequence buckled. Then the one after that.

"She's trapped in there," Dougherty said. "The only way out of there is through the furnace and she'll be cooked long before—"

Thoom! Thoom! Thoom!

The panel directly above them bent outward, farther and farther with each impact, the sound echoing throughout the engineering core. Rivets popped and metal sheared. The aluminum wouldn't be able to hold up much longer.

"I'll head for the communications center," Mira said. "If I make enough noise, she'll have no choice but to follow me, which ought to buy you guys enough time to reach the dry room. If you can get to the snowmobiles—"

"It's thirty below out there," Carrie said. "We can't—"

Something broke through the metal panel, the sharp edges tearing through unseen flesh and summoning blood.

"Go!" Mira shouted, lunging to her feet and running toward the stairs.

Thoom! Thoom! Thoom!

Mira's footsteps clanged from the stairs. Crates crashed to the ground behind her as the others dismantled the lower-level barricade. She focused on the landing above her and the door to the hallway, which she could barely see behind a stack of crates. Movement from the corner of her eye. A flash of light reflecting from the aluminum panel plummeting through her peripheral vision.

Screams erupted from everywhere at once. Mira pushed herself even harder around the tight spiral and caught a vague shimmer slither through the ragged opening in the duct and plummet toward the ground.

A shriek of agony from below her. Leo pawed at his face, half of which blistered and eroded, spilling gore down the front of his shirt. He turned around and his pained cries ceased. The pulsing arcs of blood from his severed carotid painted Sammie's features and drained down her chest, defining her form. She ripped her mouth from his neck and started toward the others, who weren't even all the way out the door yet.

Carrie screamed and tried to fight through Elroy, who bodily manhandled her into the hallway.

Mira hit the catwalk and rushed toward the second-floor barricade. If she didn't create a distraction, none of the others would make it.

"Hey!" she shouted, pounding the railing with her palms.

Sammie glanced up, her crimson face clearly revealed for the most fleeting of moments, and then sprinted toward the stairs.

Mira shoved aside the crates as quickly as she could, the clanging of footsteps spurring her on. Unlocking the door with trembling fingers, she pushed it open, squirmed between the remaining boxes, and scurried down the hallway toward the communications center.

From behind her, she heard the crashing sound of breaking wood and the thudding of footsteps on the catwalk.

She crossed the threshold and slammed the door behind her. Dragged the nearest table in front of it. Stacked anything within reach on top of it. Chairs. Computer monitors. Reams of paper. And ran toward a console that resembled the bridge of a ship.

The majority of the screens were blank. Lights that should have been flashing were now dark. Only one station appeared to be receiving emergency power. She shook the mouse to wake it, clicked on the emergency broadcast icon, and her face appeared, staring back at her from the monitor. Wild hair and even wilder eyes. Breath blooming from lips damp with mucus. She started talking and prayed to God she was able to broadcast the message in time.

Thud! The door shook in its frame.

"This is Dr. Mira Stone at Academy Station. We've lost primary power and the integrity of the complex has been compromised—"

Thud! Table legs screeched as the barricade barely withstood the assault.

"Something is in here with us. Six of us are already dead. The rest—"

Crack!

Mira glanced over her shoulder. Chairs toppled from the table. The trim splintered near the broken lock and the door swung inward, revealing the human shape at the heart of the shower of golden sparks raining from the shattered emergency light fixture. She turned back to the camera, the clamor of falling chairs and rapidly approaching footsteps behind her, and spit out the remainder of her message.

"We're going to try to make it across the glacier to Station Nord. Academy Station is lost. Do not—I repeat—*do not* attempt to reclaim—"

Mira sensed the blow coming, clicked the button to save and transmit, and dove out of the way. The monitor crashed to the floor beside her. She scrambled to her feet and sprinted toward the door. Something wet spattered the floor behind her, spurring her on. She jumped a chair, shouldered through the narrow gap, and ran for the main entrance. Open doorways blew past in her peripheral vision, the shadows within made darker by the red glow. She concentrated on the frigid air blowing in her face and the drifting snow at the bottom of the stairs—

Something clipped her heel, sending her careening to the ground, her momentum carrying her over the edge. She tumbled down the steps. Cried out when her head struck the wall. Grabbed the railing and nearly wrenched her arm from its socket. Pulled herself upright, got her feet underneath her, and jumped to the landing.

A blur from the corner of her eye, moving quickly across the wall.

She slipped on the ice and went down hard. Something wet sailed past her head and spattered the trim. She smelled burning hair and felt searing pain on her scalp, but there was nothing she could do about it now.

Mira pushed herself up and ran out into the blowing snow. She hurdled Nichols's frozen body and followed the rapidly vanishing tracks the others had left only moments prior. By the time she summoned the courage to look back, the station had been swallowed by the storm. She lowered her head and charged through the knee-deep accumulation toward the garage.

39

Five silhouettes materialized from the snow, staggering toward the garage, little more than a vague rectangular shape intermittently appearing from the blizzard in the distance. Mira hurried to catch up with them, wary of the fact that she wouldn't be able to see Sammie until she was already upon her. And maybe not even then.

Maybe Leo was right, and the chimeras were constrained by the physical limitations of their hosts, but after watching Sammie make such short work of him, Mira wasn't in a hurry to wager her life on it. Unfortunately, the moment she left the station, that was precisely what she'd done. Even with her parka and boots, she couldn't possibly last very long in this cold, which sapped the moisture from her skin and made her lips crack and bleed. It was only a matter of time before her brows and lashes knotted with ice, and once her core temperature started to drop, there was no way of bringing it back up.

Dougherty had just finished chiseling the ice from the seams and opening the door when she caught up with the others, who funneled into darkness that smelled of motor oil and gasoline. Mira slipped inside, closed the door behind her, and helped Elroy and Moore shove a tool chest against it. She switched on the ordinary white flashlight from inside her jacket and swept it across the cavernous interior. An arctic vehicle with the tread of a tank was parked right in the middle. Beside it sat the industrial snowblower and plow used to maintain the landing strip. Drums of fuel and bags of gravel and salt were stacked against the rear wall. Two figures stepped from the shadows and into the light. Carrie's face was stark white, her eyes fixed and unfocused, her mascara forming frozen black trails down her cheeks. Amy looked little better, but she recovered her composure, snatched Mira's light from her hand, and started barking commands.

"The snowmobiles are on the other side of the Sno-Cat," she said. "The reserve fuel tanks are on the shelves behind them. Strap one on the back of each and get ready to move."

The wind howled and the building groaned. Shimmering motes of dust descended from the rafters.

Amy's transceiver crackled, and Aaron's voice echoed from the garage.

"Ready when you are," he said. "I still think we should hole up in here—"

"You haven't seen what she's capable of doing," Amy said, cutting him off. "We need to put as much distance between her and us as possible. We'll radio when we're getting close. And don't dawdle. We'll be coming in hot."

She ducked behind the Sno-Cat and pinned the shelving unit behind it with her light. Dougherty rushed over to it and started passing the reserve tanks to Moore, who tied them down on the backs of the snowmobiles.

"We're going to have to open the garage manually," Elroy said. "We'll be completely exposed while we roll these things outside, so we need to—"

Thoom!

A thunderous boom reverberated throughout the

aluminum structure. Amy shone the light toward the front door just as something hit it from the other side, buckling it in its frame.

Thoom!

It wouldn't be able to withstand very many more blows like that.

"Start the engines," Elroy said. "Be ready to move the moment I raise the door."

"We're not going without you," Amy snapped, her voice cracking.

"You'd better believe I'll be on that seat right behind you." While the others climbed onto the snowmobiles, he ran to the garage door, disengaged the latch, and grabbed the chain to raise it. Motors screamed to life. Headlights stretched his shadow up the interior wall. "Don't accelerate too quickly or the tread will just spin on the concrete. Slow and steady until you hit the snow. Then don't look back."

Thoom!

The upper half of the front door folded inward with a high-pitched shriek of shearing metal. Mira's stomach sank with the realization that if Sammie had been able to strike with such strength and ferocity, they never would have been able to barricade themselves inside the engineering core.

"Wait," she gasped. "That's not Sam—"

"Go!" Elroy shouted.

He jumped and landed in a crouch, using all of his weight and strength to pull the chain. The door rattled up to the ceiling and the snowmobiles' headlights fired out into the storm. Moore went first, his tread spinning impotently until it finally gained traction and launched him into the night. Dougherty rolled out into the accumulation and rocketed away after him. Carrie lowered her head behind her windshield and chased their taillights out of sight. Amy was right behind her, screaming for Elroy to hurry up and climb on.

Over the whine of engines, Mira heard a noise that chilled her to the marrow.

A roar.

The sound was unmistakable. She turned toward the source and saw an enormous void in the blizzard, charging right at them. The ice on the creature's fur faintly reflected the glow of their headlights, limning the form of a beast she immediately recognized.

"Chinook . . . " Amy sobbed.

The polar bear lumbered toward her, haunches rising and falling, churning up the snow. A second's hesitation was all it needed. It reared up and raised its massive paw to strike—

Elroy jumped onto the snowmobile behind Amy, closed his hands over hers, and opened the throttle. The Arctic Cat rocketed forward, but the blow still struck home, knocking Elroy into the snow and toppling the snowmobile on its side. He rose from the accumulation, dragged Amy to her feet, and shoved her onto the seat behind Mira.

His terrified eyes locked onto hers, his lips framing words she couldn't hear.

"Get out of—"

Chinook struck him from behind, hammering him face-first into the accumulation. The beast pounced on his prone form with a flurry of slashing claws. Warmth spattered Mira's face, forcing her to turn away. She hit the gas and raced into the night, tears streaming down her cheeks.

Amy screamed Elroy's name and buried her face in Mira's parka as the carnage vanished into the rooster's tail of snow behind them. She moaned and sobbed, the forlorn sounds seeming to come from someplace far away.

Numbness spread through Mira's arms and legs, and for a moment, she feared she might go into shock, but she bared her teeth, forced the memories of Elroy's gruesome death from her mind, and concentrated on following the trail left by the other snowmobiles, keeping one eye on the rearview mirror and the other on the glacier. By the time she saw the red glow of taillights, she was already past the boulder field leading downhill to the lake and streaking along the ridgeline opposite Academy Station.

"Call Aaron and tell him we're almost there!" Mira shouted over her shoulder.

Amy didn't respond, but Mira felt movement against her back. She prayed the older woman was up for the task ahead.

The lake blew past, its surface white with ice, its towering islands vanishing beneath the accumulating snow. If only things had played out differently. They'd come so close to realizing their dream of reversing the effects of climate change, only to damn themselves in the process. And if she didn't figure out a way to destroy her work, then it was only a matter of time before the chimeras reached the open ocean and, from there, the rest of the arctic. How many more people had to die because of their hubris?

Moore's snowmobile skidded sideways across the ice and came to rest on the granite pinnacle overlooking the fjord. Dougherty pulled in behind him, climbed off, and rushed to the rugged trail leading down to the dam. He raised his hand to shield his eyes from the wind and looked toward the distant research center.

"I don't see them," he said. His voice was high and tight, his beard thick with icicles. "We can't risk staying here much longer."

"We're not leaving anyone else behind!" Amy shouted.

Dougherty looked at the chief scientific officer and then at the empty seat behind her. He closed his eyes, took a deep breath, and steadied his voice.

"I'm so sorry, Amy."

"Elroy didn't give his life so the rest of us could die out here," she said. "A polar bear can run at twenty-five miles an hour, but only over short distances at a time. That doesn't mean we can risk any further delay." She brought the transceiver to her blue lips. "Aaron? How far out are you?"

"We're coming as fast as we can," he replied.

"I can make it down that trail," Dougherty said.

"You can't leave us here," Carrie said.

"We're not splitting up," Amy said.

"He's right," Mira said, staring downhill at the path switch-backing down the rocky ridge. It was barely wider than their tread, and any mistake could send them plummeting into the frozen lake, but with every passing second, their lead on the beast evaporated. They were safest on the move, regardless of which direction they were heading. "We can make it. By the time they reach us up here, it'll be too late."

A roar echoed from the canyon, its origin so close that the sound reverberated in Mira's chest.

"It's already too late!" Carrie screamed. She jumped on her snowmobile, gunned the engine, and sped down the steep trail. She slewed and nearly tumbled over the edge, but she slammed into a boulder at the last possible second, righted herself, and entered the next switchback at a considerably slower pace.

Mira didn't wait to see if she made it. She climbed onto her snowmobile, felt Amy's arms wrap around her midsection, and sped over the precipice. A sensation of weightlessness, a juddering impact, and they were sliding down the narrow path so fast that her breath caught in her chest. The slope had looked so much more graceful from above. It felt like they were careening headlong down the face of a cliff. She barely had time to jerk the steering wheel before crashing into the boul-ders lining the trail and launching into the open air. The skis hit the ground with a crunch of compressing springs. She focused on keeping them aligned with the slender ledge leading to the juncture where the dam's rim met with the rocky escarpment.

Carrie hit the bottom first, the jarring impact nearly stalling her engine and bucking her from her seat. She fishtailed on the ice, gained traction, and sped out onto the dam.

"Hold on!" Mira shouted.

Amy's arms tightened around her hips, the front runner buckled, and they were momentarily airborne. They hit the icy ledge and skidded toward the edge of the cliff. Mira turned into the slide. The tread caught with a jerk, and they accelerated onto the dam. She risked a glance back just as Dougherty's snowmobile slammed down onto the rocky landing and raced out onto the dam.

Moore struggled to keep up. His right front ski hammered a boulder, buckled, and snapped off. He tumbled from his seat as his snowmobile fired from the hillside and vanished into the storm. He'd barely found his feet when a massive shape rose from the rocks behind him, ice shimmering on the fur of its broad chest, a roar bursting from its unseen jaws. It was upon him before he could even draw the breath to scream.

Mira forced herself to look away before she lost her resolve. She concentrated on the snow-covered passage in front of her, a frozen trench between low walls that did little to shield her from the storm. She accelerated and had to swerve to avoid hitting Carrie, who'd slowed to pick up Aaron and Jen. The marine biologists ducked down behind her and clung to one another as they headed back toward the building they'd just evacuated. Mira reached it first. She jumped off her snowmobile, opened the door, and ushered Amy into the research center.

"Hurry!" she screamed.

Carrie skidded right at her, going way too fast. Her snowmobile slammed into Mira's. She climbed off, blood streaming from a gash along her hairline, and staggered into the building.

"Get ready to barricade the door behind us," Mira shouted at Aaron as he passed, pulling Jen by the hand behind him.

Dougherty's Arctic Cat emerged from the blowing snow. He jerked the wheel to avoid hitting the other snowmobiles, jumped from the seat, and ran for the door.

The ground shuddered beneath the advance of the beast behind him. It charged right over the snowmobile in its way, shattering the windshield and breaking the front skis.

Mira made room for Dougherty to slip past her and slammed the door behind him. She helped Amy and Jen drag the table right up against—

Impact from the other side. A deafening roar.

Mira threw herself against the barricade, braced her feet, and fought to keep it from sliding inward as the others piled everything within reach against it, all the while struggling not to think about the fact that they were now trapped.

40

M ira stood at the window and stared down upon the frozen lake. She wondered how thick the sea ice had become. How far the underlying temperature had dropped. How high the pH had climbed. And how many billions of those infernal chimeras were down there? Their biofilm had worked better than they ever could have dreamed, but the price of success was far higher than they were willing to pay. The concrete structure beneath her feet was the only thing standing between the containment of the nightmare organisms and the utter annihilation of the global ecosystem.

How in the name of God had everything gone so wrong?

"I repeat, this is Academy Station," Amy said. "We need emergency evacuation. Can anybody out there hear me?"

Only static answered.

She spiked the handset of the long-range radio transceiver against the console and tugged her fingers through her damp hair in frustration.

"We'll be able to reach someone once the blizzard lets up," Dougherty said, gently placing his hand on her shoulder.

"There'll be fishing boats off the coast, and we should easily be able to hail Nord . . . "

His words trailed off when he saw the expression on her face. They'd all seen the doppler image on the television mounted above the window, the mass of clouds eclipsing the entire screen and the forecast showing the storm that wasn't about to break anytime soon. At least the observation center had a dedicated power supply to ensure the dam didn't fail, even if the station did. That had been Elroy's parting gift to them: a chance to survive.

They had lights and heat, running water, and even a small stash of food they'd removed from the mini-fridge after adding its bulk to the barricade. Everything in the room had been shoved against one door or the other, leaving a bare space in the center where the only thing to do was watch the snow fall and pray the polar bear had either given up his assault on the building or lost interest in the prey trapped inside. It had been nearly half an hour since they'd last seen Chinook, and not knowing where he was made the situation infinitely worse. He no longer threw his weight against the heavy steel doors or paced across the roof, each thudding footstep bringing them closer to giving in to panic.

Mira couldn't shake the feeling that this was the calm before the storm.

"I found him," Jen whispered, her voice bursting from the transceiver.

There was no need to ask where she'd seen him; there was only one place it could have been.

"I'll be right there," Amy replied.

Mira followed the chief scientist down the stairs to the observation deck, where Jen and Aaron sat in the darkness, far enough from the viewports so as not to be visible from the other side. They gestured for Amy and Mira to stay where they were.

A disturbance passed through the water, a current without a source. Bubbles and microorganisms swirled in its wake. A tapping sound from one inset window, a thump against the next. Chinook was testing the glass, discreetly, trying not to attract too much attention while he searched for a way in.

"That's not normal polar bear behavior," Amy whispered. "There's other prey out there, animals that would be far easier to catch."

More thumping and tapping as the churning water moved back across the windows. Seconds passed in silence. Minutes. The sediment slowly dispersed and hung motionless in the water again.

"He's on the roof," Carrie whispered from the two-way. The terror in her voice was palpable. "We can't stay—"

A loud thud echoed from the speaker. Carrie screamed.

"He should have lost interest and moved on by now," Amy said. "There's no reason he should still be—"

Crack!

Mira flinched, and Jen scrambled away from the viewport. They'd both heard that sound before.

"It knows we're in here," Mira whispered.

Carrie screamed again, her cry reverberating from the stairwell.

Crack!

Jen switched on her green flashlight and shone it at the inset window. A network of fissures spread through the Plexiglas as they watched, lightning bolt cracks striking outward toward the edges. A black haze hung in the water, a cloud slowly dissipating on the swirling current. There was only one thing it could be.

Blood.

A shimmering shape knifed through it. Mira caught a glimpse of a broken tusk. A bulbous face. Twin black eyes.

Crack!

The Plexiglas fractured. A fine spray of water burst from the point of impact, drilling the wall on the opposite side of the room with enough pressure to burrow into the concrete.

"It's not going to hold!" Aaron shouted.

He propelled himself from the floor and raced toward the stairs, where Amy and Mira were already scrambling upward. Jen slipped in the freezing water, struggled to her feet, and aimed her flashlight back at the window.

More snapping and cracking from the window. The cloud of fresh blood spun like a whirlpool through the rapidly expanding hole. The narwhal appeared again, its broken tusk little more than a jagged nob, the flesh on its face shredded from the underlying bone. It hit the glass with a resounding *crack!*

Glass erupted from the shattered window, hitting Jen on a column of water with such force that the impelled shards cut through her clothing and skin alike. It hammered her against the far wall, pinning her for several seconds before casting her aside into the rising water. The whale tore ribbons of flesh from its sides as it squeezed through the broken viewport. It raced through the shallow water toward Jen, its flagellating tailfin breaching the surface. It bit the hood of her jacket, flipped around—

The green light died and the narwhal vanished.

Jen went under, her hand reaching toward the surface, her legs kicking desperately. She sped backward through the water and passed through the window—

"Snap out of it!" Amy shouted.

Mira tore her eyes from the sight of Jen's body receding into the dark lake, which was funneling into the room at an alarming rate. It had already risen to the first landing and was climbing fast, filling the air with freezing spray. The temperature plummeted as the observation center flooded. Aaron urged them to climb faster, the roar of the waves chasing them toward the upper level, where Carrie's screams echoed from the confines.

They emerged from the stairwell into a new nightmare. All of the windows overlooking the fjord were cracked, as though something had repeatedly struck them from the other side. One shattered before their eyes and scattered glass across the floor at their feet.

"The barricade!" Dougherty shouted.

He rushed to the nearest door and dragged away the couch braced against it, toppling the mini-fridge in the process. The others hurried to his aid and started hurling aside chairs and cases of equipment.

Mira peered back over her shoulder as Chinook crawled through the window from above, slinking silently across the ceiling. Ice shimmered on his fur, lending substance to his otherwise invisible form. He reached straight down, planted his front paws on the floor, and lowered himself to the floor. Jagged shards crunched beneath his weight. Bloody pawprints marked his advance toward them.

"Hurry!" Aaron shouted.

Dougherty managed to open the door just far enough to squeeze through. Amy followed, dragging Carrie by the hand. Aaron pushed Mira from behind, forcing her to turn away from the frozen silhouette and squirm through the gap. The cold air hit her hard enough to steal the air from her lungs. She shielded her eyes from the blowing snow and charged out onto the slick dam.

Chinook roared from behind them. He frantically scratched at the door and walls in a desperate attempt to widen the opening far enough to pursue them.

Mira raced to catch up with the others, who were already disappearing into the storm. They'd come out the opposite side from their snowmobiles, leaving them at the mercy of their legs, and there was only one direction they could go.

Back to the station.

The realization hit her so hard that she stumbled and had to grab the railing to keep from falling. After everything they'd endured within its walls . . . after barely making it out of there alive . . .

Movement from the corner of her eye. She glanced over the side and watched Jen's body float to the surface amid the fractured chunks of sea ice. The narwhal surfaced a dozen feet away, its abdomen opened and trailing snakelike viscera. It had been so hellbent on attacking them that it had disemboweled itself in the process.

Mira averted her eyes and stared up at the research station, the silver disk fading in and out of the blizzard. The grim truth of the situation hit her.

This was where she would die.

41

Now

"What the hell was that thing?" Speedy shouts.

The SUSV bursts through a snowdrift and a solar panel shatters against its bumper, sending plastic shrapnel clattering across the windshield.

"Focus on the road!" Ryder shouts from the seat behind him.

"What road? There's nothing out here but snow!"

Another solar panel explodes before them. The research station appears from the blizzard, diagonally to their left. Speedy alters course and accelerates straight toward it.

Cameron lowers his night-vision apparatus and switches to the thermal register. An uninterrupted black landscape of ice stretches as far as he can see, save for the faint purple glow of heat dissipating from the open cargo hold of the Hercules, which fades into the storm behind them.

"Dancer!" he shouts into his commlink. "Get that plane out of here!"

"I'm not taking off until I'm certain there's nothing on board—"

"There's no way it can get into that cockpit. Take off with the cargo ramp down. If it's still back there, the pressure will suck it out with everything that isn't bolted down." The SUSV skids right up to the station. Speedy slews sideways to use the bulk of the vehicle to cover their escape. "Call for backup and get your asses to Nord Station. We'll radio for evac the moment we've rounded up the civilians."

"What about you—?"

"That's an order, Major!" Cameron throws open the passenger-side door and bounds out into the snow. "That plane's our only ticket out of here. I need you to get it off the ground right now!"

He ushers Rush and Ryder from the back seat and takes up position between the two cars, sighting down the glacier over the coupling. The running lights of the Hercules momentarily blind his lenses as the plane turns and ramps up for takeoff, the turboprops raising billowing clouds of snow. Waller and Kato tumble from the rear car and scramble for the entrance, passing through his peripheral vision in shades of gold and orange.

There's no sign of the polar bear.

Cameron nearly trips over the body of one of the station's engineers, frozen in the accumulation, as he backs toward the open doorway, through which he hears his men frantically clearing the drifted snow from the threshold. He watches the blinking lights on the Hercules' wings as it ascends—

A violet blur emerges from the storm and streaks toward the lowered ramp.

Metal crunches.

Steel shears.

The ramp catches the snow. Tears off. The wing dips,

impaling the winglet in the accumulation. The plane spins sideways, the propellers screaming—

A flash of light and a wall of heat strikes Cameron, knocking him backward. He bellows in anguish and charges toward the fiery wreckage, raising his night-vision apparatus. Deep black smoke fills the air. A broken wing stands from the snow, marking the trail of melted snow and smoldering debris leading to the twisted remains. Flames roar from the opening in the tail and engulf the fuselage. The front windshield shatters, and fire rises from the cockpit.

Cameron shouts in anguish and rushes toward the gaping maw where the crew door had once been.

"There's nothing we can do for them!" Speedy shouts, grabbing him around the chest and dragging him away from the plane.

Cameron struggles to break free, but his vehicle operations specialist squeezes even harder and turns him away from the plane. He catches a hint of movement from the corner of his eye.

"Down!" Ryder shouts.

Speedy tackles Cameron into the snow. Bullets scream past them and strike their target with a series of wet thudding sounds. Cameron scrambles out from underneath Speedy and looks for Ryder, who walks in a shooter's stance toward the nose of the plane. The rescue combat officer stops in his tracks and steadies his aim.

Cameron reseats the night-vision apparatus over his eyes and follows Ryder's sightline toward—

"Jesus," he whispers.

The violet polar bear staggers toward them, its partially decapitated head hanging limply on its neck, its orange muzzle grazing the accumulation. Golden blood pulses from its severed carotids, painting the surrounding snow. Its fur has burned to its blistered skin. Broken bones and metal shards protrude from the meat of its haunches.

There's no way it should still be alive, and yet somehow it lumbers toward them.

Ryder squeezes off a three-round burst, which pounds the beast squarely in the chest, but doesn't even slow it down.

"Go!" Cameron shouts, grabbing his subordinate by the back of the jacket and spurring him to motion. He shoves Speedy ahead of him and sprints toward the station, where Rush crouches on the roof of the SUSV, covering their retreat. The tech sergeant fires over their heads as they near, buying them enough time to round the vehicle and head for the front door. "Everyone inside!"

Cameron takes up position between the two cars once more and aims his rifle at the polar bear. It stumbles and falls, then slowly rises to its feet. The laceration across its neck has already faded to pink and the remainder of its body is nearly as dark as the ice. It produces a belching sound from its torn windpipe and raises its head from the ground, fixing its pale orange eyes on him. The beast sways, and then collapses into the snow. It doesn't attempt to rise.

A gust of wind howls, blowing a white curtain between them.

Rush drags him backward into the station, slamming the door in front of him and sealing off his view.

Cameron suppresses his emotions and assesses the situation. Under his command, six National Guardsmen and two civilians died within a matter of minutes. Only six of them remain to secure the station and rescue the missing scientists, assuming they're even still alive. And he and his men are trapped in an abandoned facility with two civilians who've been manipulating them from the start, not to mention whatever else invisibly stalks the darkness.

He turns in a circle, taking in everything around him.

Waller and Kato stand at the top of the stairs, seemingly unfazed by everything transpiring around them. The red glow of emergency lighting he'd seen on the security footage is gone, and there's only silence from the overhead ductwork. Wind screams through the hallway above him, masking all subtle sounds in the lower register of hearing.

"Speedy," he says. "I need you to restore power."

"I don't know the first thing about solar—"

"You're a mechanical engineer. If anyone can figure it out, it's you." The vehicle operations specialist takes a deep breath, thrusts out his jaw, and nods his readiness. "Rush . . . get to the communications center. The moment we have power, I want an SOS going out on every frequency. And see what you can do about accessing the security footage from the local servers. The rest of you, with me. We need to get those broken windows boarded up before we freeze to death."

"You don't think that thing out there is still alive, do you?" Ryder asks.

Cameron doesn't know how to respond. When last he'd seen it, the polar bear had looked dead, but it shouldn't have been able to pursue them with its head practically separated from its body.

"Keep your eyes open," he says, seating his M4 against his shoulder.

He ascends the stairs, sighting the hallway down the barrel of his rifle, his mind stitching together the blueprints he'd studied on the plane. A left turn and he feels the frigid breeze against his face. The entire building is so cold that he has to adjust the contrast and tolerances on his thermal lenses so he can see the fine details of the world around him. Rush branches from the hallway behind him and climbs over the fallen barricade into the communications center. Speedy ducks through the broken door on the right, his heavy tread striking the inner catwalk with a metallic clang. The entire team's survival hinges upon their success. If they're not up to the task, it won't matter if the rest of them are able to board up the windows.

Cameron sweeps his weapon from left to right as he passes through the research library and the lounge, the temperature dropping with every step he takes. He enters the cafeteria, where a blanket of snow has drifted over the broken tables and up against the eating bar. On the floor behind it is the frozen body he watched fall from the ceiling. He recognizes the chef, Swearengin. His desiccated face stares blankly at the floor, his beard and eyelashes crusted with ice, his skin the texture of peeled string cheese. The ceiling above him betrays no sign of how he'd been suspended.

"You two flip over that table and hold it up to the window," Cameron snaps at Waller and Kato. "Ryder . . . find out how many more windows we need to seal."

Cameron jerks the eating bar back and forth until it snaps from its moorings. He drags it through the snow and broken glass, stands it on end, and leans it against the wooden slab. The men from NeXgen help him cram sections of the other broken table into the gaps surrounding it. The wail of the wind rises in pitch as it seeps through the cracks, but the ferocious gales no longer hurl snowflakes into the kitchen.

"This barricade won't withstand a sustained attack," Waller says.

"Then we'd better hope it doesn't come to that," Cameron says.

"There's another one over here," Ryder calls from the dark hallway of the residential wing.

A resounding thud echoes from the lower level and the lights snap on.

Cameron instinctively raises his optical apparatus and blinks away the afterimage, which resolves into the dim red glow of the emergency lighting. Electricity crackles overhead and sparks rain from an exposed conduit, momentarily illuminating the blood spatters on the walls. He lowers his lenses and adjusts the tolerances until he can once more discern his surroundings.

"Go help Ryder with that window," he says, shouldering past the men from NeXgen and following the thumping of machinery down the corridor.

Rush bursts from the communications center and nearly barrels right into him.

"You're going to want to see this," he says.

Cameron hurries to catch up with his tech sergeant, who precedes him into a small room he recognizes immediately. The tables and chairs that Dr. Stone had used to barricade the door are right where he remembered them being. The video monitor lays shattered on the floor where it fell during her final transmission. The remainder of the communications equipment appears to have been attacked with a sledgehammer. At least from a distance. Up close, the blood smears covering it are unmistakable. Someone beat the electrical components with their bare fists.

The hairs rise on the backs of his arms.

"She disabled the transmitters so no one could call for help," he says. And with that realization, everything he thinks he knows about the situation changes. He'd believed that the organisms had turned Dr. Rantanen into a mindless monster, but the evidence of higher-order thinking and reasoning surround him. He recalls the way the organisms had tapped directly into the fish's nervous system and wonders just how deep those connections run. "Get me that security footage."

"Sergeant . . . " Rush says.

Cameron knows exactly what his subordinate is going to ask and answers before the words cross his lips.

"I don't know if she's still in here," he says, "but we're going to need those cameras operational if we're going to have any chance of finding her."

"Then I'll need more than emergency power."

Cameron turns, rushes to engineering, and leans over of railing of the catwalk. He can barely see Speedy on the lower level, his thermal signature nearly indistinguishable from the hot air gushing from the broken duct he's attempting to patch.

"I need you to restore primary power," he shouts. "We have to get those security cameras up and running again."

Speedy pauses his work, steps from the steam, and looks up at Cameron. He doesn't need an explanation as to why.

"Just buy me a little more time."

Cameron nods and runs down the hallway. The barricade over the window in the kitchen appears to be holding, as do those in two of the bedrooms, where desks have been stuffed into the holes and braced with bedframes. He finds Ryder, Kato, and Waller dragging desks and mattresses from the neighboring rooms, preparing to toss them down into the entryway to barricade the front door.

"Wait!" he shouts. "That's the only way in or out of the station."

"Exactly," Ryder says. "We need to make sure that if the polar bear survived, it can't get in here."

"But what if something's already in here with us and we need to get out in a hurry?"

Ryder's mouth opens, but no words come out. He slowly closes it and nods his agreement.

"I'm in," Rush says, his voice crackling through their earpieces.

"It's about time," Waller says.

"Excellent," Cameron says, glaring at the corporate lackey. "Make sure all of the cameras are up and running. I want eyes on every inch of this complex, especially the floor below us. Radio the moment you see anything remotely out of the ordinary."

"Yes, sir."

Cameron turns to Ryder.

"Watch the main entrance; nothing gets in or out," he says, and then speaks into his microphone. "Speedy, we need to clear that sublevel. You enter the hallway from the engineering core, and I'll head down the staircase at the other end. We'll meet in the middle."

"What about us?" Kato asks.

"Once the lower level is clear, you're on your own. Until then, you're not to stray from Major Ryder's side. Understood?"

Cameron turns without waiting for an answer and hustles toward the back staircase, knowing full well that if whatever Dr. Rantanen has become is still in the station, he's potentially walking right into the jaws of a trap.

42

Mira crouched beside Dougherty behind a row of solar panels and scrutinized the distant station through the blowing snow. The gusting wind revealed the structure just long enough for them to be able to tell that the front door stood wide open. Their tracks across the open terrain were long gone, along with any indication as to whether or not Sammie was still inside. They knew for sure that Chinook was somewhere out here with them, although with the way his occasional roar reverberated through the canyon, it was impossible to pinpoint his location. All they knew for sure was that he was getting closer by the minute, and they couldn't afford to remain out in the open for very much longer.

"I can't go back in there," Carrie sobbed from behind them.

"We'll die within a matter of hours if we stay out here," Aaron said.

"And if Sammie's still in there, we won't even last that long.

For all we know, she's sitting right inside that door, just waiting for us to walk in."

"Like a spider in a web," Mira whispered, the howling wind stealing the words from her lips.

"There's another way into the station," Amy said.

Everyone looked at the older woman, who stared at the far side of the station, where it perched on stilts over the steep escarpment.

"Are you talking about the access hatch we used to set the additional pillars to support the aquarium?" Dougherty asked.

"If Swearengin can use it to slip out for a smoke, then surely we can use it to get inside."

"And then what?" Carrie asked, the panic rising in her voice. "We'll be right back where we started."

"We'll be out of the elements, and we'll have access to all of our dry food stores," Amy said. "We can barricade the stairwell, weigh down the hatch, and wait for help to arrive."

"We don't know if Mira's call even went through."

"Even if it didn't, it's only a matter of time before the NSF notices we've failed to upload a single daily video log."

A furious roar rolled like thunder through the canyon below them, momentarily betraying Chinook's location. Mira thought about how Sammie had chased them out of the station and onto the glacier, where the polar bear had been lying in wait. How Chinook had trapped them inside the observation center, where they'd been attacked by the narwhal. How they'd been herded out the opposite side of the building from their sole means of escape and back toward the station again. Was it possible that the infected species were working together? Did they utilize a form of unspoken communication, some sort of hive-mind connection, or did they simply share the same hunting instincts? Regardless, there was no doubt in her mind that Chinook was attempting to flush them from their hiding spot and drive them like cattle to the slaughter. Whatever action they took next needed to have an element of unpredictability if they were to have any hope of surviving.

Mira studied the rugged granite cliff, its windward surfaces rimed with ice. A narrow path traversed its face and disappeared into the shadows beneath the station. One misstep and they'd plummet hundreds of feet into the frozen lake. And if the hatch was frozen or Swearengin had locked it, then that was where they would die.

"We have to take the chance," she said. "Sammie didn't know Swearengin was down there until he opened the door to the kitchen."

"But she was waiting for him when he did," Carrie said. "And you saw what she did to him."

"I don't like the idea any more than you do, but our core temperatures are dropping by the second and that bear down there won't be content with just making noise for very much longer."

Fresh tears dampened the frozen trails on Carrie's cheeks as she scrutinized the harrowing trail leading down the steep slope and between the stilts.

"Are you sure we'll be able to seal off both entrances?" she whispered.

Mira took those words as tacit approval and crawled from her concealed position onto the windswept snow. She was shivering so badly she could hardly push herself up from the ground, let alone run at full speed toward the pinnacle upon which the silver saucer perched. Her fingers and toes felt like they could snap with the slightest pressure, and her exposed skin burned with hypothermic potential. She slipped and fell. Righted herself. Slipped and fell again. A glance toward the station revealed nothing, but at least there was no sign of movement through the blowing snow or fresh footprints churning up the accumulation. She caught occasional glimpses of the interior through the patterns of ice on the windows. There was no light inside, emergency or otherwise.

Sammie could have been looking back at her from mere feet away, and she never would have known.

The wind grew stronger, the strip of land ahead of her steeper. Footing became increasingly treacherous. Hardpacked snow gave way to exposed rock slick with ice. Every step brought her closer to the precipice, beyond which she could see only a vast expanse of nothingness through snowflakes that blew sideways with such force that she wondered if they would ever land. The far side of the canyon was invisible through the storm. The frozen surface of the lake intermittently appeared from the clouds, so far down that she nearly lost her resolve.

Mira lowered herself to her rear end and scooted downhill until her heels hung over the edge. There was a narrow ledge several feet down, and another one below it. Both of them looked like the slightest application of weight would send them tumbling down the mountainside. If she could lower herself carefully enough and lean back into the solid rock, she just might be able to make it to the stilts—

Another roar reverberated from below her, the sound shaking the earth.

Mira gasped as she slid over the ledge. For a fleeting second, she saw only open air beneath her feet. She barely stifled a scream when her boots struck solid rock.

"You can do this," Aaron said. The marine biologist perched on the rocks above her and spoke just loud enough to be heard over the wind. "Focus on those support posts and keep your feet moving."

Mira cautiously lowered herself to the next ledge and scooted sideways, feeling along the uneven granite with trembling hands. The gusting wind threatened to pry her from the escarpment, but she pushed on, one step at a time, until the nearest pillar was within her reach. She hugged it for dear life and pulled herself underneath the station. The deep shadows slowly resolved into an earthen hollow mercifully preserved from the elements.

She fell to her hands and knees and crawled away from the edge, a sob of relief bursting from her chest. The metallic exterior of the station grazed her head as she pressed deeper into the darkness. She drew her green flashlight from her jacket and hit the switch. The beam revealed a square hatch above her, its edges thick with ice. She found a chisel in a shallow alcove beside a Folger's can full of cigarette butts and set to work. By the time she'd cleared the seams, Dougherty and Aaron were right behind her, helping Amy and Carrie through a triangular gap between stilts and into Swearengin's private little smoking area.

Mira got her feet underneath her, braced her shoulders against the hatch, and raised it just far enough to see inside. She raised the flashlight and, heart pounding in her chest, shone it across the floor, faintly illuminating the interior. There were bags of flour and beans stacked on pallets against the far wall. To her left: shelves overflowing with boxed and canned goods. To her right: crates stamped with their ports of origin. Racks of toilet paper behind her. There was no hint of movement, save for the motes of dust shimmering in the emerald glow.

Amy whispered something, but Mira couldn't make out the chief scientist's words over the rushing of her pulse in her ears. She raised the hatch a little bit higher and aimed her beam toward the stairs, but she couldn't see all the way to the top to tell if the door was still open.

There was only one way to know for sure.

"Stay here," she whispered, glancing back down at the others. "I'll make sure she isn't waiting for us."

"And if she is?" Carrie asked, staring up at her through eyes wide with fear.

Mira couldn't find the words to respond. They were out of options. Either they barricaded themselves inside until help arrived, or they died out here in the snow. She had to look away before she lost her resolve.

Rising on trembling legs, she swung the hatch all the way open and climbed into the silent station.

43

While the dry storage room was considerably warmer, Mira's breath still plumed from her lips as she crawled across the floor. A pall of stale cigarette smoke hung in the air, a reminder of the man who'd died while trying to escape from this very room. The green light wasn't bright enough to explore the deep shadows around her, but she didn't dare risk turning on anything brighter, at least not until they were all safely barricaded inside. And maybe not even then. The longer they evaded detection, the better their chances of survival.

Mira killed the light, crawled toward the nearest wall, pressed her back against it, and rose to her full height. Feeling her way along the smooth surface, she crept toward the stairs, planting each foot carefully so as not to make a sound. Her eyes slowly adapted to the dim light filtering from the top of the staircase. She risked a glance around the corner and saw the door to the kitchen standing open at the top. A gust of wind propelled a dusting of snow across the landing.

She needed to close that door.

Her peripheral vision wavered in time with her racing pulse

as she ascended, clinging to the railing for support. One step. Two. Her eyes never left the open doorway or the accumulation that would betray Sammie's invisible advance. Mira wished she could shine the green light ahead of her to make sure no one was there, but doing so risked giving away what she was trying to do. And if she failed . . .

She shivered at the thought, climbing higher and higher until she had to duck to minimize her profile. The bitter wind was cold on her face and carried with it a scent that reminded her of the meat freezer in a restaurant. She nearly lost her resolve when she saw Swearingen's body, but she summoned the courage to slowly push the door closed. Every subtle creak of the hinges caused her breath to catch in her chest, her hands to shake a little harder. She watched for the sudden appearance of footprints in the snowdrift below the broken window until she finally eased the latch bolt into the strike plate with a soft click.

Mira quietly stood and stuffed one of the aprons hanging on the wall against the base of the door to prevent any light from leaking out. She switched on her flashlight as she descended the stairs and held the hatch while the others climbed into the building.

Dougherty locked it and dragged a crate on top of it. While Amy and Carrie piled even more boxes on top of it, Aaron disassembled one of the shelving units, carried the wooden posts up the stairs, and braced them between the door and the angled ceiling. The moment all four were firmly in place, they started stacking everything they could find on the stairs and against the door until there was no way anyone would be able to get in or out, no matter how hard they tried.

Mira's adrenaline abandoned her, depositing her on her rear end in the middle of the floor. She wanted nothing more than to curl into a ball and sleep until help arrived, but between the terror and the cold, she couldn't stop shaking long enough to do so. The others sat on the bare wood plank floor around her. None of them spoke for fear of making any more noise than they already had.

Every sound became ominous. Every groan of the settling facility sounded like footsteps overhead, every thump of the cooling ductwork like someone trying to get in. Once, Mira thought she heard something scurry through the barricade and duck behind the wall of toilet paper.

"She knows we're here," Carrie whispered. "Can't you feel it?"

"We don't even know for sure that she's still inside the station," Amy whispered. "If she followed us out into the storm, she probably already died of exposure."

"Chinook's still out there, though."

"As long as we're in here, he can't get to us," Dougherty said.

"You can't possibly know that," Carrie whispered. Her voice started to rise, the panic she'd struggled to suppress bubbling back to the surface. "He'd break right through that door and—"

"No one knows we're here," Mira whispered. It was all she could do to keep her own voice steady. "And as long as we remain calm, we can keep it that way."

She placed her hand on Carrie's knee and gave it a gentle squeeze. The redhead took a shuddering breath, wrapped her arms tightly around her chest, and leaned back against the shelves behind her.

Mira wished she felt even half as confident as she sounded. Maybe they'd be able to survive in here for a while, but without a source of heat, it was only a matter of time before the interior temperature reached a state of equilibrium with the environment, and no amount of shared body heat would be able to save them when it did. And without a way to warn their rescuers about the dangers invisibly stalking the glacier and the halls of this station, they'd be luring innocent men to their graves. She had to figure out how to—

A faint thump reverberated through the floor, as much a sensation as a sound.

Carrie stifled a sob. Aaron cautiously crawled closer.

Mira swept her light around the room, searching for any sign of movement.

"There's something underneath us," Amy whispered, pressing her palm flat on the floor. "I can feel it moving."

Another thump. Closer this time.

"It found us," Carrie whimpered.

A rattling sound from above them. All eyes rose to the barricade at the top of the wooden staircase. The doorknob shook again as someone tested it from the other side.

"Nothing can get in here," Dougherty whispered.

"You've seen what they can do," Carrie whispered. "That acid they produce will eat right through our barricades."

Mira recalled the stomach acid Sammie had spewed onto the window while trying to break in and the spatter that had landed on the floor after striking Porter's face.

"But it can't dissolve glass or wood," she whispered.

"You can't know that for sure. What if—?"

"Shh!" Amy hissed.

Another soft thump from below them. A creak from the top of the stairs.

They were working in tandem. Sammie and Chinook. Probing their defenses. Searching for a way in.

Thud!

The crates piled on the hatch shuddered. One fell and broke open, disgorging packages of ramen noodles. Dougherty climbed on top of the remainder and added his body weight to the barricade.

Crack!

The sound of splintering wood echoed from the stairwell. A fissure formed in the door, above the point where the cribbing braced it.

Carrie clapped her hands over her ears and frantically shook her head.

"Grab another crate!" Dougherty shouted.

Amy and Aaron sprung to action, but there were simply none left.

Thud!

The impact from below toppled Dougherty from the stack. Aaron rushed to take his place.

Crack!

The flimsy wood near the top of the upstairs door broke, creating a jagged triangular hole. Sharp fragments tumbled through the mounds of crates and shelving units.

Mira cried out, set down her flashlight, and scrabbled over the precarious barricade, rushing toward the top of the stairs in the hope of sealing off the hole—

Thud!

Another blow to the underside of the hatch sent Aaron crashing to the floor, crushing a crate beneath him. He shouted in pain and rolled over, inadvertently kicking the flashlight underneath the rack behind Carrie.

Crack!

More wood splintered from the door—

The attack stopped as quickly as it had started.

Silence descended upon the dry storage room, marred only by the sounds of their heavy breathing. The green flashlight cast just enough light to limn the faces of the others, who looked at each other with expressions of shock and confusion. The barricades over the hatch and at the top of the stairs had withstood the siege. Rivulets of blood dribbled down the inner surface of the door, presumably from lacerations inflicted by the sharp wood as Sammie attempted to break through.

Mira backed down the stairs and turned in a full circle. The frenzied assault had been terrifying, but the quiet was even worse.

"They gave up," Carrie whispered, her voice redolent with hope. "We're going to be all right."

Mira tuned her out. Something was wrong. Sammie had slithered through ductwork barely wider than her shoulders to get into the engineering core. Chinook had practically torn apart the observation center to reach them. And the narwhal had nearly killed itself trying to shatter the viewport with the most sensitive organ in its body.

There was only one reason the infected would have ceased their attack so abruptly.

She retrieved her flashlight and slowly turned in a circle, driving the shadows from the corners of the room, the gaps between the shelving units, and the rubble heaped on the stairs.

A droplet of blood streaked through her peripheral vision and landed at her feet.

Mira raised her beam toward the ceiling.

And screamed.

44

Now

Cameron creeps down the stairs, cautiously placing each step to minimize the thudding of his footsteps. He rounds the landing and brushes past Dr. Porter's suspended legs. One glance at the physician's skeletal face nearly robs him of his resolve. He can't tell how the corpse is suspended until he catches a glimpse of its shadow on the wall. Filamentous strands hold the body in place, like it's been bound to the ceiling by wires.

There's no sound from the lower level. No light. No heat. No movement. Even the air is still. It's as though the facility itself is dead, a hollow exoskeleton through which he moves silently, as insubstantial as a ghost.

He descends into Dr. Stone's lab and recognizes the giant aquarium he's seen on so many video logs. Its waters are dark, its pumps and lighting arrays lifeless. Something hammers the other side of the glass with a sharp *crack* as he passes. He whirls and sights the source down the barrel of his rifle. A toad-faced fish, its form outlined in the faint purple glow of its minimal body heat, continues to strike at him as he inches deeper into the room, peeling apart the shadows, checking underneath the desks and inside the cabinets.

"First lab clear," he whispers into his commlink.

"Same on this end," Speedy replies.

Cameron returns his attention to the hallway and approaches in a shooter's stance, the sculpin a violet blur in his peripheral vision. It repeatedly bludgeons the glass, mangling its face in the process.

Crack. Crack. Crack. Crack.

He eases down the corridor and descends into the adjacent lab. It looks like every doctor's office he's ever visited, save for the dried blood all over the floor in the entryway and the bed in the back, which looks like something from a Civil War surgeon's tent. There are no heat signatures, nor anywhere for one to hide. He returns to the hallway and nearly fires at a blur of color emerging from a distant doorway before recognizing his vehicle operations specialist.

"Second room clear," Speedy whispers.

Cameron acknowledges with a nod, waves the other man into the next room in the series, and ducks into the office Dr. Madigan shares with Dr. Hudson. If there's anything down here, either he or Speedy will encounter it within a matter of seconds.

Pulse throbbing in his temples, Cameron begins searching behind and underneath everything that isn't bolted down or attached to the walls, every shadow he lays bare bringing him one step closer to—

"Climatology lab clear," Speedy says.

Cameron finishes his search of the administration office.

"Lower level clear," he says, allowing himself to release the breath he didn't realize he'd been holding.

"All of the security cameras are functional," Rush says through his earpiece, "although there doesn't appear to be any sign of where the scientists have—Wait . . . I think I might have something here."

Cameron sprints down the corridor, ducks into the engineering core, and ascends the spiral staircase, the clanging of footsteps echoing around him. He crosses the hallway, skirts the fallen barricade, and joins his tech sergeant at the communications center.

"Look right there," Rush says, pointing at the upper right corner of the monitor. A network of cracks runs through the screen, the fracture lines darkened by dead pixels. It's nearly impossible to make out the details of the darkened kitchen. "At the top of the door."

Cameron leans closer and notices ribbons of congealed blood on the wood below the gap in the broken door. The hole is barely a foot high and would have been indistinguishable from the deep shadows were it not for the ragged edges. He'd been standing in the cafeteria mere minutes ago and hadn't even noticed.

"That orifice isn't big enough for anyone larger than a child to squeeze through," he says.

"Look at the way the splinters project outward, like someone pried out the corner of the door from this side."

Cameron recognizes what Rush is trying to say.

"You think they barricaded themselves in the dry storage room," he says.

"There aren't any cameras down there, so I can't say for sure, but it does stand to reason."

"Then it's possible they're still here, that they didn't head for Nord after all."

"A premature assessment, I'm afraid," a voice says from behind him. Cameron turns to face Waller, who leans against the doorframe. The older man picks his way over the fallen table and chairs and approaches them with a smirk on his face. "There's a hatch in the floor."

"It's not on the blueprints," Cameron says.

"Yet it exists," Waller says. "I assure you."

"And you didn't bother to tell us?" Cameron snaps. He can barely contain his frustration, but allowing it to boil over will accomplish nothing. "Where does it lead?"

"Onto the cliff underneath us."

"Did the scientists know about it?"

"It wasn't a closely guarded secret."

"Then they could have barricaded themselves down there to buy themselves time to escape."

"Which means they could be anywhere by now," Ryder says.

"Or anything could have gotten in there with them," Waller says.

"If there are other pertinent details that might have slipped your mind, you'd better tell us now," Cameron says. He stares daggers at Waller, who nonchalantly surveys the ruined communications equipment. "We can't secure the facility if we don't know where all of the egresses are."

"I just told you," Waller says. He smiles and cocks his head toward the door. "So go secure it."

Cameron grinds his teeth, his jaw muscles bulging. He doesn't like taking orders from a civilian any more than he enjoys being manipulated.

"Can you transfer the security feeds to a remote viewer?" he asks Rush without taking his eyes off of Waller.

"Way ahead of you, Chief."

Cameron nods to his tech sergeant and speaks into his microphone.

"Time to find out what's in that dry storage room."

"And if there's no one down there?" Waller asks.

"Then we'll seal the hatch and the front door on our way out," Cameron says, making no attempt to disguise his contempt. He lowers his night-vision apparatus and seats his rifle against his shoulder. "You're on your own from there."

He rounds the corner and heads straight for the cafeteria. Ryder and Kato stand at the top of the distant staircase, their thermal signatures like solar flares against the dark corridor. He steps behind the serving bar and notes that there are no footprints in the accumulated snow, nor is there any sign of where the person whose blood decorates the door might have gone.

Cameron turns his back on the frozen body of Terry Swearengin, whose desiccated carcass serves as a reminder that his killer could very well be in the dry storage room beneath their feet at that very moment, and tries the knob. Locked. He throws his shoulder into the door, but it doesn't budge. Barricaded from the other side, as he'd suspected. He confirms as much with a glance through the hole, which reveals wooden planks braced against the slanted ceiling. Long blond hairs and tatters of skin cling to the sharp wooden slivers surrounding it. Waller produces a stoppered vial and a pair of forceps from the inside pocket of his jacket and proceeds to collect them. Cameron pushes him out of the way and stands on his toes so he can see into the stairwell.

"This is senior master sergeant Dan Cameron from the United States Air National Guard," he shouts, his voice echoing from the darkness. "We were dispatched in response to your call for help. We're here to evacuate you to safety."

There's no reply.

Cameron steps back and kicks the door, right beside the knob. The trim splinters, but the lock holds. The other men join him, and together they attack the slab of wood with every-thing at their disposal, widening the hole until it's large enough for Cameron to pull his torso through the gap. He knocks down the wooden posts that prevent the door from opening, drops back down, and shoulders it open just far enough for him to slide through sideways. The stairs are buried beneath an avalanche of crates, shelving units, and sacks of beans and grains. He scurries over them and jumps to the wood plank floor, taking in his surroundings as fast as he can.

No heat signatures. No sign of movement. The hatch in the floor stands open, admitting freezing air that cuts him to the bone. Wooden crates lay broken on the far side. A woman sprawls facedown beside them, stuffing material blooming from her torn parka, an amoeboid pool of blood surrounding her. There's another body propped in the corner, this one definitively male. He stares at Cameron through hollow sockets, his face absolved of flesh, his jaws still framing the scream that died on his lips.

45

8 Hours Ago

Time stopped.

In that single frozen heartbeat, Mira's eyes met those of the woman with whom she'd shared a lab for so many months, only there was nothing left of her friend inside them. Sammie's pupils had expanded to eclipse her irises, and the vessels surrounding them had burst, flooding the sclera and making her eyes appear black in the green glow. Chunks of hair had been torn from her scalp, leaving bloody bald patches slick with biofilm. Her nose was broken, her forehead and cheeks lacerated, and her mouth contorted into an expression of unadulterated rage, showcasing her broken teeth. While her body was pressed flat against the ceiling, she'd somehow twisted her neck so that she looked straight down, knobs of dislocated vertebrae tenting the skin behind her ear.

Carrie screamed, shattering the momentary stillness.

Sammie let go of the ceiling and plummeted toward Mira, who dove out of the way. She struck the ground on her shoulder, rolled onto her chest, and crawled—

Frantic thudding shook the floor. The crates over the hatch jumped, tossing aside Aaron and Dougherty. Amy rushed to their aid as Sammie alighted on the ground with her arms and legs spread wide.

Carrie scooted away from her. Kicked at the floor. Managed to stand. Turned and—

Sammie retched and a flume of fluid burst from her mouth, spattering Carrie's face and neck. She staggered another few steps and collapsed, blood pooling underneath her, a horrible mewling sound seeping from her chest.

Thud!

The hatch swung open, scattering splintered wood from the broken crates. Aaron scurried away from the trapdoor, while Dougherty instinctively lunged toward it. He grabbed the hatch and attempted to close it, but he made the mistake of glancing down through the hole, if only for the most fleeting of moments.

A geyser of stomach acid erupted straight up into his face. He cried out and staggered backward, the tissue melting from his face like wax from a candle. A scream burst from behind his suddenly exposed teeth, only to abruptly cease when his back hit the rear wall and he slumped to the floor.

Mira lunged toward the staircase. If she could scale the barricade that now served only to trap her inside—

Sammie cut her off, lashing out and knocking the green flashlight from her grasp. It hit the ground and died, stranding them in darkness marred by the wan light diffusing from the open hatch, which wasn't bright enough to illuminate the barricade, let alone the invisible blow that struck Mira's head.

She felt as much as heard a distinct cracking sound. Felt the warmth of blood in her sinuses. Tasted copper in the back of her throat. Her vision became watery. She caught a glimpse of the floor rising toward her—

Darkness.

. . .

WHEN SHE OPENED her eyes again, her forehead was stuck to the floor in a puddle of blood. It was already cold, forcing her to wonder if it was hers or someone else's, although the thought dissipated as soon as it formed. Everything hurt, and yet she couldn't seem to move. It was as though she were trapped inside her body, unable to make it do her bidding.

The faint light by which she'd momentarily been able to see darkened. She detected movement from the corner of her eye. A black shape covering the hole in the floor. It slowly slid down through the hatch, the motion little more than the passing of shadows in the night. She caught a glimpse of Aaron's bloody face, his chin banging from the lip of the hole with a clatter of teeth, and then he was gone, his limp arms trailing him into the hollow underneath the station.

She tried to call his name, but no sound passed her lips. Her eyes closed of their own accord. She heard breathing from somewhere above her, the sound's origin distorted by the acoustics.

Footsteps. Approaching. Stopping right in front of her face.

A tug on her arm and she slid toward the hatch. Her forehead bumped over the lip. She felt the ground fall out from underneath her, replaced by cold air that chilled her to the core.

Mira tumbled into space, the crown of her head striking stone, her neck buckling—

A FAINT GREEN glow passed through Mira's eyelids, summoning her from the pitch-black abyss. The pain returned in pulsating waves that rippled through her entire body but emerged from her mouth as little more than whimpers. Her fingers and toes were rapidly growing numb, although they were the least of her worries.

Memories of the siege in the dry storage room assaulted her. She watched Carrie and Dougherty clawing at the dissolving flesh of their faces over and over in her mind and wondered how in the name of God she was still alive. Why hadn't Sammie killed her? Were any of the others still alive?

There were no answers to be found in the darkness, so she attempted to open her eyes. And failed. Her head felt heavy with settled blood, her neck strained from supporting its weight as she bounced along, rocking from side to side, as though draped over a horse's saddle. Or at least that was how her mind interpreted it, but how could she be moving? The last thing she remembered was being dragged through the hatch and landing squarely on her head. With the memory came the pain where her scalp had torn and the realization that there was likely only one thing capable of causing the strange loping motion she experienced.

Chinook.

Mira panicked and again tried to open her eyes. Her lashes tore as the ice knitting them together broke. The sudden influx of light forced her to blink repeatedly. At first, she couldn't see anything, but slowly the world around her came into focus. She saw storm clouds from the corner of her eye, stained emerald by the aurora borealis, which faintly illuminated the icy strands of fur brushing against her face. She was strapped underneath his belly, spanning his girth, her hair trailing through the snow. His massive limbs moved in her peripheral vision, churning through the accumulation as though it were no more substantive than air. She struggled to push herself away from him, to kick free, but none of her appendages responded. A scream welled in her chest, although with as sharply as her neck was bent, it found no release.

She was struck by the realization that she could actually *see*

Chinook. As she'd noticed with the biofilm in the lake, the aurora borealis produced green light in the same spectral range as the aquarium hood. As long as the solar winds continued to cause the particles in the atmosphere to remain in an excited state, they'd counteract the cloaking abilities of the chimeras.

Why hadn't the polar bear killed her yet?

The question rose unbidden, but she forced it back down. Where there was life there was hope, and as long as she still had blood flowing through her veins, there was a chance she'd still be able to get out of this. She just needed to focus past the pain and concentrate on doing whatever it took to survive.

Mira tried to get a good look at her surroundings, but all she could see through the clouds of snowflakes rising from the polar bear's paws was more snow, its surface blurred by movement and the gusting wind.

Where was he taking her?

If she could just figure that out, then maybe she could come up with a way to—

The reality of the situation crashed down on her with such emotional force that it nearly drove her back into unconsciousness. She recalled how the infected sculpin had bound the other four in webbing and affixed them to the rocky walls inside the little cave. When she'd found them, three had already been drained of their liquefied viscera, their bodies rendered desiccated husks, while the fourth had yet to be consumed. A single organism could only eat so much. Had the sculpin been saving it for later consumption, like a fly in a spider's web? Is that what was happening to her? Had Sammie and Chinook sated their appetites on the bodies of her colleagues, and they were simply saving her for later? And if so, where were they taking her?

The polar bear stopped and rose to his full height.

Mira's head lolled sideways. She caught a glimpse of the silken cocoon binding her form, the cellophane-like mess tangled with the long fur of Chinook's underside. There was someone else trapped beside her, but she couldn't tell who it was.

The polar bear dropped to all fours and charged through the snow again.

Mira had seen something, though. A landmark she might have missed had Chinook not stood when he did. One that told her exactly where she was going.

The spark of hope died.

Even if by some miracle her call for help had gone through, there was no way whoever came to rescue her would know to look for her here. And even if they managed to track her across the glacier, she'd be dead long before they arrived.

The screaming wind echoed from the canyon. Mira felt the ground fall out from beneath her as Chinook barreled over the rocky ledge and dropped down to the slick trail. The side of her head struck something hard—

And she saw no more.

46

Now

Cameron cautiously lowers himself through the hatch and drops to the ground. The wind screams through the maze of beams supporting the structure, bringing with it an assault of snowflakes that feels like needles stabbing the exposed skin of his face. He seats his rifle against his shoulder and performs a quick sweep of the surrounding hillside through the thermal lenses, which reveal little more than a black landscape partially limned by a deep purple glow. There are no sources of heat within visual range, so he raises the apparatus to commence a thorough search of the surrounding area in hopes of picking up the scientists' trail.

He's surprised to find the northern lights in the sky, as they hadn't once appeared during his arctic rescue training in Kangerlussuaq. Emerald and violet ribbons wavered behind the roiling clouds, producing just enough light to see the blood on the frame through which he'd just descended. The spatters on the ground glisten where the snow has yet to accumulate upon the crimson ice. It's impossible to say just how old they are, but based on the relative warmth of the structure above him and the increasing severity of the storm, they couldn't have been more than ten to twelve hours old.

A bright light blooms overhead, casting his shadow upon the ice in front of him. He raises his hand to shield his eyes from the glare. Rush leans over the hole, spins the flashlight, and passes it down to him, grip first.

Cameron nods his thanks and uses the beam to explore his surroundings. The granite is sharply scored from the implements used to shape this part of the mountain. There's a chisel inside a nook in the rock, a can of cigarette butts toppled behind it. Deep gouges score the underside of the station, parallel gashes so deep they've torn through the silver metallic coating and penetrated the underlying insulation. The broad posts supporting the aquarium are sunken into the granite to his right. A semicircle of girders leads around the precipice to his left. He catches occasional glimpses of the distant fjord and the dam towering over it through the clouds rolling through the canyon.

"What do you see?" Waller asks, edging Rush aside to get a better look.

"There's a lot of blood down here," Cameron says. "Much of it is pooled, as though several individuals bled onto the ground for some indeterminate length of time." He crawls away from the hole, toward the sheer drop ahead, the wind steadily rising with every inch he advances. "It's smeared where they appear to have either crawled or been dragged to the northwest, where a narrow path wends up to the top of the cliff."

"Is this still a search-and-rescue mission?" Rush asks.

Cameron shakes his head. He understands what his tech sergeant is asking, but it's impossible to tell if the researchers are still alive. There are no arterial spatters or pools indicative of severe blood loss or exsanguination, so that should count for something. Of course, not finding any bodies is a promising sign, as well.

Strange markings catch his eye. He leans closer to the ground to better appraise deep linear demarcations in the ice, removes his glove, and traces the scoring with his fingertips. It's readily apparent that the gouges were inflicted by claws.

"Polar bear tracks," he says, following the nearly invisible prints away from the opening. There's no mistaking where they're heading. He turns and heads back toward the hatch. "They lead up the mountain, toward the front of the facility."

"Where we first encountered the bear," Waller says.

"True, but . . . "

Cameron's about to share his theory regarding the age of the claw marks when he notices something he missed the first time. There are faint pink discolorations in the ice. He scratches at one with his thumbnail and stares at the chips. There's no doubt that it's transferred blood, although there's something different about the configuration of toe prints in relation to the arch of the forefoot. These aren't bear tracks. They're smaller. Daintier. The bare footprints of a human being not much larger than a child. He pictures Dr. Rantanen, tucking her white-blond hair behind her nymph-like ears. The same white hair tangled in the broken wood of the door leading downstairs from the kitchen.

"What is it?" Rush asks.

Cameron crawls underneath the hole, slings his rifle over his shoulder, and climbs out of the wind. He hesitates to give voice to his fears despite the mounting evidence supporting his theory.

"Dr. Rantanen broke through that door—"

"There's no way," Waller says, interrupting.

"And yet that's what happened. She herded the survivors down here, where the polar bear was waiting on the other side of the hatch."

"To finish them off?" Rush asks.

Again, Cameron shakes his head. He's inclined to believe that the polar bear physically removed the wounded from beneath the station, but that behavior doesn't mesh with everything he knows about ursids, which begin consuming their prey where it falls, before it's even dead. He opens the channel on his microphone and speaks so that the others can hear him.

"Speedy, get that Susvee warmed up and ready to go."

"Yes, sir," the vehicle operations specialist replies.

"Ryder, there's a trail leading up to the northwest side of the complex from underneath the stilts. Find it, isolate the tracks, and see if you can figure out which direction they're heading." Cameron clicks off without waiting for a reply and begins ascending the fallen barricade. He addresses Waller without so much as a glance in his direction. "You're going to want to reseal that hatch. And I recommend barricading the front door behind us."

Waller makes no reply, but Cameron can feel the man's stare on his back as he squeezes through the doorway into the kitchen. Let him believe that Cameron has forgotten about him just as easily as he turned his back on him.

Rush jogs to catch up with Cameron, who speaks quietly and without turning his head.

"You have remote access to the security system?"

"Yes, sir."

"Good," Cameron says. "Don't take your eyes off of those pricks. Keep me apprised of everything they do."

"The signal won't travel more than a couple of miles in this weather."

"Surely they know that too, which is why we're going to need your technical expertise to overcome that problem."

Rush smiles.

"That can definitely be arranged."

The roar of the SUSV's engine guides them toward the

main entrance, where Kato stands in the open front door, sighting the vast glacier down the barrel of his M4. Speedy finishes scraping ice from the all-terrain vehicle's windows and takes up position near the driver-side door, rifle at his shoulder.

Cameron descends the stairs, sidesteps the bed frames and furniture that Kato planned to use to barricade the door, and strides out into the snow. He lowers his night-vision apparatus and raises his rifle. A flare of color from his peripheral vision guides him through the blowing snow. He finds Ryder crouching at the edge of the escarpment. The rescue combat officer rises as Cameron approaches and gestures to the west, following the rim of the canyon.

"It went that way," he says.

"How can you be sure?" Cameron asks.

Ryder waves him over and kneels over a set of tracks that's been nearly scoured away by the wind. Cameron crouches opposite his sergeant, but with the degradation of the prints, he can see little more than subtle impressions and the faintest hint of transferred blood.

"You have to take off your goggles," Ryder says.

Cameron raises his apparatus and blinks in surprise. Out here in the open, the aurora borealis reflects from the tracks, as though bits of glitter have been stomped into the snow. Not so much that he would have noticed had he not been explicitly looking for something out of the ordinary, but more than enough to confirm Ryder's suspicion as to where the polar bear had gone, hopefully with the scientists it dragged from underneath the station.

The chimeric microorganisms must have transferred from the pads of the beast's paws, much like the blood they'd used to follow its trail up the hillside.

Cameron once more lowers his lenses, raises his rifle, and heads back toward the SUSV, the wind whipping a cloud of exhaust from its tailpipe. The front door of the station is already closed. Judging by the commotion on the other side, the barricade was going up in a hurry.

Rush approaches, a poorly concealed smirk on his face.

"I mounted a signal repeater right up there on the roofline," he says. "There are five more in the Susvee. We'll just need to stop and plant them when the signal starts to fade."

"Good," Cameron says, climbing into the front passenger seat of the SUSV. "Don't let them out of your sight."

Speedy waits for Rush and Ryder to settle into their seats before accelerating across the glacier. Academy Station—along with Waller and Kato, and whatever they intend to do while they think no one's watching—rapidly fades into the storm behind them. They pass the polar bear's carcass, its lifeless body buried beneath the snow.

Cameron settles back into his seat and finally allows himself to accept that the monster is well and truly dead.

47

P *lip.*
The pain returns with such intensity that a sob bursts from Mira's chest, the sound echoing around her.

Plat.

Warmth on her face. A tickling sensation at the tip of her nose. She tries to reach for it, to wipe it away, but she can't seem to feel, let alone control, her arms.

Plip.

She can't tell if her eyes are open or closed, at least not until they slowly begin to adjust to the darkness. The dim aura of the northern lights limns her surroundings, imbuing the ice-rimed walls with an ethereal green glow. The stone underneath it is pale gray. She recognizes the spectral fossils and the earthen floor, ten feet straight down, and remembers being dragged over the edge of the cliff—

A scream tears the lining of her parched throat. She watches droplets of blood shiver from her brow, the tip of her nose, and plummet to the ground.

Pla-plat.

They dimple the surface of a puddle easily a foot wide. It's already frozen around the edges. How long has she been here?

Mira struggles to move, but none of her appendages respond. It's as though she's been bound—

Memories of Porter hanging in the stairwell and Swearingen rising toward the ceiling cut through her confusion. She realizes the same thing has happened to her and thrashes from side to side, but the bindings immobilize her shoulders and hips. Whatever material tethers her to the ceiling is far stronger than she is.

She allows her head to hang limply on her neck to alleviate the strain, summoning a rush of fresh blood from the gash along her hairline. The warm fluid falls to the floor with a pattering sound.

Plip-plat-plat.

A rapid-fire dental clicking sound, like a frustrated mother tsking a misbehaving child, echoes from somewhere out of sight, its origin impossible to divine,

Mira holds her breath and remains perfectly still, listening to the sound until it fades to nothingness. It didn't sound like the clattering of claws on stone. Not precisely, anyway. But that was as close as her mind could come to rationalizing it. Where was Chinook? And how in the name of God had he affixed her to the roof of the cavern?

She recalls the way the sculpin had used its webbing to attach the others to the underside of the rock and the condition of the carcasses upon which it had fed. If she doesn't find a way to get out of here, she'll share their fate. Panic surges through her at the thought, but she can't allow herself to give in to it. Not if she hopes to survive.

But even if she somehow escapes, where can she possibly go? She won't last for more than a few hours on the open glacier, which isn't nearly long enough to make it back to the station, assuming she can even find it through the blowing snow and without anything resembling landmarks to guide her. Nor will she be able to outrun Chinook, if it comes to that.

Those problems will have to wait, though. For now, she can only worry about getting herself out of the sticky substance adhering her to the ice and rock. She tucks her chin to her chest as tightly as she can, until the pain in her neck is more than she can bear, and visually appraises her predicament. The substance immobilizing her is definitely some kind of spider silk, although it's thicker and stickier than any she's encountered. She's bound in multiple layers resembling Saran Wrap that's been stretched in all directions at once, tearing oblong holes in the transparent sheets. Diagonal strands radiate outward in every direction, attaching her to seemingly every outcropping and fissure in the ice.

How the hell had Chinook produced it?

Mira shakes her head to clear it of all thoughts unrelated to her immediate survival. There will be time for analysis later, but only if she manages not to die inside this awful cave, where prehistoric creatures remained undiscovered for hundreds of millions of years.

Twisting her wrists as far as she can, she curls her fingers into claws and tries to tear the webbing. Her fingernails bend backward to the point they threaten to tear from the cuticles. She pulls and scratches, pushes and pokes, yet no matter how hard she tries, she can't damage or loosen the silk, which had been engineered to create a polymer with the tensile strength of steel.

She screams in frustration.

Tsk-tsk-tsk-tsk-tsk-tsk.

Mira freezes.

The sound is louder this time. Closer. She's certain of it.

A shadow diffuses through the ice wall at the very edge of

sight before fading again. Its shape is distorted, impossible to identify. More clicking sounds and it fades again.

Mira tugs harder at the webbing. There's precious little feeling in her fingers, and yet she swears she feels the webbing loosen, if only the slightest bit.

A scream erupts from the darkness, the sound reverberating throughout the cavern. Someone else is in here with her. Someone in a lot of pain.

"Aaron," she whispers, her voice cracking.

His cry fades into oblivion.

Mira holds her breath, waiting for a repeat occurrence.

Plip. Plat.

She's sure it had been Aaron's voice, only she can't tell where he is, and she fears what might happen if she were to call out for him and draw attention to herself.

Tsk-tsk-tsk-tsk-tsk-tsk.

Mira turns toward the source of the sound. She can't get her head far enough around to see it, although its shadow once more passes across the ice, vague and menacing. A wave of panic courses through her, giving her the strength to force her fingers through the webbing. She stretches and tears until it loosens enough that she feels her hips shift.

Pla-plat. Plat.

Blood trickles from her brow, forcing her to blink it out of her eyes. The sweat produced by the exertion only serves to exacerbate the flow. It strikes her that she's growing warmer, and for the first time, she realizes that her clothing is damp. The cocoon must be containing her body heat. She kicks her legs and feels the hint of movement, a subtle laxness that hadn't been there before.

Another scream. Aaron's pain is impossible to ignore. A spattering sound of fluid striking the floor and the marine biologist starts to cry.

There's a sharp intake of breath from the opposite direction.

Mira cranes her neck and tries to isolate the source. The ice distorts a dark form near the domed ceiling. A frayed length of rope appears to hang from it.

Braided hair.

Amy.

Her breathing remains shallow, but at least she's still alive.

Tsk-tsk-tsk-tsk-tsk-tsk.

Mira turns toward the sound, just in time to watch a shadow ascend the wall. She imagines where the figure must be standing for the light entering the cave to cast it at such an angle. If she twists her neck and shoulders—

A silhouette appears, its shadow creeping through the ice around it like reflections in a funhouse maze. It clings to the ceiling, upside down, by its hands and feet. There's no denying its human contours, the swell of its buttocks and breasts, the tangled hair hanging from its head. Its neck is strangely bulbous, as though swollen with goiters. It raises its hand to its face, thrusts fingertips seemingly sharpened to points into its mouth, and—*tsk-tsk-tsk-tsk-tsk-tsk*—pries a length of silk, like gooey taffy, from between its lips.

Aaron screams again, but a wet slapping sound silences his cry. He grunts in terror as the webbing seals his mouth, his frightened breath bursting from his nostrils.

They're going to die. All of them. They're going to die, right here and now, unless she can find a way to escape her bindings.

Mira twists and squirms, kicks and flails. She becomes an animal at the mercy of her primitive survival instincts: a coyote that would chew off its leg to escape a snare, a lizard that would shed its tail if it meant living beyond this moment.

Movement from the corner of her eye. A scuttling sound. The silhouette scurries across the icy rock and heads straight toward her.

Mira screams and recoils, but she can't create any more

distance between them. The shadow inches closer, its face emerging from the darkness and into the faint green light.

Her heart drops in her chest and her bladder lets go.

There will be no escaping their fate.

No hope for rescue.

Mira closes her eyes and prays that her death will be quick.

48

The SUSV cruises along the glacier, the wind hurling the sheeting snow inland from the Arctic Ocean. It blows sideways across the hood and makes the all-terrain vehicle appear as though it's sliding sideways across the ice. Progress is maddeningly slow as they can't risk turning on the headlights for fear of washing out the faint green glow of the polar bear's pawprints, which vanish before their eyes beneath the accumulation. If they don't hurry, there will be no tracks left to follow, but if they drive too fast and lose sight of the trail, they'll never find it again.

"Waller and Kato went straight to Dr. Stone's lab," Rush says. He sits behind Speedy, diagonally to Cameron's left, the glow of his handheld tablet flickering from his face. "Just as we expected."

Cameron nods. The two men from NeXgen had paced the top level of the station for a full fifteen minutes, waiting for the SUSV to travel outside of mobile video range, just as they'd expected. He's confident he knows what they intend to do, but he needs proof if he's going to go up against corporate interests powerful enough to pull Colonel Patrick's strings. There's no way in hell he's leaving this place while a single one of those organisms is alive, let alone as an escort for men hoping to further tinker with it in a lab. Too many lives had been lost already, including six men from his own team, whose families he would have to personally inform of their sacrifices.

"I'm picking up several heat signatures to the right," Ryder says from behind him. "I can't tell—Wait . . . Jesus."

Cameron lowers his thermal lenses and appraises the landscape. The polar bear's trail vanishes, and the glacier takes on an eerie black glow, the blowing snow like television static. He can't see more than fifty feet in any direction, although when the wind shifts—

"There they are," he says.

A stratified rock formation shaped like the dorsal fin of a shark fades in and out of the storm. Several indistinct pink and purple shapes float underneath it. One raises its enormous wings, revealing the yellow body heat trapped underneath, and Cameron recognizes them for what they truly are.

"Carrion birds," he says.

"They could be any kind of bird," Ryder says.

"Suspended from the underside of a rock formation without flapping their wings? They're holding onto something." Cameron fixes the location in his mind and raises his goggles. The birds disappear into the darkness. If he looks closely, however, he can see a vague green shape that almost looks like—"Stop the vehicle."

"With as fast as those tracks are fading?" Speedy says, but Cameron's already out the door and high-stepping through the deep snow, the windswept surface crumpling like Styrofoam beneath his weight.

He covers the distance in under thirty seconds, his breath bursting from his lips, the condensation freezing to his face. He shields his eyes and steps closer. The massive scavengers startle at his approach but make no move to abandon their meal. They just continue stabbing at the already cold flesh with their hooked beaks, tearing off strips of flesh and choking them down.

The white-tailed eagles resemble their bald American cousins, only the white feathers from their heads are scattered throughout their plumage, creating a marbled appearance that blends with the fur of the caribou upon which they perch. It hangs upside down from the pinnacle, its antlers swinging gently above the accumulation with every gust. From a distance, he'd feared the carcass belonged to one of the missing scientists. While he's relieved to discover that it's just a buck, the nature of the physical damage unnerves him.

The caribou seems to watch him through hollow sockets, its tongue protruding from its offset jaws. Parallel lacerations transect its snout and cheeks, although not nearly as deep as those on its broad white throat, which have nearly separated its head from its trunk. A greenish tint radiates from the wounds, as though the microorganisms had been passed from the attacker's claws. There's no doubt in Cameron's mind that the injuries were inflicted by the polar bear, but that doesn't explain the mess of webbing encircling the caribou's girth and connecting its rear hooves to the overhanging granite. It almost looks like millions of spiders had attempted to cocoon the poor animal.

"How in God's name . . . ?" he says, the wind stealing his words from his lips.

The nature of the carnage suddenly hits him, and it goes against every law of the natural world.

Predators don't leave their prey to rot. They consume every last bite of its meat and then don't hunt again until they're hungry. Cocooning an animal and saving it for later is something an arachnid would do, hence the whole reason it spins a web in the first place. He suddenly understands why the bear dragged off the scientists. It was all about scarcity. There are only so many prey species in such a remote and harsh environment, which means that the people he's searching for are likely still alive out here—somewhere—but they won't remain that way for very long.

Cameron runs back to the SUSV and jumps into the passenger seat. The warm air blasting from the console feels like sandpaper against his frozen skin.

"Hit it," he says. "We can't lose that trail."

"Not without Ryder," Speedy says.

"Where . . . ?" Cameron starts to ask, but his words trail off when he sees his rescue combat officer materialize from the snow outside his window.

"I asked him to plant another signal repeater on top of that rock formation," Rush says. "A little elevation ought to buy us another couple of miles, which just might prove invaluable. Kato put on a drysuit and got in the tank while you were out there. He's already collected several samples of the biofilm for Waller, who appears to be loading them into some kind of cryogenic unit."

"We can't let those samples leave this place," Speedy says.

"Agreed," Cameron says, "but our more immediate concern is containing the organisms that have already escaped."

Ryder throws open the door. Ice clings to the stubble on his cheeks and chin, the skin underneath raw and chafed.

"Go," he says, squeezing into the back seat.

Speedy hits the gas. The deep tread bites into the snow, and the SUSV accelerates across the glacier, the lingering green impressions of paw prints blowing past so quickly that Cameron can hardly see them.

"Rush," Cameron says. "Were you able to locate that cave I asked you to find?"

"Yes, sir," the tech sergeant says. "Dr. Keyes mentioned the discovery in one of her video logs. Do you think that's where our missing researchers are?"

"If I'm right and they were taken from the station for later consumption, then they're someplace where they can be kept alive for as long as possible."

"Give me a second to program the coordinates into the GPS."

Gambling on the cave makes Cameron nervous, but, as far as he knows, there are no other enclosed geological features and nothing at all on the map between here and Station Nord.

Speedy slows as the prints vanish and the tracks fade to little more than a shallow furrow. The blowing snow appeared to have buried any remaining microorganisms transferred from the bear's paws.

"Continue on your present course," Rush says. "I'll let you know when we're getting close."

"I can handle the directions," Cameron says. The knowledge that the tracks have been leading toward the ice cave bolsters his convictions. "I want you surveilling those pricks in the station."

Rush passes up the GPS unit. A glance at the screen confirms they're making a beeline straight toward their destination. And at their current pace, they should be there within a matter of minutes.

"Kato's out of the tank," Rush says. "He just collected something in a red plastic bag and handed it to Waller."

Cameron furrows his brow. He can think of only one thing other than the biofilm that the men would want to take.

"Damn it," he whispers, rage flaring inside of him. Their mission had been to ferry Waller and his team to Greenland, secure Academy Station, and then leave them to their own devices. Colonel Patrick hadn't said anything about bringing back living organisms. NeXgen must have already had a covert plan in place to retrieve its men and recover the biofilm. "I should have seen it."

"What was that, Chief?" Speedy asks.

"Nothing," Cameron says. Or at least nothing that his men

need to know right now. They have more important things to deal with at the moment.

A rock formation materializes from the blizzard, a tattered flag snapping on top of it, before vanishing into their wake.

"We should be right on top of it," Cameron says.

Speedy slows. A ragged crevice appears in front of them, its rocky edges standing like broken teeth from the accumulation. They pull right up to it and stare out over the canyon, the far rim lost to the storm.

"Keep the engine running," Cameron says. "And if we're out of contact for more than five minutes—"

"I'm not leaving you behind," Speedy says.

"You and Rush have the most important task. If anything happens to us, you need to make sure that none of those organisms ever leave this godforsaken place."

The vehicle operations specialist offers a solemn nod and cranks up the volume on his commlink.

Cameron grabs his rifle, climbs out into the wind, and heads for the ice cave. A few scattered pawprints remain on the frozen earth in the lees of the rocks, where they've been spared from the elements, the hint of green shimmering beneath the aurora borealis. He knows for sure that at least one polar bear is dead, but he can't rule out the possibility that any number of others have been infected. And there's still Dr. Rantanen . . .

Ryder steps up beside him and appraises the steep hillside. Neither remarks upon the frozen spatter of blood on the exposed rock.

"This isn't what you signed on for," Cameron says.

"If you think I'm letting you go in there alone—"

A scream cuts off Ryder midsentence. The distant sound echoes from the canyon.

There's no more time for words.

Cameron lowers his night-vision apparatus, seats his rifle against his shoulder, and drops down to the icy path.

49

Mira feels the warmth of breath on her cheek and turns away. The smell is more than she can bear, like a boiling stew of vomit and blood. She closes her eyes even tighter, holds as still as she possibly can, and prays the shadow will leave her alone.

Seconds pass in silence.

A finger brushes her cheek, tracing the path of her tears to the corner of her eye. She shakes her head and whimpers.

Tsk-tsk-tsk-tsk-tsk-tsk.

Mira instinctively opens her eyes and turns toward the source of the sound. A scream dies on her lips. She only vaguely recognizes Sammie. A sludge of biofilm covers every inch of her naked form, shimmering faintly green in the dim light, a ghostly apparition clinging to the cavern roof. Her elbows and knees are bent in the wrong direction to accommodate the position, the dislocated joints tenting flesh stretched beyond its limits. The chimeras appear to have knitted her skin closed where it has torn, but there are still open wounds through which her bones and tendons are visible.

"I'm so sorry," Mira sobs.

Sammie recoils at the sound, and for the first time, Mira gets a good look at her friend's face. The knobs of her dislocated vertebrae no longer bulge behind her ear, but rather seem to have been forced back into place. Her hair has fallen out in clumps, leaving bare swatches of scalp. What little remains hangs in dreadlock-like clusters, matted with blood and biofilm, the same grotesque paste that covers her face. Her eyes have become black pools, the dilated pupils indistinguishable from the hemorrhaged vessels, and yet there's still something undeniably human about them. Blood drips from her lashes with every reptilian blink.

She cocks her head and again extends a bony finger toward Mira's face. The fingertip following the trail of tears along her cheekbone feels like Velcro. Sammie draws it back and brings it to her lips, which have split so deeply in places that her gums are visible. She opens her mouth and extends her tongue to taste Mira's tears. Her brow crinkles in confusion, and she bares her teeth. Her incisors have fallen out and her canines protrude from their sockets like fangs.

Mira screams.

A hurt expression passes over Sammy's face, and for a second, she almost looks like she's going to cry, but suddenly her brow lowers, her eyes narrow, and she opens her mouth well past the point where the joint should have stopped it. She presses her tongue to the roof of her mouth, revealing pointed swellings to either side of the frenulum, where the salivary glands should have been. She reaches inside, grabs one of the tiny points, and pulls it out—*tsk-tsk-tsk-tsk-tsk-tsk*—with a gooey strand of webbing.

Mira screams and thrashes against her bindings, her entire body sliding just enough that she can almost wriggle her shoulders from the cocoon.

Sammie slaps the web over Mira's mouth. Her cry abruptly ceases, its echo reverberating into the darkness. She gasps for breath, but no air flows into her mouth and her nostrils are filled with mucus. Panic sets in. Her chest tightens, her lungs seemingly stoppered. She tries to free her hands. Attempts to bite a hole in the webbing, to blow through her nose—

Her nasal passages clear, just enough to allow for the slightest passage of air. She forces herself to calm down, to concentrate on drawing the cold air through her sinuses and down the back of her throat. If that narrow passageway closes again . . .

"Leave her alone," Amy says, her voice trembling.

Sammie moves in a blur. She scurries fluidly across the ceiling, straight toward Amy, who gasps in alarm.

Mira can't let the older woman suffer in her place. She issues a muffled grunt and struggles to free her arms. For a fleeting moment, it almost feels like she moves.

"You afraid to tangle with someone bigger than you?" Amy shouts. "Well, I've got news for you; this old bird's a lot tougher than she looks."

Sammie grabs Amy's braid and wrenches the older woman's head back, exposing her throat.

Mira squirms and wiggles and suddenly squeezes from the top of the cocoon, freeing her shoulders. The webbing is hydrophobic. That's the key. The same quality that makes it float and resist separating in the water causes her sweat to function as a lubricant between her body and the silk. She pries her arm free, tears the sticky silk from her mouth.

Sammie rears back, inverting herself from the ceiling like a cobra preparing to strike—"No!" Mira shouts—and vomits a flume of stomach acid onto Amy's face.

The older woman screams as her skin blisters, then melts from her skull. The pain in her cries is unbearable but, mercifully, doesn't last long. The acid eats through her trachea and vocal cords, releasing her dying breath as a ragged sigh through the bloody stoma.

Mira sobs and tugs at her restraints. She needs to get out of here, to find help.

A slurping sound.

She doesn't have to look to know what Sammy is doing to Amy. She kicks and squirms and—

Mira's momentarily airborne, the ground simultaneously falling out from underneath her and rushing to greet her. A cry rises to her lips, but the impact with the rocky floor knocks the wind out of her. She struggles to breathe, to push herself to all fours. The pain in her chest is crippling. She must have broken a rib, yet she manages to stand and stagger deeper into the cave.

Sammie drops from the ceiling and alights behind her, arms splayed, head still twisted backward. Her spine makes a crackling sound as her head turns all the way back around. She rises to her full height, knees popping back into their sockets.

Mira rushes toward Aaron, who's cocooned in a stone hollow, surrounded by strange ice formations. She jumps up, grabs the webbing, pulls with all her strength.

Aaron's words are muffled by the silk over his mouth. His eyes widen, and Mira realizes what's about to happen.

She twists out of the way as Sammie's hand flashes through her peripheral vision, snaring a fistful of her hair and tearing the roots from their follicles. Mira slips on the ice and narrowly ducks Sammie's next slashing blow. She scrambles to her feet and runs in the opposite direction, shouldering from one ice column to the next, leading the monster away from Aaron and into the narrow passageway.

The wind grows stronger with every step, the temperature plummeting. Mira's breath freezes to her lips. The light drawing her to the outside world grows brighter and brighter until she's nearly upon it, the scuttling sound of her pursuit closing in behind her.

A dark shape passes across the narrow crevice that serves as the entrance to the formation, momentarily eclipsing her only way out.

Mira screams and tries to stop. Loses her footing and slides straight toward the source of the movement. She rolls onto her stomach. Claws at the frozen earth. Crawls in the opposite direction.

And looks straight into Sammie's eyes as her former friend races toward her.

There's nowhere left to run.

This is where it ends.

50

A scream echoes from the other side of the wall of ice. Cameron slithers through the narrow gap into darkness so cold and complete that all he can see through the thermal lenses is a world of seamless black. Details come into focus as he pushes himself up from the frozen ground. He takes in his surroundings down the barrel of his rifle, his finger tightening on the trigger.

Bare earthen floor, covered with rocks. Walls coated with ice, masses of which form columns and formations reminiscent of speleothems. The size of the cavern is impossible to gauge, the route of penetration dictated by a narrow passageway—

A blur of color. Orange and yellow. Low to the ground. Its shape is undeniably human. Long hair. Slender. Female.

The woman screams as he approaches her from behind. Glances up at him, then in the opposite direction, toward another thermal signature racing toward them on all fours, its appendages violet streaks. Its inhuman face is an orange mask of rage, its eyes and open mouth glowing gold.

"Get down!" he shouts.

And pulls the trigger.

A three-round burst strikes the ground around the creature, sparking from the exposed stone. The colored blur dodges sideways, scurries up the wall, and races away from him along the ceiling.

He aims and fires another burst. The bullets shatter an opaque wall of ice just as the creature passes behind it and disappears into the darkness.

Ryder squeezes through the crevice and starts to pursue, but Cameron extends an arm to hold him back. He reaches down, takes the woman by the hand, and helps her to her feet.

"Get her to the Susvee," he whispers.

"I'm not going anywhere without Aaron," the woman whispers. "Not while there's still a chance he might survive."

Cameron recognizes the woman's voice from her video logs. Dr. Mira Stone. He looks her dead in the eyes and recognizes the determination. There's no time to argue.

"Then stay behind me," he whispers, "and do exactly as I say."

Cameron advances into the cavern. Thermal hand- and footprints marking the figure's passage fade into nothingness. There are no heat signatures corresponding to blood spatters. It's staggering to think that not a single shot hit its target. He finds the impact points on an ice formation near the ceiling, fractured shards dotting the path at his feet. There's no sign of where the creature might have gone, but there's only one direction to go from here.

He walks in a shooter's stance, the reflections from the ice throwing off his sense of depth perception. The movement in his peripheral vision is unnerving. He concentrates on the thermal range, searching for the faintest hint of color.

His heart beats faster, his blood rushing in his ears. He didn't get a clear look at his quarry, although there's no doubt in his mind that he's hunting Dr. Rantanen. Not after everything he'd seen on the security footage. He can't allow himself to think about that now, though. Lives hang in the balance. If he can contain the threat she poses without killing her, then he will, but if he's forced to make a choice . . .

"It's not Sammie's fault," Mira whispers from behind him, as though reading his thoughts. "Please don't kill her."

Cameron tunes her out and focuses on his surroundings. The texture of the ice changes the deeper he goes, his reflection giving way to shadows that seem to spread through the ice like smoke. He hears a wet slap and smells something metallic, a scent reminiscent of battery acid, and abruptly stops.

There's a nearly imperceptible heat signature around the sharp bend, behind a column of ice. He inches closer to get a better look. A pool of blood glows faintly from the floor, rapidly cooling around the edges. Chunks of flesh form mounds in the middle. A fresh gob streaks from the ceiling as he watches and strikes the puddle with a wet slap. He raises his eyes to the source and nearly squeezes off another three-round burst.

Dr. Madigan's body is bound in what looks like a cocoon, her head hanging limply from one end. Her face is skeletal, her long braid clinging to her skull by a strap of scalp.

He averts his eyes and scans the area for any other sources of heat or movement. There's another cocoon on the ceiling. Empty. A vague purple and orange aura beyond it, distorted by the ice.

"Waller and Kato are leaving the lab," Rush says through his earpiece. "It looks like they got what they came for."

Cameron doesn't respond for fear of announcing his location, but his tech sergeant's observation confirms his suspicions. The men from NeXgen didn't want any witnesses to their collection of the biofilm. And if he was right, there was already a plan in motion to make the samples disappear before anyone was the wiser, although he couldn't fathom how they intended to do so in this weather. Maybe another plane or all-terrain vehicle dispatched from Thule Air Base, five hundred miles away. Anywhere farther away than that and it would take at least another half a day to arrive. Regardless, he and his team need to be there when the transport arrives, but they have to accomplish their primary mission first.

He eases around the corner and hears a muffled voice, like someone attempting to speak through a gag. Dr. Aaron Wallace looks down at him from where he's bound to the roof of the cavern, the lower half of his face concealed by a mess of webbing. Tears stream from his eyes, which glance to the side and back again. To the side and back again.

"Down!" Cameron shouts.

He hits the ground and rolls. A magenta blur plummets from a hole in the ceiling and lands where he'd been standing a split-second ago.

Cameron comes up firing, the flash of discharge causing a strobe effect. Dr. Rantanen bucks backward and twists sideways. A golden spatter of blood ascends the wall behind her. She sprints behind an ice column, her injured arm hanging at her side, blood spiraling around her forearm and dripping from her fingertips, leaving a glowing trail on the rocky ground behind her.

Gunshots roar from behind him and to his left, staggering the woman and driving her back. Ryder advances from the corner of Cameron's eye and heads for the man in the cocoon. The rescue combat office draws his knife and hacks at the bindings. Cameron catches a glimpse of Dr. Wallace sliding out and draping over Ryder's shoulder as he moves to outflank Dr. Rantanen. She scrabbles up the wall before he can do so and passes right across his sightline. He takes aim at her opposite shoulder and squeezes the trigger—

"Don't!" Dr. Stone shouts, pushing his elbow.

Cameron's shots go high and wide, sparking from the wall near Dr. Rantanen's head and ricocheting into the ceiling. Fissures race through the ice from the points of impact and, with a thunderous cracking sound, a section of the roof collapses.

Dr. Rantanen leaps to the floor and scrambles out from beneath the massive chunks of ice and stone raining down on her. Veers toward Cameron. Launches herself at him before he even senses the attack coming. Ducks under his rifle. Gets into his chest. Drives him backward.

He leaves his feet and hits the ground on his back, his breath exploding from his chest. A boulder slams to the ground beside his head. He attempts to roll away, but the woman presses her advantage. She squeezes her legs around his abdomen. Forces his head back and pins it to the ground. Rears up above him and opens her mouth—

Ryder steps up beside her and pins the smoldering barrel of his rifle to her temple. A falling rock hits his weapon right as he pulls the trigger.

A flash of discharge and the world seems to move in slow motion.

Dr. Rantanen jerks her head down. The bullets tear through her hair, the expulsion of gasses singeing the clumped strands, and ricochet from the wall beside her. She rounds on Ryder and lunges from on top of Cameron. Her throat swells, and she makes a sickly retching sound. A geyser of fluid bursts from her lips.

Ryder ducks out of the way, but not quickly enough. The acid strikes his cheek and splatters on his back. He slaps his hand over the wound and stumbles backward, firing straight up into the roof of the cavern, which disintegrates in the blink of an eye. His screams are swallowed by the deafening rumble of countless tons of stone fracturing and coming apart.

Cameron propels himself to his feet, grabs Ryder by his collar, and pulls him out of the way. Mira and Aaron rush to his aid, and together they drag the injured soldier toward the outside world.

A slab of granite slams to the ground, forcing Dr. Rantanen in the opposite direction, deeper into the cave. Another boulder strikes her head, driving her to her knees. She scuttles in reverse and looks up at Cameron through the blood dripping from her brow. Her eyes meet his through the rain of earth and dust.

He releases Ryder.

Takes aim.

And fires.

51

M ira reaches for the barrel of the rifle, but she's too late. She sees Sammie's face in the flash of discharge, her ghostly features limned green by what precious little light reaches her through the haze of dust and falling debris. A crimson star bursts from her forehead, and then she's gone, the pained expression on her face vanishing beneath the avalanche of stone and ice.

"No!" Mira screams, but her words are swallowed by the roar of the earth coming apart all around her.

Aaron wraps his arms around her and drags her in reverse. She pushes him away and rounds on the man with the rifle, who shouts something into her face, although she can neither hear his voice nor make out his words. He hands her his rifle and pushes her toward the trail leading to the surface. A rock clips his head, denting his helmet. He crouches, drapes his fallen comrade's leg over one shoulder and his arm over the other, and rises in a fireman's carry.

Mira sprints ahead of him, following Aaron's dark silhouette through the narrow maze, the walls of which begin to collapse beneath the weight of the crumbling ceiling. The light from the outside world dies, stranding them in darkness so deep she can see neither the man ahead of her nor the soldiers behind her. She repeatedly trips and falls, rolling her ankles, skinning her knees and palms. Something strikes her head. Stars flash across her vision. She feels warmth seeping from her hairline, wipes the blood from her eyes with her sleeve, and fights through the dizziness—

Suddenly, she can see again. The wall of ice concealing the entrance falls like a curtain of shattered glass. Jagged rocks break loose from the ceiling and streak through her peripheral vision. One hammers Aaron and drives him to his knees, fibers blooming from a tear in his parka. She grabs him by the hand, pulls him to his feet, and drags him out onto the ledge, where the brutal wind nearly sweeps them from the icy path. The entire hillside seems to crumble at once, sending ice and earth tumbling past her.

The soldier staggers from the rubble, boulders bounding past him and plummeting into the deep canyon. Something clips his heel, and he goes down hard. He struggles to stand with the weight of the injured man on his shoulders. Cameron, the patch on his jacket reads. Blood pours from the ragged orifice in his fellow soldier's cheek, through which his rear molars and the arch of his mandible are visible.

"Go!" Cameron shouts.

Aaron rushes ahead of Mira and jumps from the ledge. He reaches back just as she leaps from the precipice, and they both tumble into the snow. The ledge collapses. Cameron barely manages to fall in the right direction, the added weight on his back driving him face-first into the accumulation as the escarpment vanishes behind him.

The roar subsides, and a cloud of dust rises into the sky. It swirls above the crater where the cave had once been before being carried away by the wind.

Mira can only stare at the rubble, beneath which Sammie's

body lays buried beneath countless tons of granite. The memory of the blood exploding from her forehead, in that frozen moment in time, will forever be a scar upon her soul. She rocks back and screams up into the night.

She should have been able to save Sammie. Should have been able to save them all. Every one of them was dead, save for Aaron, whose face shimmers with blood from the laceration running straight across the crown of his head. Ice has already begun to form in his hair.

"We have to keep moving," Cameron says.

Without so much as a hint of remorse, he stands, shifts the weight of the wounded man—Ryder, his nameplate reads—on his shoulders, and starts uphill. Mira yells in anguish and jumps in his way. He lets her beat his chest with her fists until she runs out of steam and collapses to her knees.

"I'm sorry," he says, his voice little more than a whisper. "Believe me, if there had been any other way ... "

He steps around her and ascends the slick trail, picking his way around rock formations rimed with ice.

"There's nothing you could have done," Aaron says. "There's nothing anyone could have done."

Mira understands on a rational level that he's right, but it doesn't make her feel any better. There had been numerous points along the way when she should have recognized what was happening. Had she done so, her colleagues would still be alive. She'd failed them all. In her hurry to change the world, she'd cost thirteen innocent people their lives. Thanks to her hubris, Lord only knew how many discoveries wouldn't be made, how many revolutionary technologies wouldn't be developed, and how many millions would die from the very climate disaster they'd sought to avert.

She allows Aaron to help her to her feet, but she can't bring herself to meet his gaze. All she can do is stare blankly out across the canyon as she follows him uphill toward a vehicle that resembles twin armored boxcars with snowmobile treads. Two more soldiers emerge from the front car—Rush and Rodriguez—and help lay Ryder on the back row of seats in the rear car, leaving the man who carried him all this way to collapse in the snow, his pain etched upon his face.

"What the hell happened down there?" Rush shouts. He produces an emergency medical kit from underneath the seat and sets to work bandaging the gaping wound on Ryder's face. "It felt like the whole damn mountain dropped underneath us. Had Speedy not reacted as quickly as he did and gotten us the hell out of there, we'd have probably landed right on your heads."

Cameron shakes his head as though unable to find the words to reply. Mira follows his sightline to where the tattered flag marking the cave's location now flies. Its bent post protrudes at an angle from the mouth of a pit that has to be fifty feet deep. Slabs of stone stand at odd angles from the edges, mirroring the shape of the collapsed cavern. Snow already accumulates on rocks that haven't been exposed to the outside air in hundreds of millions of years, while the wind hurls flakes down through the dark crevices between them, into the heart of the earth itself. She thinks about the bodies of her friends entombed down there and promises herself that she'll return to collect their remains, even if it means crawling down through those narrow gaps and dragging them out all by herself.

"Are they all that's left?" the man Rush had called Speedy asks, nodding in her direction. He lowers his voice to a conspiratorial whisper. "Were you able to neutralize the threat?"

Cameron rises from the snow and climbs into the passenger seat of the front car without answering.

"We need to get to the station before Waller can unload the biofilm," he says.

Speedy nods and hurriedly climbs behind the wheel.

"Why don't you two come with me," a voice says from

behind Mira. Rush offers a reassuring smile and guides Aaron and her into the rear car. He gestures for them to sit in the seats across from Ryder. "Let's see what we can do about those lacerations."

Mira dabs her fingertips into the freezing blood on her forehead. She'd nearly forgotten about the injury. The reminder brings on a fresh swell of pain, dispelling the numbness that had settled over her. She wants nothing more than to curl into a ball and wish the whole world away.

The engine growls, and the vehicle lumbers across the glacier. Mira watches the rubble fade behind her through the ice-etched window while the soldier swabs her laceration with a topical antiseptic. She wants to thank him and ask how he managed to find them, but no words will form. Coldness spreads outward from her core, and her vision goes out of focus. The blowing snow shifts directions, and, for the most fleeting of moments, she could swear she sees a spectral green figure. She only vaguely understands that she's going into shock.

Rush closes her wound with a handful of butterfly bandages and sets to work on Aaron, who stares at the injured man lying on the bench seat across from him through glazed eyes. Ryder's pasty white from blood loss, and his chest barely rises with his labored inhalations. If he dies, his death will be Mira's fault as well. A man she's never met, but one who traveled thousands of miles to rescue her, only to find hell waiting for him in a dark ice cave—

"They're tearing down the barricade," Rush says. He abruptly grabs the tablet propped on the seat beside him and swings the microphone attached to his helmet in front of his lips. Mira catches a glimpse of the screen. She hardly recognizes the main entrance of Academy Station. Desks and bed frames have been haphazardly piled against the front door. Two men she's never seen before are attacking the mound with their bare hands, hurling aside the debris. "How far out are we?"

The response through his earpiece is loud enough that Mira can hear it, even over the rumble of the tread.

"What's going on?" a voice responds.

"Waller's making his move," Rush responds. "And he appears to be in a hurry."

Mira recognizes the name from the long line of signatures at the bottom of the form approving her request to use the purple marine bacterium for her study. What in the world is a bigwig from NeXgen doing all the way—?

And then it hits her.

She recalls watching Sammie's final video log. Her partner had described the presence of hydrolytic enzymes in the dead sculpin's wounds and signed off with the words "I await advisement." This must be the man she'd been addressing, a man who'd dropped everything and traveled to the arctic when he recognized the significance, a man who'd barricaded himself inside the station while everyone else searched for survivors. He'd realized what the chimeras were capable of doing.

"He's come to collect the biofilm," she whispers.

The vehicle accelerates, churning up clouds of snow. The world passes in a white blur as Mira contemplates the ramifications. If her chimeras were to fall into the wrong hands, they could very well be responsible for the extinction of every higher order of life on the planet. She feels sick to her stomach. Had she ever been in control of her own project?

They needed to destroy the chimeras, along with every last bit of her research, and scour this entire area from the face of the planet.

Lake Tranquility streaks through her peripheral vision, its frozen islands standing like gravity-defying icicles from the vast field of snow. Academy Station winks through the storm, reflecting the green of the northern lights, which have begun to fade to a diffuse purple haze. The tank treads bound over imperfections in the ice, launching from buried features that haven't seen the light of day since the dawn of time. Aaron scoots higher in his seat at the sight of the approaching station, his feet uselessly scraping the floor in an effort to create as much distance as possible between him and the facility.

In the distance, two figures lower their heads against the wind and stagger away from the open front door. They disappear behind the rows of solar panels, only to reappear near the top of the staircase leading down to the lake.

The vehicle slews on the ice and grinds to a halt. It has barely come to rest when the men in the front car jump out and give pursuit.

"Stay here," Rush says. "This shouldn't take too long."

He reaches for the rear door, but Mira grabs him by the sleeve before he can throw the latch.

"There's still a polar bear out there," she says.

"Not anymore."

Rush extricates his arm from her grasp, throws open the door, and hopes down into the snow. The wounded soldier groans and tries to sit up, the movement causing him to open his eyes and bare his teeth in agony. His bandages darken with blood, ribbons of which dribble down his neck from behind his ear, iridescing in the waning green glow.

Mira gasps and climbs out before Rush can close the door. She pulls him aside and speaks just loud enough that he can hear her over the wailing wind.

"Your friend's infected. I saw—"

The words die on her lips as something catches her eye, right at the edge of the vehicle's roofline.

A pale red smear.

Blood.

52

Cameron runs through the snow toward the edge of the cliff, where the clanging sounds of heavy boots striking the metal steps reverberate from the canyon. He shields his eyes against the ice crystals blowing inland from the fjord and sees the men from NeXgen, who're nearly all the way to the bottom and descending at a measured pace. Neither of them glances up the switchbacking stairs to make sure they aren't being followed, allowing Cameron to close the gap behind them at a rapid click.

He glances back at Speedy as he rounds the second landing, planting his feet near the edges to minimize the clamor of his footsteps. The vehicle operations specialist recognizes what he's doing and follows suit. As long as the men they're chasing continue making more noise, they won't notice—

The racket abruptly ceases.

Cameron crouches against the railing and signals for Speedy to do the same. The clanging echoes away into oblivion, swept away by the rising wind.

"Chief," Rush says through his earpiece. The tone of his

voice makes Cameron's blood run cold. "There's something up here you need to see."

Cameron doesn't respond for fear of betraying his presence to the men below. Besides, he has complete confidence in his tech sergeant's ability to handle anything that comes his way.

He risks a peek over the side and watches two figures streak out from underneath him onto the slick talus. One of the men slips and falls. The other doesn't even slow down.

"Where are they going?" Speedy whispers.

Cameron shakes his head. He was wondering the same thing. He'd been certain that Waller had arranged for the arrival of an overland vehicle or a second plane, but he and Kato were heading in the opposite direction from the landing strip and moving with the purpose of men who knew their destination. Where could they possibly be going?

Colonel Patrick's words from Cameron's initial briefing rise unbidden.

We're talking about Peary Land in Greenland, the northernmost landmass on the planet. The temperature's currently thirty below and Nord is reporting whiteout conditions. There's no way they're reaching it across a hundred miles of open arctic terrain.

Cameron tunes him out and concentrates on the memory of that conversation. Why was his mind dredging it up now?

This will be a search and rescue mission, Lieutenant Colonel Andrews had said. *We've been in contact with a Canadian Coast Guard cutter on Baffin Bay and several commercial vessels in the Greenland and Norwegian Seas, but they lack your team's medical training and experience under these conditions.*

And then it hits him. It wasn't something that either of his commanding officers had said, but rather the words spoken by Dr. Carter Young, the representative from NeXgen.

One of our subsidiaries operates a shipping fleet out of Norway. We could dispatch a SAR team, but even if they set sail right now, you'd still beat them by a good eight hours.

But if that vessel had been put to sea when the NSF first received Dr. Stone's call for help . . .

Waller hurries along the treacherous trail toward the distant observation center, which flirts in and out of the storm.

"We can't let them reach the dam," Cameron says.

He pushes off from the rail and jumps down to the next landing, abandoning all attempts at stealth.

"What's going on?" Speedy asks, but before Cameron can answer, the conning tower of an icebreaker materializes from the mist shrouding the fjord.

MIRA WALKS around the side of the vehicle to get a better look at the smeared blood. It almost looks like a palmprint. Below it, there's another smudge that resembles the ball of a foot, with teardrop-shaped impressions where the toes would have been.

"Chief," Rush says from behind her, speaking into his microphone. "I think we might have a serious problem up here. Acknowledge, over."

Only static crackles from his earpiece in response.

The world seems to tilt on an unseen axis as Mira climbs up onto the running board and stares at the roof of the rear car. There's blood everywhere. She recognizes a vaguely human shape, like a crimson snow angel, and recalls the shadowed gaps between the fallen stones at the site of the cave-in, the very same openings through which she'd promised herself she would crawl to recover her friends' bodies, if she had no other choice. Is it possible that Sammie had somehow survived and used them to reach the surface?

Rush says something from behind her, but she can't make out his words over the whooshing of her pulse in her ears.

She climbs down and walks around the tailgate to the opposite side of the vehicle, where there are still dimples in the snow from footprints that the wind hasn't entirely erased. Faint pink droplets mar the snow between them, leading toward the station.

No, not toward the station.

Around it.

Mira leans into the wind and follows the rapidly disappearing trail as though in a trance. Her eyes guide her as her mind transports her into memory. She sees herself reaching for the barrel of the soldier's rifle, but he pulls the trigger before she can stop him. Sammie's head snaps back and to the side. Blood bursts from her forehead where the bullet strikes, and she vanishes behind the rubble falling from the collapsing ceiling. There's no way she could have survived the gunshot wound, let alone being buried underneath tons of granite, and yet the blood guiding Mira past the station and over the precipice tells a different tale.

A rumbling sound draws her attention to the fjord, where an icebreaker cuts through the black waters in the distance. The enormous ship must be three hundred feet long, with a seventy-foot-tall bridge crowned with satellite antennas and golf ball-like radomes. A helipad platform dominates its foredeck, while its aft deck bristles with cranes. She's never seen a seafaring vessel travel this far inland.

Her breath catches in her chest.

"Oh, God," she whispers, glancing toward the rounded edge of the station, which hangs out over the escarpment, perched precariously on stilts. A faint green shimmer passes between the girders, then vanishes again. She breaks into a sprint and races toward the narrow path traversing the rim of the cliff and wending into the shadows underneath the facility. "No!"

Rush calls to her from behind, but she doesn't dare slow down to reply. Not while there's still a chance of catching up with Sammie before she can—

Mira slips, lands on her hip, and slides over the edge. A glimpse of open air, the frozen lake, far below—

Whoof.

Her breath bursts from her lips as she slams into a boulder and flops to the ground. She gasps for air, but none will come. Pushes herself to her hands and knees. Crawls. Casts a panicked glance down at the fjord.

Water parts before the icebreaker, waves riding up its hull. It veers toward the southern side of the channel, its momentum slowing as though in preparation of docking with the dam.

The pressure in Mira's lungs breaks and frigid air floods into her chest. She sobs in relief and scrambles through a gap between stilts into the deep shadows. Only the faintest hint of the northern lights passes through the storm, imbuing the ice surrounding her with violet and emerald—

Movement overhead.

A spectral form scurries upside down across the silver siding and out over the nothingness. Broken bones protrude from Sammie's misshapen appendages, her torn flesh sealed by webbing that positively glows with chimeric microorganisms.

"Sammie!" she shouts.

Her friend stops and twists her head all the way around so she can see Mira. There's nothing left of Sammie inside those cold black eyes. Her mandible appears to have fractured right down the middle. It opens outward like chelicerae, revealing her fanglike teeth and the swollen ducts underneath her tongue. Her forehead's a craterous ruin where the bullet took a bite out of her frontal bone, the ragged edges of which are knitted together over her exposed brain like fibrous stitches.

"Let me help you!" Mira calls, loud enough to be heard over the wailing wind. She wraps one arm around the nearest support post and reaches for Sammie with the other. "Take my hand! We'll figure this out together!"

Sammie's brow furrows, and a crimson tear squeezes from the corner of her eye.

She lets go and plummets into the canyon.

"No!" Mira screams.

CAMERON HURDLES the last flight of stairs, hits the landing, and lunges onto the icy path. He slips on the loose rocks. Rights himself. Accelerates again. He can't risk slowing down, even under such hazardous conditions. The thought of someone like Waller tinkering with that organism in a lab pushes him even harder.

He hears Speedy's footsteps on the slick trail behind him, but he can't spare a glance back for fear of losing sight of the men from NeXgen, who intermittently appear from the blowing snow ahead of him. Waller's almost to the final straightaway leading out onto the dam, a silver canister clutched under his arm like a football, while Kato trails him by a good fifty feet, a red plastic bag swinging at his side.

Kato abruptly stops and looks straight up—

A blur of motion materializes above him, like the slipstream of heat trailing a comet, and he collapses to the ground. Bones break with an audible *crack!* He screams and struggles to crawl out from beneath a faintly green shape. A wet slapping sound and the skin on his face begins to blister. He turns toward Cameron as his flesh melts away from his cheekbones and teeth. His eyes widen in panic and he reaches—

Another emerald blur, and his cries cease.

Cameron pulls down his thermal lenses and the world turns black, save for the purple and orange figure crouching over the fallen man, whose golden blood floods out across the ice. The figure rises and stares at him through eyes like twin glowing suns.

The ground falls out from underneath him.

There's no mistaking Dr. Rantanen, nor the massive wound on her forehead where he'd shot her.

Cameron raises his rifle and pulls the trigger, but his target's already on the move. Bullets ricochet from the ground behind her heels as she propels herself from all fours to two feet, moving far faster than he can. She runs out onto the top of the dam, her head and shoulders barely visible over the raised concrete sides, heading straight toward the observation center. A second figure is nearly already upon it.

Waller.

The conning tower of the icebreaker rises above the structure's roof, an orange cloud of exhaust diffusing into the storm behind it.

Cameron knows exactly what he needs to do.

He charges onto the dam and fires indiscriminately at the colored silhouettes streaking away from him, driving them to the ground. He rounds on the icebreaker, aims at the windows of the pilothouse, and fires until his magazine runs dry.

Glass shatters and light overwhelms his optics. The vessel's engine roars. Water churns from its stern as it attempts to maneuver out of range.

Waller climbs up onto the rail, the silver canister held high like a trophy, and prepares to jump to its deck, but Dr. Rantanen is upon him before he has the chance. The container slips from his grasp and falls into the fjord as she drags him down. He lands squarely on his back and opens his mouth to scream, but she tears into him before he can do so. Golden spatters fling from her slashing fingertips and burst from her snapping jaws.

Cameron stops, loads a fresh magazine, and steadies his rifle.

Dr. Rantanen rounds on him, her face glowing with Waller's blood.

He forces aside his reservations and takes careful aim.

Something breaks inside of him as he squeezes the trigger.

53

T he echo of the final gunshot fades beneath the howling wind.

Mira sobs as she runs from the bottom of the stairs. She slips and falls. Pushes herself back up, only to fall again. Rush helps her to her feet, but she shoves him away. Her eyes never leave the spot where she'd last seen Sammie, her naked form limned with blood, rushing out onto the dam.

The icebreaker swings away from the shoreline, making a wide turn toward the far side of the fjord, its silhouette merging into the storm. The roar of its engine grows more distant by the second.

She skirts the dead man's remains, the surrounding earth glimmering with crimson ice, and hurries across the windswept rock.

The lone figure standing on the dam drops to his knees and vanishes behind the raised concrete wall. She doesn't see him again until she's racing out onto the dam.

Cameron turns at the sound of her approach, rises to his feet, and hurries to intercept her. Wrapping his arms around her, he attempts to turn her around and steer her in the opposite direction. She catches a glimpse of Sammie's body over his shoulder and moans in anguish.

Her friend lies on her back, legs crumpled underneath her, arms flung out to her sides. Rapidly cooling blood gives substance to her transparent form, the faint green iridescence fading with the northern lights in the sky. The gunshot wound between her breasts leaves little doubt as to her condition.

Mira beats her fists against the man's chest until she's overwhelmed by exhaustion. She slumps to the ground, a flood of emotions rising within her and spilling from her eyes as tears. Memories of death overwhelm her.

Porter hanging in the stairwell. Anthony's body sprawled on the floor of the lounge and Laurie's propped against the wall in the hallway. Nichols's blue corpse disappearing beneath the accumulation outside the front door. Swearengin lying behind the serving bar. Blood pulsing from Leo's severed carotid. Elroy sacrificing himself so they could escape the garage and Moore falling beneath the polar bear's claws. Jen's body floating to the surface of the lake amid the broken sea ice. Carrie and Dougherty crumpled in the dry storage room, their skeletal faces absolved of flesh. Amy's final breath burbling from the rapidly eroding wound in her throat. And now Sammie, who'd been responsible for so much suffering, but who'd never deserved this fate.

Of the fifteen of them who'd called Academy Station home, only she and Aaron remained.

This was all her fault. She should have been the one bleeding out on the ice.

She should have been able to save them.

Rush and Speedy reach underneath her arms and lift her to her feet, drawing her away from Sammie as gently as they can. Her legs go numb, and she has no choice but to allow them to drag her back toward the shore. She watches her friend's body fall away behind her until she passes Cameron, who looks at her with a tortured expression on his face. He lowers his eyes and stares at his hands, as though expecting to find them covered with blood.

CAMERON STAGGERS from the dam onto the rocky ridge, the wind battering him from seemingly every direction at once. He can barely see the conning tower of the icebreaker in the distance as it heads back out to sea. It doesn't matter now, though. He'll find that vessel if it's the last thing he does and make sure that someone is held accountable, even if it leads him all the way up the chain to Colonel Patrick, or his bosses at the Pentagon.

In fact, a part of him hopes it does.

Whether personally or professionally, his commanding officer had been in bed with a private corporate entity whose interests didn't align with his country's. Because of them—because of their shared greed—six men under his command had died. Six good men. And then there were the scientists, whose remains he'll soon have to collect. While their bodies can't be returned to their families, their loved ones need to know what happened to them. He won't be party to some grand cover-up.

Nothing like this can ever be allowed to happen again.

Cameron stares up at Academy Station, perched precariously overhead. It's only a matter of time before someone on that icebreaker alerts the powers that be to their failure—if they haven't already—and another team is dispatched to collect samples of the microorganisms. There needs to be nothing left of the facility when they arrive. Surely, between the SUSV and the arctic vehicles in the garage, there's enough fuel to burn this whole place to the ground. He'll be damned if he's going to allow more lives to be lost in the pursuit of profit when his sole mission has always been to save them.

Forcing aside his anger and guilt, he inhales a deep breath and takes charge of the situation.

"Rush: take Dr. Stone back to the station. See what you can do about moving Ryder and Dr. Wallace into the medical suite. Tending to the three of them is your sole priority. Speedy: siphon as much gasoline as you can from every vehicle you can find. I want to turn this entire complex into a bonfire you can see from space. I'll begin gathering bodies—"

"Drop your weapons."

Cameron turns to face the speaker, knowing full well to whom the voice belongs.

Waller shove Rush out of the way and grabs Dr. Stone around the neck. He produces the knife from the sheath underneath his left arm and presses the tip into the side of her throat, summoning a trickle of blood. She tries to speak, but he gives the blade a slight twist and she manages only a gasp.

"You don't want to do this," Cameron says, narrowing his eyes.

Deep lacerations crisscross Waller's face and neck. The surrounding skin is pale to the point of translucence. He sways as though struggling to maintain consciousness and bares his teeth against the pain.

"Your guns," he says. "I won't ask again."

Cameron holds his M4 at arm's length, sets it down on the ground, and slowly raises his empty hands. Rush steps around from behind him, but he signals for his tech sergeant and Speedy to follow his lead and relinquish their rifles. Waller kicks their weapons from the path and down the rocky slope.

"Listen carefully and don't test my resolve," Waller says. "You and your men are going to take off your boots and throw them down onto the lake while Dr. Stone and I return to the station, where we'll barricade ourselves inside and await transport back to the States. If you so much as think about trying anything stupid, I'll sever her carotid, and you'll have to watch her bleed out, knowing there's nothing you can do to stop it."

Cameron wants nothing more than to tear Waller apart with his bare hands, but he's not willing to risk the lives of any more innocents, even if it means sacrificing his own.

"Take me instead," he says. "I'll go willingly, and my men will do exactly as I say."

"You might not care about your life, but I know you care about hers. As long as I have Dr. Stone, you'll obey my every command. Now . . . take off your boots."

Cameron stares down Waller for several seconds—his jaw muscles clenching and unclenching—before dropping to one knee. He catches a hint of movement from the corner of his eye as he unties the laces of his right boot.

"You'd kill us all," he says. "And for what? Money?"

Waller scoffs.

"You don't have the slightest idea what I can do with this organism, do you? The future of warfare is biological. You think COVID was an accident? It was a deliberate shot across our bow by our most dangerous enemy, one meant to demonstrate its prowess and its willingness to deploy such a weapon, even if it had to use its own citizens as vectors. Such wars were not meant to be cold, with labs stockpiling viruses capable of wiping out the population a thousand times over. They must be won quickly and decisively, and with the utmost prejudice."

Waller slowly starts backing away, dragging Dr. Stone with him. He's unsteady on his feet, the blood loss beginning to take its toll. The tip of the knife slips deeper into her neck. She cocks her head away from it, her eyes widening in panic.

"Imagine releasing these chimeric organisms in the heart of Beijing or Moscow," he says. "How long would it take before the infected were slaughtering everyone and everything in their way? We could eliminate all of our enemies in one fell swoop and make sure they never rise against us again. And all without firing a single shot."

"If you release it, you'll destroy every life form on the planet," Cameron says, slipping off his boots. The cold cuts right through his socks and burrows into his feet. Again, he senses movement from his peripheral vision, but he can't risk drawing attention to it. At least not yet. "There will be no way to stop its spread, no hope of containing it without catastrophic loss of life."

"As it stands now, maybe. But give me time to work with it. Give me a chance to map its genome, to engineer it to do what I want it to do." He carefully crouches and retrieves the red plastic sack Kato dropped. "Give me a year with this"—he holds up the biohazard specimen bag, its contents roughly the size and shape of a fish—"and I'll give you the most powerful weapon the world has ever known. One for which only we will have the cure."

Cameron detects a faint shimmer to his right, like steam seeping out from behind the concrete wall lining the top of the dam. He meets Dr. Stone's gaze, then deliberately looks to his right, drawing her attention to the source of the movement. Her eyes widen in surprise.

He hopes to God she's ready for what's about to happen.

MIRA WATCHES the transparent figure stagger from the dam, its outline partially silhouetted in blood. She suppresses the urge to scream and again meets Cameron's stare. He offers a subtle nod. His hands drift away from his boots and he plants them in the snow, his legs tensing in anticipation.

She has to distract the man with the knife in her neck.

"You can't control . . . an organism . . . like this," she says through bared teeth, every word seemingly causing the blade to sink deeper into her flesh. "This species evolved . . . before our very eyes. Who's going to stop that . . . from happening again?"

"I am," Waller says, his eyes never leaving Cameron. "Now toss those boots."

The three soldiers comply without argument. Their boots tumble down the incline and land near their rifles, just past the shoreline of the frozen lake. Their toes won't last an hour in these conditions, which is presumably what Waller is counting on. It will take time to climb down and collect them, buying him enough time to reach the station first.

A twist of the knife gets Mira moving. One foot behind the other as he pulls her backward, alternately glancing at the path leading uphill to the station and the national guardsmen behind him. His hands begin to tremble.

Mira looks to her left, where the figure collapses to the ground. It rises again like steam from a sewer grate, its body taking form from nothingness. A massive gunshot wound, framed by a starburst of blood, mars its chest. Ice has already formed on its shoulders, in its hair and lashes, on its cheekbones and the bridge of its nose. A glass-like image of Sammie materializes from thin air, although her friend is long gone. The chimera's head lolls on its neck, as though the creature lacks the strength to hold it up.

Waller stumbles and nearly falls, jerking Mira so suddenly that his blade slices her skin all the way back to her ear. A freshet of blood pours down her neck and soaks into her collar. She slaps her hand over it and desperately attempts to hold the laceration closed.

He turns and freezes. His entire body grows unnaturally still.

Waller must have seen Sammie.

The pressure on Mira's neck suddenly relents. Before she realizes what's happening, Waller jabs the tip of the knife into her side, cutting through her parka and prodding her ribs. He ducks behind her as though attempting to use her as a human shield.

Mira glances at Cameron, who shifts his weight forward, just waiting for the right moment to make his move. To her left, Sammie lumbers closer, her disjointed movements reminiscent of the way the sculpin had tried to crawl across the floor after its death, the microorganisms that animated it firing their final electrical commands through the wiring of its nervous system. Her head rocks back and she makes a retching sound that Mira recognizes immediately.

She drops like a sack of potatoes. Waller's knife slices straight up the side of her jacket and through her hood. The moment she hits the ground, she starts to roll.

Fluid spatters behind her.

Waller screams as the acid burns through his face and chest. He claws at his liquefying flesh, even as Sammie throws her arms around him and opens her mouth wide enough to engulf the entirety of his lower face—

CAMERON SEIZES THE OPPORTUNITY. He leaps over Dr. Stone and plows into Waller and Dr. Rantanen, wrapping his arms around them. The three of them hit the ground and tumble toward the edge of the escarpment overlooking the fjord. Their momentum carries them over the precipice.

A sensation of weightlessness.

The scream of air rushing past his ears.

A fleeting glimpse of the black water rising to meet them.

Cameron lands on top of Waller, the impact with the rugged shoreline knocking the wind out of him. Waller's head strikes the edge of a boulder, the granite edge opening the back of his skull like a hatchet. Dr. Rantanen lands on her back, her neck folding over a rock formation with a sharp *crack*, severing her spinal cord. Her body slumps over the side and starts to fall toward the shallows, but Cameron grabs her arm before she splashes into the water.

His breath returns with a lurch. He rolls over and looks up into the storm, the wind assailing him with sleet that feels like needles stabbing his bare skin.

From the corner of his eye, he sees a red plastic bag drift inland on the current and sink beneath the waves.

EPILOGUE

Mira winces as Rush applies the butterfly bandages to the wound on her neck. They'd found some Dermabond tissue adhesive in the medical suite and used it to hold the edges of the laceration closed, hopefully minimizing the scarring. She wasn't overly optimistic, but, unlike so many others, at least she was still alive.

Fortunately for Ryder, his wounds appeared to be less severe than they'd initially suspected. Rush had irrigated his chemical burns, applied salve, and bandaged the side of his face. He now slept in the bed across the room from her, an IV delivering a cocktail of painkillers and fluids into his arm and every blacklight they'd been able to find shining down on him. The green flashlight confirmed that the chimeras that had infiltrated his wounds had already begun to die off. They'd run his blood through a UV sterilizer when they returned home, just to be sure.

The others grew increasingly worried about the fates awaiting them stateside. With all of the survivors in stable condition, they'd decided to wait for as long as possible before calling for retrieval, buying themselves enough time to sanitize the facilities. Cameron was understandably concerned about the consequences of her microorganism falling into the wrong hands—or any hands for that matter—as Waller and the men from NeXgen had already demonstrated. They'd been willing to let every single one of them die just to get their grubby little mitts on her chimeras.

A part of Mira mourns the loss of her research and everything she could have used it to accomplish, but not so much that she wouldn't happily be the one to strike the match and set this whole infernal complex ablaze. As long as she lived, there was still hope, and she fully intended to make sure she didn't waste the opportunity afforded her by the sacrifices of her colleagues. She would find another way to combat climate change, and she'd be damned if she didn't succeed, if for no other reason than to honor their memories.

Mira nods her thanks to Rush and rises without a word from the desk that once belonged to Dr. Porter, whose dried blood still decorates the floor. Aaron pushes himself up from the chair opposite hers and starts to follow her. She turns around and gently squeezes his hand.

"Thanks," she says, "but I need to be alone for a little while."

"I'm here if you need me," he says, although she suspects he likely needs her more than she needs him. He'd been here for nearly two years by the time she arrived and had lost everyone he held dear, but she's of no use to anyone like this. She promises herself she'll make an effort to be there for him when all is said and done. For now, she needs to be able to think without being constantly reminded of everything that had transpired over the last seventy-two hours, especially if she's going to make sure it never happens again.

The hallway smells of gasoline. She hears Speedy's footsteps overhead as he carries tank after tank of fuel into the station. As soon as Ryder's ready to move back to the SUSV, they'll douse every last inch of Academy Station and burn it to the ground. Before that happens, however, she has to make sure that everything in her lab is as it should be. The last thing she wants to do is spend the rest of her life wondering if anything had been removed prior to its incineration. As it is, she's going to have a hard enough time deleting all of her video logs and the data she'd uploaded to the system, although Rush seems confident that he can pull it off.

Mira's heart breaks as she descends into her lab for the last time. She remembers the day she'd first arrived. Walking into her lab had been like stepping into a dream from which she never wanted to awaken. The equipment, set up to her precise specifications. The aquarium, like something ripped straight from her wildest imagination. And Sammie, who'd rushed to greet her like they were already old friends. They'd been convinced they were going to change the world. It's staggering how quickly the best of intentions can turn to ashes.

She tosses all of the notebooks and folders and laptops into a pile in the center of the room. She grabs every bottle of chemicals from the cabinets and dumps them onto the mound to ensure that everything burns hot and fast. When she's done, she slips Sammie's lab coat from the back of her chair, carefully folds it, and sets it right on top of the mound, her embroidered name proudly displayed.

Mira's eyes blur with tears as she surveys the wreckage of her life. She can bear the sight for only so long before turning and heading for the door. Something crunches underfoot. She glances down and stares at the burned carcass of the sculpin she'd exposed to the UV rays. She'd assumed that Kato had collected it and that its remains had been in the biohazard bag.

A thought strikes her like a bolt of lightning from the sky, nearly stopping her heart in her chest.

If the fish's body is still here, then what was in Waller's sack?

. . .

CAMERON STARES down upon the fjord, where white waves crest against the black sea. These would be his final moments of peace before he forces his life through the shredder. He'll be detained as soon as he sets foot on American soil and stripped of his rank before he can raise a single objection. On the positive side, he's confident that Colonel Patrick won't seek a dishonorable discharge or push for a court-martial, if only for fear of what Cameron might say. He'll want to wash his hands of this whole mess as quickly as possible and make everyone involved simply go away. Not that it matters. As long as Cameron's able to destroy every last bit of evidence of what happened here, there's nothing they can do to him that's worse than what they've already done. By robbing him of his faith in the institution he'd sworn to defend, they've taken away half of his reason for living.

Granted, he'll still be able to save lives as a paramedic or a firefighter, but it won't be the same. At least he'll be able to walk away knowing that in his own small way, he'd helped save the world from itself.

Unfortunately, there are still monsters like Waller out there, men who've become so ingrained in the institutions of power that it will take a complete overhaul of the system to carve them out. Maybe that will happen someday, although he doesn't hold out much hope. No one man can burn down the establishment, unlike the station lording over the cliff above him.

The wind shifts and the smell of death overwhelms him. He turns and grabs the gas can from beside the pile of bodies he'd collected from the ice cave, the station, and the surrounding environs. He tries not to look at their faces as he sloshes the accelerant onto them. They deserve better than this.

Or at least most of them do.

He strikes the emergency flare and tosses it onto the remains. Flames engulf them and issue deep black smoke that billows out over Lake Tranquility, where Speedy's currently in the process of running the power cables from the main solar-powered generators into the boathouse. A few minor alterations and several hundred thousand kilovolts will pass through those cables and into the lake, using the conductivity of the biofilm to electrify the water and kill every living thing within it. He forces aside all thoughts of the whales, as those that aren't yet dead are undoubtedly infected, and it's only a matter of time before they start ripping each other apart.

The thought makes him sick to his stomach.

At least he'd recovered the cryogenic storage dewar Waller had dropped while attempting to jump to the deck of the icebreaker. More importantly, even after falling twenty feet onto the rugged shoreline, he'd managed to keep Dr. Rantanen's remains from rolling into the ocean, where the microorganisms in her contaminated blood would have flooded the ecosystem. A few bottles of bleach and some direct exposure to UV light had seen to the eradication of any that might have survived on the rocks where she'd died. And yet he can't get the image of the red plastic bag Waller had dropped into the shallows out of his mind. There'd been something inside of it, something that had looked a whole lot like a fish. But if it hadn't been the sculpin from the lab, then what in God's name had it been?

He prays they never have to find out.

Cameron turns his back on the fjord and heads toward the station. The plane from Thule Air Base will arrive in eight hours and there's still much to do, especially if he intends to be basking in the warmth of the burning station when it lands.

THE BIOHAZARD SPECIMEN bag races inland on the current, which drags it down beneath the calving front of the glacier. It passes through complete darkness, tumbling across stones polished smooth by eons of flowing water. Eventually, it comes to rest and sinks into the sediment, a cloud of which billows around it as the sculpin, once immobilized by its brethren's webbing inside the hollow rock, emerges from its cocoon. It thrashes against its constraints and sinks deeper and deeper into the soft earth. Its agonal respirations slow until it has exhausted its finite supply of air.

Slowly, ice begins to form on its scales. The layer grows thicker and thicker with each passing moment, preserving the fish until the sea becomes warm enough to thaw its frozen carcass and release the chimeras into the environment.

A ticking biological timebomb, just waiting to go off.

AUTHOR'S NOTE

I'd love to take credit for the idea of splicing the silk-producing genes of a spider into a marine bacterium, but in this case, real life is even stranger than fiction. A team of scientists in Japan achieved this feat in the summer of 2020, and while their reasons for doing so were unrelated to climate change, I believe the potential applications are limitless.

Academy Station is based on the Belgian research station Princess Elisabeth Antarctica. Its green technologies were developed by the International Polar Foundation, in conjunction with private commercial interests. Thanks to its unique design, the station became the first research facility to operate exclusively on renewable energies.

I hope you enjoyed CHIMERA and take a chance on some of the other books from my catalog, where you'll find more adventure, science, history, and nightmarish creatures.

ACKNOWLEDGMENTS

Special thanks to Alex Slater at Trident Media Group; Jeff Strand; Joe Hempel; Andi and Kimmy; Justin Robbins; Shannon Marshall; Douglas Preston; James Rollins; Kim, Jovana, and Milo at Deranged Doctor Design; my family; and all of my loyal readers, without whom this book wouldn't exist.

ABOUT THE AUTHOR

MICHAEL McBRIDE was born in Colorado Springs, Colorado to an engineer and a teacher, who kindled his passions for science and history. He studied biology and creative writing at the University of Colorado and holds multiple advanced certifications in medical imaging. Before becoming a full-time author, he worked as an x-ray/CT/MRI technologist and clinical instructor. He lives in suburban Denver with his wife, kids, and a couple of crazy Labrador Retrievers.

Printed in Great Britain
by Amazon

82895523R00212